# OTHER BOOKS BY KATE L. MARY

**The Broken World Series:**
*Broken World*
*Shattered World*
*Mad World*
*Lost World*
*New World*
*Forgotten World*
*Silent World*
*Broken Stories*

*Collision*

*When We Were Human*

*Alone: A Zombie Novel*

*Moonchild*

**The College of Charleston Series:**
*The List*
*No Regrets*
*Moving On*
*Letting Go*

**Zombie Apocalypse Love Story Novellas:**
*More than Survival*
*Fighting to Forget*

**Anthologies:**
*Prep For Doom*

D1522813

12/2016

TWISTED Book One

# TWISTED
# WORLD

A *Broken World* Novel

# KATE L. MARY

Copyright © 2016 by Kate L. Mary
ISBN Number: 978-1537556598
Cover Art by Kate L. Mary

For all the fans of the *Broken World* series who refused to let go of Axl, Vivian, and even Angus. I hope everyone is satisfied with how things have turned out, even if it isn't all unicorns and rainbows. The zombie apocalypse never is.

# CHAPTER ONE

## Meg

THE air that swept over me was warm and sticky, and as suffocating as the wall I was sitting on. It caught my dark hair and whipped the locks around my face and neck until I felt like they were trying to strangle me. I brushed them aside almost absentmindedly, my eyes still glued to the distant horizon.

Below me, the landscape was green and lush and overgrown, the houses that had once held what I imagined were happy families had long ago been overtaken by nature. Even in the fading orange glow of the setting sun, it looked like a jungle. Occasionally, something moved. It could have been a bird or some other animal brave enough to venture out into the open, but at this distance, it was impossible to know for sure. Most likely though, it was one of the dead.

They were still out there. Moving across the deserted country like they actually had a purpose. How they kept going was a mystery that I doubted anyone would ever be able to solve, and not one I wanted to waste what little free time I had thinking about. Plus, it wasn't like I had scaled this wall hoping to get a glimpse of the walking dead. The world out there was what I was interested in. Or, more accurately, the world that *used* to be out there. It was gone now, as extinct as malls and movie theaters, and a thousand times more intriguing. I'd never set foot in that world for real—hell, I'd never even set foot outside the wall I now found myself sitting on—but the answers to so many of my questions about the past were hidden in those ruins.

Mom was my age when this whole thing started. Just Twenty years old. Not my biological mother, but the mom who raised me. Vivian Thomas. Young and full of life, her future had held the promise of something better than what I currently found myself living. Then the virus hit and the world around her began to die, but she was a fighter, and somehow, through months of struggle, she made it here. To safety.

If it hadn't been for the virus, she and Dad would never have met. In the world that was before, they never would have crossed paths, and even if they had, she probably wouldn't have given him more than a second look. But after the virus, everything was different, and they were perfect together.

The smashed car underneath me rocked, making the whole wall groan. Even though I knew the wall was secure, I found myself gripping the rusty metal for support. The car shook again just as Jackson Star came into view. He pulled himself up and flopped onto his belly at my side, a grunt forcing its way out of him from the effort. Then he rolled onto his back and grinned up.

"Thought I'd find you here," he said, pushing himself up so he could settle in next to me.

I rolled my eyes even as I returned the smile. "You say that literally every time you climb this wall."

"It's our thing." He nudged me with his elbow before looking out toward the horizon, but the sigh he let out didn't match my mood. It was more like exhaustion from climbing the wall than longing. "Today?" he asked, nodding toward the world in front of us.

"Shopping," I replied, my voice coming out so soft that it sounded more like an exhale. "My mom and I are at the mall shopping for dresses. There's a movie premiere this weekend. My first starring role."

My biological mother, Hadley Lucas, was a celebrity during an era when most people had so few problems they could waste time reading about the lifestyles of the rich and famous. She'd been worshiped, and I was enthralled by the idea of her. I'd dug through hundreds of old magazines just hoping to catch a glimpse of her face, and watched hours of old movies with Jackson at my side, pretending that it helped me know who she was just a little bit more.

My obsession was only partly about her, though. Yes, Hadley was my mother, but I had a mom. A mom who'd held me when I was sick and cooked dinner for me every night. She'd taught me how to kill a zombie in the most effective way, and told me stories about what life was like before the virus wiped out most of the population. I didn't need another mom. Not like that.

"First movie premiere?" Jackson cocked an eyebrow in my direction.

"She didn't want me to be one of those bratty child actors," I said, lifting my chin.

My obsession with Hadley Lucas was about the past. About being able to envision what my life would have been like if all of this hadn't happened. I was luckier than most people my age in that aspect. I had documentation of who my mother had been and how she'd lived her life. Pictures even. Most people my age didn't have a clue what their lost parents had looked like. They were shadows in their lives, always in the back of their minds, but never to have a face.

Jackson laughed and shook his head, and his brown eyes sparkled like one of the stars that dotted the dark sky above us. The little bit of light left on the horizon gave his brown hair a reddish tint, and when he turned his face toward mine, the shadow that cut across his profile made his features seem sharper.

Jackson was handsome. He wasn't a tall man, but his broad shoulders made him seem larger than he was—of course, next to me everyone seemed large—and his skin had taken on an earthy bronze tone thanks to the harsh New Atlanta sunshine. Then there were the freckles on his nose and that little dimple in his right cheek. Those two things, coupled with the smile that he could turn on and off in the blink of an eye, helped soften his features just enough to make him approachable. As fun as it was for me to dream about who I would have played on the big screen, Jackson was the one who actually looked the part of a movie star.

"You could never be bratty," he said, sliding his arm around my shoulders.

Next to his solid body I felt tiny, and it wasn't just my petite frame. Jackson had a knack for making me feel young and helpless. Childish even.

I had curves that somehow got lost in my small frame, and arms that were thin and wiry despite the hard work I'd known all my life. My mother had been a slim woman, and I'd gotten that from her. Along with her smile and smooth, pale skin. Even her green eyes. But my hair was my father's. Jon Lewis. All I knew about him was that he'd had dark hair and had loved my mother more than his own life.

"Anyone can be bratty given the circumstances," I said, ducking out from under Jackson's arm.

He frowned and shook his head, and then let out a deep breath that I mimicked.

This had been our life for the past year: him trying to love me while I shied away from it. Love was a killer. That much I knew for sure. I'd seen firsthand what it did to people in this world and I wasn't sure I had the fortitude to be able to get through it. Husbands died while trying to clear the country, and wives gave up. Kids lost their parents and ended up in the slums, settling for the scraps of an already threadbare life.

Dad disappeared and Mom turned into a shadow of herself.

No. Love lifted you up only so it could drop you farther, and when you hit the ground it was like being thrown from the tallest building in the world. It didn't just break you; it shattered you. Even my one attempt at romance had proven that to me. Although I wasn't delusional enough to think that I had loved Colton, it had still stung when he died.

No. Romance and love weren't things I was interested in.

I exhaled while shaking my head, hoping it would clear the memories and erase the pain. It didn't, though. It never did.

"I need to get home," I said, scooting away from Jackson before twisting my body around so I was facing the other direction.

With my back to the outside, New Atlanta loomed in front of me. The city was dark and gray despite the lampposts on the streets and the lights shining from windows. Everywhere I looked were living quarters on top of living quarters, with all of them so crammed together it was impossible to distinguish where one ended and the other began. My family had arrived in the beginning, shortly after the wall was built, so we'd been lucky enough to get an apartment. But many of the refugees who came here weren't so fortunate. The existing spaces had filled up faster than they could build new ones, and people had found themselves living in tents on the street. Soon, they began making their own shelters, bringing in supplies from outside the wall, which resulted in dwellings that were little more than shacks. Barely able to sustain a family, let alone keep the weather out.

"It's only temporary," I muttered, shaking my head again.

That was the motto of this new government: *We'll pull together, we'll rebuild. Soon things will go back to normal.* The only problem with that was the fact that *soon* never seemed to come. I didn't believe they intended to do anything about the slums any more than the people living in those shacks believed it. Not after all this time.

"What?" Jackson scooted over to sit beside me, his arm flush with mine.

His skin was warm, and I'd be lying if I said the thought of being with him wasn't tempting. Lately, I'd found myself feeling more and more alone with each passing day, and Jackson had been my best friend since he saved my life when I was only eleven years old. There were moments, especially when we were alone, when thinking about the two of us together seemed as natural as breathing.

But right now, I wasn't ready for that step, and I was starting to think I never would be. All losses I'd experienced over the years had piled up inside me, building a wall around my heart that was even taller than the one I currently found myself sitting on.

"They keep saying they'll do something about the living conditions in the city," I said as I inched away from him, "but they haven't."

"It takes time." Jackson's voice took on the hard tone he always got when I criticized the way things were run, and his expression was even harder. No wonder he intimidated people. "You need to let the people in charge do their jobs."

"It's been twenty years!" I shook my head when my voice echoed across the night sky. "We're running *out* of time. Every few years some new illness spreads through the city, killing more people. There are so few of us left as it is. How long can we go on like this?"

"What can they do?" When Jackson turned to face me, his brown eyes captured mine. "The zombies are still out there. Almost Twenty-one years, Meg. How the hell are they still moving?"

"I don't care," I muttered, tearing my gaze from his.

"You should. We all should. That's the key: Doing everything we can to figure out how those things work. They go and go and go, outliving those of us who are actually *alive*, and no matter how many crews we send out to fight them off, it's never enough. The CDC creates a vaccine and things start to look up, but the virus mutates and before we know it, even that doesn't work!"

He sounded just like his dad, reciting the same lines everyone's heard a million times before, and I had to bite back the urge to ask him if he was gearing up to take his father's place as Regulator of New Atlanta.

Instead of saying anything against Jackson's father, I chose to let out a snort. "Don't talk to me about the vaccine. It was my uncle, remember?"

Jackson slammed his mouth shut and looked away like it would take back the words he'd just thrown at me.

"Forget I said anything." I scooted to the edge of the smashed car before once again twisting my body.

I caught a glimpse of him as I lowered myself down. He was still sitting on the car and his mouth was still clamped shut, but his eyes followed me as I climbed down the wall. They were cold enough to send a shiver down my spine, but somehow apologetic at the same time. I was seething, though. So angry I couldn't bring myself to tell him it was no big deal.

I didn't even know why I was mad. I'd never met the man who gave his life to help create a vaccine, and from what I'd been told by Uncle Al and Aunt Lila, Angus had been a bit of an asshole. True, in the end he'd done the right thing, and Dad sure as hell had never had anything bad to say about him—not really. The negative stuff was always said jokingly, like a pill that had been covered in chocolate to help it go down easier. It was obvious he'd loved his brother, and from everything Mom told me, he should have. Angus practically raised Dad.

Angus gave humanity a fighting chance, and even though he'd died in the process, my uncle was something even bigger than a legend to most people. I'd grown up hearing stories about him from Mom and Dad, as well as everyone else in my little extended family, but it was the people in the colony who'd made him seem larger than life to me.

Most of time, people treated me differently the second they found out who my uncle was. There were moments when it was nice, but mostly it had made me feel strange. Secluded. Maybe that was why I'd formed so few real relationships outside my close-knit little family. Other than my one boyfriend and Jackson, that is, and both of those had come later. Jackson had popped into my life during a time when I'd felt totally alone, giving me exactly what I'd needed in that moment: comfort. Colton, too, but in a different way.

I was so lost in thought that I made it down the wall without even realizing it, and the second my feet hit the ground I took off running. Suddenly, I felt like a kid again. Rushing home after a disagreement with a classmate or acquaintance. Only, back then I'd had someone to run to. If Dad was home, he'd listen silently to what I had to say, ready with advice that sounded wise despite the slight drawl marring his speech. Mom's reaction, however, had usually been the opposite. She'd interject and ask questions. Calmly try to get to the root of the problem so she could help guide me in the right direction.

Now though, no one at home would be willing to listen to my petty problems.

I darted down the dark alley that led away from the wall, jumping over trash and other debris as I went. Anymore, most of the wall was impossible to scale, but Jackson and I had our special little place. Tucked behind a couple buildings, somehow it had been overlooked when they'd cemented the rest of the wall together a couple years ago. Or maybe, knowing how much I liked sitting up there, Jackson had talked his dad into leaving it.

I made it out to the main road and kept jogging. People waved as I passed by, and I nodded to the ones I recognized. The population had gotten so big that at times I could go a whole day without running into someone I knew personally—which was weird considering how few people had been left behind by the virus. It was nearly impossible for people not to recognize *me*, though. Between my relationship with Jackson and my last name, most of the time I found it impossible to hide who I was, and oddly enough, there were times when being recognized made me feel even more alone. Like now.

When I turned onto my street and the shantytown came into view, I finally slowed to a walk. The houses here were small and square, and the roofs so low that they barely left room for an average size adult to stand up straight. I'd never been inside one, but they couldn't hold more than a couple mattresses for sleeping—my bedroom was bigger than some of them—and yet whole families found themselves crammed into the tiny spaces.

I reached the shrine halfway through shantytown and ducked my head, hoping to hide my face behind a curtain of hair. Candles were lit, their lights flickering across the darkness, and under them a few notes were held down by rocks. The small stone statue was of a man, although I doubted it looked anything like the person it was supposed to portray. I didn't know for sure, though, because I'd never bothered to ask. No one seemed to know who had taken the time to carve the statue, but it's been in this same spot almost as long as I could remember. The subject of this weird little religion was something my family did our best to avoid talking about, though. It was just too creepy. Even for me, and I'd never even met Angus.

My gaze was still focused on the statue when a woman stepped out of her makeshift home right in front of me, holding a bucket in her arms. The curtain she used for a door got wrapped around her shoulders, and even though she managed to shrug it off, she also succeeded in sloshing the contents of her bucket onto the road. The scent of urine filled my nostrils just as the liquid splattered across my shoes.

I jumped back, letting out a yelp. "Watch it!"

"Just a little piss," she muttered, tossing the rest of the urine aside. It splashed onto the street, narrowly missing a woman and her two children. The mother glared at the woman, then hurried her children along.

"On my shoe," I said, coming to a complete stop.

The woman's eyes focused on my face and recognition flashed in them. Her gaze moved to the statue as her mouth scrunched up, and she shoved a few strands of greasy hair out of her face.

"Oh, I see how it is. Little Miss James has it too nice. She don't want to see how the rest of us live." The woman took a step closer, the bucket tucked under her arm. This time when she opened her mouth, I was so close that I could see the rotten nubs of teeth sticking out of her gums. "Can't hide from the truth forever, girlie. This is the life most of us have these days, and it ain't much better than what the zombies are living on the other side of the wall. We sleep in filth, we eat in filth, and we live with filth. This is the world!"

Her voice rose above the surrounding noise, causing people to stop what they were doing. Even though she was nasty and hateful and a total bitch, heat crept up my neck and over my cheeks. Every hair on my scalp tingled, and I stepped back, but the woman didn't let up. She took a step too, and then another and another until she was so close that she was the only thing I could smell. And it wasn't good. Urine and sweat, dirt and rotting teeth. Every inch of her reeked, and even though she was foul and repulsive and being near her made me gag, she was right. The life these people were living wasn't much better than the zombies.

"Take a good look around before you go back to that apartment you've been living in," she said, the words hissing through the holes in her mouth where her teeth used to be. "Then tomorrow, when you see your boyfriend, remember this. That father of his can do something about the way things are, but he's choosing not to."

I wanted to tell her that Jackson wasn't my boyfriend, but of course that didn't matter and she wouldn't care. Not to mention the fact that no one believed me when I did bother to say it. We'd been lumped together for years, and I had a feeling it would probably always be that way. Even if we each got married to other people, there would probably always be whispers about Jackson and me meeting up on weekends. When you didn't have much to distract you, gossip was an easy thing to grab onto.

Instead of bothering with silly details that didn't matter to anyone but me—and probably Jackson—I took a step back. "I'm sorry, but this isn't my fault, and I don't deserve your anger."

The woman's mouth scrunched up, and I cringed away, waiting for her to spit in my face or fling more hate-filled words at me.

Before she could say anything else, a familiar voice cut through the air from behind me. "What's going on here?"

I turned just as Al pushed his way through the crowd. He frowned at the woman before shooting a wink my way, and even though relief surged through me, I couldn't help feeling a little guilty. Not only did I know people in every important position, but they were my family. It seemed like every time I had a problem someone swooped in to rescue me. Despite the longing I had to return to the way things used to be, my life hadn't been hard. If anything, I'd lived the cushy existence that came with knowing people in the right places.

"It's not a big deal, Uncle Al." I gave him a smile that probably made me look like I was in pain. "Just a misunderstanding."

Al didn't look at me, and when his eyes narrowed on the woman holding the bucket, his frown deepened. For him. My uncle typically had a smile on his face, so even the smallest frown gave off the impression that he was furious.

"You giving Meg a rough time, Suzie?" Al shoved his hand under his hat and scratched his head. His other arm, most of which he lost back in the beginning days of the zombie apocalypse, was decked out in a sword contraption of his own making. It hung loosely at his side and was menacing despite the fact that Al was cuddlier than a teddy bear.

The woman in front of me shook her head so fast that more of her stringy hair fell across her face. This time, though, she didn't push it away. "Just trying to educate the girl."

"No need for that," Al replied. "Meg is as smart as they come."

He glanced around, his gaze only stopping on the shrine for a split second, and almost reluctantly the crowd that had gathered to watch our altercation began to disperse.

Only they didn't go around us. They went *through* us, pushing their way between Suzie, Al, and me. Elbows and shoulders poked at my ribs as I was shoved to one side, then the other. I took a step back, trying to distance myself from the mob, but it was

10

impossible. The crowd around me thickened until I couldn't see my uncle anymore. A handful of people shot angry looks at Suzie, but the majority of them sent me glares that could wilt a head of lettuce.

I twisted away from a particularly evil scowl, once again trying to break free of the crowd, but it was impossible. They had me pinned. We were packed together so tightly that a thousand smells flooded my senses, each one more pungent and foul than the last. I turned away from a man whose mouth was so scrunched up that I was sure he was preparing to spit in my eye, only to find myself staring at the chest of another man who was so close that I could see how threadbare his shirt was. I tilted my head back so I could see his face, and smoky gray eyes met mine. They were piercing, but so bloodshot that it looked like the owner hadn't slept for a month. At least. Still, there was something familiar about—

Before I even had time to think about it, the man moved closer. I tried to take a step back, but his fingers wrapped around my wrist, holding me in place. His gray eyes were the same shade as the hair on his head and face, and his beard was thick and unruly, reminding me of a movie Jackson and I had watched last week about a man who'd gotten stranded on a desert island after a plane crash.

The gray man's fingers dug into my flesh, and my arm jerked back almost on its own as I tried to break his hold on me. Before I was able to, his free hand found mine, and something soft was shoved into the palm of my hand.

He leaned his head down, practically putting his lips against my ear. "Take it," he hissed, his voice barely audible over the crowd still swirling around us. "Don't read it 'til you're alone."

His fingers fell away and I stumbled back, bumping into someone behind me who cursed. I blinked, and like magic the man was gone, melting into the sea of stinking bodies surrounding me as my fingers tightened around the paper in my hand. It barely crinkled and it was as soft as a piece of cloth, like a dozen different people had wadded it up a dozen different times. The way I was squeezing it probably wasn't going to do it any favors, either.

What could this crazy man who looked like he was on the verge of dying from exhaustion have to say to me? I was nobody, not really. I might have known people in important positions, and

I carried a last name that made people do a double take, but I was still just a kid in so many ways.

I glanced around, my gaze moving over the faces surrounding me so quickly that I barely even registered what I was looking at. Then, at the back of the crowd, I caught sight of Jackson. A mixture of relief at seeing a familiar face and terror at knowing I couldn't keep a secret from him shot through me as I shoved the paper into my pocket. It was probably nothing more than the ramblings of a crazy man, but maybe not. There could have been more to it.

"Meg!" Jackson called as he forcefully shoved people aside so he could get to me.

He reached me at the same time that Al did, and together the two men escorted me through the throng of people. They towered over me, and between them I felt lost even though I should have felt like salvation was on its way. My heart, which was already beating wildly thanks to the confrontation with the woman, pounded even harder now, and beads of sweat had broken out across my forehead and upper lip.

"You okay?" Al asked when we'd made it across the street.

Now that we'd put some distance between Suzie's shack and ourselves, the stink of urine had faded, but it couldn't be avoided completely. Not when walking through this section of New Atlanta.

"I'm fine," I said, forcing out a laugh. It nearly got caught in my throat and ended up coming out sounding more like a cough. "It isn't a big deal, really."

I grabbed a chunk of my hair and twisted it around my hand, working to calm my heart and slow my breathing. It wasn't easy, but thankfully, the two men in front of me seemed to attribute my anxiety to the confrontation. They would never suspect that one of the members of the mob had slipped me a message.

Al shook his head, and his usual easy smile was replaced by a frown that was deeper than almost any I'd ever seen on his face. The only exception might have been the days we'd had to deal with death and loss in our family.

"The streets are getting dangerous," Al said.

"They're just trying to live," I replied, suddenly remembering the anger Suzie had mistakenly aimed at me. I wasn't the right target, but she hadn't been wrong. Something needed to be done for these people. "Things have gotten bad. You can't blame them for being upset."

"They don't have to live like this," Jackson said, shaking his head. There was a look of disgust on his face as his gaze moved over the shacks. "They're choosing to live in filth. If they worked harder, they could make a better life for themselves. They're a drain on society."

Al frowned, his gaze moving over Jackson slowly as if he were trying to see through him, right to his dark soul. My uncle shook his head and looked away, but his usual smile seemed to have been wiped from his face.

My own mouth morphed into a frown at the sound of the Regulator's words coming out of Jackson's mouth. He was better than this and I knew it. He just had to fight against his father's influence so he could be the man he needed to be.

"How?" I whispered, keeping my tone calm so it would reach him and not make him shut down.

Jackson opened his mouth, but slammed it shut a second later. His eyes moved past me, back toward the shacks we'd just fled, but he didn't say anything. He never did. His loyalty toward his father was unyielding, which probably had a lot to do with why I couldn't take that next step with him.

I wasn't ready to give up on Jackson, though. Even the striking man in front of me, who had been brought up by a power-hungry politician in a post-apocalyptic society, had to see that this wasn't okay. It had been at least two years since any new housing units were built, and nothing was being done to help the people living in these shacks. The Regulator's house, however, was pristine. No other homes inside the walls of New Atlanta compared to it. Not even the houses of the council members, who often had to share their large homes. Two families to a house was normal these days, except when it came to the Regulator. He was above the law because he made the law, not just here, but across the rest of the country. All sanctioned settlements bent to Garret Star's will.

He'd been in charge since before the walls went up, quietly at first, and then stepping in to take control like he was saving the world from certain doom—at least according to my parents. Slowly, his influence had spread to other settlements as they popped up around the country. During the early days of

13

reestablishing the government, Garret Star had the foresight to send crews out to oil refineries so fuel production could continue. He'd also trained crews on how to get the electricity running again, then sent them to other areas to help out. If the settlement in question cooperated—meaning they adopted the laws Star had put into place—they got help. If they didn't, they were on their own. If they didn't play by the rules they got no help from the new government, no vaccine when it was finally created, and no fuel. Nothing.

I had high hopes for Jackson, even if I couldn't see us together, but deep down I suspected that he wasn't ever going to meet his potential. His father's reach was too wide, his influence too great. Jackson would never be as bad as the greedy man who had raised him—at least I hoped not—but I doubted he'd be the man he could be. The man he was with me.

Al was the one to break the silence. He twisted his head so he could glance down the street before settling his gaze once again on Jackson. "I'm late for patrol. You can make sure Meg gets home okay?"

My uncle gave him a studying look, one that said he didn't fully trust the man in front of him, but he thought that same man at least had my best interest at heart.

"I'm fine," I said.

Even though I loved that Al was trying to get along with my best friend—my family had been famously anti-Garret Star for as long as I could remember, and none of them loved that Jackson and I were so close now—I had no problem walking through the streets of New Atlanta by myself. Especially not when my own apartment building was practically in sight.

Despite my assurance that I was okay, neither Jackson nor my uncle looked my way.

"I can make sure she gets there," Jackson said, and I couldn't help wondering if he was somehow immune to the tone of my voice.

My uncle nodded as he scratched at his round belly, which seemed out of place on his still lanky frame. "Thanks."

He, too, seemed to be unable to hear my overly feminine voice.

If I wasn't so anxious to get away from Suzie and the mob, I'd remind my uncle of how many times my mom—both of them—had saved his ass.

Al, now assured that I would be okay with the big, strong man at my side, turned to look at me. "Be more careful."

He grinned, which was disarming in itself, and then shot me a wink that helped ease the annoyance inside me. It was impossible to stay angry with Al, who was more like a large child than an adult most of the time. Especially when he switched his sword out for a hook and walked around impersonating Captain Hook—complete with an eye patch and a stuffed parrot on his shoulder.

My uncle hurried off, most likely headed for the extra night shift he'd picked up. Something he'd been doing more and more of lately.

Only a second later, Jackson had his arm around my waist and was leading me down the street. I let him even though I was still irritated from our conversation on the wall—which I still couldn't pinpoint *why*—and the fact that he thought I needed him to save me. Yes, that was how we'd started our relationship, but I'd been eleven then. Things had changed. I'd survived loss that would have crippled most people these days and come out on the other end stronger. At least in my opinion.

"I'm sorry," Jackson said after less than ten steps. "I was stupid for bringing your uncle up."

His apology caught me off guard and my eyes were instantly filled with tears, which seemed to contradict the very things I'd been thinking right before he made his apology. I shook my head, unable to talk, and my dark hair swished over my shoulders, tickling my arm and probably Jackson's as well.

"No. It was dumb for me to get upset, and it wasn't even really about Angus."

"I know," Jackson said.

Of course he did. He knew almost everything about me. Had seen me at my worst moments. Hell, he'd held me at my worst moments.

I couldn't form words well enough to let him know that I forgave him, but he knew. Together we walked in silence, Jackson's strong arm around me every step of the way, almost like he was holding me up. His fingers were firm on my waist and felt so natural that I started to wonder if everyone else might have been on the right track about us. He was my best friend. Sometimes, it felt like he was my only friend. There was a serious shortage of people our age and forming relationships had never been easy for me.

When the virus hit twenty years ago, billions of people had died and come back as zombies, killing thousands maybe even millions more. Most of the babies born in the early years following the outbreak had died, but Jackson and I were some of the few to make it. He'd been here in Atlanta, which meant he got the new antibiotic the CDC had created. Me... Well, nobody really knew how I survived. Luck, probably. My biological father died before I was even born, and my mother only a few days after. If it hadn't been for my parents—Vivian and Axl James—I wouldn't have made it here at all. But I did and they raised me, and I had a good childhood despite the walls and the zombies and the death that surrounded us.

Only now, Dad was gone.

"I miss him."

The words popped out before I had time to think them through, but I couldn't regret saying them. I did miss Dad, and talking about him at home only made it worse because Mom's delusions had taken over our life, making it harder and harder to get through a day without screaming.

Sometimes, I had a hard time forcing myself to go home at all.

Tears filled my eyes and spilled over before I could stop them, and Jackson stopped walking. He wrapped his arms around me, and seconds later my face was pressed against his chest. Even Jackson, who wasn't a tall man, seemed to tower over me today. It may have had to do with my mood, though. I wasn't that short, three inches past five feet, but at the moment I felt like a dwarf in Jackson's arms.

"Jackson, I—" I tried to pull away even though his embrace was comforting. "I don't want to..."

"Shhh," he said, holding me tighter so I couldn't escape. "This isn't romantic. I know how you feel about that and I promise not to try and kiss you—even if it kills me." The teasing in his voice made me smile through the tears clouding my vision.

"You're too good to me," I said, using his shirt to wipe my damp cheeks.

# CHAPTER TWO

## Meg

**MOM'S** panicked voice greeted me the second I shut the door, and in an instant all the tension Jackson had managed to ease away was back.

"Megan? Is that you?"

"It's me," I called, even though I shouldn't have had to. There was no one else. Not anymore.

She came out of the kitchen with her hand on her chest like she was trying to calm her pounding heart. It was a cliché, but also probably not far from the truth. She'd been increasingly more paranoid since Dad disappeared.

"I've been going crazy! Your shift ended hours ago." Her brown eyes, which at one time had sparkled with life, were big and round and dull as they moved around the room. It was like they were always searching for something—or, more accurately, for someone. "Where have you been?"

"With Jackson," I said, crossing my arms.

Mom's lips pressed together and I could tell she was torn. She wanted me to be happy, even in her slightly delusional state, but my parents had never been thrilled with the relationship. It wasn't just the fact that he was the Regulator's son, either. Dad had always said that Jackson acted like he was wearing a mask. My father had never gotten the chance to see the real Jackson, though. Not like I had.

Of course now, anyone connected with the Regulator or the CDC was suspicious to Mom.

"I'm fine," I said firmly. It wouldn't be enough to end this conversation and I knew it, but I had to try and steer the conversation in another direction.

Mom shoved her hand through her dark blonde hair, which was in desperate need of a wash, then crossed her arms over her chest. She looked like she was trying to pull herself together. It wasn't working. She was about to unravel. I knew it. She knew it. Hell, probably every neighbor we had knew it.

"Did you go to work today?" I asked against my better judgment.

"You know I can't," she hissed.

I squeezed my eyes shut while mentally tabulating my own credits. It wouldn't be enough. Not even with the credits Dad had stashed away.

The image of Suzie's slum flickered through my mind and a shudder shook my body. No. That would *not* happen. I'd sell myself in the entertainment district before I allowed that to happen to us.

When I opened my eyes, Mom hadn't moved an inch.

"We're going to lose our apartment," I said, hoping to talk some sense into her. I needed her help. I couldn't do this alone.

"Is that what you're worried about?" she snapped, her eyes somehow growing larger.

"Yes, and you should be too."

*Don't scream, Meg. Don't do it. Someone will call the Judicial Officer and Parvarti will show up. It will put her in an awkward position.*

"I can't worry about an apartment!" Mom hissed, her voice quieter this time. Her brown eyes left my face only to dart around the apartment again. It was like she thought someone was listening in on us. "Your father is missing. *They* took him."

"No one took him," I said even though I had no idea what had really happened to Dad.

Mom nodded so fast that her hair fell into her face, covering her eyes. She didn't push it back. "The CDC has him. They had Angus there. They used him for years. Kept him alive even though they told us he was dead. Just so they could create a vaccine. It worked for a while, but when the virus mutated they had to start all over. Then he finally died and it mutated again, and they needed someone else. Someone new. *Your dad.*"

It wasn't the first time she'd thrown the crazy theory at me, but it didn't get any easier to hear. Even though I didn't believe it for a second, the idea that someone was holding Dad captive and using him like a lab rat made me physically sick.

"Stop it," I moaned, choking back the tears. "Please."

"I can't!" Mom threw her hands in the air, and for the first time I noticed how thin her arms were. Almost skeletal.

She wasn't eating. I'd suspected as much, but seeing all the weight she'd lost sent a shiver shooting through me. I'd already had so much taken from me, and I wasn't sure if I could stomach losing her too.

Only, I didn't know if she could be saved at that point.

"Dad isn't immune," I said calmly. "They would have told you when you got here. Joshua said it a thousand times —"

The second the words were out I knew they were a mistake, but it was too late. The trigger was there and she was ready to pull it, blowing a bullet through the last bit of hope I had that she wasn't losing her mind.

"He said it, but that was *before*. Then Axl disappeared and no one had a clue where he went. How does no one know? It doesn't make sense. Then Joshua started looking into it, and next thing you know we're being told there was an accident. An *accident!*"

She paced as she talked, her fingers picking at the hem of her dirty shirt. Her mouth moving so fast that the words spilled out like a waterfall, flooding the room and my head until I felt like I was on the verge of drowning.

I backed away until I was at the front door, and when I slipped out, she was still pacing. Still jabbering away like something was eating at her brain. Chomping on it until the Mom I knew didn't exist.

I shut the door, but her words didn't fade completely.

In the safety of the hall, I exhaled and sank to the floor. My head fell back, bumping against the door. I focused on the ceiling. It was a textured pattern that was so familiar I probably could have drawn it in my sleep. Row after row of two inch white sunbursts spread from one end of the hall to the other, only interrupted by the recessed lights and smoke detectors. The familiarity of it was soothing, so I started tracing them with my gaze. Focusing on the lines while my heartbeat slowed.

"How is she?" I'd only made it a few rows before Lila's musical voice broke through my thoughts. I looked up to find her standing only four feet away from me, her brown eyes sad. How I didn't hear my aunt walk up was an utter mystery.

"Horrible," I said, hauling myself to my feet. A piece of paper taped to the door caught my eye and I pulled it off without thinking about it. "I was a couple hours late and she lost it."

Lila's eyes moved to the door at my back and she frowned, her beautiful face marred by the creases that seemed to have grown deeper in recent weeks. She was part of this family, and for her the loss of Dad and Joshua had been like losing brothers.

"She's suffered so much. It doesn't seem fair," Lila mumbled, her eyes still on the door.

"Everyone has lost people," I pointed out, my hand tightening until the paper I'd just pulled off the door crinkled in my grasp. "Both of your parents died when the virus hit."

Lila's gaze moved to my face, and I could feel her mental chiding. "I've never lost a child."

The words were nicer than I deserved, but that had always been Lila's way.

"You're right." I looked down as heat spread across my face. Red print started up at me from the paper in my hand, but I couldn't read what it said. "She's been through a lot," I mumbled, smoothing the paper out. It was an invitation.

"Two kids." My aunt's words pulled my attention away from the paper and I looked up to find her shaking her head. A second later, she sighed and turned toward her own apartment. "How does anyone survive that?"

Images of my sister flashed through my mind, but I pushed them away. Even after all these years there were times when the pain felt so sharp that it took my breath away. Like now, standing where we had once played, feeling as if her ghost was still hanging over me. Sometimes, if I stood still long enough, I could almost hear the tinkle of her laughter echoing through the hall.

"Come on," Lila called, holding the door open for me.

I followed, the invitation still clutched in my hand. My legs were heavy and my head felt like it was floating above my shoulders. Mom's voice was still audible, but I knew I'd be safe from it in Al and Lila's apartment.

It was one of the only safe places I had left.

"Charlie should be in her room," Lila said as she headed toward the kitchen. "Have you eaten?"

"I'm not sure we have any food in the apartment," I replied. "I'm not even sure we'll have an apartment much longer at this rate."

Part of me hated throwing my problems on my aunt's shoulders, but I also knew I wouldn't be able to hide them from her forever. The credits I made had to go toward rent, leaving nothing for food. I did my best to eat at Jackson's, or pop into Lila and Al's. Even Parvarti's if I could catch her at home, which had been less and less frequent now that Joshua was gone. But I needed to be sure to take some home to Mom, which left little for me. She wasn't the only one who'd lost weight.

"We won't let that happen," Lila said firmly.

"You have your own family to worry about. You have Charlie and Luke."

"You won't have a choice." Her hands went to her hips. "Luke is barely home anymore. I'm pretty sure he's seeing someone, and if he gets married he can apply for an apartment. And Charlie has her own job. Hopefully she starts that apprenticeship soon, too." Lila rolled her eyes before turning to head into the kitchen. "She may spend most of her credits in the entertainment district, but she'll pitch in if we need it. I won't have any freeloaders in this house."

Despite my shitty day and horrible circumstances, I found myself smiling. All my life I'd heard stories about how wealthy Lila's family had been before the virus. It was funny to try and picture her in that role. Especially now that she was a frugal post-apocalyptic housewife who regularly lectured her eighteen-year-old daughter about wasting credits on frivolous things.

"We'll get by," I said, and then hurried to Charlie's room before Lila could stop me.

I rapped my knuckles against the door, but only paused a second before pushing it open. Charlie, who was a perfectly gorgeous combination of her parent's Asian and Mediterranean lineage, looked up from where she was sprawled across the bed.

"Thank God," she said, tossing the book she'd been pretending to read aside. Charlie didn't read. "I've been dying of boredom."

"No big plans for this evening?" I said, lowering myself onto the bed at her side.

Charlie snorted as she tossed her dark hair over her shoulder. "Nope. I spent all my credits. I can't wait until pay day so I can go out!"

"Yeah," I muttered.

*Sure. Go out. That's what I'll be doing with my credits.*

She looked down, and a second later plucked the invitation I'd all but forgotten about out of my hand. "What's this?"

"I don't know," I said dismissively. "An invitation. I barely looked at it."

She pressed her lips together and narrowed her eyes on the paper as she read. "It's to Dragon's Lair. That's where they're holding that big fight."

My focus was on her threadbare comforter and a loose string I was desperately trying to pull out, so I was only half paying attention when I said, "Fight?"

"Yeah. Special release program. The prison colony in DC is getting full, so they set this program up to allow some of the lesser offenders a way to earn their freedom." Charlie shrugged like it was no big deal, but a shiver went through me. "I thought you'd heard. Everyone's been talking about it."

Who's idea was that? "I've been a little preoccupied."

"Oh, yeah. Right. Of course." Pink spread across Charlie's cheeks and she looked away.

"Anyway, I hate going to fights and I don't have a single credit to spare." I went back to plucking at the string.

"You don't have to watch the fight." She frowned when she realized she didn't have an argument for the second part of my statement, but a second later her brown eyes lit up. When she turned them on me, I knew what she was going to say before the words were even out of her mouth. "We *could* go you know. All you have to do is ask Jackson to go with us."

Sometimes, I wondered if Charlie even liked spending time

with me, or if she only did it for Jackson's connections.

I plucked at the loose string harder, thinking it through. My goal was to not lead Jackson on, but the idea of getting out for a bit—even if going to the entertainment district wasn't something I typically liked to do—did sound appealing. Between Dad's disappearance and Joshua's death, followed very shortly by Mom slowly losing her mind, I was beginning to feel like everything around me had started to fall to pieces. Maybe a few hours in the entertainment district would do the trick? Jackson had unlimited credits and I knew he wouldn't mind paying...

"Come on." Charlie waved the invitation in my face as if that would motivate me to make the decision. "You could take the opportunity to get to know Jackson better."

"What are you talking about?" I asked, narrowing my eyes on her. "I've known Jackson for years."

Of course, I knew *what* she was implying, what I didn't get was *why*.

Charlie sighed and shook her head. "You aren't going to want to hear this, but I'm going to say it anyway. I know things are tough for you right now, but if you don't take some initiative, they're going to get worse. Jackson is in love with you. He has been for years. And he's rich. He has more credits than he knows what to do with, and he lives in the biggest, nicest house inside these walls. Maybe inside any of the settlements." Charlie narrowed her eyes on my face like if she just concentrated hard enough, I'd take her advice. "If you marry him, all your troubles are gone."

"That's ridiculous. I'm not going to marry Jackson."

Charlie arched her eyebrows, making her look more like Lila than ever, but she didn't say anything else.

She did have a point. The second I let Jackson know I wanted to be a couple all my problems would evaporate. But I wasn't *in love* with him, and I just couldn't do something like that.

When I didn't say anything, Charlie let out a deep sigh. Her serious expression disappeared a second later, and she nudged me, smiling. "You can at least let the rich guy buy us a night in the entertainment district."

With my head spinning, I got to my feet. "Yeah. I can do that much at least."

Charlie had given me something to seriously think about, but I had time before Mom and I found ourselves out on our asses. There had to be something I could do to make this thing work other than throw myself at Jackson. There was a way, I just had to find it.

If not, I could call this plan B.

# CHAPTER THREE

## Meg

CHARLIE bounced on the balls of her feet as we wove our way through the tightly packed bar, her boobs threatening to spill out of her low cut top with every little hop. The combined scents of alcohol, tobacco, sweat, and death filled the air, making my head pound. It would only take a couple drinks for it all to fade, though. Hopefully, once I had a good buzz I'd be able to relax. It would be nice if, just for a few hours, I could do something other than worry about where I was going to get the credits for food, or what I was going to do to keep Mom and me off the streets.

"The fight's going to start soon!" Jackson yelled from behind me.

He pushed forward, grabbing my hand as he went by and pulling me faster through the crowd of people. I slipped my free arm through Charlie's on the way past, dragging her along. Around us, people who towered over me by sometimes a foot turned to glare as we nudged our way through. Jackson didn't slow or even blink, though. He was used to getting his way.

When we finally broke through the crowd, I found the ring

looming in front of us. Surrounded by a chain link cage with only one way in or out, the once white floor was splattered with black and brown spots, trophies left behind by previous fights, and just seeing the stains sent a shudder down my spine. I didn't know why people enjoyed this kind of thing, because just thinking about it made my skin crawl.

"Over here." Jackson pulled me forward faster, past the ring and the glares of other patrons who had gotten here early so they could earn their front row seat for the fight.

Despite the evil looks shot our way, no one questioned us. They all knew Jackson. Or, more accurately, they all know his father. There wasn't a single place Jackson went inside the walls of New Atlanta where he wouldn't be recognized.

On the other side of the ring, a roped-off seating area was perched on a low platform. Eight chairs with red cushions sat only four feet from the fence, all of them empty and just waiting for a VIP to show up. Jackson pulled the rope aside and behind me, Charlie squealed. The smile on his face seemed forced, though, not like the Jackson I knew, and for some reason my father's words rang in my ears. I pushed them aside, wanting to think about anything but my family at the moment.

Jackson gave a dramatic bow and waved toward the seats, motioning for us to enter. Charlie bounced toward the chairs like she owned the place. I went in a little more hesitantly.

"I really just wanted a drink," I told Jackson after he'd replaced the rope and taken a seat next to Charlie. I was still standing because the thought of watching a fight at all made my stomach roll, but watching it without a drink or two in me made me want to run. Especially this close to the ring.

"Sit down." Jackson patted the empty seat at his side. "The waitress will take care of it."

"There's a waitress?" Charlie sat up straighter.

Jackson shot her a wink as he leaned closer. "When you're a VIP there is."

Her brown eyes lit up, and when they met mine, she nodded toward Jackson. It wasn't subtle, but the only indication that he saw it was a slight twitch of his lips. He almost looked pleased with himself.

I rolled my eyes and Charlie made a face that reminded me of when we were kids and she would get mad because she wasn't allowed to make up all the rules to whatever game we were playing. I half expected her to stick her tongue out at me, but she just nodded her head toward my best friend again. In a much more dramatic way this time.

*Yes, Charlie, I get it. Marry the guy while I can.*

I squirmed in my seat while I waited for the waitress. The bar was just to our right, but a wall of people separated us from the booze.

Thankfully, it took less than a minute for a woman to come out from behind the counter. She was so short that only the top of her pink head was visible through the crowd, but the people swarming the room stepped aside as she passed like she was Moses parting the Red Sea. Almost every set of eyes in the room followed her progress as she headed our way, and when she finally came into view, I could see why. The outfit she was wearing was little more than a few strategically placed strips of material, crisscrossing over her body in a way that covered the important parts while at the same time giving off the impression that at any moment something just might pop out. Her exposed skin shimmered with sweat, but it also sparkled under the lights shining down on her from above. She must have slathered herself with body glitter before coming into work.

She stopped just outside the ropes, almost like she would never dare cross the barrier separating the VIPs from the *little people.*

"What can I get you?" she called, expertly raising her voice so she could be heard over the roar of voices and laughter filling the room.

Her gray eyes slid over Jackson, but it was a different look than I was used to. Typically, women looked at Jackson like they were trying to figure out how to snag him, but she seemed almost hesitant when she looked him over.

"Moonshine." His gaze took in every inch of the waitress, starting at her lean legs and slowly moving up. He sat up straighter, grinning. "Three."

The eye-fuck he was giving her made me squirm. It wasn't jealousy though; at least I didn't think so. It felt more like I was getting a glimpse of a side of him that I'd never seen before, and something about it made me uneasy. If I hadn't been feeling nauseated before, I certainly was now.

"I'm going to need something stronger," I called. "Get me a couple shots."

Jackson tore his gaze away from the bare flesh in front of him, blinking when he glanced my way. Almost like he'd just remembered that I was next to him. He didn't look embarrassed, but he did shrug.

I just rolled my eyes. He was free to do whatever—or whoever—he wanted.

"Two shots." This time when he ordered, he managed to keep his eyes off the mostly nude girl in front of him.

The waitress shot me a look, her gray eyes sliding over me slowly. Next to her skimpy dress, my jeans and t-shirt probably made me look like I was getting ready to go on a supply run and I wanted to protect myself from getting ripped apart by zombies. She couldn't be much more than seventeen, which was the legal age for working in the entertainment district. Still, I could tell she was trying to look older. Her makeup was caked on, but under it her skin looked smooth and healthy. When I took a closer look, I noticed that the light brown roots of her pink hair were nearly an inch long. She was pretty, though.

Her lips were puckered when she headed off. Like everyone else she probably assumed Jackson and I were together, but there was no disappointment in her eyes. I was used to women acting like they were trying to pry Jackson and me apart, but she just looked curious. Odd.

I pulled on my t-shirt as I took a good look around the room, and it hit me that I was probably the only woman in the place not wearing something tight and revealing. Charlie, sitting on the other side of Jackson, had on a shirt low-cut enough to be dangerous, and her jeans could have passed for a second set of skin. Most of the other women, though, were wearing clothes similar to the waitress's. Dresses that had so little material they left nothing to the imagination, which was probably the point. A lot of the girls here were on the job, hoping to make enough extra credits so they could buy their family food or a better life. It happened a lot.

"I bet she gets lots of tips." Jackson's eyes were glued to the waitress's ass until she'd disappeared through the crowd. Then, almost like he was trying to make excuses for her he said, "You have to do what you can to survive in this world."

I had to bite my tongue to stop from pointing out that he wouldn't know a thing about that. Of course, there was a good chance he was saying it for my benefit. Almost like he and Charlie were on the same page. My Dad was gone and I was practically alone now that Mom was losing it, and survival might mean finally giving in to his advances.

But he couldn't want to get me that way. Could he?

I didn't know for sure about that, but I did know Jackson was right about one thing: The waitress probably did get a lot of tips. Just a couple hours ago I'd sworn to myself that I would sell my body before Mom and I ended up on the streets, but maybe it wouldn't have to come to that. Maybe all I needed to do was get a job in a place like this and show a little skin.

I gnawed on my lip while I scanned the crowd crammed into the room. Most of the people in this room could be put into two categories: The young, like Charlie, who were just out for a good time, and the dregs of society. The men and women who worked in the entertainment district, the ones who dealt in the black market, and the zombie slayers who had grown accustomed to being dirty, both inside and out.

The second group was the one I focused on because I'd gain nothing from the first if I worked here. Young people didn't have the extra credits to throw away on tips. Not that the people working in the entertainment district should either, but they did it anyway. Many of them would rather use their money for drinks than bother wasting it on food and silly things like a visit to the dentist or the bathhouses.

It was easy to pick their kind out, even in a room this packed. Men or women, they were typically more worn-looking, usually covered in tattoos and piercings. Sometimes they had missing limbs or eyes or teeth, and they were never without a drink in their hands. These were the people who would help keep me off the streets. I just had to figure out how to go about getting a job here *and* how the hell I was going to stomach it.

The waitress came back just as a man stepped into the ring in front of us. He was shirtless, and his dark skin glistened under the lights as he lifted his arms above his slick head. He turned in a circle, slower than necessary, and the crowd cheered, drawing a smile from him that revealed gaps where his two front teeth used to be.

Jackson passed me a shot and I downed it, barely feeling it with all my attention focused on the man who still hadn't stopped spinning. Even though it was slow, I couldn't understand how he hadn't gotten dizzy yet. Between the stink and the lights, I would have fallen on my ass by now.

"Who's that?" I asked, having to raise my voice over the cheering crowd.

I passed my empty glass to Jackson and took the second shot from him, throwing it back. The second one burned, but it also coated my stomach when it went down. I blinked when I started to feel it. The alcohol didn't take long to work its way through me since I'd had almost nothing to eat today.

Jackson took my second empty glass before handing me the moonshine. "That's Dragon, the champion. He does the introductions when he isn't fighting. This is his place."

I studied Jackson out of the corner of my eye, wondering how he knew that. He'd never mentioned to me that he came to see the fights, but it was possible. He had other friends — the kids of council members — and I knew he went out without me at times. It was still hard to picture him hanging out in a place like this, though.

"He looks like a dragon," Charlie said before I could ask Jackson if he'd been here before.

He chuckled as he handed the waitress a wad of credits, and I wasn't sure if it was the buzzing in my head or not, but I swear his gaze slid over Charlie like he was imagining her naked.

The waitress's eyes lit up when she took the credits from Jackson, and based on the way she bounced back through the crowd — with every eye glued to her ass — I guessed she'd just earned more in one tip than she would have the whole night otherwise.

"Welcome!" Dragon's deep voice cut through my thoughts and I found my eyes once again glued to the ring.

The man was facing the other way when he finally stopped spinning, giving me an excellent view of the tattoo on his back. It stretched from his shoulder blades down to his waist, disappearing into his loose-fitting pants. True to his name, it was the image of a dragon with its wings spread wide, almost like it was preparing to take flight.

"Tonight we have a special guest, all the way down from the DC prison system."

The crowd went wild, some people cheering while others hurled boos and insults through the air. Something moved to my left and I turned just as the crowd parted and a couple burly men pulled a cart forward. On top of it, chained to a post, two zombies snarled and jerked, trying to get at the people gathered in the room. The closer they got to the ring, the louder the crowd roared, cheering and throwing things at the zombies as they passed.

I shifted uncomfortably in my seat. "I hate this part."

"Don't worry." Jackson put his hand on my leg, two inches north of my knee, and for once I let him. "They're required to have the vaccine behind the bar just in case someone is bitten."

"What about the fighter?" I asked, craning my neck to get a better look at the zombies even though my stomach flipped uncomfortably. "He could get infected from just a scratch."

"One injection a week has been proven to work in most cases."

Most cases? Sounded like an awfully big risk. Of course, Jackson would know. Not only was his dad the Regulator, but he'd been director of the CDC when the initial virus broke out. He had several medical degrees to his name, and extensive knowledge when it came to how viruses worked. Plus, he was a genius. Something Jackson had in common with his father. He'd started an apprenticeship at the CDC at the age of fifteen and hadn't looked back. Jackson, whether he chose to follow in his father's footsteps as leader of the new government or not, would be a great man one day. I just hoped he chose to be a good man, too.

"A lot of good it will do if these assholes are carrying the mutated virus," I said, even though my knowledge of how this all worked was child's play compared to Jackson's.

The whole thing made me uneasy. Why people liked watching something this sick I'd never know, but it took a twisted kind of person to really enjoy something like this. Suddenly, I found myself wondering how the hell I had ended up here in the first place.

Jackson squeezed my leg. "It'll be fine."

I was too focused on the zombies to push his hand away, even if it had now snaked up to my thigh.

The beefy men had finally reached the ring, and I leaned forward when they unhooked the zombie's chains. The creatures fought their handlers as they were dragged forward, but it didn't seem to take much effort to pull them into the ring. They got closer to where we sat and the stench of death became overwhelming. I had to focus on breathing out of my mouth so my stomach didn't jump up and spill its contents all over the red carpet at my feet.

The men pulled the zombies to opposite corners of the ring, clicking their chains into place before heading out, being sure to keep a safe distance from the claws of the dead. The creatures went crazy as all around them more cheers rang through the air, and the clink of metal against metal was so loud it felt like it was echoing through my head.

Dragon grinned, his eyes sweeping across the throng of people gathered around the ring as he turned in a circle one final time. "Are you ready?" The walls seemed to vibrate with the roar of the crowd. "Do you want to meet our fighter?" More cheers pulsed through the air. "Bring him out!"

Dragon pointed to my left and a man stepped through the door the zombies had just come out of. He kept his head down as he made his way through the throng of people, and I found myself standing so I could get a better look at him. The crowd was too thick, though, and no matter how I twisted nothing was visible except the top of the fighter's head.

I shifted from foot to foot, waiting for the man to come into view. Finally, after what seemed like an eternity, he stepped into the ring and took his place at Dragon's side. Still, though, I couldn't get a good look at him because both men had their backs to me.

"Donaghy!" The crowd went wild when Dragon announced the fighter's name.

The man still didn't lift his head. His hands clenched into fists at his sides, and the muscles in his arms flexed. Almost every inch of them were covered in tattoos. Dark black lines crisscrossed one another, circling his forearms and biceps as they moved up and curled around his shoulders and back. From there the lines moved

34

down, stopping just above his waist. The design was so intricate that it was nothing short of a work of art. I couldn't imagine that he'd gotten it in DC—not based on the rumors I'd heard about the living conditions in the prison settlement.

Dragon's arms were still raised when he turned to face me, and his mouth was stretched wide with a smile that made him look like he was on the verge of going insane.

The fighter turned too, and I was finally able to get a good look at the convict. He was younger than I'd thought he would be, only twenty-five at the most. His dark hair had either been cut close to his head or was just growing back after being shaved. I'd heard stories about problems with lice in the DC prison system, so it was possible they'd resorted to shaving the heads of all the prisoners.

Donaghy's eyes stayed on the floor and his square jaw twitched as Dragon talked, highlighting the fighter's victories in DC before joining the release program. Since then, he'd excelled in both the Baltimore and Dayton settlements.

The room went nuts, and finally the fighter pulled his eyes away from the ground. They were ice blue and colder than December when they scanned the crowd. He didn't smile, and he didn't look proud of his accomplishments in the ring. At his side, his hands were still clenched into fists, and every time he tightened his jaw, the scar that cut across his chin puckered.

Seeing it made me sit back in my chair.

Dad had a scar in the exact same place. I was so used to it that most of the time I didn't even notice it, but with Donaghy in front of me, it felt like I'd been slapped across the face. It was harsh and unexpected, and enough to make my head spin.

"Are you ready?" Dragon called as he walked backwards, moving toward the door.

I shook my head, trying to rid myself of the image of my father as all around me the crowd once again cheered. Donaghy barely blinked.

Dragon was still grinning when he ducked through the open door, shutting it behind him. The click of metal against metal was so loud it could be heard even over the roaring crowd. In the ring, Donaghy turned to face the zombies, his back once again to us as he flexed his hands. Making a fist, then relaxing his fingers, then repeating the gesture. In front of him, the dead fought against their chains, while outside the ring their handlers got ready to release them. All it took was a flick of a switch and the chains fell away, freeing the dead. And then they charged.

These two must have been newer than their putrid skin made them look, because they were fast. Too fast to have been turned for long. When the first one reached Donaghy, the fighter easily kicked him back, sending the creature's rotting body flying into the side of the cage. A metallic clang echoed through the room and the crowd went wild. The second zombie reached the fighter, who once again tried to kick him back, but in a move so fast that it took my breath away, the dead man's hand closed around Donaghy's ankle, stopping him mid-kick.

Gasps and cheers broke through the crowd when the fighter went down, his back slamming against the floor of the ring, and suddenly I was on my feet. My heart was pounding like crazy and even though I didn't want to see this man—or any man for that matter—get ripped apart, I couldn't make myself look away.

Donaghy kicked his trapped leg, trying to break free while the first zombie approached him from behind. The creature's collision with the fence hadn't even fazed him, and he gnashed his teeth as he tore across the ring, intent on ripping the fighter's throat apart.

"He's out," Jackson hissed at my side, his voice low and primal and brimming with something that reminded me of glee.

I shook my head. "No."

In the blink of an eye, the fighter was on his feet and the zombie that had been holding him was down. It happened so fast that I couldn't figure out *how*. All I knew was that the zombie who'd had the upper hand a second ago was on the ground and Donaghy was slamming the heel of his boot into the creature's legs, one after the other, over and over again. Even over the roar of the crowd, the sound of splintering bone was deafening.

The second zombie was almost on top of him when the fighter spun its way. His hand wrapped around the dead creature's throat, stopping the thing in its tracks. The zombie gnashed his teeth but Donaghy didn't move. His fingers tightened, sinking into the decaying flesh. Black blood poured over his hand and ran down his arm, dripping onto the already stained floor of the ring. In seconds, the fighter's entire hand had disappeared inside the zombie's throat. Lost in a sea of gray, rotten flesh.

Donaghy twisted his wrist, and just like that, the zombie's head detached from its body and fell to the floor. His milky eyes were still open, and his rotten teeth still chomping when its body landed next to the head.

The crowd went crazy, and I was right there with them, cheering for this man without even thinking about it.

"Did you see that?" Jackson elbowed me and I turned to find a strange kind of excitement gleaming in his eyes. "That was amazing."

My dark hair fell across my face when I nodded, and even though I didn't understand the expression shining in my friend's eyes, I couldn't deny the truth. It had been amazing.

The second zombie was still on the ground, struggling to get up despite the shattered bones in his legs. Now that his friend had been taken care of, Donaghy turned his attention to the writhing creature. With both legs snapped, the poor thing couldn't do much more than reach for the man in front of him, so it wasn't much of a fight. Donaghy shook his head, pausing in front of the zombie and studying it for just a second. It was almost like he hated to put an end to the thing. He didn't hold back, though. He slammed the heel of his boot against the zombie's skull. Two stomps was all it took, and then the second zombie met the same fate as the first one. Dead. Finally.

Donaghy's shoulders heaved as he stared down at the now motionless creatures, his icy blue eyes looking at them like he felt sorry for them. Like he wished he could have given them a more dignified death. It was a strange scene, watching this hulk of a man stare at the piles of rotting flesh at his feet as the crowd cheered and Dragon, still beaming, returned to the ring.

"Give this man a hand!" the bar owner called, grabbing Donaghy's arm and lifting it above his head.

Once again, the fighter didn't react to the praise, and if I didn't know any better, I'd think he was a robot.

The crowd was still cheering when he exited the ring.

The second he was gone, two men rushed in. One was carrying a shovel while the other had a bucket and a mop. I stood frozen in place, watching as the man with the shovel scooped up the remains. He tossed them into a wheelbarrow just outside the cage, then turned back for more. The man scooped up the head of the first zombie Donaghy had taken out, and the things' mouth was still chomping away. The man laughed as he said something to his friend. They chuckled together, and I found myself wondering what they were talking about. Whatever it was, it struck me as irreverent. These may have been zombies, but they had been people at one time. People who'd had lives and loved ones. People who were missed. They deserved better than this. We all did.

I turned away when the man with the bucket started mopping up the ring.

All around the room, people exchanged handfuls of money, settling bets made before the fighter had taken the ring. On the other side of the room a man was shoved through the crowd. Curse words flew through the air when a second later a fight broke out. I watched as the two men tried to beat each other senseless, but got nowhere thanks to the thick mass of people packed around them. The two hulking men who had brought the zombies out of the back room pushed their way through the crowd, and seconds later the offenders were separated and dragged from the bar.

"What'd you think?" Jackson asked, and I turned my attention to his grinning face. Everything about his expression said that he wanted to please me.

On the other side of him, Charlie was in the middle of throwing herself at a guy nearly twice her age. Despite the buzzing in my brain from the alcohol, he looked vaguely familiar. I was fairly certain that he worked with her dad, which meant she was probably trying to charm her way into convincing him not to mention this whole thing to Uncle Al. It would work, of course. Charlie always got her way.

"Did you have fun?" Jackson asked when I didn't respond to his first question.

"It was better than I thought," I said, lifting myself up on the tips of my toes as I scanned the crowd for the waitress.

The top of her pink head was visible, and I raised myself up higher, hoping to get a better look. Like me she was short, making it hard to see anything she was doing. Then the crowd shifted, giving me a perfect view of the stack of credits in the waitress's hand. Seeing all those tips cemented my decision. I needed to figure out how to get a job here. It was the only way.

"We can come more often, if you want." Jackson grinned and nodded to the rope at my side. "VIP seats."

"Yeah," I said reluctantly. "Maybe."

The last thing I wanted was for Jackson to come here more often, but I needed to be subtle about it. I couldn't let him know what I was thinking or he'd do everything in his power to stop me.

I looked back to find the waitress grinning as she shoved her credits down her dress, somehow managing to find a place to hide them within the tiny strips of fabric.

I took one step toward the rope, ready to head over there, but stopped when Jackson got to his feet.

"Are you ready to go?" he asked.

"Not yet." Since I didn't want him coming with me, I waved for him to sit back down. "I need to use the bathroom."

He frowned as his gaze moved across the room. "Here?"

He had a point. The place was squalid even by the entertainment district's standards. Now that the crowd had thinned out some, I could see how much dirt and blood—both zombie and human—were caked on the floor. The few tables in the place were so wobbly I was surprised they were still upright, and the brown tint to the walls wasn't paint. It was years and years of dirt and neglect.

"When you gotta go, you gotta go," I said, trying to sound confident even though my stomach had turned inside out.

Jackson frowned, but didn't argue when I ducked under the ropes and headed off. More importantly, though, he didn't follow.

I passed the bar where the waitress was chatting with Donaghy, the newly crowned champion of Dragon's fight club. At his side, holding a vial and syringe, stood a second waitress who had skin so wrinkled and tan she looked like she'd spent her life wandering the desert. The fighter was dotted with the black blood of his victims, but there wasn't a single scratch on him as far as I could tell, and he didn't even wince when the older waitress plunged the needle into his arm.

Hopefully, Donaghy decided to go clean up soon. When I came back out I wanted to be able to talk to the pink haired waitress privately.

The hallway I headed down was thick with darkness, but I

was able to locate the bathroom by smell alone. There was only one, used for both men and women, but thankfully it was empty when I stepped inside. Four urinals lined one wall while five stalls stood against the other. Only one had a door on it, and even that was barely hanging on. The toilets were so dirty that I was pretty sure a person could catch the zombie virus just from sitting on them.

"Gross," I muttered, staring at the nearly black toilet.

I didn't really need to go, but I'd had to make up some excuse to get away from Jackson. A couple minutes of standing in the bathroom should be all I needed.

I'd just turned to face the door when a man stepped through it.

He froze when he saw me, pausing just inside and blocking my escape completely. His eyes, which were hazy from alcohol, slid over me, and the expression in them was enough to put me on alert. But it was the smile that stretched across his face that set alarm bells off in my head. He was older than me by at least thirty years, and slightly hunched over. The wrinkles lining his leathery face were deep and dark, probably filled with years of dirt, and what little bit of hair he had was greasy and matted to his scalp. He probably hadn't bothered to make a trip to one of the city's bathhouses in months, instead spending his free time and credits in places like this.

"I was just leaving," I said, trying to use my size to my advantage and duck past him.

His hands closed on my shoulders before I'd managed to squeeze by, and I jerked away, but didn't get anywhere.

"Hold on now, girl," he said, his mouth so close to my face that even over the stench of moonshine I could smell the food rotting between his equally rotten teeth.

"Let go." I made the words as hard and menacing as possible, but I doubted there was much about me that would intimidate this man. Even with his hunched frame he towered over me by nearly five inches.

His grin stretched wider and his grip tightened on my shoulders. I slipped my hand around my back and pulled out my knife—I never left home without it—but the blade didn't make it even halfway to his throat before his free hand had swatted it away. The knife flew from my hand and clattered across the floor, and the man slammed my back against the wall. He pressed his whole body against mine.

My heart was pounding like the beat of a drum when the guy put his face against my neck, moving his nose down over my breasts. "This night's gonna be better than I thought."

I screamed and tried to raise my knee, hoping to get him in the balls, but he just pushed closer to me. His body was flush against mine now, and he had me pinned. I squirmed and growled, probably sounding like a zombie, but made no progress. This man was bigger than me, and he had the upper hand. Even worse, I couldn't hear a single sound from the bar, so I knew they wouldn't be able to hear my screams. We were too far back, and the cement walls were too thick.

# CHAPTER FOUR

## Donaghy

THE waitress who called herself Glitter wouldn't shut her damn mouth even though I hadn't said more than two words to her. Okay, four, but they were *get me a drink*. Not exactly an invitation to chat.

The other waitress, Helen, gave me the vaccine with a grin on her face, her eyes moving between me and Glitter like she expected to hear an engagement announcement any day now. Right. Even if I wanted to get involved with this girl I couldn't. I was a convict, which meant anything I wanted to do was off limits. I couldn't even walk out the front door.

"I've really never seen anything like it," Glitter said as Helen walked away. The girl pushed her barely covered chest forward and her tits threatened to spill out. I stared at them as I took another sip. Anything so I didn't have to focus on the words pouring out of her mouth. "Are you that good all the time, or was it just an easy fight?"

I blinked and pulled my gaze away from her flesh. The girl batted her gray eyes in my direction and disgust rolled through me. She was young, probably barely legal, which meant she was

Patty's age. Shit. I wasn't about to screw some chick who was the same age as my sister. I didn't care how willing she was or how amazing it would feel.

"I'm good." I threw the rest of my drink back as I got to my feet, slamming the glass on the bar with so much force that I was shocked it didn't shatter. The blood on my arms had started to dry, and I wanted to wash it off. There was a small bathroom and shower in the back room, but I'd seen Helen and Dragon head in there. The way they'd been making out made my skin crawl. No way did I want to walk in on that.

"There another bathroom in this place?" I asked Glitter. "I need to clean this zombie shit off me."

The waitress frowned, but pointed to a dark hallway that seemed to stretch on forever. "That way."

I nodded before turning away.

The few light bulbs hanging from the ceiling were out, which was probably a good thing. I doubted the people coming here would be surprised to see the roaches and rats running up and down this hall, but that didn't mean they wanted to have a spotlight shining down on them. Filth was a normal part of life these days, and you couldn't escape it no matter how hard you tried. The best thing you could do was go about your business and pretend it didn't disgust you.

I'd made it halfway down the hall when something that sounded like a scream bounced off the walls around me. I froze, but only because I was trying to figure out where it had come from. My ears perked up and the blood pumping through my veins moved faster while I waited. It didn't take long.

"No!" a woman screamed, her voice trembling with fear.

This time, I didn't hesitate. I took off after the sound, charging down the dark hall with my fists already clenched at my sides. There was no mistaking that sound, but I still wasn't prepared for what I saw when I charged into the bathroom.

A man who was so filthy he could have been mistaken for a zombie had a girl up against the wall. Her shirt had been torn open and his hands were already working on her jeans. She fought and kicked and struggled, but he was too strong and she wasn't making any progress.

Red spread across my vision, painting the room and the man

44

and the girl he was pawing at until it looked like everything was covered in blood. Something inside me snapped, and before I knew what was happening, the asshole was on the ground. He snarled up at me, but anything he might have said was cut off when my boot slammed into his face. Just like with the zombies in the ring, my heel made contact with his nose not once, not twice, but three times. Blood sprayed across the already red room and pooled on the floor under the man's head, spreading. Filling the cracks in the old cement floor as the rage that had taken over me started to fade. He wasn't moving when I stepped back, and my shoulders were heaving. I stared down at the bloody mess in front of me. My whole body was tight and my hands were clenched until it felt like my bones would break.

I'd done it again.

Shit.

Sobs drew my attention to the girl. She was leaning against the wall, her shoulders shaking as she pulled at the tattered remains of her shirt, trying to cover her breasts but not making any real progress. Seeing her like that knocked the wind out of me. Made me think of Patty and how she'd looked that day. Made me want to throw up or kill the asshole on the floor all over again.

"Hey—" I reached for the girl, but she shrank away. I didn't blame her. Why would she want a beast like me near her? "Are you okay?" I asked even though I doubted she wanted me talking to her.

"Y-yes." She nodded as tears rolled down her cheeks. "Th-thank you."

I nodded in response because I couldn't think of a thing to say.

Her shirt was so ripped that it didn't cover much. I looked away, trying to give her some space so she could pull herself together. If only I had a shirt I could give her.

The girl took a couple deep breaths that seemed to echo through the room, but I kept my eyes on the floor.

"Could you—" She hesitated. "I have a couple friends in the bar. We were in the VIP area."

Of course this girl was a VIP. That's the way my life went. It should make me hate her, living the life of ease while the rest of us had to struggle, but I couldn't. Not with her trembling hands covering her body the way they were.

"Yeah." I cleared my throat as I headed for the door, but I didn't have anything else to say.

The VIP area was empty when I reached the bar. Before and during the fight I hadn't paid enough attention to know who'd been sitting where, and the VIP area was the last place I'd ever look. I'd learned my lesson and I knew that those were the kind of people to avoid if you wanted to stay alive. They were worse than the damn zombies.

It only took one look around the room to figure out who the right person was, though. He was young, but carried himself like he owned the world as he leaned against the bar, flirting with Glitter. The waitress was talking to him, but she wasn't as excited as she had been with me. She seemed hesitant. A little afraid. Like she wanted to get away but was scared to offend him. He must be the son of someone pretty high up if she was acting that way. Great. What the hell had I gotten myself into now?

I cleared my throat when I stopped behind the guy. He turned my way, his gaze moving over me with something that looked like appreciation, which made no damn sense. I was nobody to this asshole, but he looked like he wanted to pat me on the back.

"Donaghy." He stuck his hand out. "Hell of a fight."

His tone was cordial, but something about the gleam in his eyes made me squirm. Like he was still thinking about the violence I'd inflicted on the dead, or even worse, like the same kind of violence lived inside him. Like he thought we had some kind of a bond that only men who beat people down on a daily basis would understand.

He was wrong.

I didn't take his hand even though I knew from experience what a bad idea it was to piss off the rich kid. "You have a friend? A girl?"

The guy in front of me blinked and dropped his hand to his side. "I'm sorry?"

"There's a girl in the bathroom who needs help. She said she was sitting in the VIP section with her friends."

He shook his head twice before what I was trying to say finally sank in, and when it did something else flashed in his eyes. Surprise. Not worry.

"Meg?" he said after a second.

46

"Didn't get her name." To be honest, I probably couldn't have described her even if someone held a gun to my head. When I'd walked into the bathroom, all I could focus on was the rage. Afterward, when the prick had been dead and bleeding out, I'd done my best to avoid looking at the sobbing girl.

"Shit," the guy in front of me muttered, then hurried off.

An Asian girl at the end of the bar ran after him, but I stayed where I was. I'd done my duty. Now all I had to do was wait and see if saving the girl's life had earned me a one-way ticket back to DC.

"Get me a drink, Glitter," I said, sliding onto a stool.

The waitress headed off without responding. She almost looked relieved to be free of the rich guy. At least she was smart. He may have been at the top of the food chain, but she was better off here where at least she knew what to expect from people.

# CHAPTER FIVE

## Meg

I lost it the second Donaghy left. My legs gave out and I sank to the filthy bathroom floor. Shaking. Holding my tattered shirt against my body even though it didn't come close to covering my breasts. The man who'd tried to violate me was lying on the floor less than a foot away. Dead. A bloody mess that didn't even look human. I spit on his corpse, and then burst into tears.

Coming into this bathroom alone had been dumb and I should have known better. There was a reason DC was as overrun as it was. Men—and women—had turned feral. They were worse than the zombies.

I was still a blubbering mess when Jackson came rushing into the room. He paused in the doorway, his eyes going from me to the dead man as Charlie skidded to a stop behind him. The second she saw me she started crying.

Charlie ran back the way she came while Jackson dropped to his knees at my side. "Tell me Donaghy stopped him."

I nodded, trying to get words out through my sobs, but finding it nearly impossible.

Jackson put his hands on my shoulders. "Breathe, Meg."

Slowly, I sucked in a deep breath, filling my lungs. When I blew it back out, I somehow managed to regain my composure. Crying and losing control, those were two things I didn't typically do. I prided myself on being strong. It was how I'd been raised. Of course, this was a situation I'd never found myself in before.

"I'm okay," I finally managed to get out.

Jackson sighed, but I wasn't looking at him. I was staring at the corpse that had been my attacker, and it suddenly hit me that Donaghy could get sent right back to DC for killing this man. For *saving* me. Justice was swift and harsh these days, and self-defense was rarely an excuse. Especially if someone already had a reputation for being a troublemaker. He could get the death penalty this time.

Not if I had anything to say about it.

I dragged myself to my feet, brushing Jackson off when he tried to help me. "I said I'm fine, but Donaghy might not be."

"Are you seriously worried about him?" Jackson shook his head. "After what you just went through?"

"Yes." I turned my back to Jackson and slid the remains of my clothes off. The bra was done for, so I tossed it aside, but the shirt I slipped on backwards so the tear was in the back. "Tie my shirt closed."

Jackson sighed, but did as he was told, and I took the opportunity to gather my strength. What had almost happened here was horrible and traumatic, but I was okay. Donaghy had gotten here before any real damage was done, and right now he was the one in danger. Not me.

"Let's go," I said when I'd turned back to face Jackson.

"Seriously?" He was still shaking his head when I headed out of the bathroom, but it only took him a second to hurry after me.

I wiped my hand across my face as I headed back down the dark and stinking hall, trying to get rid of any remaining tears. I needed to look as strong and put together as possible. As strong as my biological mother had been and as strong as Vivian Thomas had raised me to be. Being weak in this world would get you killed.

The enforcers had just arrived. At the bar, Donaghy was slumped over his drink like he knew he might be enjoying the last few moments of freedom he'd ever see. If they sent him back to DC now, he was right. He'd either die within the walls of that retched city or he'd be put to death an hour after he got back. My guess was the second one.

"We had a report of an attack," the head enforcer called.

I recognize him right away. It was the leader of Al's crew, and it only took two seconds for me to locate my uncle in the crowd of men. Damn. Charlie must have been really freaked out if she called her dad.

"The body is in the bathroom." Charlie was shaking when she pointed down the hall, and Uncle Al was at her side in a second as two other guys headed to the back to check it out.

"What happened?" Al asked his daughter, forcing her to look up at him.

Charlie swallowed and said, "Some guy attacked Meg."

Al's eyes moved my way, and the second he saw me his daughter was forgotten. He crossed the room and pulled me against him, and I tucked my head under his chin. Being in my uncle's arms wasn't as comforting as it would have been to have Dad here, but it was the best I was going to get. I squeezed my eyes shut and let out a deep breath, blowing the rest of the tension out of my body.

"Fucking great," Donaghy muttered just loud enough for me to hear.

I pulled away from Al, but didn't take a step back. "You have to listen to me. That man would have had his way with me, and probably killed me when he was done. Donaghy—" I jerked my head toward the fighter without looking his way. "—saved me. You can't let him get sent back to DC."

Donaghy twisted to face me and Jackson stepped up so he was standing at my side. Dragon and the older waitress stood behind the bar, watching the scene unfold while behind Al, Charlie's bottom lip quivered. My uncle's eyes were focused on me, though.

"You're alright?" It was rare that I saw Al looking so serious, and twice in one day must have been some kind of record.

"I'm fine," I said firmly. "Did you hear what I said? Donaghy saved me."

Al's gaze moved to the fighter, and his lips tightened as he looked the big man up and down. "Meg said *back* to DC, so I'm guessing you're here as part of the release program."

"That's right." Donaghy's ice blue eyes moved toward me, and his gaze was so intense that it made the hair on my scalp prickle.

At my side, Jackson stiffened and moved closer until his arm was pressed against mine. It would have been nice if I'd thought he was doing it to comfort me, but it felt more like a possessive gesture than one that revolved around concern for my well being. Plus, the expression in the fighter's eyes wasn't threatening. If anything, he was looking at me like I was a puzzle he needed to solve.

"Eyes on me." Al's voice was thick with authority.

Donaghy complied but his jaw twitched like he wished he could argue. He clenched his hands the way he had in the ring.

"Good," Al said. "You got lucky, because this is my niece, and any man who risks his neck to save her deserves a medal in my book. Not a trip to the gallows."

Donaghy's back stiffened but he looked uncertain. He didn't answer right away, and I got the impression that he might be waiting for a punch line.

Finally, the fighter's hands relaxed. "Thank you."

"No," my uncle said firmly. "Thank you."

Al gave my shoulder a squeeze before heading back toward the bathroom. Jackson hurried after my uncle without telling me why, but I didn't care, because right now I had too many things I wanted to say to Donaghy.

I turned to face the man who had saved me, forcing out a smile that was shaky but sincere. My eyes filled with tears, but I blinked them back. "Thank you."

The fighter's gaze met mine, but it was hesitant. Confused. "Why?"

"Because you saved me."

"No." Donaghy got to his feet.

He was so tall that when I tilted my head back so I could look up at him, it hurt my neck. My gaze narrowed in on the scar that cut across his chin. Something about it made him seem so vulnerable. Despite his size and his muscles and the tattoos, and even the knowledge that he was a convict.

"Why did you stick up for me?" he asked, and I moved my gaze from the scar to his eyes.

"Because you saved me, and because it's the right thing to do," I said it like it should be obvious.

He didn't respond, and his blue eyes held mine for what felt like hours. It was just the two of us, Donaghy and me, silently trying to figure each other out.

Jackson stopped at my side, popping up out of nowhere and bringing us back to the present. Once again, he stood too close to me. Made his presence too known. He cleared his throat and the fighter tore his gaze from mine somewhat reluctantly. Donaghy took another drink while I shuffled my feet, and neither man said a word as they sized each other up. I felt trapped between them, their bulk overpowering me. It was like I was a tiny pawn in a game I didn't know how to play, but I wasn't sure what to do about it.

"I want to thank you for helping Meg." Jackson straightened himself to his full height, which was nothing compared to the fighter's, and thrust his hand at Donaghy. "You could have walked away, and these days a lot of people would have, but you put your neck out there. You're a good man." The fighter stared at his outstretched hand until Jackson finally dropped it to his side. Irritation flashed in his eyes, but he didn't back down. If anything he seemed to straighten his back even more, making himself a bit taller. "Where are you staying while you're in New Atlanta?"

Donaghy tore his gaze away from where Jackson's hand had been just a moment ago, once again focusing on me. "There's a back room here. Dragon set up a few cots."

A shiver ran through my body at the way the fighter was staring at me. He kept his gaze on my face, his eyes sweeping over my features slowly as if he was trying to memorize every line and contour.

"I'd like to offer you a room." Jackson turned on the charm, flashing the fighter that signature smile of his. The way he straightened his shoulders made it seem like he was waiting for a pat on the back. "My father is the Regulator here, and we have plenty of extra space. We'd be honored to have you stay in our home."

"Not interested." Donaghy didn't take his eyes off me long enough to look at Jackson.

"I'm sorry." Jackson's smile didn't falter, but he blinked and shook his head. He wasn't used to hearing no, except from me, so I was sure he didn't have a clue how to respond to that.

"Donaghy." I touched his arm and the fighter's muscles contracted under my fingertips while at my side, Jackson's body stiffened even more. "Sometimes when people offer to help you, they're being sincere."

The fighter's eyebrows pulled together, but his gaze was focused on my hand, still resting on his forearm. I held my breath, hoping this man would take Jackson's offer of goodwill. If I could repay him for what he'd done I would, but the truth was, there was absolutely nothing I had that would be a sufficient thank you. Jackson had everything, though, and a room in the Regulator's house would be more luxury than Donaghy could have ever hoped for in this world.

Finally, the fighter nodded. "Okay."

"Excellent." Jackson let out a breath, but his body didn't relax. "I'll make the arrangements."

He hurried off, leaving Donaghy and me alone yet again, but the fighter turned back to the bar. I shuffled my feet, not sure what to do or where to go, but knowing my conversation with Donaghy was done. At least for now.

When I looked up, I found the pink haired waitress staring at me from the other side of the bar. Dragon and the other waitress were behind her, talking quietly to each other. I'd almost forgotten why I'd decided to risk my life in the first place, but finding myself suddenly alone, it seemed like the perfect opportunity to talk to her.

I headed over, my heart thumping even harder than it had in the bathroom. It got even worse when the bar owner and the waitress at his side turned my way.

"Hi," the young waitress said quietly, her gray eyes oddly innocent when they looked me up and down.

"Hi." My throat suddenly went dry, and all the conviction I'd come over here with melted away. I wasn't sure how to go about this, and trying to have this conversation with my uncle, Charlie, and Jackson around was risky. "I was wondering how you got a job here," I said, keeping my voice low.

The girl's eyebrows shot up, getting lost under her pink bangs. "You need a job? I thought you were with the Regulator's son."

"Not exactly." I glanced around, and once I was sure the coast was clear, I went for it. "I need the money, and it seems like you do pretty well here."

"Tips are good as long as you didn't mind..." The waitress looked down at her dress and shrugged. "If you want a job, though, you're going to have to talk to Dragon." She nodded behind her. "I'm sure he'll hire you. Finding girls who want to work here and still have all their teeth is tough."

I almost shuddered, but managed to control it. Beggars couldn't be choosers, and right now I was as close to becoming a beggar as I'd ever been. It was this or nothing.

She turned to face her boss, and when I looked up, I found him staring at me, a thoughtful expression on his face.

After a few seconds he said, "You're a tough girl. Pulled yourself together awfully fast after that business in the bathroom. We need tough people around here. Especially when they look like you." His gaze moved over me slowly, causing every hair on my body to stand on end. Despite the fact that I desperately needed a job—and he seemed on the verge of offering me one, oddly enough—I had the sudden urge to run. "What's your name?"

"Meg," I said, the word almost getting stuck in my throat. "Megan James."

Dragon's shoulders stiffened, but something about the expression in his eyes told me he already knew that. Not a surprise, most people knew who I was before I introduced myself. Still, I found myself squirming under his gaze. Hopefully, he wasn't some religious nut. I needed a job, but I refused to work for a crazy person.

The smile returned to Dragon's face, but something about the expression had changed. He was looking at me like we were old friends, and there was respect in his expression that made me stand up straighter. It wasn't the same kind of respect that came from zealots—they usually had an excited gleam in their eyes that made me feel like they were on the verge of dropping to their knees and praying to me. No, Dragon seemed like he was taking me seriously.

I held my breath as I waited to find out if he was going to start asking me weird details about the uncle I'd never met. It happened—a lot—and every time it did I walked away feeling like the world had taken a nosedive into insanity.

After a second of silence, Dragon said, "Be here tomorrow at six. And be sure you dress sexier than that."

He turned away and the older waitress hurried after him. His words didn't leave me feeling any better about the situation. So he wasn't a religious nut job, didn't mean there weren't other ways he could totally creep me out.

# CHAPTER SIX

## Donaghy

**THE** girl, Meg as it turned out, traded a few words with Dragon before he headed off, and now she was whispering with Glitter like they were old friends. Which didn't make any sense. She was here with the Regulator's son, sitting in the VIP section. Why the hell would she be talking to the waitress, and why the hell would she be sticking her neck out for me?

I wasn't used to having people care about me, and I sure as hell wasn't dumb enough to think the Regulator's son had made that offer out of the kindness of his heart. Despite what the girl seemed to think. Hell, that asshole's heart was probably so black that if I cut it open, it'd look like the inside of a zombie. Rotten. No, the bastard had done it to impress the girl.

Glitter ran off, leaving Meg alone at the end of the bar, and even though I knew I needed to stop staring at her — that rich prick was all bent out of shape over it — I couldn't make myself do it. She was small, not just thin, but short as well, but she was strong. Strong enough to pull herself together after what had almost happened in the bathroom and strong enough to stand up for me. But she was also vulnerable right now. I could see it in the way she gnawed on the inside of her cheek. Something major was eating away at her, only I didn't know what it could be. With her connections — the Regulator's son just dying to get his hands on her and her uncle high up in the ranks of the enforcers — she should have been sitting pretty.

I gauged her to be around twenty, meaning she was born after the virus and could still have two living parents. That right there would be enough to make anyone special in this world. On top of that, she was healthy. A little thin, but in a nice way. She still had curves in all the right places, I knew because I'd seen them firsthand in that bathroom, and her skin was soft and pale. Unmarred by the rough world we now lived in. Even under the shitty lights in this bar her dark hair shined, which was a good sign that she hadn't suffered from poor nutrition. It was the worry in her green eyes that had me bothered, though. That expression didn't have a damn thing to do with the attack.

Glitter came back and held out a piece of paper. Meg looked around as she took it, almost like she was afraid someone was going to see her. She shoved it in her pocket and a frown turned down her lips. When she pulled her hand back out, a different piece of paper was resting in her palm. This one was dirty and crinkled, and based on the expression that crossed her face, I'd say it was important.

"It's all set!" the Regulator's son called.

Meg shoved the paper back in her pocket as he headed over, but his eyes were on me. He looked like he was ready to pat himself on the back for being so fucking great, or for coming up with such a perfect way to impress Meg. I wasn't sure which one. Chances were, it was both.

He stopped in front of me and smiled, but there was something very fake about the expression. Like he stood in front of the mirror every night practicing the gesture, but hadn't perfected it yet.

"Dragon knows the plan and your guards will see to it that you get to the house safely. Please give this to the men at the front door."

The rich little prick handed me a card and I flipped it over.

*Jackson Star*. Figured. The guy acted like he thought he was the star of the whole fucking world, so it made sense that would be his last name.

"Thanks," I muttered even though I didn't really give a shit. After DC, the little cot Dragon had set up for me would have been a dream come true.

Jackson turned to Meg, who had both hands shoved in her pockets now. If I hadn't seen her get attacked with my own two eyes, I never would have guessed it had happened. That was how put together she looked. This chick was badass tough.

"Charlie's staying with her dad, but Al asked me to walk you home." Jackson put his hand on her arm and I found myself flinching for her. After what she'd just gone through, he should be more careful about touching her. Thoughtless asshole.

"Yeah," Meg said stammering over the word, but not sounding nervous or scared, just anxious. "That's a good idea. I should check in on Mom. Make sure she ate."

She lived with her mom. Maybe her family was on the council and that was how she had her connections. It had to be something big, otherwise people wouldn't be falling all over themselves to make sure she was safe.

Meg shot Glitter a look before heading off with Jackson. The VIPs nodded my way when they passed, but I barely looked up from my drink. I was too busy thinking about everything that had gone on tonight.

The fight had gone down the same way it usually did. I always won and the crowd always acted like it was some kind of major victory. Right. Two zombies out of the two million still left roaming this country. How ridiculous. After I'd put the dead down, all I had really wanted to do was get some rest. These assholes liked to act like I was a big shot when we got to a settlement, pretending this release program wasn't just a more creative way to kill off the prisoners crowded into DC, but when we were out on the road, it was chains and work. When we got stuck in the mud yesterday, I was the one who'd had to dig the truck out. When raiders from an unsanctioned settlement attacked last week after we left Dayton, you better believe your ass the guards left me chained inside the truck while they took cover. Bullets flying everywhere. Nowhere for me to hide. Shit, I came so close to getting hit that I started saying my prayers.

Yeah, the fight went the way it always did, but this business in the bathroom wasn't normal. The entertainment areas were always seedy, and things like that happened more than they should, but if it had been anyone else I'd rescued, the enforcers would have shot me or thrown cuffs on me the second they arrived. Meg had pull in the settlement that didn't make any damn sense.

"You looking for a little company?" Glitter's voice broke through my thoughts, and when I looked up, she was practically on top of me.

"I'm good." I took a sip, still looking at the waitress but thinking only about Meg. "Tell me something," I finally said, setting my glass down. "What were you and that girl talking about?"

"The one who got attacked?" Glitter's eyebrows shot up when I nodded. "She wanted a job. Just didn't want the Regulator's son to find out."

"A job here?"

"Yeah. A job *here*." Glitter put her hands on her hips and for the first time I noticed the scars that ran up the inside of both her arms, heaviest in the crook. Junkie. I should have figured. "Something wrong with working here?"

"Not a damn thing," I said with a shake of my head. "These days, you have to do what it takes to survive."

"No kidding." Glitter snorted before heading off, obviously tired of me telling her no.

*You have to do what it takes to survive.* It had become my damn motto over the past year, going back to Patty and what had happened with her. I'd done what I had to because that's what we did now. Then I got sent to DC, and every day I had to do what it took to stay alive. In there they didn't give a shit if you killed each other, which meant that if I wanted to make it out of that place one day, I was going to have to get my hands dirty.

Then came the fights. I started working my way up the ranks of convicts, getting extra privileges and eventually earning my way into this release program. All of it coming down to one thing: surviving. And I didn't have plans to stop surviving any time soon, either.

# CHAPTER SEVEN

## Meg

THE piece of paper in my pocket felt like it weighed a hundred pounds on the walk home. Jackson wouldn't leave my side no matter how many times I told him I could make it back on my own. He was so damn determined to make sure I was okay that he wouldn't hear me when I told him I was fine.

How the hell had I forgotten about the note, and what was in it?

That was the main thing going through my head as we reached the edge of shantytown. It had to be after two o'clock in the morning, but this section of the settlement was never completely silent. Not with the shacks crammed so close together and the people living in them determined to do whatever it took to survive. Which meant grunts and moans filling the empty space between Jackson and me, letting us know that nearby some woman was earning a living on her back—or on her knees.

"You okay?" Jackson asked, just as we made it past the shrine that signaled the center of the pathetic little neighborhood.

"I'm fine."

He nodded and shoved his hands in his pockets. "I just want to make sure. After what almost happened, hearing that..." When he broke off, he looked away and I could practically hear him blushing.

This was the Jackson I knew and loved, even if his concern was misguided at the moment. When he was around other people or in public, he became his father's son. Bossy and important. Always throwing his weight around. Like he had at the bar when dealing with Donaghy. Jackson did a nice thing, offering the fighter a room, but he also craved the praise the good deed would bring. That was his father's influence. When it was just the two of us, though, Jackson was caring. Sensitive.

"I'm fine," I said more firmly. "That asshole didn't even get close. Donaghy made sure of that. Plus, I'm not oblivious to what sex is."

The tightening of his lips told me not to push that subject. Jackson never had liked my one and only boyfriend, and the guy I had given my virginity to. In fact, we'd barely spoken during the few months that I had dated Colton. But Jackson had been there to comfort me when my boyfriend had gotten killed on a supply run, and after that we'd fallen back into our easy friendship. Almost as if Colton had never existed to begin with.

"I should have been the one to take that scumbag down." Jackson's tone was cool, and as hard as stone. Something about it made me shiver even more than the memory of what had almost happened in that bathroom.

"Let's just forget about it," I said, wanting to shrink away from him but stopping myself. "Okay?"

"Yeah. Okay."

We reached my building, but I stopped at the door. "I'm good from here. You should get home before your dad gets worried."

"Yeah. It is pretty late." He glanced past me, into the lobby. "The elevator is working? I don't want you going up that dark stairwell by yourself this late at night."

"It's working." I didn't know for sure, but I did know that I needed him to give me some alone time. If he walked me to my apartment, I'd go right from him to Mom, and who knew when I'd get a chance to read the note.

"Okay." Jackson shoved his hands back in his pockets. "I'll see you tomorrow?"

"I'm not sure," I said elusively, thinking about the meeting I had with Dragon tomorrow evening. "I have some errands to run and I have work. I'm pretty busy now that Dad's gone."

The lump that always formed in my throat when I thought about never seeing Dad again returned, only this time for some crazy reason, so did the image of Donaghy's scar. Why had that scar left such a big impression on me?

Jackson and I said our goodbyes and I hurried inside. Thankfully, the lobby was empty and most of the light bulbs were working.

As soon as I was sure he wasn't going to follow me in, I pulled the note out of my pocket and unfolded it with shaky hands. The words scrawled on the paper danced across my vision, making it hard to grasp their meaning. Or maybe, just hard to accept the meaning.

*Your dad is immune and he's still alive.*

My knees, already unstable, gave out and I slumped to the floor. The note was still in my hands and I couldn't look away from the words.

What the hell was going on? Mom had been ranting about the exact same thing for weeks, ever since Dad disappeared, but I'd assumed that she'd lost it. It didn't make any sense. If Dad were immune, why wouldn't they have told him? They could have just asked him to donate his blood. Angus had done it.

"No." I shook my head and balled the paper up, crushing it in my palm.

This couldn't be right. This was just some crazy person who had heard a rumor and wrote it down. Or someone who was trying to push me over the edge right along with my mom.

But what if it *was* true? What if Dad was alive and they had him somewhere in the CDC? Using him. Experimenting on him like he was a rat.

"No," I whispered again, tightening my hand on the note.

"No."

It didn't matter how many times I said the word, though, there was a part of me that thought Mom might not be crazy after all. That my dad was still alive and if I could just find him, I could save him.

How, though, and who did I turn to?

Jackson wasn't someone I would ever consider. I trusted him, but I also knew that he put way too much faith in his father, who was the most corrupt person I'd ever met. If I told Jackson about this note, he'd insist on telling his dad, and that would be the end of my dad. Assuming he *was* still alive.

Mom? No. She was already struggling, and even though it might help her a little to think that I believed her, this confirmation of her suspicions might push her over the edge completely.

Parv? She was the Judicial Officer of New Atlanta, putting her in charge of all law enforcement. Something like this could put her in a sticky spot. Not to mention the fact that she didn't seem to be dealing well with her own husband's death. She put on a brave face, but since Joshua's accident she'd been home less and less.

Uncle Al was the obvious choice. He'd listen to what I had to say. Be objective and helpful. He was pretty high up, so he could do some snooping around, but not so high up that anyone was keeping tabs on him. Yeah, Al was the person I needed to talk to for sure.

Of course, he was on patrol right now and most likely wouldn't be back until morning. Charlie had stayed with him, so there was a chance he'd walk her back at some point, but more than likely she'd tag along while he patrolled the entertainment district. She liked to pretend she was interested in his work, but I suspected that she just craved the drama that came with the job.

I'd have to talk to him tomorrow. After I got off work, but before my meeting with Dragon. It didn't leave me much time, but it wasn't like I had another choice. I couldn't sit on this for too long or it was going to eat away at me like it had been eating at Mom. If I lost my mind too, we were done for.

I hauled myself up off the floor and headed for the elevator, my legs heavy with exhaustion and the weight of the note making things worse. At this rate, I was only going to catch a couple hours of sleep, but it was rest I was going to need if I wanted to get through tomorrow. Six hours of work, then a few more hours at Dragon's bar, assuming he didn't change his mind between now and then. I had some serious doubts about that man's sanity. Just thinking about tomorrow made me even more exhausted than before.

I slammed my thumb into the up button, but nothing happened. Great. The elevator was broken. Again.

Guess it was the stairs for me.

# CHAPTER EIGHT

## Donaghy

IT had practically killed my pride to accept that asshole's offer, but half asleep and lying in a bed softer than the fur of a damn cat, I couldn't bring myself to give a shit. I could have stayed here forever.

The sound of someone knocking on the door jerked me awake and I grabbed the pillow — a fucking feather pillow of all things — and pulled it over my head. It had to be early afternoon by now, but I didn't plan on getting my ass out of this bed until I had to be at Dragon's. Maybe if I ignored whoever was at the door, they would get the point and go away.

A minute went by and my body started to relax, but I was once again jerked from sleep when the asshole on the other side of the door knocked again. This time louder.

"Shit," I muttered, shoving myself off the mattress and practically falling out of bed.

The hardwood floor was cold under my bare feet as I made my way across the room. The curtains were drawn over the windows, blocking out ninety percent of the light, but a few rays had managed to break their way through the cracks. They were bright, confirming my earlier suspicion about how late it was. I hadn't slept this long since before the apocalypse, and back then I had been a dumbass kid who hadn't appreciated it.

I ripped the door open and the light in the hallway was so bright that it nearly blinded me. I squinted and shielded my eyes with my hand, trying to force the world to come into view. When my gaze focused on Jackson's face, I had to fight back a growl. I'd expected my guards, not this asshole.

"What?" I barked, my eyes still half-closed.

Jackson's eyes narrowed as they swept over me. "Do you want me to give you a minute to get dressed?"

"I'm fine," I grumbled. "What do you want?"

"I'd be more comfortable if you put something on." The prick pressed his lips together and waited like he was expecting me to jump at his command.

"I'm fine." I crossed my arms and leaned against the frame. In DC you couldn't go for more than twenty minutes without seeing somebody butt ass naked, or a whole day without somebody seeing you. Last thing I was going to worry about was this asshole's penis envy.

Jackson cleared his throat, and what flashed in his eyes had nothing to do with discomfort. Penis envy, maybe, but I wasn't sure.

"Fine," he said coolly, his gaze moving to my forehead. He wouldn't look down, but he was too good to look me in the eye. "I wanted to thank you again for last night, and make sure you had everything you needed."

I blinked. "Everything I needed?" Was this guy for real? If I had a roof over my head and a few cups of water, I considered it a good day.

"Yeah," he said.

"Yeah," I repeated. "I have everything."

His gaze met mine, and I did everything I could to stare him down, but he didn't waver. I was bigger than him, but he had a chip on his shoulder that was bigger than this damn house. There was something else, too. Something in his eyes that made me uneasy, and right now, the only thing I really needed was for him to get the hell out of here. First, because the bed was calling my name, but also because he gave me the creeps like no one ever had before.

"Good." Jackson took a step back. "We just finished with brunch and I told the cook to save the leftovers. There should be a plate in the kitchen for you."

*He's throwing you his scraps like you're a dog.* The muscles in my arms tightened when I clenched my hands into fists. "Thanks."

"Sure thing." Everything about him looked smug as he took a step back. His eyes flickered down and his lips twitched. "Have a good fight."

I watched him from the doorway as he headed down the stairs, and when he finally disappeared from sight, I pushed myself off the wall and headed back inside my temporary room.

What a disturbing prick. I've met some scary ass people in my life—DC was crawling with them—but this guy was king of the creeps. I hadn't liked him last night, but it had more to do with his position than anything he'd done. Sure he'd only offered me a room to impress the girl, but that was normal. Now, after just a couple minutes of interacting with the dude, I could tell I was spot on in my dislike. He was as much of an ass as every other person who had a position of importance these days, maybe more so—I couldn't forget that his dad was the Regulator of New Atlanta, and that dude ran this sorry excuse of a country. Even more than all that other stuff combined, though, was the feeling gnawing at the back of my mind that told me Jackson had a seriously disturbing side to him.

I pulled on a pair of pants before venturing out into the hall. My guards dragged themselves up off the floor, grumbling as they did it. I knew that they saw a piece of scum when they looked at me, and that they thought it was a total waste to allow me any sort of luxury. Not that they should be complaining. Jackson giving me a room got them in the big house, too.

The place was a damn palace. I'd been too dead tired last night to really appreciate it, but as I headed down the stairs, I couldn't help admiring it now. Marble floors and pillars, a huge curved staircase. The double front doors at to be at least nine feet tall and the most elaborate things I'd ever seen. Outside these walls people were living in filth, barely surviving, and here this house sat. Lavish. Air Conditioned. Clean. Worst of all, so empty that my footsteps echoed through the rooms.

I found the kitchen easy enough, and when I pushed the door open the greasy scent of bacon still clung to the air, making my stomach rumble loudly.

The room was thick with darkness, and I paused just inside the door so I could wait for my eyes to adjust. The second they did, though, the light flickered on and I had to squeeze them shut.

"We got electricity, dumbass," one of my guards said from behind me.

"Not used to it," I mumbled.

The other guard snorted, and when footsteps crossed the room, my eyes were still shut tight. "The animals in DC don't get lights. Remember?"

The familiar sound of silverware clinking against a plate forced my eyes open, but I was still squinting when my guards came into view. They were leaning over a plate like vultures picking apart a rotting carcass. My plate.

"Shit," the one said through the mouthful of food that was meant for *me*. "I haven't had bacon in twenty years."

"I ain't never had bacon," the younger of the two said.

"That's mine," I growled when my eyes had finally adjusted to the light.

The older one looked up. One hand was still digging through the food on the plate while the other moved to the gun on his hip. "What you gonna do 'bout it?"

*Break your neck.*

That's what I thought, and it's what I wanted to say and do, but I stepped back before my temper got the better of me.

"Nothing," was the only word that made it out of my mouth.

They went back to shoveling the eggs and bacon into their mouths, the younger one not even bothering with a fork. And they called me an animal. These two were so filthy you'd think they had just crawled out of a gutter. The older one's beard hung to the center of his chest, and the thing was riddle with specks of dirt and food—none of which came from the plate in front of him. The younger guy's dreadlocks were probably crawling with bugs, and the dirt under his nails was so thick it had most likely been there for years.

I turned my back on them and dropped to the floor, channeling all the hate and rage in my body into my pushups. The muscles in my arms tightened when I pushed myself up and down, moving faster with each pass. A fork scraped against the plate as I propelled myself up, the sound of lips smacking together rang in my ears on the way down.

"The streets are crawling with them." The booming voice of a man penetrated the door at my side, and I slowed, but didn't stop. "Scum. We get more and more of them every week."

"We're going to have to do something about the population," a second man said, his voice softer and slightly nasal. "It's getting out of hand again."

"When was the last flu?" the first one asked.

"Going on five years now."

There was a pause before the man with the deep voice responded. "It's not too soon?"

"Never too soon to take out the trash."

The two men chuckled and I realized I'd frozen mid-pushup. My gaze darted to the left, but my guards were too busy stuffing their faces with the rest of my food to notice the conversation going on in the other room. I went back to my pushups, slower this time so I could hear. Keeping my eyes on the guards and my ears focused on the other room.

When the laughter had died down, the first man asked, "Any change in our test subject? I was in the lab late last night and didn't have a chance to check on him."

"No, but we both know we can't keep him this way for long." The other man's nasally voice was farther away now, and I had to strain to hear him. "We're going to have to do something more permanent soon."

"Go ahead and take him out of the coma. He's not going anywhere."

"I'll let his doctors know." The man with nasal voice cleared his throat. "And the rest of the family? We can't keep dragging this out."

"I'm in a sticky situation and you know it." The first man snapped. "We have plans for the girl and Jackson assures me it's going well."

"You're really going to let your son's sex life risk everything we're trying to accomplish?" This time, the nasal tone was accompanied by annoyance. "No one but the brothers has had this kind of immunity, not even the girls. You know this guy's blood could be the key to everything we've been trying to accomplish. He very well could be the only chance we have. All our other efforts went nowhere. Your son, on the other hand, can find someone else to screw."

"Don't push me." The man with the deep voice growled, and the sound of feet scuffling against the floor made me freeze again. "Understand? And this has nothing to do with Jackson's sex life. We've had this plan in place for years, and I'm not about to throw it away because it's taking longer than we expected. We need the name this girl brings with her. Otherwise, I'd take care of the whole thing in one day. I'll do what needs to be done when I'm sure there's no other option."

"Fine." The other man huffed, not sounding very put off by his friend's anger. "You just let me know when you decide to take the next step."

They kept talking, but their voices got fainter and I was only able to catch a word or two of the conversation, until finally the voices faded away completely.

I pumped my arms up, and stopped, holding the position while I tried to figure out what I had just heard. Talk about a flu, and then some man who was immune. Jackson and a girl. I had to assume they were talking about Meg, but why? And what the hell did her name have to do with it?

"Get up," one of my guards growled.

A boot banged against my side and my arms gave out. Somehow, I managed to brace myself before I slammed face-first into the tile floor. I rolled onto my back and found both guards standing over me, licking their disgusting fingers like the animals they were.

"We're supposed to get you to Dragon's soon," the older of the two said.

"It's still early," I mumbled from my place on the floor.

I could jump up and snap their necks. Make a run for it. There was no way they were stronger than me, and they were too stupid to have their weapons ready. But then what? If the stories about security in New Atlanta were true, I wouldn't make it far. Maybe to the wall, but all the way over? No. They'd catch me and shoot me on sight. Then I'd never make it back to Patty.

"Don't give a shit what time it is," the older guard said. His beard was dotted with little yellow specks of scrambled egg. "Dragon told us to bring you over, so that's what we're gonna do. Get up."

I rolled back to my stomach, then hoisted myself up. The kick to my side hadn't been hard enough to leave a bruise, but it still ached when my muscles tensed. Thanks a lot, asshole. It wasn't like I had to fight zombies tonight or anything.

I walked ahead of the guards, out through the kitchen door and into the dining room. It was empty, just like I knew it would be.

"We drop this dude off, then maybe we can squeeze in a few free hours," the younger guard said. "Find us some tail."

"Forget that." The old guy let out a belch that sounded wet. "I wanna get wasted."

My gaze moved up and down the halls as we headed toward the stairs so I could get dressed. Whoever I'd heard talking was gone now, and the house once again felt empty.

All the people living on the streets, and this was how the Regulator was living. He was an asshole. Must have been where his son got it.

# CHAPTER NINE

## Meg

**THE** trek up the stairs was twice as torturous after a six hour shift. Last night I'd had to hold on to the railing so I wouldn't fall on my ass, I'd been that tired, but today it felt like I was climbing a mountain after running from a horde of zombies.

Six hours on the maintenance crew was draining on its own, but add to that the worries constantly swimming around inside my head, and by the time I had finished my shift I felt like could curl up in bed and sleep for days. Between Mom and Dad, the bills that had to be paid, and my upcoming night in Dragon's Lair, my brain didn't have a moment to rest all day long.

Reaching the third floor gave me a second wind, but I didn't feel any perkier than I had any other day in recent weeks. Al was most likely between shifts, which meant I'd be able to talk to him about the note. Hopefully, once I spilled my guts to my uncle, he could help shoulder some of the burden and I wouldn't feel so weighed down.

I paused outside Al and Lila's long enough to shoot a quick

look toward my own apartment. The hall was silent, but I could almost hear Mom's nervous chatter and constant pacing from where I stood. It could have been my imagination, but I doubted it.

When I rapped my knuckles against the door, the sound echoed through the hall. I shot another look toward our apartment when my heart beat faster. If Mom heard, she could look through the peephole and see me standing here. The last thing I needed right now was a confrontation.

My aunt and uncle's door opened and I let out a sigh of relief at the sight of my Uncle Al.

"Megan?" He looked over my shoulder like he expected someone to be with me. Who, I didn't know. I was pretty much alone in this world right now. "What's going on?"

"Can I come in?" I slipped my hand into my pocket and fingered the paper. It felt like a piece of cloth, but seemed to weigh a hundred pounds. "I have something I need to talk to you about."

Al pulled the door open wider and stepped aside so I could enter. The note was out of my pocket before the door had even clicked shut behind me, and I held it out when I turned to face him.

My uncle's gaze moved to the paper in my hand, amusement in his dark eyes. Of all the people I knew, he was one of the few who didn't seem to struggle to laugh in this world. Everyone else had baggage so heavy it seemed to weigh their souls down until they were practically hunched over from the pressure of it all.

"What's this?" Al took the note, his mouth twitching like expected it to contain a joke.

He balanced the piece of paper against his stump as he unfolded it with the hand he did have. The sword he wore while at work was off, which was normal when he was at home. I was used to seeing the stump, but as I waited for him to read the note I couldn't stop from thinking about that missing arm and what it must have been like when he'd lost it. I'd heard the story, both from my parents and from Lila, and I knew how terrible that day had been for them all. They've seen the world change so much in their lives, and it must have been hard for them to keep hoping it would get better when nothing ever seemed to.

It had been pretty early in the apocalypse when Al was bitten, and my family found themselves faced with a horrible choice: try to save him by cutting off his arm, or let him die. They didn't even know for sure if it would make a difference, but Joshua did it anyway at the insistence of Al, who'd only been seventeen at the time. Thankfully, it stopped the spread of the virus and he made it through.

In front of me, the expression on my uncle's face changed slowly. His smile grew stiff, then melted away as his gaze moved over the words. He must have read the note six or seven times while we stood there in silence, and with each passing second, the frown on his face grew deeper until the man who stood in front of me looked nothing like my fun-loving Uncle Al. The person who looked up had troubled eyes, and a face that was etched with lines so deep it gave off the impression he was on the brink of dying from old age.

"Someone gave this to me yesterday," I said by way of explanation. "On the streets, right after my confrontation with that woman."

Al's hand was shaking so hard that if the paper hadn't been so worn, I probably would have been able to hear it crinkle in the silence of the apartment.

"Who?" he asked.

"I don't know. Some old man. How he knows anything about Dad is beyond me, but after all Mom's ranting, I can't help wondering if there's some truth in this." I nodded toward the note in my uncle's hand. "What if Dad is alive? What if he's immune?"

Al's eyes darted around and his hand shook harder, making my heart speed up. He knew something. He wouldn't be acting this way if he didn't.

When my uncle looked back at me he was smiling, but it was nothing like his normal smile. It was forced and it didn't reach his eyes. It looked drawn on, and the lines on his face hadn't disappeared.

"You can't trust a crazy man on the streets." The laugh that popped out of his mouth wouldn't fool the dumbest person alive. Al balled up the paper and shoved it in his pocket. "I know it's hard to accept, we all miss your dad, but he's not alive. There's no conspiracy here."

Every inch of my uncle was tense, which was nothing like him. It felt like I was standing in front of a stranger. He was lying.

Even worse, he was nervous. Almost like he thought someone might be listening to us. He reminded me of Mom...

"Al?" A million questions flipped through my head, but every one of them could be deadly if someone actually *was* listening to us right now.

My uncle laughed again, which wasn't only forced but inappropriate considering we were talking about my father who was missing and presumed dead.

"We can't feed into your mom's fears." Al's voice was firm, and he shoved his hand in his pocket like he was guarding the note. Like he was afraid I would grab it and run from this room, waving it above my head as I tore through the streets of New Atlanta. "Let's just keep this between the two of us. Okay?"

I didn't move right away, but neither did Al. His eyes held mine as his lips twitched, making it look like he was struggling to keep the smile on his face. The pleading in his gaze spoke volumes, though. He was begging me to listen to him. To walk away and not ask any more questions. At least not here.

"Yeah," I said, backing toward the door on shaky legs, unable to stop myself from scanning the room. Was someone watching us right now? Was I in trouble? "You're right. This is nuts, and we can't let Mom know about it. We'll just keep it between the two of us."

Al let out a sigh as he nodded, but he was still tense. "Good."

"I have to go." I stopped with my hand on the doorknob. "I have somewhere to be."

"Good then." My uncle nodded. "So do I, in fact. More work. Have to keep busy." His lips twitched again, and I finally turned away so he didn't have to keep the smile on his face.

"Thanks, Al."

I couldn't breathe until I was in the hallway and the door was firmly shut. The worries that had been swirling through my head all day long had only grown, and with the way things were going, they weren't likely to get better any time soon.

"I'll have to think about it later," I said, pushing myself off the door and heading toward my own apartment.

As much as I'd love to sit around and mull over the mystery that had become my life, I had a new job to get to, and I had to get ready. Which meant taking a shower and squeezing myself into the little black dress I'd bought today. Glitter had given me the name of a place to go — I'd never had the need for a slutty dress before — and buying the thing had meant using up the last of my credits. But with any luck it would just take a few hours at Dragon's and I'd come out ahead.

THE ENTERTAINMENT DISTRICT OF NEW ATLANTA HAD been restricted to two streets, but they were both packed to the brim. Bars, clubs, strip joints, and pool halls lined the road, just waiting for the good people of the city to come in. The signs were mostly hand painted, but a few places had actually managed to scavenge electric ones. Their flash was enticing when it was dark. Like a promise that within those walls you'd be transported to the past, taken to a time when zombies didn't rule the world and people didn't die of starvation on a regular basis. *Come in*, they seemed to say, *we can make you forget that you live in this hell.* They couldn't, but that was the trick. These days, people would do anything to feel like things were normal, even spending credits that should have gone toward food or clothes or healthcare. Whatever it took to forget the zombies for just a few hours.

It was early evening, so the electric signs hanging in windows were off as I headed down the street, but the area was still bursting with life. Laughter and music flowed from open doors as I passed them, and usually the sound of clinking glasses or balls slamming into one another on a pool table. The sickly sweet smell of trash hung in the air, but it was the scent of ammonia that burned my nostrils when I passed an alley. Black bags, teeming with garbage, lined the sidewalks, baking under the hot sun as they waited for trash day. The city's garbage got collected once a month, and then taken outside the walls to be disposed of. Where, I didn't know, but I had no doubt I'd find out soon thanks to my new job on the maintenance crew. Trash week was coming up very soon.

Angry words cut through the air and a second later a man stumbled out of a bar in front of me, his lips flapping as he screamed over his shoulder, "Didn't want your ale anyway! Tastes like piss."

He stumbled over his own feet or the cracks in the sidewalk or

79

possibly even the trash lying around, and I dodged him just before he slammed into me. The man kept walking, not even noticing me as he mumbled to himself about how he just needed a drink so he could sleep. Just one more drink.

I walked faster, wrapping my arms around my stomach and keeping my eyes down as I passed men and women who were leaning against walls, smoking bootleg cigarettes. Some whistled my way while others asked if I was looking for a lay or a job. A few said nothing as their gaze followed my progress down the sidewalk.

At the end of the street, nestled between a strip club whose music seemed to make the entire building vibrate and a stack of smashed cars that helped make up this part of the wall surrounding New Atlanta, sat Dragon's Lair. The brick building was black and windowless, and above the red door an elaborate mural of a dragon had been painted. The creature was midflight, it's green scales radiant against the blue sky as it breathed fire into the air.

I took a deep breath, working to calm my pounding heart as I stared up at the picture. Whether it had been here before the apocalypse or after, I didn't know, but I did know that once the sun went down no one would be able to see it. There were no working lampposts in the entertainment district and no light was mounted above the door. Last night when Jackson, Charlie, and I had arrived, it had been so dark that the mural had been invisible.

After a few minutes of staring at the image, my heart hadn't slowed, but I knew I couldn't put this thing off anymore. The longer I stayed outside, the more my shirt stuck to my body, so I pushed the door open and went in.

Three men sat at the bar, all of them leaning over half-empty glasses that seemed to have an almost hypnotic effect on them. None of them looked up when the door shut behind me, and other than the drunken men at the bar, the place felt deserted. Between fights the crowds must have been minimal, but I knew that in just a few hours the place would be brimming with activity. Dragon's Lair was the only bar in the district that had a ring.

Even nearly empty the atmosphere was stifling. The Georgia humidity had seeped inside the cement walls and mixed with the remnants from last night's crowd until the air was thick and difficult to swallow. I sucked in a deep breath, hoping to fill my lungs, and it nearly choked me. The foul odor of death had mixed with the coppery scent of blood and the stink of dozens of unwashed bodies, eliminating what little bit of refreshment the humidity hadn't already stolen from the air.

Working here was going to be fun.

My heels clicked against the floor when I forced my legs to move, but the men at the bar still didn't bother looking my way. The staff was nowhere in sight and the place was totally silent, sending a shiver down my spine.

"Hello?" I called, and my heart jumped to my throat when my voice echoed back to me.

Where the hell was Dragon? I was right on time—maybe even a few minutes late—so he should have been waiting for me.

There was no response, not even from the drunks, so I moved deeper into the building. Glitter wasn't behind the bar and neither was the other waitress I'd seen working last night, and none of the other employees seemed to be around either. The long hallway that led to the bathroom was dark and as soundless as the rest of the place. Not that I'd be stupid enough to go down that hall by myself more than once.

I turned away before the memories from last night made me lose my nerve. I needed this job, and it didn't matter what had almost happened here or how much I was going to hate serving the scum that came into this place. Credits were credits.

"Dragon?" I called as I headed away from the dark hallway and back toward the room Donaghy and the zombies had come out of last night.

The door was cracked and I paused long enough to rap my knuckles against it. Once again, the sound echoed through the room, but no one answered. When I pushed the door open, the hinges creaked, and a second later the stink of rot slammed into me. My legs trembled as they begged me to run. I didn't, though. I stayed the course, pushing the door open the rest of the way and stepping inside.

The room was dark, and before my eyes had time to adjust to the sudden blackness, I was greeted by the snarls of the dead. My feet rooted themselves to the ground even as I reached for the knife I had strapped to my thigh. I didn't pull it out as I waited for the room to come into focus. When it did, I found four zombies chained up inside the cages that lined the walls. The clink of metal as they fought to get free grew until it nearly drowned out their moans and growls. The sounds only became more violent when I stepped further into the room.

I headed for a door that was just past the cages, but thankfully out of the reach of the zombies. It seemed to be the only room that Dragon could have been hiding in.

Once again, I paused outside the closed door and knocked. The thud of footsteps on the other side was barely audible over the zombies. Every move they made had the hair on the back of my neck prickling even more. Standing with my back to them felt wrong. Dangerous, and so opposite of what I'd always been told to do that I was having a tough time not pulling out my knife and stabbing them in the head.

In front of me, the door was pulled open and I almost jumped back when the cool, blue eyes of Donaghy greeted me. "It's you."

"Yes." I glanced toward the zombies, who were fighting against their chains like crazy. "Is Dragon here?"

Donaghy's eyebrows shot up and he stepped aside so I could enter. The room was small, with three cots and a tiny, stinking bathroom to the left. No door on it as far as I could tell. Just past the beds was yet another door. Probably Dragon's office.

At my back, the door clicked shut, muting the sound of the zombies.

"Dragon's busy." I turned when Donaghy threw himself onto one of the cots. "They've been at it for fifteen minutes, so I'd be willing to bet he's about done."

"They?"

Donaghy lifted his eyebrows as he stretched out on the bed. "Helen."

Helen? That must have been name of the older waitress I'd seen last night.

"Oh."

I crossed my arms over my chest and hugged the plaid shirt I was wearing closer to my body. Underneath, my new dress clung to my curves. Next to the one Glitter wore last night it probably didn't look very provocative, but even with the shirt covering it I felt naked.

82

Donaghy put his hands behind his head and stared at ceiling.

Silence fell over us, disturbed only when the sounds from the rooms on either side of ours grew louder. Moans. The clink of chains. Grunts from Dragon's office. Growls. Gasps of pleasure. Wood scraping against the floor. Helen's raspy voice begging for more.

"You fighting tonight?" I asked when I couldn't stand the noises anymore.

My arms tightened around my chest as Donaghy tore his gaze from the ceiling and looked my way. The plaid shirt made me sweat, but it was soft and comforting against my skin.

"It's Friday, which means two fights." His tone was bored, or maybe resigned. It was hard to tell.

"You don't get nervous?"

Donaghy pushed himself up so he was sitting, his eyes never leaving mine. "No reason. Zombies are dangerous, but predictable. Nothing I can't handle. It's people you have to worry about."

He sounded like my family. It was what I'd grown up hearing, and even though I didn't know everything that had happened to my parents after the virus hit—or my biological parents for that matter—I did know that at times, men had turned out to be more of an enemy than even the zombies had.

Donaghy couldn't be old enough to remember all the uncertainty of those first few months, though. He was maybe twenty-five, meaning he had probably been around five years old when the virus had broken out. Too young to have more than a vague recollection of what went on. Maybe he was older, though.

"How old are you?"

Donaghy's eyebrows shot up, but he didn't blink before saying, "Twenty-six."

I was close. "Do you remember what it was like before the virus?"

It was an odd question to pop out of my mouth because it wasn't what I'd been wondering about at all. I'd been wondering how he handled the outbreak, or more importantly, how he'd survived. Instead, I asked him about before. Figured.

"I remember some things, but to be honest it's hard to pin down which memories are real." He pressed his lips together and frowned as he looked me over, making my skin prickle. "You can't be older than nineteen, right?"

"Twenty," I said.

Donaghy nodded and his head was still bobbing when the door behind me opened. I spun around just as Dragon stepped out, still in the process of zipping his pants. Helen was adjusting her black crop top, a grin on her face as she sauntered by. She was tall and thin, and she'd probably been an attractive woman at one time, but now she just looked worn out. Her tan skin was so wrinkled and tough that it reminded me of leather, and her short hair had been bleached until it looked white.

She winked when she walked by, and despite the disgust rolling through me at the thought of her and Dragon, it was a welcoming gesture that I was pretty sure had been meant to put me at ease. And it had.

"You made it!" Dragon's smile stretched wide as his gaze moved over me, revealing the gap in his mouth that was shockingly dark against his white teeth. "Wasn't sure if you'd have the nerve."

"You have to do whatever it takes in this world."

Dragon's eyebrows shot up and his gaze went over me again. "Very true..." His smile widened when his eyes met mine. "Most of the people who come through the doors of my bar can attest to that."

"I'm just looking to serve drinks." I uncrossed my arms and stood up straight. Show no weakness. I'd been taught that from an early age and now was no exception.

Dragon chuckled. "Whatever you say."

The tone of his voice made it seem like he had more in mind for me, or like he expected me to do more when desperation took hold. He was probably only speaking from experience. These days, desperation was an epidemic even more destructive than the original virus had been.

Dragon headed for the bathroom where he washed his hands. As he ran his hands under the water, the muscles under the tattoo covering his back flexed. His head was up, and he used the cracked and filmy mirror in front of him to study me. I squirmed, waiting for him to say something, but he didn't.

When he finally flipped the water off and turned to face me, his hands were still dripping. "Take the shirt off so I can see what

I'm working with."

I shook my head and pulled my shirt tighter against my body.

"Not for that." He waved his hand dismissively. "You look healthy enough, but I want *quality* waitresses."

The bar owner's smile didn't fade, and I couldn't look away from the black gap where his teeth used to be as I unbuttoned the flannel shirt covering my dress. Behind me, the growls and snarls of the zombies were deafening, but they didn't drown out the pounding of my heart. I took a deep breath and slipped the shirt off, allowing it to drop to the floor like I was undressing for a lover, not in the middle of a job interview. Dragon pressed his lips together as he looked me over and I had to resist the urge to cross my arms. It didn't matter that my legs were trembling, I needed to appear strong and in control in front of men like this.

"Turn around." Dragon spun his hand in a circle as if he thought I wouldn't understand the words coming out of his mouth.

I did as I was told, stealing a look at myself once my back was to him. The black dress was skin tight and sleeveless, the neckline coming down to a deep V that accentuated what little cleavage I had. In the back, the V was even lower, ducking down my spine and stopping less than an inch above my waist. The dress was tight and short, going only two inches past my ass. The knife strapped to my thigh peaked out, a warning to any man who thought he was going to get something other than drinks from me. I'd never owned anything like this dress before—never had the need—and being in it made me feel naked. Especially with the way Dragon was studying me.

My gaze met Donaghy's as I turned back to face Dragon, and the way the fighter's jaw was clenched made something inside me buzz. The expression in his blue eyes was similar to the one from last night when he found me in the bathroom. It was like he was considering ripping Dragon's head off.

I tore my gaze from his and focused once again on the man I was hoping would be my new boss.

"Looks good, and the knife is a nice touch. You won't need it, though." His smile didn't waver, but his eyes did cloud over. "Working for me means no one will touch you. If they do, I'll rip their limbs off."

85

I swallowed at this savage tone, but it was oddly comforting. And for some crazy reason, I believed him. I wasn't sure if he was doing it to be nice or if it was just his possessive nature coming out, but it made me feel a hell of a lot better about working here.

"Thanks," I muttered.

Dragon nodded once before heading toward the door Helen had disappeared through a few minutes earlier. "Follow me." Almost as an afterthought, he added, "Both of you."

I followed my new boss into the other room, pausing just long enough to swipe my shirt up off the floor, and behind me Donaghy got to his feet. The zombies went nuts when we walked past them, growling and reaching for us, their mouths chomping at air. I made a wide arc around them, staying at least four feet out of their reach, but Dragon got so close their fingers almost brushed his arm. He snarled back at them, and then chuckled before heading out into the bar.

"Prick," Donaghy muttered behind me.

I glanced back, but his eyes were on the floor.

"We have an hour to get you some training before things start getting busy. Shouldn't be hard. We only have three options, after all." Dragon lifted three fingers, ticking the options off as he listed them. "Moonshine, Ale, and shots of whiskey."

"Seems easy enough." A total lie. There wasn't going to be an easy second of working here.

We stopped in front of the bar where Helen was serving the three men already trying to kill themselves with booze, while at her side Glitter was busy getting ready for the night. The younger girl lined glasses up along the bar top so they were easy to fill, then pulled bottles of amber and clear liquid out from under the counter. She counted them, her lips pressed together in a purse that, oddly enough, reminded me of my dad.

The thought caught me so off guard that I found myself staring. Then, out of nowhere, I found myself thinking about the scar on Donaghy's chin. I stole a glance at the fighter as Dragon went over my duties—which didn't include much more than filling glasses. Donaghy was leaning against the counter, staring across the open room toward the ring, as silent as usual.

"I get ten percent of any tips you make." Dragon's voice boomed through my thoughts, and I turned to find his brown eyes narrowed on me. "Don't try to cheat me or you'll be sorry."

I swallowed. "Of course not."

Like I would ever consider cheating this guy out of anything.

He nodded once, satisfied that I was taking him seriously, and then turned and headed over to where Helen was standing. "Glitter can take it from here."

I didn't move for a second, watching my new boss walk away. The interview had been even shorter and easier than I'd thought it would be, but knowing that I had the job didn't make me feel any less uneasy than I had before I set foot in the place. If anything, my stomach was tighter than before.

When I turned to face the bar, Glitter was staring at me, her gray eyes glittering with unconcealed interest. "We need to go down to the basement before things get too busy."

"Basement?" I shivered, thinking about how disgusting the rest of the place was. If it was gross up here, I was sure the basement would be crawling with things that until now had only haunted my nightmares.

"Yeah." She nodded as she came out from behind the bar, calling over her shoulder, "You got it from here, Helen?"

The older woman nodded. "You know I do, sugar."

Glitter smiled as she headed toward the long hallway that led to the bathroom. I followed, my heels clicking against the stone floor, and to my surprise, footsteps echoed after us. I glanced back to find Donaghy two feet behind me, his demeanor as stony as ever, but his blue eyes on me.

"Thought you could use some help."

"Aren't you a sweetheart." Glitter's voice echoed through the hallway.

Donaghy didn't respond, and he didn't look away from me. His expression was an odd mixture of protective and curious, and it made the hair on my scalp stand up.

Glitter's footsteps came to a halt, and I stopped just short of slamming into her. In front of us stood a door with a keypad next to it. I shuffled my feet anxiously as the waitress typed a few numbers in. Donaghy was standing so close to my back that every breath he let out brushed against my bare skin, and the combination of his nearness and body heat made me to break out in a sweat.

The door unlocked with a hiss and I had to move back so Glitter could pull it open completely. I ended up bumping into Donaghy, who grabbed my hips to keep me from falling.

"Sorry," I said, twisting slightly to face him, but not enough that he had to let me go. His hands felt impossibly large on my body, and I was sure that if he wanted to, he could crush me with them. Just like he had last night with the zombies in the ring.

Donaghy only nodded.

Glitter's voice had an edge of annoyance to it when she said, "This way."

She headed down the stairs, which were cloaked in shadows and ended in an abyss so black all I could think to compare it to was the gap in Dragon's teeth.

Reluctantly, I pulled out of Donaghy's grasp and headed after Glitter. She was less than a foot in front of me, but halfway down her pink hair got lost in the shadows. Darkness engulfed me, and I was forced to hold onto the rail to make sure I didn't fall. In front of me Glitter's heels clicked against the steps, matching my own and the pounding of Donaghy's boots at my back.

The pink haired waitress stopped walking and I froze on instinct. This time, Donaghy was the one who bumped into me. His chest was level with my head when he grabbed my bare arms, and the rough callouses on his palms were oddly soothing against my soft skin.

"Just a second." Glitter's voice broke through the darkness and I jumped. Donaghy didn't move, but the pounding of his heart against my head increased.

It didn't take more than a second for the light to click on, and when it did it was so bright that I found myself blinded by it.

Donaghy's hands left my arms, probably so he could shield his eyes from the brightness, and behind me he swore.

"Sorry," Glitter said. I cracked one eye to find her heading across the basement. "I keep telling Dragon to put a light at the top of the stairs, but he's too cheap." Something like amusement, or maybe even affection, rang in her voice.

She was moving again before my eyes had a chance to fully adjust, but I did my best to follow her. The room was only slightly in focus, but I was shocked by how sterile it was. No dirt or bugs or rats, and no cobwebs clogging the corners. The walls and ceilings were starkly white, making it even more difficult for my eyes to adjust, and the floor was a black and white checkered tile. Stainless steel tubs and barrels were lined up along one side of the room, with tubes going in and out of them, and the other side was lined with shelves. Glass bottles by the hundreds were crammed into the space, filled with brown, amber, and clear liquid.

"Holy shit," Donaghy said from behind me.

"Dragon is a neat freak." Glitter shrugged when she stopped in front a shelf.

She pulled a couple bottles off and passed them to me, and I took them even though I was still surveying the area. There were two doors on the other side of the room, one was steel with another keypad next to it, but the other was made of wood.

"What else is down here?" I asked, nodding toward the doors.

Glitter handed Donaghy a couple bottles, her gaze moving quickly to the doors before she grabbed more booze off the shelf. "Dragon's apartment."

"He lives down here?" I turned my full gaze on her.

"Yup." She pressed her lips together, giving off the impression that she was holding something back, then she said, "This area is off limits. Only Dragon, Helen, and I have the code." Her dark eyes held mine when she turned to face me, four bottles cradled in her arms. "We should go up. The place is going to get busy real soon."

She headed toward the stairs, passing Donaghy and me without another look. My gaze met the fighter's and he shook his head. He gave the spotless room one more look before following Glitter, and I was right behind them.

This wasn't what I had expected to find in Dragon's basement at all.

# CHAPTER TEN

## Meg

**AFTER** the pristine atmosphere of the basement, Dragon's Lair felt even more depressing. The poorly lit room reminded me of a dungeon, and the stink of death was pungent enough to make my stomach roll.

Glitter set the bottles she'd carried upstairs on the counter, then motioned for Donaghy and I to do the same. The fighter set his down without a word, and before I'd even had the chance to put my own bottles down, he was heading across the room toward Dragon's office.

I watched him go, memorizing the way his muscles moved as he walked. It made his tattoos appear to have a life of their own, rippling over his skin like waves rolling out to sea. It must have taken hours to draw the lines on his back, and every second of it had been worth it as far as I was concerned. Donaghy was like a walking work of art. In more ways than one

"You ready for this?" Glitter asked, drawing my attention her way.

Heat flooded my cheeks at being caught staring, but when I turned she wasn't looking at me. Instead, the waitress was focused on lining the new bottles up under the counter. With her head bowed, I got an even better view of the long roots poking out of her pink hair.

"I think so." I shifted my weight to my right foot, hoping to give the left one a little break from the heels. Already my feet were killing me and the night hadn't even started yet.

"She'll be fine," Helen said in a scratchy voice, coming over to join Glitter and me. The older woman smiled fondly at the younger girl, then turned the same look on me. "Just pour and take credits, right?"

Glitter shoved her pink hair out of her face and nodded. "Pretty much all there is to it."

"I can handle it," I said firmly.

Helen grinned even more, but Glitter's gaze moved over me slowly, doubt clogging her expression.

"You sure about that?" the younger waitress asked.

"She'll be fine." The skin on Helen's face wrinkled even more when she looked me over, but her blue eyes were bright and friendly. "This is Megan James. Surviving is in the family name."

Glitter blinked and something flashed in her eyes, but before I could figure out what it was, the look was gone. It was almost like she wanted to hide that she knew who I was. It was a nice gesture, although pointless. Everyone knew who I was.

"That's right. I'm a survivor," I said, looking back and forth between the two women. "Plus, I don't have a choice. It's this or the streets."

"We all know a little something about that." Glitter frowned as she ran her hand through her pink hair.

With her arm raised, the lights shining down from above highlighted the patches of scars that ran up the inside of both her arms, darker in the crook than anywhere else. They were faded, but there was no doubt what they were from. Track marks. Scars from intravenous drug use. It was a miracle she was alive and healthy considering how many there were. Clean needles were few and far between these days, and most people who turned to drugs ended up dying a pretty fast and horrible death from infection, overdose, or some other communicable disease.

"Being a survivor or the streets?" I asked even though I knew I should mind my own business. The scars had me intrigued. Glitter didn't seem like she was still using, which was good, and she looked healthy enough, but she had obviously been into it pretty heavy at some point.

"Both." Helen answered for the young girl, patting her on the back in a comforting gesture.

The older woman looked over her shoulder at the few patrons already sitting at the bar. There was only a handful more than there had been before we'd gone down to the basement, but more trickled in every minute or so. They talked and laughed as they headed for the bar, ready for a night of drinking and gambling. It was going to get busy fast.

"Need to get to work." Helen nodded once and then turned away, leaving Glitter and me alone.

"When Dragon found me on the streets I was out of my mind. Bleeding." The young girl pursed her lips and for the second time a jolt of familiarity went through me at the expression. She glanced toward the scars on her arms. "I don't remember a lot from before he found me, though." She poured herself a shot and threw it back, and her eyes squeezed shut for a second before she continued. "He saved me. I'd be dead if he hadn't brought me back here. I was young, but pretty far gone. Dragon got me cleaned up, gave me a job, and a place to live."

Glitter ran her hands over the scars on her arms, her eyes not meeting mine while she waited for me to respond. She probably thought I was going to judge her. Last night I'd been here with the Regulator's son, sitting in the VIP section. From the outside my life probably looked peachy. The problem with that was, looks could be deceiving.

"You got lucky, then," I said.

Glitter lifted her head, her pink hair a curtain over one eye. "Yeah."

"Let's get some drinks poured!" Dragon's voice boomed through the room and I jumped.

Glitter winked before turning away, a small smile now on her lips. The boss man didn't seem to intimidate her very much. Maybe he was all bark and no bite.

Donaghy was doing pushups in the middle of the ring and on the other side of the bar, leaning against the wall, Dragon stood watching him. The boss's arms were crossed and he had a smile on his face as the fighter pushed his body up and down. A few other men stood at Dragon's side, and I recognized them from the night before. The two hulking men who had brought the zombies out—and broken up any fights—as well as the men who cleaned the ring up after Donaghy's fight.

"Here." Glitter held a shot glass out to me. "Makes the night go easier."

I took the glass, my hand shaking just a little, then threw the shot back. The liquid burned its way down my throat to my stomach, coating everything inside me in a warm blanket. From the other end of the bar, Helen threw me a smile as she tossed her own shot back.

At least everyone who worked here seemed friendly. That was something I hadn't expected.

I slid the now empty glass across the counter to Glitter just as a wave of filthy men swept through the front door.

"Here we go," she said, turning to fill a few glasses. "People are getting off work and it's going to get busy real fast. Let's get some ready to go. They're going to come in thirsty."

I followed her lead, filling glasses with moonshine while she took care of the ale. Men filed in, already loud and rowdy, most of them filthy after a day of work. My gaze moved over the crowd, stopping on Donaghy as he crossed the room toward me. Sweat had beaded on his chest and his skin shimmered under the lights, but once again it was the scar on his chin that I found myself staring at. It had a strange pull on me, and even though I tried to tell myself it was because it made me think of my dad, I knew that wasn't true. Something about Donaghy was comforting.

"I need a drink," he said when he stopped in front of me, his gaze moving from mine to the men filling the room. "A shot."

I filled the small glass and slid it across the bar toward him. "You ready?"

"Told you—" He threw the shot back, slamming the empty glass down when he was done. "—there's nothing to worry about."

I almost laughed.

At my side Glitter giggled as she served drinks, and Helen was batting her eyes like she was a sixteen, not pushing sixty. I knew I should be helping them, both because they needed it and because I was missing out on tips, but I couldn't seem to walk away from the man in front of me. The fighter's silent strength had a strange hold on me. Plus, just hearing the lewd comments the men were throwing the other waitress' way made me want to run for the door.

Donaghy's eyes searched mine for a second before he finally said, "Why are you here?"

I forced out a smile. My insides were more uneasy than they'd ever been and small talk — or heavy talk — was the last thing on my mind, but this man had saved me and I felt like I owed him something.

"Working."

He shook his head. "That's not what I mean. Why?"

"I need the credits?" I wasn't sure what he was asking, but with his blue eyes trained on my face, I was having a hard time figuring it out.

He took a step closer. The bar separated us, but I could feel his body heat anyway. It was sweltering in the already stuffy building. All around him people shifted, trying to make room as more and more sweaty bodies filled the space. After Donaghy's impressive win last night, Dragon's Lair was going to be packed.

"You have connections," he said, lowering his voice like we were having an intimate conversation. "The Regulator's son—"

"Is a friend." My voice was firm, but quiet. "Just a friend."

His brows pulled together and something flashed in his eyes. Confusion or maybe relief. Seeing it sent a shiver shooting through my body, but again, I didn't know why.

"Friend?" he finally said.

A smile curled up my lips even though his eyes were still on me and it felt like he hadn't blinked once. "You know, a person you spend time with."

The fighter didn't crack a smile. "I know what a friend is. That's not what I meant."

"I know what you meant." His gaze was making me want to squirm. "Jackson may want more out of me, but that isn't going to happen. We're just friends."

Donaghy's eyes moved from my face for the first time, and when he dragged his gaze across my skin, every inch of me grew warm. The look was all searching, though. Like he was trying to figure out where I fit into the puzzle he'd been working on.

"Be careful here," he said when he was once again looking me in the eye.

"You heard Dragon. Now that I'm an employee, being here is less dangerous. He can't afford to lose one of his girls."

Donaghy's eyebrows shot up. "That's a comfort to you?"

"Enough of one."

The expression in his eyes had grown in intensity until eventually I was forced to look away. My gaze moved down. A muscle in his cheek twitched, nearly hidden by the dark stubble that covered his face. His square jaw gave his looks a rugged intensity that was matched only by the severe way he held himself. He pressed his lips together just as my gaze stopped on his chin, and his scar puckered just a little. It ran from the right side of his bottom lip to the point of his chin. Staring at it brought back so many thoughts of my dad that I found myself unable to look away. Even worse, my fingers tingled and I had to stop myself from reaching out to touch it.

Donaghy shifted under my gaze, and for the first time since I met him, he almost seemed uneasy. "What are you staring at?"

"Your scar," I said, tracing it with my eyes. "It makes me think of my dad."

"I remind you of your dad?" Something that might have resembled a smile turned up his lips.

I let out a laugh, and just like that the spell was broken. When my gaze met his again, curiosity flashed in his icy blue eyes.

"No. Not at all, actually. Just the scar." This time when my gaze moved to the scar, I allowed my fingers to trace the line. His skin was warm under my touch and his jaw scratchy. "He had one in the same place, just a little smaller."

"Had?"

"Yeah." I let out a sigh as I looked around. The place had really started to fill up and I knew I couldn't put it off any longer. "I should get to work. Good luck."

"No luck." Donaghy took a step back. "They're zombies. I already told you. They aren't who we have to worry about."

He walked away, leaving me staring after him.

His words were terrifyingly similar to the rant I'd been hearing from mom for the past few weeks.

"Meg!" I spun to face Glitter, who was nodding toward the bar. "Get some more drinks poured."

"On my way."

The work was mindless. Someone asked for a drink, I poured it, and then I did the same thing for the next person and the next and the next. The only time I changed it up was when the bar counter got too crowded with empty glasses.

"We do it like this," Glitter said as she grabbed a dirty glass in each hand and dipped them into a bin of murky-looking water.

She held them under to the count of five, and then put them upside down on the counter so they could dry. It didn't look the least bit sanitary, and it had me questioning how Dragon could be a neat freak but also allow something like that to happen in his bar.

"Help me," she said, grabbing two more.

I did as I was told and in less than a minute almost all the empty glasses were rinsed—not clean—and drying on the counter behind us. Then we went back to helping Helen serve drinks.

The tips were few and far between—although good when they did come—but the nasty looks and lewd comments flew like a waterfall. The first time a man tossed me a very descriptive comment about what he'd like to do to me, I flinched away from him.

Glitter had my back, though.

"Say that again and I'll jump over this counter and cut your balls off," she shot at the man, not missing a beat as she poured moonshine into a glass. "Then I'll toss you in the ring and let Donaghy have a go at you."

The man chuckled. "You know I'm all talk, pinkie."

He winked before turning away, pushing through the crowd until he was swallowed up by the mass of filthy bodies.

"You have to stand up for yourself," Helen said, pausing long enough to elbow me. "That's all."

Glitter nodded in agreement. "Most of these guys are just trying to get a reaction out of you. If they really are dangerous, Dragon will take care of it."

I wasn't sure how to tell the dangerous men from the ones who were just fooling around, but I took the other two women at their word. From then on out, I worked at shrugging off any comments thrown my way, sometimes shooting out a comeback and other times just telling them they'd have to settle for doing me in their dreams. It helped take the edge off things.

"The fight is going to start in five minutes," Glitter called over the crowd. "Then we'll be able to catch our breath."

I nodded as I poured moonshine into a barely dry glass.

The air that had been humid when I arrived was now practically dripping. Almost as if the building itself had started to sweat. Even in the skimpy dress my skin was moist, and for the first time since walking into the building, I was envious of the strips of fabric covering Glitter's body. Right now, I would have been happy to serve drinks in the nude.

I shoved a mass of sticky hair out of my face and let out a deep breath when I caught sight of Dragon walking into the ring.

"Good Evening!" His deep voice boomed through the bar less than a minute later, and like magic the crowd in front of me began to thin.

When I glanced toward Glitter, she smiled. "Told you."

"Thank God. Is it always this crazy?" The roar of voices had been replaced by a low hum as people made final bets while they waited for Dragon to bring the champion out.

"Not always. It depends on who's fighting." Glitter ran her hand through her pink hair.

Helen leaned against the counter at her side, lighting a cigarette as she stared across the room at the ring. Her stomach was visible between her crop top and the tight, black skirt she wore. Just like the rest of her, the skin was dark and wrinkled, but her stomach was flat. She didn't seem to have an ounce of extra fat on her body—other than her breasts, which I suspected weren't real. The woman must have lived on cigarettes alone.

"Dragon likes to be the one to fight—" Helen took a long drag off her cigarette. "—but people were getting tired of seeing it. That's why he finally agreed to the release program." Smoke floated around her head when she talked.

"Needed some new blood," Glitter said just as Donaghy came out of the back room.

"Exactly," Helen replied.

Just like last night, the zombies were already chained up inside the cage. From where I stood, I was able to see the two men who were waiting to release them, but only the top of Donaghy's head was visible as the crowd parted for him. I stood on my tiptoes, hoping to get a better view, but until he stepped into the ring, I couldn't see more than his dark brown hair. When he climbed into the cage, he turned to face the bar. Last night his eyes had been down. Not focused on anything in particular, and especially not looking at the crowd. Tonight, however, he was looking right at me.

Dragon droned on at Donaghy's side, talking about his impressive win the night before, and the entire time he spoke the fighter's blue eyes held mine. They were so focused and captivating that I couldn't look away. Not when a shiver moved up my spine. Not when my scalp prickled. Not even when Dragon backed out of the cage.

The second the zombies were free Donaghy ripped his gaze from mine. Before I could even blink one of the dead was down. The second one charged the fighter, and a waterfall of black blood sprayed across the ring as he joined his friend. The crowd went wild and my view was cut off when hands flew in the air, waving credits around as the men cheered for more blood.

"What do you think he did?" Glitter said behind me.

I didn't look away from the ring. "What do you mean?"

"To get sent to DC. What do you think he did?"

"These days—" The sound of Helen sucking chemicals into her lungs momentarily cut off her words. "—it could be anything or nothing."

I stood on the tips of my toes when the back of a zombie's head came into view. The other one was nowhere to be seen, but from here I couldn't tell if he was out or just injured. "He's alive, so that tells me it wasn't anything too violent."

"True." The shudder in Glitter's voice made me rip my eyes away from Donaghy.

I turned to find her hugging herself, her skin pale and sweaty. The faraway look in her eyes told me she was remembering something bad. Or trying not to remember it, more likely.

"You okay, sugar?" Helen asked, her tone soft despite her scratchy voice.

Glitter nodded, but her arms tightened. "Yeah."

The word was nearly drowned out by the cheer that rose up behind me. I turned to find Dragon opening the door to the cage, his grin wider than it had been even after he'd come out of the office earlier today.

He grabbed Donaghy's arm and lifted it above his head. "The champion!"

Donaghy's shoulders heaved, but when he looked up, his eyes found mine for the second time. Every hair on my body stood on end and I had to force myself to look away. When he stared at me like this, it felt like he was trying to see inside me.

The second I wasn't focused on the fighter anymore, my gaze was captured by another familiar face. Luke. Brown eyes held mine as he headed toward me, frowning in a way that made him look exactly like Uncle Al.

"Shit," I muttered just under my breath.

I crossed my arms and hugged myself as heat flooded my cheeks at the sight of Charlie's older brother, and I couldn't stop myself from taking a look around to make sure my uncle wasn't with him. I could just imagine the two of them coming here together so they could drag me out of the bar like I was a ten-year-old who had gotten caught doing something wrong. Sure, Luke wasn't my brother biologically, but we'd grown up together, and there had been stages in our childhood when I'd spent more time with him than Charlie, who had been a selfish and moody child at times.

"Megan." Luke stopped in front of me and I was relieved to find that he was alone. He shuffled his feet, and like me looked around. Almost as if he had the same worries going through his head that I'd had. "What are you doing here?"

"I got a job."

I sunk my teeth into my bottom lip while I waited for a lecture, but Luke seemed almost relieved when he let out a deep sigh.

"Oh." The chuckle he let out was nervous. "I saw you here last night with Charlie and Jackson, but ducked out before you could spot me. I wasn't sure if they'd come back with you. Charlie would tell Mom and Dad for sure."

"Tell them what?" He couldn't mean that Charlie would tell her parents about seeing Luke here, because that wouldn't do much more than get Charlie in trouble. Luke was twenty, only ten months younger than me, and as far as my aunt and uncle were concerned, he was an adult.

"About my apprenticeship," Luke said.

"You got an apprenticeship?" This was the first I'd heard of it, so I doubted his sister knew. "Wouldn't that make your parents happy?"

"Not exactly..." He glanced over his shoulder before meeting my gaze again. "I'm working with a zombie slayer. They don't know yet and they aren't going to be thrilled about it either. You know how we grew up. Always being told that we were lucky to be here. Hearing that things in New Atlanta weren't perfect, but that we needed to be grateful. I couldn't go a week without hearing some story about how awful life after the virus was. Mom and Dad are going to think I'm nuts, but I can't do this anymore. I'm leaving. I can't stay in this city. Only, I wanted to be ready for anything that might happen out there. That's why I got the apprenticeship."

"Leaving." I said the word like I'd never heard it before, but I was having a tough time wrapping my brain around it. It felt wrong. Luke had always been a part of my life, and I didn't like the idea of him not being here anymore.

"You have to know why," Luke said. "Things were bad enough, but after what's happened recently, there's no way in hell I'll stay here and let this government disappear me the way they have your dad and uncle, or kill me like they did with Joshua."

"Luke, I—" I wasn't sure how to respond. He'd never spoken to me like this before, and hearing him say *out loud* that he agreed with my mom made me wonder what he'd seen that I had been missing all these years. "What are you talking about?"

Luke leaned forward and grabbed my hand. "This thing with your dad is just the tip of the iceberg, and I know you have to sense it too. Things are going to get worse before they get better, and I'm not going to stick around for it. I'd ask you to go, but I know you can't. Not while you don't know for sure what happened with your dad, but—"

"Did your dad tell you something?" I looked around after the words were out, but no one seemed to be paying attention to us. The bar was still crowded, waiting for the second fight to start, but the men gathered in the room were too busy drinking and gambling to pay attention to what Luke was saying to me.

"No." Luke shook his head and his hand tightened on my arm. "Why? Does he know something?"

I wasn't sure if I should tell him about the note or not. On one hand, he was more likely to believe me than anyone else, but I didn't want to put him in danger.

"No," I said almost hesitantly. "There's nothing to know."

Luke's frown told me he didn't believe me, but before he could say anything a man came up to stand beside him. It was obvious just by looking at him that he was a zombie slayer. He was tall and his shaggy hair went down to his shoulders. It was a combination of dark blond and gray that matched his close-clipped beard. I judged him to be close to fifty, possibly a bit younger; although it was hard to tell thanks to the miles he wore on his tan skin. Years of living outside Atlanta had given him the weathered appearance that I was used to seeing on zombie slayers, and the hard, blue eyes that looked at me were filled with death.

"You ready to get the hell out of here?" the zombie slayer asked, obviously talking to Luke, but looking at me.

"Yeah." Luke nodded, then drummed his fingers on the counter like he was trying to decide what to do. "This is Megan."

The zombie slayer's eyebrows lifted as he looked me over a second time. "James?"

Great. Even the crazy zombie slayers who lived outside the city knew who I was.

"That's right," I said, trying to sound casual about it even though I was already gearing up to tell this asshole to keep his intrusive comments to himself.

"I knew your parents." The zombie slayer nodded slowly. "Long time ago."

I blinked and studied him more closely. Nothing about him was familiar, so I knew I'd never met him, but something in his expression told me he was telling the truth.

"You did?"

"Jon was a real good man." His mouth scrunched up and he tore his gaze away from me so he could look around the room. "Died coming to this shit hole. We would have all been better off if we'd stayed where we were. Me especially."

"This is Jim." Luke's tone indicated that the name should mean something to me, but it didn't. I'd never heard of a man named Jim, and I had no idea how he knew my biological parents who had never even made it all the way to Atlanta to begin with. In Colorado, I'm assuming, but still... This man was a stranger to me.

"Need to go," Jim said.

He didn't look at me again, and I got the impression that something about seeing me brought back bad memories. A lot of zombie slayers were running from things, so maybe thinking about my parents brought back the memories of whatever this man was trying to forget.

Luke nodded and took a step away from the bar. "Yeah. We're heading out in an hour."

"You're staying out there overnight?" A shiver ran down my spine. I'd never even set foot outside the city, and Luke was planning on spending the whole night out there. Among the zombies and marauders.

"Need to get his feet wet." Jim slapped Luke on the back but still never looked my way.

"It'll be fine." Luke grinned like it was a game, not a matter of life and death.

I had the urge to reach out and grab his hand, but stopped myself. I didn't know this zombie slayer, and I didn't want to make Luke look weak in front of the man.

"Be careful," I said instead, trying to sound strong.

Jim turned away, heading for the front door as Luke nodded. I watched from behind the bar as he followed the other man to the door. He would be okay. He was tough and resourceful—like his dad—and I had no doubt in my mind that he'd make it out there. Still, I didn't like knowing that I was about to lose one more person I cared about.

# CHAPTER ELEVEN

## Donaghy

**THE** crowd was still cheering when the men rushed into the ring after the second fight. The excitement surging through the air wasn't real, though, and it sure as hell wasn't for me. The people were just bored, possibly a little pissed off, and seeing me beat the shit out of a couple zoms was a good way to kill some time. They knew it wasn't difficult, and I knew they didn't give a shit about me. If one of the zombies had managed to sink his teeth into me, the crowd would have reacted the exact same way they were right now.

People moved aside as I headed for the bar. They slapped me on the back and told me I'd done a good job. Women rubbed their tits against my arm when I went by. I didn't look at any of them, though. Now that both fights were over, I just wanted a drink. Hopefully, people would get the hell out of here and give me some room to think, too.

"Drink?" Meg asked when I finally stopped in front of her.

"Moonshine."

She nodded and grabbed a glass that was still smudged with other people's filthy fingerprints. Her eyes were so glued to mine while she poured it that I half expected the liquid to end up all over the counter. Instead, she managed to stop it at exactly the right spot. Three quarters of the way full, just like Dragon had told her.

When she slid the glass my way, there were so many questions hanging over her head that I could practically hear the gears in her brain turning.

"What do you want to know?" I asked before taking a sip.

"Excuse me?" Meg's eyebrows shot up and she leaned closer.

I tried not to focus on the curve of her breasts as she leaned against the bar, but it was impossible. The V was so deep that it left little to the imagination, and the fabric was thin. Thin enough that I could make out the hard points of her nipples.

"I can tell you're dying to ask me something. So just do it." I dragged my gaze up her body and a flush spread across her already red cheeks. Her dark hair was sweaty and matted to the sides of her face and neck, and for a brief second all I could think about was what she would look like spread out underneath me. Her skin glistening with sweat and her hair plastered to her face as I worked her over.

I cleared my throat and focused on my drink.

"What makes you think I want to ask you something?" she asked.

I looked up. "Because you do."

"Why were sent to DC?" She took a small step back like she was afraid I was going to hit her.

Did I look that scary?

My gaze moved from the girl in front of me and down over myself. Black zombie blood was splattered across my arms and chest, and there were scars on my knuckles from fighting. I was sure the expression on my face didn't help give off a warm fuzzy feeling either. I typically tried to keep it somewhere between bulldog and pissed off teenager. It made me less approachable.

Only, I wasn't sure if I wanted this girl to stay away. Ever since I'd come across her in the bathroom and she'd stuck up for me the way she did, I'd found it more and more difficult to maintain an air of indifference.

I smoothed out my features, which took a hell of a lot more effort than it should. "I stood up for someone I loved."

106

Meg's expression waivered and she blinked. "How?"

"Doesn't matter." My hand tightened on my glass.

I expected her to argue, but she just nodded before saying, "Where are you from? Before DC, I mean."

"Dayton." My grip loosened on the glass. "I was born in Ohio. The virus killed my dad, but Mom and I made it. When things got bad, after the dead came back, she took us to Wright-Patt. They'd already started to fortify the area, and by the time they made contact with Atlanta, the walls were secure. We were pretty happy there. As happy as people can be, I guess."

"Your mom is still there?"

I should have anticipated that question, but it caught me off-guard. It had been so long since I'd told anyone a damn thing about myself that I'd forgotten the natural progression of conversations. Someone asked a question and you answered, which led to more questions. It should have occurred to me that Meg would want to know where Mom was now.

"No." The word came out firm and final.

Even though Meg lifted her eyebrows, she didn't seem offended. "You don't have to talk about anything you don't want to."

I didn't want to. Did I? I hadn't had a real conversation with anyone since I got sent to DC, but something about this girl made me want to keep it going.

I was still trying to decide when Meg said, "How was your night at Jackson's?"

Just like that, the walls inside me that had started to crumble went back up. This girl might have been struggling, but I couldn't forget who her friends were. I was almost certain that sooner or later she'd give in and marry that asshole, if for no other reason than so she didn't have to slum in places like this. I couldn't even blame her. With the way the world was, you had to do whatever you could.

"Like a dream." My voice had returned to its normal tone, coated in indifference. "Haven't slept in a bed in a year, and never one that soft. If I'd gotten some food it would have made the place better than heaven."

Meg frowned. "Jackson didn't feed you?"

"It was late when I got up. He left me a plate of food, but my

107

guards ate it." I shrugged. "Doesn't matter. Dragon gave me a prepackaged meal."

Meg shook her head a few times. "Speaking of Jackson...." She gnawed on her lower lip like she wasn't sure what to say. "I'd appreciate it if you didn't mention that I got a job here."

My shoulders stiffened. "What do you think happens when I'm at his house? You think I hang out in his room, gossiping about the settlement or some dumb shit like that?" My words were laced with more vengeance than this girl deserved, but I couldn't stop it from spewing out. The idea that the Regulator's prick son would ever stoop to having a conversation with me was the most absurd thing I'd ever heard.

"Of course not." Meg glared at me, all the uncertainty of a moment ago gone in the blink of an eye. "I just wanted to make sure you didn't accidentally mention it in passing. Where I work is none of Jackson's business, but he wouldn't see it that way."

"I guess he wouldn't like the idea of his future wife slumming it, would he?" I held her gaze while I took a drink, so I didn't miss the fire that blazed in her eyes.

"I'm not going to marry Jackson."

I set my glass down, still watching her. "Why not?"

"Because we're just friends. Which I already told you."

"You have to admit it would make your life easier." I lifted my eyebrows, challenging her to argue with me.

"Comparatively, yes. But I don't love him, and I'm not dumb enough to think that marrying someone you're not in love with wouldn't bring on a whole new list of problems."

"So you're waiting for the fairy tale?" I almost rolled my eyes. Every time I thought I had a little bit of this girl figured out, she threw me for a loop. If she thought she—or anyone else for that matter—was going to find some magical happy ending, she was delusional.

Meg looked down, frowning at the marked-up bar top in front of her. "There's no such thing as fairy tales."

"No shit." I snorted before finishing off my drink, then slid the empty glass over. I'd reached my limit of free drinks for the night, but she refilled it anyway.

"Don't tell Dragon," she said, looking around.

The bar had emptied out, most of the patrons having moved

on to strip joints or pool halls now that the fights were over, and it made it easier for me to think. Plus, it gave me more time to study the girl in front of me.

Meg turned to help Glitter clean the glasses while Helen gathered the ones that had been left around the room. I sipped my drink, knowing I couldn't take another free one from Meg, and watched as she learned her new duties. On first glimpse, the dress she wore wasn't as revealing as Glitter's, but now that I'd gotten a better look at it, I noticed that every time she stopped under one of the lights the fabric became almost transparent. I was sure she didn't have a clue that the thing was as see through as it was, but I wasn't about to tell her. The swell of her breasts and the curve of her ass were about the best things I'd seen in a year, and I was going to soak up every second of it while I could. The next dump these assholes dragged me off to probably wouldn't have waitresses nearly as young or attractive as this one did.

"Need to come up with a side business." Dragon's voice boomed through the bar and I tore my gaze off Meg to find his dark eyes focused on Glitter. "How do you feel about stripping?"

The girl narrowed her eyes at him. "You know exactly how I feel about it."

"Just asking." Dragon winked as he shot her a toothless grin. "I thought you might have come to your senses."

Glitter just snorted.

My back stiffened when the man's gaze moved to Meg. It was ridiculous how protective I felt toward her. Insane. We barely knew each other, and here I was ready to jump up and snap that asshole's neck the second he stepped out of line.

"Don't even think about it," Meg barked as she rinsed glasses in a bin of murky water.

Dragon let out a loud chuckle and turned his focus on Helen, who was leaning against the bar at his side.

The older waitress ran her fingers up his arm, grinning past the cigarette perched between her lips. "You know I'm up for anything."

"Darling," Dragon said, grabbing her hips so he could pull her against him. "If I thought the assholes who came into this place would be smart enough to appreciate you, I'd say go for it."

"Men never know a good thing until it grabs them by the

balls," she said, emphasizing her point by grabbing Dragon's crotch.

The man growled, and I turned away when he started dragging Helen across the room.

Glitter slid over to stand next to Meg, who had her tips from the night spread out in front of her. Seemed like a decent amount.

"You do okay tonight?" The girl with the pink hair nodded toward the stack of credits in Meg's hand.

"I think so."

She counted the bills while I took another sip of my drink. She'd done well, which wasn't a surprise. She may not have the charm that Helen seemed to be an expert at turning on and off, or the dress that was barely a dress like Glitter, but Meg was sexy without even trying. Just standing there, gnawing on her lip while she stared at the stack of credits in her hand caused nasty thoughts to flip through my head.

It would be a bad idea, though. Me and her.

"I'm leaving in a week."

It wasn't until Meg looked up, her eyes full of questions, that I realized I'd said it out loud.

"What?"

"Shit," I chuckled to myself while I downed the rest of my drink. "The alcohol must have pickled my brain. It's been too long since I drank."

Meg smiled, but she still looked confused.

"Where do you go after this?" Glitter asked, leaning her hip against the counter.

"Key West. It'll be the first time I've ever seen the ocean."

A smile lit up the young waitress's face. "I've always wanted to see the ocean. Do you think it's as blue as it is in pictures?"

"Can't be." I shook my head. "Nothing's that clean-looking these days."

Meg exhaled as she mimicked the other waitress's stance, only she looked more exhausted. Like she needed the counter to hold her up while Glitter was just trying to relax.

"My mom grew up in California," Meg said.

"California?" The name was distantly familiar, like a place I had once heard existed but had forgotten all about. "No settlements there, right?"

"No."

"Let's see," Glitter lifted a few fingers. "There are settlements in Oklahoma, Texas, Key West, Dayton, Baltimore, Colorado, Minnesota, South Carolina, and here. Right?"

"Sounds about right," I muttered.

She was forgetting the prison settlement in DC. It was a cesspool, and as far as I was concerned, we'd all be better off if everyone forgot it.

"I read an article in the *National Newspaper* last week about how they're going to be building trains soon." Glitter turned her eyes on Meg. "Has Jackson's dad mentioned that?"

"I don't talk to the Regulator." The tone of her voice made me look up. Meg was frowning, and there was something that looked a little bit like disgust in her eyes.

"Oh." Glitter pressed her lips into a pout. "Dragon said it's bullshit, but I don't know. Wouldn't it make everything easier if there were trains? We could move supplies more quickly, which would mean expanding the walls or making better living quarters."

"Dragon's right," I said, pushing the stool back so I could stand. "It's bullshit. But even if by some miracle they do end up building these trains, they sure as hell aren't going to use them to make our lives better."

Meg nodded like she agreed, but Glitter just frowned. The more I talked to the girl, the younger she seemed. Naïve too. It was as if someone had tried to protect her from everything in this world, or like she'd been hidden away for a lot of her life and hadn't experienced much. It didn't make sense though, not with the track marks on her arms.

"I'm beat," I said, turning to face the door. "I hope those dumb ass guards of mine get here soon so I can hit the sack."

# CHAPTER TWELVE

## Meg

**BY** the time I dragged myself out of the bar, I was pretty sure I knew exactly how the zombies felt: Dead on their feet. The street was dark, but not deserted, and the echo of music and voices bounced off the walls around me. It was impossible to tell where they were coming from, though. Here and there a glow broke through the darkness when someone lit a cigarette, and every shadow that moved seemed threatening.

I pulled my plaid shirt tighter against body and kept my head low as I walked. Thankfully, Donaghy and his guards were right behind me, because I hadn't even made it to the end of the street before someone called out to me from the shadows.

"Fifteen credits for a blow."

I reached for my knife, but before I'd even had a chance to wrap my fingers around it, Donaghy was at my side. "If you want to keep your dick intact, you'll shut your mouth."

The man, barely visible in the darkness, slinked back until he was nothing more than a memory.

"Thanks," I said, shooting Donaghy a smile as I picked up the pace.

It was so dark that I could barely distinguish more than an outline of the man next to me, but I could see it when he nodded. "You're welcome."

We were silent once again as we moved side by side down the street. Donaghy's body heat was oddly comforting. Not because the night was cold—it was hotter than hell on steroids—but because it once again reminded me of Dad and how soothing his silent presence had always been.

Maybe the two men shared more similarities than just a scar.

We reached the end of the street and turned right, but when we made it to the next intersection, I paused. My apartment building was in the northern part of the city, but Jackson's house was south.

"I go this way," I said, turning to face Donaghy.

The spotlights from the nearby wall were just bright enough to illuminate the intersection, but they also threw deep shadows across the area and made the man at my side seem twice as big. The fighter's gaze moved from me to the street at my back, almost like he was trying to decide if it was safe enough for me to go on my own, and I appreciated it more than he'd ever know. I hadn't felt like anyone cared what happened to me since Dad disappeared. Anyone other than Jackson, that was, and his concern could be suffocating at times.

"Maybe we should go with you," Donaghy said, his icy eyes moving back to mine.

I opened my mouth to tell him that it wasn't necessary, but before the words could make their way past my lips one of the guards stepped forward. "We don't got time for that."

With the shadows stretched across the street the way they were, it was impossible to know which one of the men said it, but I couldn't miss the fury that flashed in Donaghy's eyes just before he turned to face the men.

"You do what I say," he hissed.

The man who'd spoken moved his hand toward his waist, and even though it was too dark for me to see what he was doing, I could only imagine that he was reaching for a weapon.

"It's okay." I stepped between Donaghy and his guards. "I know how to defend myself." The uncertainty in the fighter's expression probably had a lot to do with how we'd met, but I squared my shoulders. "I was raised by survivors. They taught me how to look out for myself."

Donaghy's hand wrapped around my wrist, firm but gentle at the same time. "Be careful."

"I will." My heart pounded so hard that I was sure it would send me into orbit.

"Let's go," the guard at my back growled.

Donaghy nodded, his gaze still holding mine. A second later his hand slipped away, and I turned to watch him follow his guards down the street.

Suddenly, I felt more alone than I had in my entire life. The darkness surrounding me seemed heavier somehow. Oppressive.

The fighter faded into the shadows, his form getting darker and darker until he was barely more than an apparition. Just before he disappeared, he glanced over his shoulder, and the look was enough to make every inch of my body hum.

When the three men disappeared for good, I turned away, heading toward my apartment. I had my knife out before I'd made it even a block. Just in case. Guns were prohibited inside the walls—even though everyone knew you could get them on the black market—but knives were a survival staple.

Unlike the entertainment district, this part of the city was silent. I passed apartment buildings with only a handful of windows illuminated, and businesses that were cloaked in silence. It stayed that way for two blocks, and then I turned the corner, making my way past the shantytown that led to my neighborhood. Most of the shacks I walked by were silent, but occasionally the hum of someone breathing or a moan of ecstasy broke through the quiet.

Tonight, the sound sent a shiver down my spine. Just twenty-four hours ago Jackson had been concerned that these same noises would flick some kind of switch inside me, and I had dismissed his worries like they were infantile. Now, though, as I passed a shack that's walls were practically vibrating, heat flooded my body. It wasn't a bad feeling, though. I wasn't thinking about that asshole from the bathroom or what could have happened. No, I was thinking about Donaghy. About his intense gaze and how it had felt to have his body pressed against mine as we made our way into the dark basement. About his firm grip on my hips.

"Get a grip, Meg," I whispered as I walked faster.

Despite my confrontation with Suzie yesterday and the stigma of living in the shantytown, I'd never felt threatened walking past these little shacks. Even now, nearly two o'clock in the morning with almost no light, I was walking fast more out of habit than fear. Most of the people living in these shacks didn't want to hurt me. They were just trying to survive.

My apartment building came into view, and I slowed. Out front, leaning against the wall like he didn't have anything better to do, stood Jackson.

"Shit," I muttered as I worked to come up with an excuse as to why I was out this late.

There wasn't a good one and I knew it. Other than Charlie, I didn't have friends. Especially not any I would go to the entertainment district with, and based on the hour and my attire, there was no way I'd be able to convince Jackson that I'd been anywhere else.

My last name had always been a hindrance when it came to relationships. Often when people heard the name James they treated me like I was someone special, bending over backwards to do anything and everything for me. Other times, however, they avoided me. Whether it was because they didn't know how to talk to the niece of the savior of the human race, or because they thought I was too good to talk to them, I wasn't sure. I just knew that whenever someone new found out who I was, I had to prepare myself for one extreme or the other.

I was still fifteen feet away when Jackson pushed himself off the building. "Where the hell have you been? I looked for you on the wall, but you weren't there. I thought maybe you'd gone home to check on your mom, but she was out of her mind with worry when she answered the door."

Out of her mind with worry, or just out of her mind?

"Charlie and I went out." I pressed my lips together and held my breath, hoping that he bought the lie.

It was unusual, but it would be an easy lie to pass off. Charlie had stayed behind with her dad last night, which would explain her absence now, and I knew she'd be willing to lie for me if I asked her to. Plus, Jackson had been around long enough to know that Charlie was constantly begging me to go out with her.

"Why didn't you call me?" I'd expected him to be hurt to learn that I'd gone out and not invited him, but instead something that sounded a lot like anger coated his words. Jealousy even. "Who else were you with?"

The accusation was as bright as day: he assumed I'd been out with another guy. I guess it was an easy assumption for him to make. The only other time during our friendship that I'd gone out with someone other than Jackson was when I'd dated Colton, and that hadn't gone over well. In fact, Jackson had acted exactly like he was now. At the moment, I was too exhausted to sooth his ego. I'd never tried to lead Jackson on and I wasn't about to start now.

"Jackson, I love you. You're like a brother to me." I exhaled, dragging it out while I chose my words. I wanted to tell him that he had no right to ask me questions or tell me what to do, but I doubted that would go over well. "This is getting to be too much. I need space. I need to be young and single and not feel like I'm constantly working to buffer your ego."

It was the truth as plainly as I'd ever dared speak it, and even though there was some relief in saying the words, there was a part of me that was scared. Afraid of how he would react and what he would do. Which was nuts. This was Jackson. He was my friend.

"Seriously, Meg?" He took a small step toward me and I forced myself to hold my ground even though I wanted to shrink away from him. "I've done everything for you! I've been patient and understanding. I've listened to all your bullshit about how my dad isn't doing everything he can for this settlement." The venom in his voice was so thick that this time when he stepped toward me, I couldn't stop myself from flinching away. He paused and looked me up and down before saying, "Are you scared of me?"

"No." My voice shook, giving me away, and even though it was dark, I swear I saw a little bit of glee in Jackson's eyes.

All day my brain had been so full of Donaghy that I couldn't help comparing the two men right now. Jackson was the son of someone powerful and my closest friend, but there were times when I felt like a switch inside him flipped, and I couldn't help wondering if he'd been playing a part this whole time. Like he was hoping I'd fall for the charade long enough to get trapped in his web. Donaghy, however, was a convict, but being with him made me feel secure in a way that I'd never felt with anyone other than a family member. Almost like I knew that the fighter would do anything he could to keep me safe. Even risk his own life.

Did I think Jackson would do that?

No. I didn't.

"I'm not afraid of you," I said, squaring my shoulders even though something in the back of my head told me I should be. "And I'm not going to let you bully me into being in love with you, either. I don't know who I want, or if I will ever want anyone, but I know you aren't the right person for me.

"I'm not trying to bully you," he whispered, the words pushing their way through his teeth and sounding a lot like the hiss of snake.

"I know." I reached out, my hand shaky, but he backed away. "I want to be your friend, Jackson, but if that isn't enough for you, then maybe we need to spend some time apart."

I pressed my lips together while Jackson stared at the ground. His jaw twitched and his hands were clenched into fists. It only took thirty seconds for him to turn away from me. His eyes were still down and something about him reminded me of how Donaghy looked when he was in the ring, right before he ripped a zombie apart.

Jackson didn't even look back at me when he said, "I don't know why I wasted all these years on you. I'm *Jackson Star*. Who are you? Nobody. You may have the last name, but you don't have the blood. You're nothing."

The sting of his words was sharp and painful. He didn't look back once as he headed down the road and into the dark night. Even though the shantytown didn't scare me, I tensed when he reached the edge. He was right about one thing, he was Jackson Star, and I had no doubt that there were plenty of people in those shacks who would slit his throat and piss on his corpse and not lose any sleep over it.

I stayed where I was, my fingers flexed around my knife until he had finally disappeared around the corner. Once he was out of sight, I exhaled and headed into my building. Thankfully, the elevator was working, and once I was inside I pulled off my heels and wiggled my toes. Tomorrow I was going to have to make sure Charlie covered for me with Jackson or anyone else who asked, but I'd worry about that later. Right now, all I wanted to do was get some sleep.

The lights on our floor flickered as I headed down the hall, and I braced myself for a fight when I opened our front door. The apartment was silent though, and I'd only taken one step inside when I realized why. Mom was passed out on the couch, fully dressed and snoring with her mouth hanging open.

Something about it brought to mind the time Charlie, Luke, and I had gotten our hands on a bottle of moonshine. We'd been young—Luke and I just fifteen, and Charlie only thirteen—and by the time the booze was gone, Charlie had been passed out on the floor, her mouth hanging open just like Mom's was now. Only, that couldn't be right. Mom didn't drink. Her dad had been an alcoholic, and so had Dad's mom. Booze had always been a rarity in our house.

I sighed as I slipped my knife back into its sheath. "I'll get her to bed, then I'll sleep."

When I shook Mom's shoulder, her lips moved and she shifted, but she didn't open her eyes. If I didn't know better, I'd have wondered if someone had drugged her.

"Mom," I said, kneeling at her side. Once again, it was useless.

It took everything in me to lift her off the couch. She was dead weight, but manageable since she was nothing but skin and bones at this point. Her head flopped to the side when I lifted her, straining under the weight, but I made it to the bedroom.

There I dropped her on the bed, and when her head flopped to the side for the second time, there was something about it that hit me as wrong. I couldn't seem to wrap my brain around the situation, though. People didn't sleep this soundly. Not without drugs of some kind. Only, there were no drugs in this house. I knew because I'd torn the place apart looking for any credits that might have been hidden away by my parents. And I seriously doubted that Mom had left the apartment so she could buy some. She was way too freaked out to risk going out there. But what other explanation could there be? Nothing that I could think of.

I closed my eyes and exhaled. "I'll see you in the morning," I muttered as I headed out of the room, shutting the door behind me.

In my own room I stripped, leaving my dress on the floor when I crawled under the covers. The bed was warm and inviting, and my body heavy with the need to sleep. But my brain was humming. Thinking about my new job, coworkers, and most of all Donaghy. The fighter. The convict. The person who had saved me and had a scar just like my father's. For some reason, I couldn't get him out of my head.

# CHAPTER THIRTEEN

## Donaghy

**MY** guards were on my ass to walk faster the whole way back to the Regulator's house, and even though I was so tired I could barely lift my feet, I kept my pace slow. The last thing I was going to do was give these assholes what they wanted.

The walk was kind of nice, too. Atlanta was silent but active. The apartments we passed hummed with life even though there was really no audible noise. I couldn't explain it, really. I just knew that there was a peacefulness to this city that didn't exist in DC.

There it was never silent. The population was restless. Waiting. Like everyone slept with one eye open, either looking for their chance to get out or expecting someone to try and slit their throat in the night. Almost an entire year I spent there, and not once did I wake up feeling rested.

Here, though, it was different. And it wasn't just because of my temporary room in that mansion. This was a real city. It may have been depressing at times, and it was definitely oppressed by this shit show of a government that had sprung up, but the people here had a fighting chance.

We made it back to the Regulator's house, which was silent

and slightly cold compared to the rest of the city, and the second I set foot inside I was ready to crawl into bed. Here I had it slightly better than my guards, which was something special. They had to curl up on mats outside my door while I got a real bed. Usually, it would be the other way around. Me sleeping on the floor while they got cots.

"Up the stairs," the younger of the guards said through a yawn. "And you better sleep in again. I'm dead tired."

I didn't miss how bloodshot his eyes had looked when he picked me up at Dragon's, or how vacant his companion's were. The older man hadn't said a word since we left the bar. Whatever he was on must have been some strong shit.

I trudged up the stairs, not because these assholes wanted me to, but because now that I was in the house, I couldn't stop thinking about how soft that damn bed was. Honestly, I could have died in it and been happy.

The creak of hinges made me pause at the top of the staircase, and I held my breath when footsteps pounded down the hall in my direction.

"Jackson?" The booming voice was familiar, but in my tired state it took me a moment to figure out where I'd heard it. This morning when I was in the kitchen, this asshole and the dude who had sounded like he was talking out of his nose had discussed some serious shit.

The memories were enough to wake me up.

"No," I said, the word almost getting caught in my throat.

The man came into view, and the second I saw him I almost busted out laughing. His voice might have been deep, but he was small. Almost a foot shorter than me and probably not much taller than Meg. His shoulders were broad and he carried himself like he owned the world, but I knew without a doubt that I could take him down with one punch to the gut.

He stopped in front of me and the light from downstairs was just bright enough to illuminate his face. His son resembled him a lot, although younger and a hell of a lot bigger. They had the same good looks that would make most women spread their legs without a second thought, and an air of importance that probably made men follow them with no questions asked.

"You must be the fighter." He blinked while he searched for

my name. "Donaghy?"

I cleared my throat. "Yeah."

The Regulator stuck his hand out. "Good to meet you. My son told me about what happened in the bar. Horrible business. I have a mind to shut the whole entertainment district down, but you wouldn't believe what a resistance I've gotten to that idea. It's a damn shame."

I stared at his outstretched hand for a second too long and his eyes clouded over. Like his son, this man gave off a creepy vibe, only it wasn't as intense as Jackson's.

"Thanks," I said when I finally took his hand in mine. "I appreciate the room." My tone came out less enthusiastic than I wanted, but the Regulator didn't seem to care.

"Anytime." He dropped my hand and looked past me, past my guards and down the stairs. "I thought you were my son."

"Haven't seen him," I said even though he wasn't asking me where Jackson was.

The Regulator nodded twice, his eyes still looking past me. When he waved to the hall at his back, everything about him was dismissive. "I'm sure you're tired."

"Yeah," I said, moving past the small man with my fists clenched. "Thanks."

The Regulator didn't answer, but I didn't give a shit.

Staggered and shuffling footsteps followed me to my room, and before I'd even had a chance to open the door, both of my guards had plopped down on their mats. Briefly I considered giving the older one a kick in the gut as payback for this morning. He probably wouldn't even remember it in the morning. Instead, though, I turned toward my room.

I froze when the sound of the front door opening cut through the silence in the house. My own door was cracked, allowing me to hear it a second later, the Regulator's deep voice echoed up to me.

"Where the hell have you been?"

"Out," Jackson snapped at his father.

"Don't raise your voice to me," the Regulator said.

His son sighed. "I'm not trying to fight. It's late. I'm tired and I had a shitty night."

"Fine." Footsteps moved through the house, getting closer. "I met the convict you brought to my house. Honestly, Jackson, I know why you thought it was a good idea, but it wasn't. His guards are so wasted he could plow right over them, then slit our throats while we slept. You need to think things through a little better in the future."

"Shit. I forgot the asshole was here." The footsteps stopped. "Well, he can go back to Dragon's tomorrow. I'm starting to think this whole thing with Meg has been a waste of time."

"The girl isn't cooperating?" The Regulator's voice was as cold and hard as stone.

"I know you think we need her name, but I don't know if it's as important as you think it is. She isn't even related by blood, and I'm starting to think she isn't going to cooperate anyway." Jackson blew out a deep breath. "Tonight she made it pretty clear that she doesn't want me, and I think there may be someone else."

Something inside me tightened. Meg. They were talking about Meg again. What the hell did she have to do with anything, and what exactly did this prick have planned for her?

"We have to get her to see how much she *needs* you, that's all. It has to hit home just how bad her circumstances really are. And how much worse they can get."

"Exactly how are we going to do that?" Jackson asked. "Things are shitty enough. After the last couple weeks, I expected her to be begging me for help at this point, but she hasn't asked once."

A crack echoed through the house, like the Regulator had slapped his son on the back, and a second later the footsteps started up again. "You leave that to me. I know exactly what to do. She'll come around. There are very few people in this world who will hold onto their pride in the face of starvation and death."

"If you say so." Jackson's voice was doubtful, but not upset at the prospect of Meg facing whatever the Regulator was referring to.

The footsteps drew closer, so I backed into my room, shutting the door carefully behind me.

At first listen, the conversation sounded like a normal father son talk about unrequited feelings, but I knew better. Something was up. I wasn't sure what had happened between Meg and Jackson tonight, but I couldn't stop thinking about the conversation I'd overheard this morning. When I replayed it in my mind, the uneasiness in me grew. Something was off about that man, but he wouldn't hurt Meg. Right? What would be the point? Sure she was well connected, and he'd said something about needing her, but she couldn't be anyone that important. She was too young and obviously broke. She should have been nobody.

Still, I couldn't shake the feeling that something bad was about to happen. As long as I was here, I'd have to keep an eye on her.

# CHAPTER FOURTEEN

## Meg

THE sun was barely over the horizon and I was dragging my feet thanks to my late night. Even half asleep the memory of everything that had happened over the last two days flipped constantly through my mind.

Donaghy's blue eyes flashed through my mind, and my stupid heart did a little dance. The fighter was a nice distraction, which I more than needed at this point in my life, but that was all. The tattoos on his back, and the sweat that beaded on his muscled chest after a victory against the zombies, his—

"Holy shit, Meg, you need to get a grip," I whispered to myself as I pulled my work jumpsuit out of the locker.

The last thing I needed right now was the complication a schoolgirl crush would bring to my life.

"James!" My boss's voice echoed through the room.

I jumped and spun around to face him, my jumpsuit still in my hands and Donaghy still swimming through my mind.

Hanson scratched his round belly as his brown eyes moved over me, almost like he was trying to size me up. His thin hair was plastered to his sweaty scalp, moist and dark and so sparse he might as well shave it off.

The corner of his mouth turned down just before he said, "Get some leather on."

The jumpsuit turned to lead in my hands, becoming so heavy I had a hard time holding it up. "Leather?"

Hanson rolled his eyes like I was the dumbest person he'd ever spoken to. "You heard me. We got a weak spot and I need to send a crew out to fix it. You take the lead."

He walked away before I'd had a chance to respond. Not that I would've had anything to say to that. Me take the lead? I was the newest person on the maintenance crew and he'd never sent me outside the walls before, let alone had me *lead* anything. It seemed like he would want to put someone more experienced in charge.

I was like a robot as I put my jumpsuit back in the locker, and the automatic movements continued when I headed for the office. The turn of events had my mind spinning in circles. Before Dad disappeared I'd had a cushy job that didn't require much effort. It had paid just enough credits to give me a little extra spending money—being second in command behind Parvarti, Dad had made a good living. Even though I've known for the past couple years that I needed to get started on an apprenticeship, deciding what I wanted to do with my life hadn't been as easy as I'd thought it would be—there weren't a lot of options in a post-apocalyptic world—so I'd been dragging it out. Floating through life. I'd thought I had plenty of time to decide.

Then Dad disappeared and Mom stopped going to work, and I had to figure something else out. An apprenticeship at the CDC didn't seem like a possibility anymore, not with Joshua gone, and the idea of working with Al and Parvarti had hurt too much. Plus, starting out at the bottom of a career like that didn't pay as much as some of the dirtier jobs did. People who didn't have the desire or aptitude to continue their training chose one of the many menial careers the settlement had to offer: maintenance, undertaker, or runner. They were all dirty and dangerous at times, but the majority of their duties were mindless. Of all the menial jobs in the settlement, the maintenance crew paid the best. Mostly because it is the least desirable.

So that's what I did. Last week when I'd realized that I was reaching the end of the credits Dad had stashed away, and that

Mom wasn't going to come around anytime soon, I'd gone out and gotten a job on the maintenance crew. *Me.* Megan Hadley James, niece of the infamous Angus James, niece of the Judicial Officer, and best friend to the Regulator's son. It didn't seem real. The boss—that asshole Hanson—had looked at me like I was nuts when I'd told him who I was, but it was real nonetheless, and now I was about to be sent *out there.* Outside the wall that had kept me safe for the past twenty years. For all the times I'd imagined what it would be like to grow up in a world that had no walls, this was the last thing I thought I'd find myself doing.

Locating the leather wasn't tough. There was a shelf in the office lined with jackets and pants, and I dug through them until I found some that would work. They were big on me, even over my other clothes, but that was to be expected. I had a feeling it wasn't normal for them to send a twenty-year-old girl who was barely over five feet tall out to patch a hole. Especially one who had never set foot outside the walls before.

Why the hell had he picked me?

Once I was covered in leather, I headed out of the office. Already my skin was slick under the clothes and the sun was barely up. In the distance, an orange glow had begun to spread across the sky. Soon, it would light everything up, bringing with it a heat so intense that it would take my breath away and cover every inch of my body with sweat.

I found my boss by the truck. At his side stood four men dressed in leather, all of them towering over me. The expressions on the men's faces told me that they didn't understand what the hell was going on any more than I did.

The boss waved at me impatiently. "Let's go! You move that slow out there and you're going to be zombie chow." Something flashed in his eyes that made me slow instead of walk faster. Almost like me becoming zombie chow was *exactly* what he had in mind.

"Shit," the guy in front of him muttered as he turned and headed for the truck. "You put her in charge and we might as well kiss our asses goodbye."

I moved faster even though inside my chest, my heart was beating to a rhythm that reminded me of the background music to a horror movie Jackson and I had watched last month. Something wasn't right here.

"Why are you sending me out?" I asked when I stopped in front of Hanson.

He scratched his stomach while his eyes focused on a spot just above my head. "Always do. You're new, but you gotta get your feet wet sometime."

He had a bad poker face and he knew it. Funny thing was, he didn't seem to give a shit. I couldn't question him without getting canned, and we both knew I needed this job. Which put me in a *damned if I do, damned if I don't* kind of situation.

I wanted to argue, but my head told me to keep my mouth shut. This man wasn't interested in what I had to say.

When I turned away, I found the rest of my crew waiting at the truck. None of them looked very thrilled about what we were about to do.

"Who did you piss off?" the guy in the driver's seat asked when I slid in next to him.

He was probably close to thirty, which meant he had been around ten when the virus hit and most likely had memories of the world as it was before. Even though every now and then I found myself longing for the past, most of the time I was glad I didn't really know what I was missing.

"What do you mean?" I asked.

In the second row, the other two guys stared at me, the same question swimming in their eyes.

"You obviously pissed somebody off or you wouldn't be here." The driver lifted his eyebrows as he reached for the key already dangling from the ignition. He turned it, and when the engine roared to life, my stomach dropped. "My suggestion: figure out who it was and be sure you kiss their ass from now on unless you want to end up dead."

Ice coated my body inside and out. "What do you mean?" I repeated. I should have been able to come up with something—anything—else to say, but I couldn't. My brain wouldn't focus on anything long enough to form another sentence.

All three of my crewmembers looked at me like I was nuts.

"He means," the guy behind me said. His eyes were small and beady in his thin face, but they got even tinier when he narrowed them on me. "When they want to get rid of someone, there's only

"Megan James." My name came out as a whisper, but it was loud enough to make my heart beat faster.

"Shit." The blond guy in the back hadn't spoken this entire time, but when he swore, it drew my attention his way. He didn't say anything else, though. He just shook his head.

"Axl James was your father?" the driver asked.

"Yeah." I looked back and forth between the three men, but they all looked away. "What?"

"Nothing." The driver turned and shoved the door open. "We have work to do."

They were hiding something from me. Just like Al had been yesterday when I showed him that note. But what? What did these people, and my Uncle, know about my Dad that they weren't sharing?

I pushed the questions aside as I stepped out of the truck. Later. I'd ask later. Now, though, I needed to focus on what we were doing so my boss didn't get his wish: Me ending up a zombie snack.

"You can cover us while we work?" the driver called as he lowered the tailgate and started pulling supplies out.

"Yeah."

I put my back to them and tightened my grip on the gun. The wind blew, but it wasn't refreshing. It was thick and humid and hotter than a damn oven. Thankfully, though, it wasn't laced with the scent of death.

The three men got to work while I kept watch. I was so focused on my surroundings that I barely registered what was going on behind me until the sound of a blowtorch cut through the silence. I looked over my shoulder long enough to see the two guys who had been sitting in the back holding a sheet of metal against the wall while the driver used the blowtorch to secure it.

I was still watching them when the sound of another engine made me spin around. My gun was already up and only a couple seconds later, a truck came into view. I moved my finger to the trigger, but didn't fire. It was probably just another crew or a group of zombie hunters. Maybe even runners who were on their way to another settlement. Still, being prepared was the smart thing to do. It wasn't common for marauders from unsanctioned areas to attack Atlanta, but it also wasn't unheard of. They never got inside the city, but taking out a crew or two so they could snatch their supplies would be enough for them. Although, the runners were the ones who usually had to worry about stuff like that. That's what had happened to Colton.

The truck slowed to a stop in front of me, and the doors flew open. Two men who looked slightly familiar stepped out, but it wasn't until Donaghy got out of the truck behind them that I realized who they were. Dragon's cronies. The ones who cleaned the ring up at the end of the night. All three of the men were decked out in leather, just like my crew and I were.

I lowered my gun when thoughts of last couple nights in the bar slammed into me. The fighter was the last person I expected to see right now.

"Any dead around here?" The younger of the two men yelled. "Need to grab a few for tonight's fight."

Donaghy crossed his arms and leaned against the truck. He hadn't looked my way, so I wasn't sure if he even realized I was here. Or if he'd care. He looked bored. Bored and annoyed at being out here so early.

"Not yet," I called.

Donaghy's head jerked my way just as a moan broke through the silence. His eyes meet mine, sending a tingle of excitement shooting through me, and he shoved himself off the truck.

He looked around before taking a step closer to me. "What are you doing out here?"

"Maintenance." I nodded to the wall at my back where the rest of my crew was still working to patch the weak spot.

Donaghy's gaze flitted their way, but it was brief. When he was once again focused on me, his expression was intense. Searching. Like he had a million questions going through his head at once and he couldn't grasp hold of even one.

A strangled moan cut the hold he had on me in half, and I raised my gun as I turned in a circle, slowly. Scanning the area as I went. There was nothing at first, though. Not even when a second moan broke out, or when more followed and goose bumps popped up on every inch of my skin.

"Incoming!" I called, still scanning the area.

My eyes were straight ahead as I blocked out every thought that didn't have to do with survival, pretending I was back on the

134

practice range. How many times had Mom or Dad taken me there when I was growing up? Too many to count, that was for sure. The shooting range was the only place inside the walls where normal citizens could legally get their hands on a gun. Mom and Dad had made sure I was prepared in case the unthinkable happened. As soon as I was able to lift a gun, they had me there. Learning to defend myself against the dead. Getting in target practice with every weapon they could get their hands on. I'd never set foot outside the walls until now, but that didn't mean I didn't know what I was doing.

"We're almost done!" one of my guys called from behind me.

I didn't bother looking to see which one.

"You got this?" Donaghy's voice was as serious as a heart attack.

"Survivors raised me and they made sure I was one too."

Thank God.

The first wave rounded the corner only a few seconds later. Six zombies, all so rotten and old that it looked like they were struggling just to lift their feet. There would be more, though, and we all knew it. These things ran in packs now—or shambled in packs, anyway. It was the only way they'd been able to survive this long. If we only came across one or two at a time, we'd be able to take them out without a problem. But twenty? Fifty? A hundred? Numbers like that were a lot harder to control.

I took aim, exhaling to ease the tension in my shoulders. When I squeezed the trigger, a gunshot echoed through the silence like a crack of thunder. A split second later, the zombie closest to us went down.

"Nice!" Donaghy called.

"Stop shooting." One of the men with Donaghy muttered as he grabbed a pole out of the back of the truck. A loop of rope hung from the end of it. "Son of a bitch. Dragon's going to kick our asses if we don't bring a few back."

"Fine." I glanced toward my crew. The guy with the blowtorch—I needed to learn their names—was almost done welding the metal sheet to the wall. "I'll cover you!" I called as Donaghy's guards jogged toward the advancing zombies.

The fighter looked like he wasn't sure what to do as he glanced back and forth between the zombies and me. We'd only known each other for two days—and I wasn't even sure I could say we *knew* each other—but I'd never once seen him look uncertain. Even going into the ring with the dead he looked almost bored.

"I'll be fine." I nodded once and tightened my grip on the gun.

Donaghy shook his head but jogged toward the advancing dead with the other two men anyway.

I stood ready, aiming at the nearest zombie as the three men approached it. The thing gnashed his teeth, but he was moving so slowly that it only took the driver thirty seconds to slip the loop over the creature's head. Once he was secure, they dragged him toward the truck. Donaghy didn't follow and his eyes were still on the dead headed his way.

When he stepped forward, I squeezed the gun so hard that my fingers ached. The urge to shoot nearly crushed me.

Donaghy ducked behind one of the dead and wrapped his arms around the thing's torso, pinning his decaying limbs to his sides. The zombie growled and snarled and twisted his head, trying to get at Donaghy, but he couldn't. Once the fighter was sure he had him, he dragged the dead man toward the truck.

"Shit boy," the older of the two men said. "We got a pole for that."

"I can handle it." The leather covering Donaghy's body bulged as his muscles flexed under the zombie's struggles. "And the sooner we have these bastards, the sooner we can get out of here."

The two men shook their heads, but helped Donaghy drag the zombie to the truck where he was chained in the back next to the first one. The creatures fought and struggled, and the chains holding them down clanged against the truck bed, but they didn't make any progress.

"Dragon wants at least two more," the older man called.

Together the three men jogged back. Just as they'd reached the remaining three zombies, another group rounded the corner. This one was at least four times bigger.

"More!" I called.

This time, I didn't hold back. I squeezed the trigger and the gunshot rang in my ears as a zombie dropped to the ground. Donaghy and his guards managed to wrangle two more of the dead and were just dragging them back toward the truck when another wave rounded the corner, bringing at least twenty more zombies into view.

Shit. If we didn't get out of here now, we were going to be in real trouble.

"You almost done?" I called before firing again.

My gaze moved to where Donaghy and the other two men were working to get the last of the four zombies into the truck bed. This one seemed to be newer—and a lot faster. Donaghy's face was bright red as he worked to keep the thing in his grasp.

"Almost!" one of my crew yelled from behind me. I didn't bother looking back to see who.

I fired again and again, barely pausing between shots. When my gun clicked, I released the empty magazine, then slammed a new one in place before firing again.

The zombies in front of me fell, but I knew I didn't have enough bullets to take them all out. I backed away, keeping the dead in my sights as I headed for my truck.

I'd only taken two steps when a scuffle to my right drew my attention, and I looked over to find the younger of the two men struggling to control the zombie. The other man stood off to the side like he wasn't sure what to do, but Donaghy pulled himself into the back of the truck. The younger man backed up, trying to dodge the zombie's jaws, but all he managed to do was back right into one of the dead men chained up inside the truck bed.

The zombie's hand wrapped around his leg and the man tried to jerk free. He fell to the floor, twisting his body to the left while the zombie attempted to pull him closer. His pant leg slid up, exposing the skin at his ankle, and the zombie saw his chance. It leaned forward, mouth wide open, and a second later the creature's decaying teeth sank into flesh. The scream that ripped its way out of the man echoed through my head.

"Son of a bitch!" Donaghy said as he grabbed the zombie that wasn't chained up and slammed it against the ground.

Metal clinked and a few seconds later the fighter was back on his feet. He grabbed the newly infected man, who was huddled on the floor of the truck bed trying to stop the blood from seeping out of the bite, and dragged him from the truck.

All this happened so fast that I barely had time to take it in between shots, and with each second that passed, the horde got

137

closer to us.

Donaghy shoved the injured man into the cab of their truck, then turned my way, his eyes moving from me to the crew at my back. "Go!" The fighter slammed his hand on the hood of the truck before running over to join me.

The men who had most likely been charged with keeping an eye on the convict didn't even hesitate. The truck's tires squealed against the pavement, and a second later it was speeding off, leaving the rest of us behind in a trail of dust.

I only got off one more shot before it hit me that Donaghy had no way to defend himself against the approaching dead. "You aren't even armed!"

"Never needed a weapon before." He didn't take his eyes off the advancing dead.

I shook my head and squeezed off one more shot, then pulled a knife out of the sheath at my waist.

Donaghy's eyes grew to twice their size when I held it out to him. "You could get in big trouble for arming a convict."

"I have connections, remember?"

He frowned, but took the knife from me anyway. "I wouldn't count on Jackson's help if I were you."

Jackson?

My gaze went from the zombies in front of me to the convict at my side, then over my shoulder to my crew. It looked like they were just finishing up, which meant we'd be able to get out of here soon.

I squeezed the trigger, letting off one final shot before backing toward the truck. "What does Jackson have to do with anything?"

"I don't know if he does, I just know he was pretty pissed off when he got home last night." Donaghy stayed at my side, his back stiff and the knife in his hand. "What the hell happened between you two?"

The zombies were getting closer. The wave that had rounded the corner last must have had quite a few fresh ones in it, and they had passed up the slower ones in their need to rip into my flesh. I glanced over my shoulder again and found my crew jogging toward the truck, but it was impossible to feel any relief at the situation we now found ourselves in.

"Get in the truck!" the man who had driven us out here called.

"Get it started!"

Was he joking? I'd never driven in my life.

"Shit," I muttered and fired again.

Less than six feet of space separated us from the horde now.

"What are you waiting for?" one of my men screamed from behind me.

I glanced toward Donaghy. "Can you drive?"

The fighter shook his head, but grabbed my arm and pulled me toward the truck anyway. "No, but I'm willing to give it a shot."

He ripped the door open and shoved me in, then climbed in after me. By the time he had the door shut, the dead had gained another foot. They were now so close that I could actually see the maggots crawling through their rotting flesh.

The keys hung from the ignition, and the second Donaghy turned them, the engine roared to life. The passenger door was yanked open and the cab was filled with shouting as the men in my crew yelled at each other to get in. Next to Donaghy, a zombie slammed into the side of the truck and a scream ripped its way out of me. My crewmembers climbed in, two of them throwing their bodies over the seat to get in the back row, while the third yelled at them to hurry. He climbed in next to me, and the second he was safely inside, slammed the door shut.

The horde had converged on the truck. They were all around us, banging on the sides and the windows. One crawled onto the hood and another somehow managed to get himself into the bed of the truck.

"Go!" one of the men behind me yelled, his voice echoing through the cab.

Donaghy threw the truck into gear and we lurched forward so fast that my whole body slammed into the back of the seat before being thrown forward. The fighter's hands gripped the steering wheel as we plowed through the dead, the tires bouncing over bodies while black and brown blood splashed across the windows. Donaghy pressed his foot down harder on the gas, and before I knew it, the dead were behind us.

"Holy shit," I breathed out.

My heart was pounding so hard that it almost drowned out the sound of the crewmembers behind me as they shuffled and swore.

"We have a stowaway," one said.

Something slammed against the window at my back, and I spun around. The zombie who had climbed into the bed of the truck had his face smashed up against the little window. His milky eyes peered at us through the glass as his mouth opened and closed like he was imaging what it would feel like to sink his teeth into us.

"Slow down," the guy with the beady little eyes said as he twisted in his seat.

Donaghy eased up on the gas and the truck lurched awkwardly, throwing everyone forward.

"Shit." Beady eyes narrowed on the back of the fighter's head. "Keep it steady."

"Sorry." Donaghy's hands tightened on the wheel. "It's my first time."

"Why didn't you drive?" the guy at my side asked.

"Because I don't know how." I turned to face him even though heat had crept up my neck to my cheeks. "Until today, I've never set foot outside the walls of the city."

All three crewmembers cursed at the same time, throwing out a rainbow of profanity that filled the small cab. Donaghy tilted his head and his neck cracked as his hands tightened even more on the steering wheel. I kept my head up even though I felt slightly ashamed for putting my crewmembers in danger. It hadn't been my choice, though. Hanson, or whoever it was that had it in for me, had made the decision to send me outside the city with no experience and little training.

"Gotta take care of this guy," the crewmember with the shifty eyes said from behind me.

I twisted in my seat as he eased the little window open, giving himself just enough room to stick the barrel of the gun through the hole. The zombie's fingers worked their way in, reaching for us. The thing opened his mouth and my crewmember took the opportunity to shove the barrel between the creature's decaying teeth. When he pulled the trigger, the zombie's head exploded, sending down a waterfall of dark brown blood, brain matter, and bone.

"He was a fresh one," my crewmember said, pulling his gun

back inside and shutting the window. "The virus must have just turned him."

He was right. The thing's blood still had a brownish tint to it, which meant he hadn't been dead long. Maybe only a matter of hours.

Back before the virus mutated, people died and then turned, and by the time they came back, their blood was thick and black. Now, though, the virus turned them slowly, making them monsters before they had even died. It was torturous watching the change, but at least it gave us a better shot at saving people who got infected. If we could get them the right vaccine before the virus got too far, that is. Problem was, the virus had mutated so many times now that we didn't always know what strain we were dealing with. The vaccines they'd made from my uncle's blood weren't always good, and Angus was dead now. There was no chance for them to create a new vaccine when they didn't have the blood of someone immune to work with...

Unless that note was telling the truth and Dad *was* immune. Then it might make sense that they had him.

I turned to face the men in my crew, looking them over slowly before asking, "How did you know my dad?"

The guy at my side looked away. "Everyone knows your family."

"That's not what I mean and you know it. When I told you who my dad was, you acted nervous. What do you know that you aren't telling me?"

"Nothing," the guy behind me snapped. "We heard he died. We felt bad." His beady eyes were narrowed on my face when I turned to face him. "That's it. Don't go looking for trouble unless you want it to find you."

I looked the three crewmembers over, but none of them would meet my gaze. There was definitely something going on that I didn't know about, but these guys didn't know me well enough to share it. I needed to get them on my side if I wanted them to trust me.

"Have you guys met Donaghy?" I asked, jerking my head toward the fighter who was driving us—a little slower than necessary—back toward the gate. "He's fighting at Dragon's Lair tonight and I'm serving drinks. You should stop by."

Donaghy's head turned my way long enough for him to give me a puzzled look, but I ignored it.

"You're serving drinks at Dragon's?" the crewmember at my side said doubtfully.

"Yeah."

Despite the tension still lingering in the car, the man with the beady eyes grinned. "Gotta see that."

"Good," I said, faking excitement. "I'll see you tonight then?"

When they nodded I felt like letting out a sigh of relief. I'd get answers from them tonight. After a few drinks, people were always more willing to share their secrets.

# CHAPTER FIFTEEN

## Donaghy

**MEG'S** been on my mind ever since I drove back through the gate this morning. She wasn't really out of her element out there—she'd handled herself a lot better than I had expected her to—but she wasn't totally prepared either. I couldn't for the life of me figure out why the hell someone sent her outside the walls in the first place. The other people on her crew were all men, and it was obvious just by looking at them that they'd been outside more than their fair shares. But Meg was clueless.

Then there was the conversation on the way back in. Meg asked the crewmembers questions about her dad, and she was right to act suspicious—they were clearly hiding something. Plus, they said that everyone knew her family, which pretty much confirmed my suspicions: Meg had connections. I didn't know exactly what was going on, but it was obvious something big happened to Meg recently or she wouldn't be working here—or on the shitty maintenance crew. I'd be willing to bet my right nut it had something to do with her dad and how she kept talking about him in past tense.

I was in the ring doing pushups when the sound of the front door shutting echoed through Dragon's Lair. I pushed myself up the rest of the way and paused, watching from the darkened ring as Meg walked across the room wearing the same black dress she'd had on last night. Her heels clicked against the cement floor, but even from all the way across the room I could see how shaky her legs were.

When she was no longer in my range of vision, I went back to my pushups. Gritting my teeth and trying to focus on what I was doing. Not on what happened this morning. I had to get this girl out of my head. I couldn't get involved in her mess. I had my own troubles. My own life. She could handle herself.

It was impossible, though. No matter what I did, thoughts of Meg refused to stay away, and after only ten more pushups, I gave up.

I flopped down on my stomach, ignoring the black and brown stains on the floor while I caught my breath. My heart pumped a spastic rhythm that had barely eased by the time I got to my feet.

Meg was behind the bar when I stepped out of the ring. She lifted a glass of moonshine to take a drink, but her hand was shaking so hard that the liquid sloshed out.

"Shit," she muttered, but the mess didn't stop her from taking a drink.

"Bad day?"

"Holy mother—" She practically slammed the glass on the counter before turning narrowed eyes on me. "Don't sneak up on me like that."

"Sorry." I slid onto the stool in front of her. "You okay?"

"Fine." She pressed her lips together before grabbing a grungy looking rag off the bar and wiping up the mess she'd made. "And you know what kind of day it was. You were there."

"True." I drummed my fingers against the counter, trying to think of something to say. She was jumpy, but I didn't think it had a lot to do with the zombies. Even though she shouldn't have been out there, Meg had taken the dead out pretty easily. No. There was more going on with her.

She poured me some ale without even being asked. When she slid it across the bar, I wrapped my fingers around the cloudy glass before she'd had a chance to let go. Our fingers touched and she looked away when her cheeks turned a bright shade of pink. "Thanks."

Meg nodded, but a second later closed her eyes and took a deep breath before blowing it out. When she opened them again, she was looking over my head.

Even in the skimpy dress she looked out of place in this bar. The walls were so cracked that I wouldn't be surprised if the whole place collapsed, and there was a layer of dirt covering everything that was probably at least twenty years old. I bet if we wiped the walls down, we'd find splatters of blood that dated back to the early days of the zombie outbreak.

Why the hell was this girl here?

"Why are you here?"

The question I'd been dying to ask slipped out before I could stop myself, but I didn't give a shit. I had to know. It had been a long time since I'd allowed myself to get involved in anyone's business other than my own, but the moment I'd saved this girl, I was involved, and there was no going back now.

She didn't look my way. "You already asked me that."

"But you never answered."

Meg exhaled and slumped against the bar. It pushed her breasts together until they threatened to spill out of the dress and I had to fight to keep my eyes on her face. It wasn't as hard as it should have been, though, not when I saw the tortured expression in her eyes.

"My life has turned into a shit storm," she said, the words coming out like a sigh, "and this was the only way not to get soaked."

My lips twitched with something that could almost be a smile, but I wasn't sure. Smiles had been few and far between for me—I actually hadn't been sure if I *could* smile anymore until I got here. Then the image of what a *shit storm* would actually look like popped into my head, and it was so graphic and repulsive that I found myself chuckling. *Me.* Laughing. Who the hell was this girl?

"I seriously doubt it's as bad as you think it is." The half-grin on my face felt foreign and awkward, but a part of me liked it. Like how it felt to know that I still had feelings other than rage and hate and bitterness buried deep inside me.

Meg stood and crossed her arms, her green eyes crackling

when she focused them on me. "Why's that exactly?"

"Don't get all pissy." I was still grinning when I took a sip, and my gaze was still on her. Her eyes were blazing like she was seriously considering punching me in the throat. I almost laughed again. "I'm just pointing out that anyone who is *friends* with the Regulator's son and has an uncle high up in the ranks of enforcers — in New Atlanta — isn't doing too bad."

"My aunt is also the Judicial Officer," she fired at me.

Shit. This girl was even better connected than I thought. "You're shitting me."

"No." Her arms dropped to her sides. "But none of that helps find my dad, or brings my mom back from the edge of the cliff she's about to jump off of."

My smile faded and I hated that it was gone. "There are no cliffs around here, so I'm assuming you're talking metaphorically."

"You assume right."

The conversation from earlier popped into my head, and once again I found it impossible to keep the questions inside. "What happened to your dad?"

"I don't know." She exhaled and her body slumped forward once again until her arms were resting on the bar. "He disappeared about three weeks ago. Left one morning and never came back. They told us he went out on a run and got cut off from the group, but they never found him. Never found any signs that he'd been killed or injured or even taken by another group. He just vanished. But you know how it is. These days, if they don't find you in twenty-four hours, you're presumed dead. And with good reason."

Damn. I'd kind of thought her problems were all in her head. The drama of a girl barely out of her teens who didn't know what it meant to have real issues. Not the kind of problems that threatened to kill you when you weren't looking — or worse.

"I'm sorry."

"It's not your fault."

"Are you going to tell me it's no one's fault? Just the way the world is now?"

The bitterness in my voice surprised even me. I was sick and tired of the assholes who ran this country using the zombies as an excuse to fuck everyone over. Apocalypse or not, people still had the ability to choose to be decent human beings.

"No." She lifted her gaze to hold mine. "In fact, I'm starting to think my mom's insane ranting isn't as crazy as I thought it was."

"You're going to have to elaborate on that for me."

Meg looked around like she was afraid someone was listening as she leaned closer. "Ever since Dad disappeared, my mom's been raving like a lunatic. Talking about how they took him. Just like they took my uncle." She blinked. "I guess I need to go back further than that."

"Further than what?" She'd lost me. Maybe her mom wasn't the only one slightly unhinged.

"My uncle was Angus James."

She said the name like it was some major revelation, but it still took a moment for it to sink in, and even then I thought I had to be wrong. "Angus James?"

"Yeah, Angus James. He was the first immune person to arrive in Atlanta and the CDC used his blood to help create the original vaccine, as well as the two others they needed when the virus mutated."

Damn. This girl was like apocalyptic royalty. Literally. At this exact moment there were probably hundreds of people saying a prayer to the great Angus James, hoping he would save them from starvation or sickness or the zombies. Hell, probably even the government. And Meg was *here*. Working in this shit hole excuse for a bar while begging for leftovers from the scum of the city.

"You can't be serious." For the first time since they arrested me in Dayton, I found it impossible to maintain even a little bit of my air of indifference.

"I am. Even though my parents saw my uncle's body for themselves, there were always rumors that Angus was actually alive. That the CDC was keeping him in a chemically induced coma so they could use him however they wanted. It was far-fetched, and there was nothing to support it, but the rumors didn't stop until—" Megan's voice broke and she looked away. "I was eight when he finally died."

There was more to the story, but I didn't push her. Whatever it was that she was holding back, it made her face contort until she looked like she was about to break into a million pieces.

"What does any of this have to do with your dad's

disappearance?" I asked instead.

She sucked in a deep breath, then blew it out like she was trying to steady herself. When she spoke again, her voice was thick with tears, but her eyes were dry. "A few people speculated that Dad was immune too, so when he disappeared it seemed to set something off in my mom's brain. She lost it. Started having delusions that the CDC had taken him. That they were using him to create a new vaccine. The virus is genetically engineered to mutate every few years. Did you know that?"

"No." But how did she know that?

"My uncle Joshua worked at the CDC," she said, almost like she was reading my mind. "He was a doctor."

"So you know someone in every important position?"

"Not anymore. Joshua is dead, which has only pushed my mom's delusions farther. She thinks he discovered something about my dad and that the authorities killed him to keep him quiet."

I drummed my fingers on the counter, studying her face for a second while I decided what to say. There was a lot that could be said to all this. It sounded far-fetched, but it didn't. Honestly, I wouldn't put much past the people in charge. Would they keep someone hostage for years so they could use him like a lab rat? Probably. Does that mean they did?

The question I settled on was: "What do you think?"

"I don't know. At first I was thought Mom was losing her mind, but then someone gave me this crazy note and now..."

Her eyes darted around when her voice trailed off, but the place was nearly empty. There were a few guys sitting at the other end of the bar, their hazy eyes focused on Helen as she babied them. I'd noticed that was her thing — trying to mend the wounded men who wandered into this building. Glitter and Dragon hadn't made an appearance yet, my guards had cut out the second they dropped me off, and the bouncers were back on the cots, sleeping.

I gave Meg a second to calm down before reaching across the counter to take her hand, pulling her attention back to me. "What did the note say?"

Meg looked at her hand in mine, then lifted her head her gaze was holding mine. "That my dad is alive, and that he's immune."

My first thought was that she might be as crazy as her mom,

but then the conversation I overheard in the Regulator's house came back to me, and doubt crept in. They couldn't have been talking about Meg's dad, right? It was hard to remember all the details, but they'd said something about a man who was immune. And something about taking him out of a coma...

Meg's eyes narrowed as the silence stretched out between us. "What?"

"I overheard something strange yesterday."

I gave her the details I could remember, and the more I said, the bigger her eyes got. Even though some of it still didn't make sense—the conversation about the flu, for example—I had to admit that the rest was pretty incriminating in the light of Meg's story. Even worse, I couldn't help wondering if she found herself outside the wall today because of what Jackson's father had said last night. Although, that part of the story I kept to myself. No point in freaking her out even more.

"It can't be," she said when I'd finished. "If my dad was immune, someone would have told him. Right?"

I didn't know about that. "I think the people in charge will do whatever it takes to reach their end goal. The problem is, I'm not really sure what that goal is. Before I overheard that conversation, I would have said eradicating the zombies. Now, though, I'm not so sure. Let's face it, they've been telling us for twenty years that they were trying to reestablish a democracy, but we haven't had a real election yet. Every time we get close something happens to distract people."

Like a new flu outbreak...

Shit. I couldn't believe I hadn't made the connection before now. The Regulator and his crony talking about taking out the scum of this settlement and bringing up another flu outbreak as if it was the answer to all their problems. Like population control or something.

"And they would have taken him earlier," Meg mumbled, shaking her head and staring at the bar counter like she hadn't heard a word I just said. "No. That can't be right. Angus died nearly twelve years—" Her mouth moved, but no words came out for a few seconds. When they finally did, they were softer. "Right after Margot disappeared."

"Who's Margot?"

"My sister."

I sat up straighter. Usually, I wasn't one for conspiracy theories, but it seemed a bit odd that both her sister and her father would disappear. "Your sister disappeared just like your dad did?"

"No." She still wasn't looking at me. "She was killed during a breach."

So much for that theory.

"We never found her body, though. Just her book bag. It was torn and bloody. We all just assumed..."

Of course. Why wouldn't they?

Meg's head snapped up. "But what if? What if it was staged? What if she inherited the immunity and they took her to create a new vaccine?" Her eyes grew to twice their size as they darted around the bar. She looked like she thought someone may be eavesdropping, but that didn't stop her from spewing out the ridiculous theory. "We never did figure out how the zombies breached the wall. They just showed up and started killing people. Mom was walking us home from school and people came running down the street, screaming. It was like a wave washing us away from her. Margot and I were together at first—I was holding her hand—and it felt like someone ripped her away from me. There were so many people around that I couldn't figure out what happened, so I kept running. Moving with the crowd. The stink of rot was everywhere..." Her lips moved just a little after the words had trailed off, and even though no sound came out, I was pretty sure she whispered her sister's name.

I felt for the girl, I did, but this story had gotten so crazy and far-fetched that it didn't make a bit of sense anymore. If her father was immune, why not just tell him? Ask him to cooperate? We all knew the story of Angus James, and we knew that he died trying to get here to save the world—which was the main teaching of The Church. I was sure Meg's dad would have done the same thing.

"Look," I said, pausing to take a gulp of ale while I chose my words. "I'm the last person who would ever stick up for this shit show of a government—I don't trust half the things they do—but even I know that theory is nuts."

Megan's eyes flashed like she was once again considering punching me. "Are you calling me nuts?"

"No. I'm saying that you've lost a lot and you're struggling to make sense of it. Only it can't make sense, and what you're suggesting is just a touch past crazy." More than a touch, only I wasn't about to tell her that.

"You said yourself that you heard the Regulator talking about someone who was immune."

"I don't know it was the Regulator, I'm just guessing. It sounded like the prick, but nothing is certain in this world. Hell, for all I know it could have been that guy talking." I jerked my thumb toward the end of the bar where a guy who couldn't weigh more than ninety pounds was slouched over a glass of moonshine. His eyes were so bloodshot and sunken that it didn't take a genius to know he was trying to kill himself with booze. "Whatever I heard may or may not have had to do with your dad, but my guess is it didn't. Your uncle isn't the only person they've found who was immune."

"No." Megan gnawed on her bottom lip. "That's true. There have been others."

I found myself hoping that I was getting through to her. She seemed like a nice girl, and I hated to see her lose her shit and start throwing around rumors that wouldn't accomplish anything other than get her killed or shipped off to DC.

"I'll keep my ears open," I said, softening my voice. "Just promise me you won't repeat this story to anyone else."

Meg's eyes glistened with tears. "You will?"

"Sure." It wasn't going to hurt for me to pay attention, and hopefully when I didn't hear anything else, she'd come back to reality.

The smile she gave was more than enough incentive to help her out. Since the moment she stuck up for me, I'd been drawn to her, and the more I got to know her, the stronger that attraction had become. It was stupid and I knew it. In a few days I'd be gone, dragged off to Key West to fight again, then some other place. It wouldn't stop until I was dead and I knew it. Even if I found myself hoping against hope that I'd make it back to Patty one day, deep down I didn't really think I would. I'd have a better chance of sprouting wings and flying away.

Meg was still smiling at me when Dragon called my name.

I turned, frowning when I found my guards standing in the

doorway. They typically didn't show up until after the fights, and they didn't look the least bit happy to be here now.

Dragon waved and I headed over almost reluctantly. Something told me I was about to get some shitty news.

"What's going on?" I asked when I stopped in front of the three men.

My guards looked ready to rip my head off, and even though I knew I didn't do anything, their anger was aimed at me.

"Regulator told us to take a hike when we went back to his place," the older guard said. "Guess we ain't welcome under his roof no more."

Shit.

Until now, I'd assumed that Jackson was talking out of his ass last night. The guy had so obviously been trying to snag Meg that I figured it would take a lot more than a little argument to make him back off. Guess I was wrong. Whatever she had done or said last night, it must have really pissed Jackson off. At least I didn't have to worry about whatever messed-up plan he had cooked up for her anymore.

"Bound to happen," I said, glancing back at Meg.

I sure as hell was going to miss that bed, but more than that, I was sorry I couldn't keep my promise to keep my ears open. I'd have to let Meg know that it wasn't going to work out. Later, though, after the fight.

"We have the cots in the back," Dragon said, already turning away. "It'll be fine."

He left, but my guards didn't. Apparently they thought if they glared at me long enough, it would kill me. Wrong, assholes. I was tougher than that.

"Dragon's right," I said as I turned my back on them. "It will be fine."

# CHAPTER SIXTEEN

## Meg

**EVEN** after Donaghy headed into the back room and the bar started to fill up, I couldn't stop thinking about everything I'd just heard. To me it seemed like proof that Mom wasn't losing her mind, and that the note that crazy old man had given me had at least a little bit of truth in it.

People crowded into the bar and the air grew thicker while Glitter, Helen, and I served drinks. I could hardly focus on what I was doing. The other waitresses seemed to notice that my mind wasn't exactly on the job, because they each sent questioning — and somewhat concerned — looks my way. Even if I could have explained over the crowd of people begging to get wasted, I wouldn't want to. Donaghy was right. I couldn't go around repeating this story to anyone unless I wanted to end up dead or shipped off to DC.

My crew popped up in front of me only a few minutes before the fight was scheduled to start, and just seeing them had my brain buzzing more than ever. I couldn't forget the way they'd acted when I mentioned my dad, or how they wouldn't meet my gaze when I asked them questions. They knew something, and I was going to get it out of them.

"Hey guys!" I called, ignoring how the younger of the three — the one with the beady eyes — gaped at my cleavage. I still hadn't gotten their names, but it was something I planned on fixing. Tonight after the fight if I could manage it. "Drinks?" I smiled and batted my eyes, which earned me another look from Glitter.

"Moonshine." The guy ogling my tits managed to look me in the eye long enough to order.

"You got it."

I poured three glasses and slid them across the bar top, slyly waving away the credits they tried to hand me. Out of the corner of my eye, I saw Glitter shoot me a look, but I didn't turn long enough to be able to figure out what she was thinking. I wasn't sure if Dragon would fire me for giving out free drinks, but I did know that I needed these guys at least a little loosened up.

"Thanks." The oldest of the three guys winked as he took his glass.

He was the best looking of the three, even if he was about ten years older than me. Not that things like that mattered much anymore. The apocalypse made for strange bedfellows.

"See you after the fight?" I replied, smiling.

The guys nodded just as Dragon's voice bellowed over the crowd. The blond guy gave me a little wave before heading off after the other two, and I watched as they pushed their way through the crowd in hopes of getting a better view of Donaghy and the zombies.

All around us, the crowd moved toward the ring just like my crewmembers had. Glitter came up beside me but I didn't look her way. I wasn't sure if she was going to rat me out to Dragon — they seemed to be close, so anything was possible — or what I'd do about it if she did. I needed this job, but the idea of getting on Dragon's good side made me cringe.

"You going to tell me what's going on?" Glitter asked when I didn't turn her way.

On the other side of the room, the zombies were being carted toward the ring, and I kept my eyes on them as I shrugged. "Just need some information. Thought I'd grease the wheel."

Glitter grabbed my arm and forced me to turn. "You have to be careful about handing out free drinks. Not because of Dragon, but because these guys will kill each other over shit like that." I shot her a doubtful look, but she nodded. "I'm serious. The wrong guy sees you giving out a freebie after he's used his hard-earned credits, and the next thing you know it's a bloodbath in here."

Shit. She had a point. On the streets, I'd seen fights break out over much smaller things, and that was when alcohol wasn't involved.

"I hadn't thought about that."

"I know, that's why I'm telling you." Glitter's gray eyes moved over me and her lips pulled into a purse. "What else is going on?"

"I just have a lot of crazy family stuff going on, that's all."

She shoved her pink hair off her forehead and looked away, and I suddenly felt like a piece of shit. This girl had no one but Dragon and Helen in her life. Compared to her, I'd had it easy.

When she turned her head, the lights shining down from above hit her just right, casting shadows across her face that highlighted the dark circles under her eyes. I hadn't noticed them before, probably because she'd tried to cover them with makeup. She'd done a good job too, but standing right under the light like this made it impossible to hide them.

"You feeling okay?" I asked, wondering if anyone had ever looked out for this girl before. She claimed Dragon had saved her life, talked about him like he was a father figure, but I had a hard time picturing him as the paternal type. Helen, maybe.

"I'm exhausted. I have dreams. Strange dreams that are fuzzy, but terrifying at the same time. In them I'm always getting poked and prodded, and I'm tied to a bed. When they get really bad, I have a hard time sleeping." She looked my way, and when her eyes met mine, they were big and round. "I'm sure they're just leftover hallucinations from my druggie years."

I shivered at the thought of having nightmares like that. "What do you remember about your life before Dragon found you?"

"Not a whole lot." Glitter's gaze moved to the ground like she didn't want to look me in the eye.

I stared at the scars on her arms, trying to imagine a life where a person had become so dependent on drugs that their past had been totally washed away. It seemed crazy, but these days there was a lot of that.

"How old were you?" I whispered, my eyes still on the scars.

Glitter covered them with her hands and I looked up to find her gray eyes swimming with tears. Helen stood behind her, listening to us as she smoked. There was a frown on her face, but something else flashed in her eyes. Anger. No, more like rage.

"As far as Dragon could tell, I was ten."

Ten? It seemed crazy to think that this girl barely remembered the first ten years of her life. Like she had just dropped out of the sky or something. Even crazier: I couldn't believe she was still standing here if that was how the first decade of her life had gone. Addicts didn't usually make it more than a few years. There were just too many illnesses and bad drugs out there.

"How long have you been with Dragon?"

Glitter gave me a sad smile. "I'm legal."

"That wasn't what I asked," I said defensively.

"Eight years." Helen finally came over to stand next to Glitter, putting her wrinkled hand on the girl's shoulder.

"Dragon let me start tending bar two years ago even though I wasn't quite legal. It gave me something to do." Glitter's smile morphed from something sad to something a little more genuine. "Before that I spent my days learning to read and write, catching up on all the things I'd missed out on."

"Her parents were probably junkies too," Helen said. "They probably started her out on drugs at young age so they could sell her on the streets."

I shivered, but Glitter didn't bat an eye. Helen's hand had tightened on the girl's shoulder, and she leaned into it like it was a lifeline.

"It happens," the older woman said, as if I needed an education in how rough this world was.

"I know. Doesn't mean I have to like it." I reached out and touched Glitter's arm. "I'm sorry that happened to you."

The girl's gray eyes shimmered with unshed tears, but she swiped them away. "Me too. If Dragon hadn't found me, I don't know what would have happened."

"He's been like a father to you," I said, a sudden appreciation for Dragon coming over me. He may be an odd man, but he obviously had a good side to him.

"No." Glitter stood up straighter. "Not a father. Just a guardian."

Helen gave her shoulder another squeeze, and they shared a look that I didn't get.

The older woman turned her gaze on me, and here eyes were like laser beams, burning into mine. I got the feeling she was trying to tell me something without saying it out loud. What, I didn't know. About Dragon? Maybe.

"Is Glitter your real name?" I asked, knowing it wasn't, but hoping to ease the pain surrounding us.

"No." Glitter laughed and her body relaxed. "I picked it out, and even though Dragon tried to talk me out of it, he let it go. Sometimes when memories come back to me, they're shiny. Sparkly almost. The first few months with Dragon that was pretty much all I could focus on, so it seemed like an obvious name for me. I'm glad I picked it, though. It makes me feel like there's a glimmer of hope."

The crowd roared, and I turned away from the girl in front of me to find that not only had the fight already started, but had come to an end. In the ring, Donaghy was splattered with black blood, his shoulders heaving with pent up rage and energy. He had his hands clenched at his sides as he stared down at the bodies, but a second later he looked up, and when his gaze met mine, his muscles slowly began to relax. Even from this far away, the air between us crackled with energy.

"He likes you," Helen said.

"But so does the Regulator's son," Glitter whispered, her tone oddly foreboding.

I turned to face them. "Donaghy and I just met. We hardly know each other."

"That doesn't mean anything," Helen said knowingly. "When you meet the right person, you just know."

Glitter was frowning toward the ring. "The first time I met you, I thought you were with the Regulator's son."

"No. It's never been like that with us."

"I flirted with him." Glitter turned to look at me. "I thought you were together, so I flirted with him. I wanted you to catch him so you'd know what he was like."

"Who?" I shook my head. "Jackson?"

Helen grabbed Glitter's arm and gave a tiny shake of her head when the younger girl looked at her.

"What's going on?" I asked. Why the hell did it always feel like people were hiding things from me these days? "Do you know Jackson?"

"He's the Regulator's son." Helen waved dismissively as she snubbed out her cigarette. "That's all. People get nervous around him. Besides, Donaghy likes you."

"And he's hot," Glitter piped in, only this time, she wouldn't look me in the eye.

"Life rarely hands you happiness," Helen said as she pulled a new cigarette out from under the bar. She lit it, her blue eyes on me as she slowly inhaled. When she blew the smoke out, she pointed the cigarette at me as if to emphasize her words. "Be sure you don't pass it up when it comes your way."

I had a hard time believing that a convict who fought zombies was my ticket to happiness, but I let the older woman have her sage moment without argument.

The bar began to clear out, and I started to worry that my crew was going to head out too, but when the crowd thinned, I spotted them sitting at a table. I wasn't sure whether or not they were waiting for me, but I did know that I needed to head over before they decided to go to a strip club or something.

"I need to talk to them." I said nodding toward the three guys. "I think they know something about my dad's disappearance."

Helen's eyebrows shot up, but when I tried to catch her eye, she looked away.

"We'll cover for you," Glitter said, drawing my attention to her.

"Thanks." I ventured a look at Helen as I poured four glasses of moonshine, but she had moved to the end of the bar where she was saying something to Dragon.

I tensed, waiting for the bar owner to charge over and fire me for giving away free drinks, but he just nodded and looked toward the three guys waiting for me.

More secrets. What the hell was going on around here?

Donaghy was nowhere in sight when I made my way across the bar, but I had to assume he'd gone to clean himself up. I missed the fight, but the blood in the ring seemed particularly thick tonight. He was probably more covered than usual.

When I reached the table, I slid into the empty seat and set the four glasses down. "I think it's about time we got to know each other," I said with a smile.

"Thanks," the three guys replied almost in unison.

I raised my glass, urging them to drink up. I needed loose tongues tonight.

The youngest of the three, who didn't seem to realize that I had a face, called himself Ticker. At first I wasn't sure if it was his real name, but after less than ten minutes of sitting with him I decide it couldn't be. His right shoulder jerked up every minute or so, like a tick he couldn't control and probably wasn't even aware of. Most likely someone had given him the nickname when he was younger and he hadn't been able to shake it. Ticker was thin and wiry, but muscular from a life of manual labor, and his brown, beady eyes made him look slightly unhinged. Luckily, the thick mop of hair on his head helped shadow them, otherwise he'd probably scare the shit out of most people.

The older guy, Matt, was laid back and charming. His deep set blue eyes were intelligent and focused on my face the entire time we talked. He was the type of guy who walked around with a constant five o'clock shadow, giving off the impression that he'd just spent a couple days in the wilderness where he didn't have access to a razor. He wasn't only the best looking of the group, but the tallest, tannest, and most muscular. The last two I attributed to being on the maintenance crew the longest. It was strange, because there was a stigma associated with the guys who worked the crew. They were the dumbest people in the settlement. The people who had the least to contribute to society. Talking to Matt, though, I could see that wasn't always the case.

The third guy barely said a word. His age was hard to determine because he was big and bulky, but had a baby face that was nearly hidden by wisps of pale, blond hair. It took some time to learn his name since he didn't even try to get a word in — plus Ticker seemed to like hearing himself talk — but I finally discovered that it was Jimmy. True to the stereotype of the maintenance crew, Jimmy seemed to be a few cards short of a full deck, but he was gentle and had a friendly smile.

"How long have you worked here?" Ticker asked, his

shoulder jerking as he took a drink, and his constantly blinking eyes never leaving my cleavage.

"Just this week."

Matt lifted his eyebrows. "Do you have a death wish? You get a job on the maintenance crew one week, and a job in this dump the next. Aren't there enough ways to get killed these days?"

"You have to do what you can to survive," I said.

"Can't argue with that," Matt mumbled into his drink.

I tapped my toe on the floor while Ticker rattled off some story he'd heard about a zombie attack that supposedly happened outside Dayton last week. This wasn't what I wanted to talk to them about, but now that they were in front of me, I was having a hard time figuring out how to broach the subject of my dad and his untimely—and suspicious—disappearance. It didn't take long for me to decide that I just needed to be upfront about what I wanted. If I wasn't, I may never find a good opportunity.

"What do you know about my dad?" I blurted out, cutting Ticker off mid-sentence.

The words died on the guy's lips but he didn't shut his mouth. It hung open as he looked back and forth between Matt and me. Jimmy stared at his hands.

Matt didn't look at the other two guys as he leaned forward, his gaze holding mine. "You keep running around asking questions like that and you're probably not going to like what happens."

I slammed my mouth shut as Matt's warning rang in my ears. What the hell was going on? First Mom started having a mental breakdown, then Al freaked out when I showed him that note, now this. Had the whole world gone insane?

"What do you know?" I said again, not caring if the whole bar heard me at this point. People around here knew something, and I wanted to get to the bottom of it.

Matt exhaled and shook his head, but he leaned closer. "You sure you want to go down this road?"

"Wouldn't you?"

"Point taken." He leaned back a little, taking a look around before turning his gaze back to me. "I don't know a whole lot, but I know the story they're throwing around is bullshit. Never happened."

"What?"

That didn't make sense. Dad went out with a group and they were overrun. He was cut off from the others and they never found him. It happened sometimes. It wasn't that farfetched.

"There was no run that day," Ticker spit out.

"No run?" I blinked and looked between the three men.

Jimmy's eyes were still down, but the other two were staring at me, waiting to see my reaction. Only, I couldn't wrap my brain around it all. It just didn't make sense or seem real. Why would they lie unless they needed to cover up what had happened to Dad?

"Here's what I know," Matt said, drawing my gaze back to his. "Your dad was second in command of the enforcers. He'd been in the city from almost the beginning, was a good shot, and people trusted him. Knew him. They don't send guys like that out on guard duty. It would be a waste." He paused, letting that little bit of information sink in before saying, "Plus, no groups left the city that day. *None.*"

"How do you know?" I whispered.

Matt leaned closer to me again. "Because I was working and I remember hearing about your dad the next day and wondering how the hell he disappeared on a run when there were *no runs.*"

The air in the room grew thicker and I squeezed my eyes shut, trying to wrap my brain around the whole thing. If there were no runs like Matt claimed, then there was no way Dad disappeared outside the walls. Which meant he never left the city. Which meant he could very well still be *in* New Atlanta. Alive.

"What the hell is going on?" I muttered, my eyes still closed.

I opened them to find all three guys staring at me. They were strangers. Until today, I'd only seen them at work in passing. Had never even spoken to them. Could I trust what they were saying?

Normally, I probably wouldn't, but right now the evidence mounting up around me was too damning. Between the note and what Donaghy had overheard at Jackson's, as well as this little morsel, it all pointed to one thing: Someone was trying to cover up something big.

"That's all?" I asked when no one spoke.

"If there's more information out there, I don't have it." Matt shrugged. "I'm not going to pretend I'm more important than I am,

I just know that when they started spreading around the story that Axl James disappeared on a run, it was a lie."

Silence settled over us that wasn't just heavy, but disturbing.

We were still quiet when Donaghy came out of the back room. His gaze moved across the bar, not stopping until he found me, and as he headed my way, his eyes stayed locked on mine.

"Everything okay?" he asked when he stopped in front of us.

"Yeah." Matt let out a deep sigh. "Nice fight by the way, man."

Donaghy glanced the other man's way, his icy eyes raking over him like he was seeing him for the first time even though technically they'd met earlier. Well, not met exactly. Ran from the dead together was more like it.

"Thanks." When the fighter finally spoke, it didn't sound the least bit sincere.

"Sit down," I said, nodding toward the empty chair at my side.

Donaghy complied, not saying a word. His body was stiff when he lowered himself into the chair across from Matt. With him here, we were squeezed in so tightly that the fighter's leg was touching mine. The small table wasn't big enough for five people, but with Donaghy practically pressed up against me, I couldn't complain.

"Aren't you supposed to be working?" Ticker asked me, his shoulder jerking up like it was punctuation the words.

"The busy part of the night is over. It's not like Dragon is paying me by the hour." I glanced over my shoulder to find Helen and Glitter talking with the few men still sitting at the bar. Less than ten of them. Nothing they couldn't handle without me.

"So what's your next move?" Matt asked when I turned back to face him.

Next to me, Donaghy stiffened, and suddenly his leg was pressed more firmly against mine under the table. I didn't know why, but again I couldn't complain.

"I don't know." I exhaled. "I need more information, but no one seems to have anything but theories."

"I'm going to be useless," Donaghy said, and when I turned to face him, the intense expression in his eyes made me shiver. "Jackson revoked his invitation. I've been sentenced to a cot in the back room."

"There goes the only edge we had," I said.

"Maybe you should try to make up with him..." He stretched out the sentence in a way that made me turn on him with narrowed eyes.

"What exactly do mean *make up with him?*" Was he telling me to sleep with Jackson? If so, that wasn't going to happen.

"Nothing like that," Donaghy said. "I just overheard him last night. He was pissed about something that happened between you two."

"Who's this?" Matt asked before I could respond.

I looked up to find him watching me. Ticker's eyes were glued to my chest, and Jimmy was back to staring at his hands.

"The Regulator's son," Donaghy said, once again speaking before I could utter a word. I was starting to feel like I didn't need to be here.

"Shit." Matt whistled between his teeth. "Are you telling me you pissed off the Regulator's son, but were shocked when you got sent outside?"

"It's not like that," I said, sitting up straighter, which only pressed my leg more firmly against Donaghy's. "Jackson and I have been best friends since we were kids. We had a fight. That doesn't mean he wants to have me killed."

"You're fooling yourself." Ticker tore his eyes away from my chest long enough to meet my gaze, pointing his glass at me to emphasize his point. "That dude is nuts. Ticker knows him from school." His eyes went back to my chest the second he was done talking.

"School?" I asked, shaking my head.

Ticker tore his gaze from my cleavage once again, and his beady little eyes focused on my face. "Yeah." The guy's shoulder jerked as he nodded. "School. The regulator's son tortured Stevie. Beat the shit out of him." He kept nodding as he tried to take a drink, but the alcohol sloshed out of his glass.

"Stevie?" Even though it didn't make sense, I had a feeling he was referring to himself.

Ticker just nodded in response.

"Jackson Star," Matt said slowly, "is the very definition of a sociopath. If you think otherwise, you're fooling yourself. Or he's been fooling you. Not sure which." Matt jerked his thumb toward Ticker, who was back to staring at my chest, his shoulder twitching more than ever. "Ticker isn't the only person that asshole tortured, although I'd say he's the worst case—that we know of. Head injury." Matt tapped his finger on the side of his own head. "He spent a month in the hospital, almost died. After that his mom wouldn't let him go back to school. He's never been the same."

"Ticker..." I mumbled, trying to place him. He was probably about the same age as Jackson and me, but I didn't remember him, which was nuts because, there weren't a lot of kids in school when we were growing up. I should have some recollection of this kid if he'd been around. "I don't remember any of this and I've known Jackson forever."

"Stevie." Ticker rocked, his shoulder jerking harder. "Stevie Jones."

"Stevie Jones?" My mouth fell open as a memory clawed its way to the forefront of my brain.

I remembered him now, only I didn't remember anything like that ever happening. He'd been in our class one week and gone the next. I'd honestly had no idea what had happened to him, but that was also around the time that Margot died, so it made sense. I'd had other things to worry about.

"I didn't know..."

I shook my head, totally dumbfounded. How could Jackson have done something like this, and how had I not known? It made me think of all the comments Dad had made about Jackson wearing a mask. Hiding who he was. Especially from me. But why? Why go to so much trouble?

"I'm sorry, Stevie," I said, feeling like I was somehow responsible even though I'd played no part in it.

"Ticker." He shook his head. "Not Stevie. *Ticker.* Jackson killed Stevie. Did it after school in a dark alley. With a bat. Stevie is dead. I'm Ticker now."

"Holy fuck," Donaghy muttered at my side.

Matt's jaw clenched as he nodded. "Yeah."

Jackson had been my friend for years and I'd always trusted him, but *this*... This made me see him in a whole new light. All the excuses I'd made for him. All the times I'd convinced myself that Jackson was just misunderstood. That he was better than his father.

That I was the only one who saw the real Jackson Star. Had I been kidding myself all this time? Was he really no better than his father? It seemed that way.

There was no denying the fact that if the Regulator had his way, he'd rule the country for the rest of his life and we would never again be a democracy. But was Jackson a part of all that? Was he planning on following in his father's footsteps as some kind of dictator of this new zombie world?

Had he been playing me for a fool?

I looked at Ticker, whose shoulder hadn't stopped jerking. It was hard to deny the truth when it was staring you in the face.

Jackson was a monster.

Tears filled my eyes and I pushed my chair away from the table. "I'm sorry. I really am." I squeezed my eyes shut and tried to get a hold on my emotions, but it was no use. "I have to go," I said as I turned away.

# CHAPTER SEVENTEEN

## Donaghy

**MEG'S** sniffles were the first thing I heard as I approached the back room, and when I stopped outside the cracked door, everything inside me was at war. She was upset, struggling, and I wanted to go to her. If Patty were the one crying in the back room of some rundown bar, I'd want someone to be there for her.

Then again, getting involved with Meg would be the dumbest thing I could ever do. I was only here for a few more days, and the chemistry between us was getting out of hand. The last thing she needed was for me to make her life more complicated.

I started to turn away, but had only taken one step when my gut clenched. Shit. Turning my back on Meg after saving her in that bathroom just didn't feel right.

I took a deep breath and pushed the door open, knowing that doing this was probably going to end up being something I would later come to regret.

The back room was dark, making the outline of the zombie cages just barely visible in the black shadows, but the stench of death left little to the imagination. She wasn't in the holding room, so I moved farther into the darkness, toward the room with the cots. When I pushed the second door open, her sniffles got louder.

"Meg." My voice seemed unnaturally loud in the small space, but when she turned to face me, she didn't seem surprised that I was here.

"I'm sorry." She sniffed again. "I like to think I'm stronger than this, but the truth is, I don't think I'm handling this all that well."

"You're strong," I said, closing the space between us so I was standing in front of her. "This is a shit show you didn't see coming."

When she looked up, a wisp of a smile was just visible through the darkness. "You say that a lot."

"What?"

"Shit show."

"Oh."

Her smile faded, and she wiped her hands across her eyes as she let out a big sigh. "This whole thing just keeps getting worse and worse, and I'm not really sure where to go from here."

"You just have to keep looking for clues."

She nodded, but a second later shook her head. "It isn't even that. Not totally. Jackson had me fooled. All these years I trusted him. Finding out that it has all been a lie has me questioning everything in my life. I always knew his dad didn't give a shit about anything other than getting his hands on more power, but I never realized just how deep this all runs."

"What do you mean?"

"Well, if they really did have my uncle as a prisoner, I can't help feeling like there's more to what the CDC is doing than just finding a vaccine. I mean, if they were willing to do something as drastic as keep a man against his will for *years*, lying to his family and the whole world that entire time, there has to be something they're not telling us." She sucked her bottom lip into her mouth and chewed on it, her eyes turned to the floor as she thought it all through.

Even though I didn't know for sure what this government was up to, I had to admit she had a point. And it answered the big question I'd had about this whole thing: If they were just trying to find a way to stop the zombie virus from spreading, why wouldn't they be upfront about it?

"Maybe they're the ones in charge of the mutations."

Meg lifted her head, her eyes narrowed on me. "What?"

"Think about it. Every few years this thing seems to change, and we've all been told that the virus is mutating on its own. But how do we know that's true? What if the CDC is responsible for all of it?"

She shook her head, but even in the darkness, I could tell that she thought I might be right. "Would they do that?"

"I have no idea what they'd do for sure, or why, but I know this: The conversation I overheard in the Regulator's house made it sound like they had motives that went way beyond finding a cure."

A shiver shook her body and she crossed her arms over her chest, hugging herself. "Shit."

I nodded, unable to talk with my head spinning the way it was. The theory seemed crazy, but so did half the things I'd seen over the last year. All those prisoners in DC, crammed together like rats. Most of them were scum and the world would be better if they were just killed, but for some reason this government was holding onto them. They liked to talk big, saying executions were common, but it was a total lie. It rarely happened, and usually only with the men they didn't seem to be able to contain. No. It was almost like they wanted to keep all those prisoners alive. Like they were saving them…

I shook my head to get rid of the thought. It was even more insane than any of the things Meg had suggested.

She was still hugging herself when she said, "This whole thing has me feeling so alone. I'm not used to that, you know? I've always had people to watch my back. Now though, it feels like the world is about to fall on my head." She swallowed. "I always knew Jackson's dad was no good, but I had to hope that the government wasn't totally corrupt. If all this is true, though, it means they have been lying to my family for years. They've stolen everything from us. From me."

The urge to drop my baggage at her feet slammed into me, but I didn't know why. It sure as hell wasn't going to make her feel better—not with how fucking depressing it all was. Maybe, though, it would help her feel just a little bit less alone. Knowing there were other people out there who had been screwed over by this government.

"You're not alone in all this." Meg nodded like she knew where I was going with it, but I shook my head. "I mean, being screwed over by the government."

Meg's gaze held mine while she waited for me to elaborate, but for a second I couldn't. Not when the memories of the past year came screaming back. It had been a nightmare. Even worse, I didn't have a fucking clue how Patty was holding up back in Dayton.

"I have a sister," I said finally, still in the grasp of Meg's gaze. "Patty. She's seventeen. After Mom and I got settled in Dayton, things were normal for a while. We had an apartment. We got over the loss of Dad and tried to make a life. Mom worked, I went to school. The world started to feel normal. Even this dumbass government made it seem like things were looking up. Someone was in charge and we had hope that the country might recover.

"We'd been settled in for about a year when Mom got remarried. A man named Kurt who was quiet, but nice. I liked the guy, and when my baby sister was born it made the whole thing even better. Made it seem like things could be better.

"Patty was only six when the flu took Mom, along with a shit ton of other people. Kurt had always been there for us, but I guess that was too much for him. Losing his first wife to the virus, then Mom to the flu. Afterward, he started drinking. Just checked out. Seven years later, another flu swooped in and took him. It sucked, but Patty was thirteen by then and it wasn't like my stepdad was contributing all that much, so we forged on. I was twenty-one and had a good job with the enforcers, and for the next few years things were okay.

"The end came for us a year ago. Patty was sixteen and had gotten to know the JO's son. Not only was he nineteen and too old for her, but he was an entitled prick. I couldn't stand the guy. No matter how many times I told her to stay away from him, though, she wouldn't. He had this hold on her..." I swallowed. "A little over a year ago, he raped her. Patty wasn't ready to sleep with him, so he took it anyway.

"When she told me, I wanted to kill the bastard, but instead I went to his dad. I honestly thought there was real justice in this world. I thought the guy in charge would be sure to make his son pay for what he'd done to my sister. But his dad told me it was Patty's word against his son's, and that no one would believe her. They'd been seen all over the settlement together, and everyone knew she was trying to sleep her way to a better life. He told me to go home and forget about it.

"When I realized this kid was going to get away with what he'd done, I snapped. I didn't think about my actions or how they would affect my sister, I just hunted him down and let out all my rage. I barely remember it, really. Everything was red, and hitting him felt amazing. He would have died if people hadn't pulled me off him, and I wish he had. Now I'm a convict who has to treat every single day like it could be my last, Patty is all alone, and that asshole is free. I saw her when I was in Dayton. Just from afar, but she snuck into the bar the last night I was there. She looked... Younger. Thinner. Scared and broken. It made me hate myself even more."

When I finished talking, I kept my eyes on the ground. My fists were clenched from the memory, and if that little shit had been in front of me, I would have finished the job I started back in Dayton.

Meg stepped closer and I didn't flinch away when her hands touched my arms. She ran them up over my biceps, tracing my tattoos briefly before moving her hands to my shoulders. She kept going, though, until my face was between her palms and I was forced to tear my gaze away from the floor and look her in the eye. The heels she was wearing made her taller, but she was still short. Tiny. Her head barely reaching my shoulders.

God, I wanted to protect her. From Jackson and the zombies, from what was happening with her dad and mom. From the whole, fucking world. Only I couldn't. I couldn't do anything because I'd fucked up my life so bad that I was a prisoner. I was scum. Nobody.

"You deserve better than what you got," she whispered.

"We all do," I said, squeezing my fists tighter when the urge to pull her against me hit.

Meg's gaze moved to my lips, and I found myself leaning toward her. She lifted herself up on the tips of her toes, and my hands were on her hips before I even realized it, and then I was

171

pulling her against me.

"When I saw you in that bathroom," I said, my hands gripping her hips like I wouldn't ever let her go, "it was like Patty all over again."

"You saved me," Meg said.

She rose up higher, her breasts flush against my chest, and she was so close that when she exhaled I could feel her warm breath on my lips. That was all it took for me to let go. To lean down and meet her halfway, pressing my lips against hers.

Meg's body melted into mine as she returned the kiss. I moved my hand up, over the bare skin of her back. It was warm and soft under my palm, and inviting. Her lips opened, and I followed her lead, plunging my tongue into her waiting mouth. Meg's hands were still on my face, pulling me closer like she couldn't get enough of me, and I wanted so badly to drag her across the room and throw her onto one of the cots so I could rip her clothes off.

*That would be an asshole thing to do.*

The words were nothing more than a faint idea in my mind, but I couldn't push them away. I was leaving in a few days. There was no future for me, especially not here.

When I pulled back, a gasp broke its way out of Meg. "What?"

"I'm an asshole." She shook her head and I tried to step back, but extracting myself from her arms wasn't as easy as it should have been. "I'm leaving, and doing this would be me taking advantage of the situation."

"No it wouldn't, because I know you're leaving and I don't care." Meg held onto me when I tried to pull away again. "There's nothing wrong with grabbing a little piece of happiness when you can."

Shit. When she put it that way, it was hard to say no, and all I could think about was grabbing a piece of her and how good it would feel. How right.

But then I'd leave and it would probably tear me in half, and who the hell knew what it would do to her. She was already feeling abandoned, and adding my name to the list of people who had left her would be the shittiest thing I could ever do.

"I'm sorry." It took all the strength I had inside me to pull away, but this time I managed it. "I've been the asshole enough in my life, but just this once, I need to be the good guy. Need to do the right thing."

Saying it that way seemed to get through to her, because she nodded. "Okay."

"You going to hate me now?" I cringed, realizing how much the idea of her hating me hurt.

"No." She gave me a shaky smile, then hesitantly stepped closer. When she put her arms around me this time, there was a difference in the embrace. It still felt amazing to have her body against mine, but it was comforting, too. "You're not an asshole, Donaghy. Don't let anyone tell you otherwise."

I hugged her back as memories of other hugs hit me. Mom and Patty, and all the years when the world had looked good and promising. It seemed like so long ago now.

# CHAPTER EIGHTEEN

## Meg

THE apartment was dark and silent when I got home, and I did my best not to make a sound when I shut the door. My head was still spinning from all the new information I'd gotten today—and from that kiss. The last thing I needed right now were Mom's conspiracy theories clouding the facts. Especially because at this point, I might actually believe everything she spouted off.

But I'd only taken one step down the hall when the sound of Mom's mattress groaning broke through the silence. "Megan?" Her voice was muffled from sleep, but something in her tone made me pause. "Is that you?"

"It's me."

I headed down the hall, dread growing in my stomach with each step I took. Dread because Mom sounded like *Mom*. There was no paranoia in her voice or panic or anguish. It was like time had been reversed and she was the woman I'd grown up with. Only I didn't believe a switch could be flipped that quickly, and I didn't want to get my hopes up. I didn't want to believe that she had pulled herself out of this only so I could step into the room and be greeted by the same wide, terrified eyes as before.

The lights were off and I could just make out her silhouette in the darkness. She sat up when I stopped in the doorway, and a second later the lamp on the bedside table clicked on. Light flooded the room and Mom squinted, but even as she waited for her eyes to adjust, I could tell something was different.

"Where have you been?" She held her hand at the side of her face to block out the light from the lamp, and her eyes moved over me. Slow and alert. "What time is it?"

"It's late." I ventured further into the room, my heart pounding harder with each step I took.

Mom blinked and her gaze moved over me again, this time the corners of her mouth turned down. The hair on my arms stood up, and my scalp prickled the way it had when I was little and I knew she was about to catch me in a lie. I crossed my arms, trying to cover myself. Until now, I'd forgotten all about my skimpy dress.

"What are you wearing?" Mom asked as she put her feet on the floor.

Every move she made seemed to be slow. Muddled. Like she was waking up for the first time in weeks. That was how it felt to me, too. This was the most coherent she'd been since the early days of Dad's disappearance. Back when we had finally accepted that he wasn't going to come home ever again.

I tugged on my skirt, trying to make it longer, but gave up when all it did was expose more of my cleavage. "I got a job in the entertainment district. It was that or lose the apartment."

She pressed her lips together and my back stiffened while I waited for her response. My whole life my parents had worked hard to protect me from the darkness in this world. I'd grown up surrounded by death, but there had always been safety and security in this house. I knew my parents would be here for me. Never doubted that they'd die just to protect me from the horrors of this world. Now, I was knee-deep in it. The entertainment district was the epitome of everything dirty in this world. It was where people went when there was no hope left.

After a few seconds, Mom let out a deep sigh and shook her head. "I'm sorry. I know I haven't been very helpful. I don't know what's wrong with me, but I can't seem to control...*anything*." She put her hand to her head like it hurt. "Nothing seems real anymore."

"Are you okay?" I stepped farther into the room and reached out, half-expecting her to lash out at me. To scream about how none of us were okay as long as *they* are in charge. Whoever *they* were. I didn't think even she knew who she was talking about.

"My head is pounding —" Mom's fingers rubbed her temples. " — and my throat is so dry it feels like I've been walking through the desert for days."

"Let me get you a drink."

I swiped a glass off the bedside table and hurried to the bathroom. My hands were shaking when I held it under the faucet.

Mom was back.

I'd almost given up hope of ever seeing her again, but she was back. I didn't know how or why, but I did know that with her here, I had a better chance of making it. Of finding out what had happened to Dad.

But...

Maybe telling her about the note wasn't a good idea. At least not until she'd had a chance to pull herself out of this funk. If I told her everything that was going on, it might send her right back to her obsessive paranoia. I could lose her again.

"I need to wait," I whispered to my own reflection.

In the dim light of the bathroom, my green eyes were huge. So big and round that they seemed to take up half of my face. They reminded me of Mom. Of how she'd looked in full-on paranoia mode. Odd considering we weren't biologically related.

I went back into the bedroom to find Mom sitting in the same place. When I held the glass out she took it, but confusion clouded her vision. Only it was different than it had been before. She didn't take a drink. She just stared at the glass like she was trying to remember something.

"Are you okay?" I lowered myself onto the bed at her side and the old mattress groaned under my weight.

Mom nodded as she gulped the water down, and in less than thirty seconds the glass was empty. She still didn't look away from it, though.

"The last few weeks are hazy. It almost feels like a dream." She shook her head and her brown eyes filled with tears. "I've experienced more than my fair share of loss, but this is different.

This is more than the usual ache of losing someone. That's still here—" Her free hand went to her chest. "—but there's something else too. Something..."

"What?" I leaned closer.

"I can't even describe it." Mom let out a sigh, and when she looked my way her gaze moved over me from head to toe, making every hair on my body stand on end. "Where did you get a job?"

I pulled at my skirt and looked away. "Dragon's Lair."

"I don't know that place. Is it a strip club?"

"No!" The word popped out with so much force that I was surprised it hadn't knocked her over. "I'm just serving drinks between fights."

"I'm sorry I haven't helped." Her fingers tightened around the glass in her hand. "How long has it been since I went to work?"

"I'm not sure." I tugged harder on my skirt. "At least two weeks."

"Hopefully, I still have a job I can go to."

"You're not disappointed in me?" I stole a glance her way, not brave enough to meet her gaze completely.

"About the job?" When I nodded, she put her free hand on my knee, the glass still in her other hand like she couldn't seem to part with it. "No. Even before zombies took over the world I believed in doing whatever it took to survive. In fact, I was a stripper."

I turned my whole body toward her. "What?"

"I was. After I left California."

A laugh forced its way out of me. I couldn't believe my mom had ever worked as a stripper. It seemed so far-fetched, thinking about who she was—or had been before Dad disappeared, anyway. Strong. Tough. Determined. I'd always thought that no matter what came her way, my mom would be able to bend the circumstances to fit her will with little to no effort. It had always seemed like that to me growing up, anyway.

Mom exhaled and stared back down at the glass in her hand. "I had the weirdest dream."

"What was it?" I asked, only half paying attention to her. My mind was still too wrapped around the idea of her being a stripper, and I found myself wondering what else I didn't know about my mom.

"Angus was here."

I turned to face her again. *That* had my full attention. "He was?"

"It's weird, because I haven't dreamt about him in years. When he first died I did, of course. He'd been a major part of my life for so long that it almost felt like something was missing. But over the years the dreams became less and less frequent, and eventually they stopped altogether. And this was different. So *vivid.*"

I didn't know why, but a buzzing had started in my stomach. Low and soft, but constant. "Did he say anything to you? In the dream, I mean?"

Mom's mouth scrunched up and it caused a pang to shoot through me that only made the buzzing more insistent. Dad always did that when he was thinking. Puckered his lips. Damn. There wasn't anything as painful as the ache of a lost loved one. Not even a zombie bite could rival it.

"Angus was older," Mom finally said. "Thinner than he'd been the last time I saw him. And he had a beard. It was gray, and so was his hair. It's weird. People don't usually age in dreams, do they?"

She looked up, her eyes searching mine like she was begging for answers. Answers to what, I didn't know. Maybe she just wanted some reassurance that she hadn't lost it completely.

"I'm the last person to ask," I said, putting my hand on top of hers.

"Yeah." Mom nodded a few times. "He helped me sit up." A smile curled up her lips and it almost made me burst into tears. I never thought I'd see her smile again. "He called me Blondie and told me to get my shit together. Angus always had a knack for getting under my skin, but he had a soft side too. It would come out at the most random moments, taking you by surprise."

The sad smile on her face made my throat tighten. "Maybe it was just your subconscious trying to get you to snap out of it?"

"Yeah..."

Mom's smile faded and she looked down at the glass in her hand. When she shook her head, she acted like she wasn't sure. Which was crazy. Angus died years ago. There was no way he'd popped up here tonight. It had been a dream. Nothing else.

"Where did you get this water?" she asked after a few

seconds.

"The bathroom."

"I can't remember…" Her voice trailed off. "Was there something wrong with the water? Did you tell me something was wrong?"

Years ago we couldn't drink the water, but it had been awhile now. Five years at least. Back then, the government told us not to drink anything that we hadn't boiled. Even from the faucets. People who had extra credits could buy pre-boiled water, but most couldn't. Or chose not to. Mom and Dad never would buy it even though they made enough credits. The government fixed the problem by creating filters. You just screwed one onto the faucet and the water ran through it. It sure as hell made getting clean water easier. Mom must have still been confused.

"The water is okay now," I said gently. "Remember?"

"Yeah…" Mom's voice trailed off again, her eyes still focused on the glass.

I exhaled and my shoulders slumped, and it suddenly hit me how exhausted I was. But the thought of leaving Mom now that she was finally coherent caused an ache to move through me. Still, if I didn't get some sleep, I'd be exhausted tomorrow.

"I need to get to bed," I said through a yawn.

Mom blinked a couple times and shook her head. Her gaze moved to the bed and she finally put the glass down. "I'm tired too. I know I shouldn't be, but I am."

I swallowed, suddenly feeling like I was five years old all over again. Back then I'd gone through a phase where I was scared of the dark and the idea of going to sleep in my own bed had been terrifying. That's how I felt right now, scared out of my mind at the idea of going into the other room and sleeping in the dark all by myself.

"Can I sleep with you?" I asked, almost embarrassed to say the words out loud. "I don't want to be alone."

"Of course."

Mom held her arms out and I fell against her. When she pulled me close, I almost burst into tears.

"I've missed you," I said against her chest, feeling younger than ever. "I've felt so alone."

"I'm so sorry, Megan." Her lips moved against the top of my

head as she rubbed my back. "I'll do better. I don't know what's going on, but I'm going to fight this thing. I'll be here for you. Tomorrow, I'll go back to work and things will get better. You have my word."

I squeezed my eyes shut and tried to hold onto the promise. It was hard to believe, though, especially after everything that had happened.

THE ROOM WAS STILL DARK WHEN I OPENED MY EYES, but the light breaking through the curtains told me it was almost time to get up. I wasn't quite ready, so I twisted my body away from the window, hoping to block out the sun's rays.

On the other side of the bed, Mom was still out cold. Her mouth hung open and her breathing was heavy. The glass sat on the bedside table, half full. She must have gotten up to get a drink in the middle of the night.

I didn't want to disturb her just yet, so I made sure I was quiet when I slid out of bed. Mom moved, but just a little, and she didn't make a sound. I'd try to wake her up in a bit. Hopefully, she'd go into work today.

I was in the middle of making breakfast—dry toast since that was all we had—when Mom stumbled out of the bedroom. Her eyes were half-closed and her movements sluggish, but hopefully it was nothing a little bit of caffeine wouldn't take care of.

"Coffee?" I called as I turned to pour some into a mug for her.

"No." The word was slurred, but it was her tone that made me freeze.

I put the carafe down and turned to face her, the trembling in my body growing with each passing second. "Mom? Are you going to work today?"

When she looked up, she was frowning. "Go to work?"

"Last night you said you were going to."

"I can't go to work!" Her eyes darted around the room, big and round and terrified. "I have to find your father. Axl is missing, and I know they're lying to us. Just like they did with Angus."

Even though I knew it was useless, I took a step closer to her. "Mom?"

Her gaze stopped on my face for only a second before her eyes were once again flying around the room. The way they bounced back and forth made me dizzy, and I couldn't understand how she stayed upright.

She started pacing, pulling at her shirt while she talked to herself. "If they took him, that means he's still alive. In the CDC. We have to get in there. But how? How do we break into the CDC when..."

Her words trailed off, too low and fast for me to catch them. Not that I wanted to. I'd heard all of this over and over again the last few weeks, but after last night, they were more devastating than ever before. Why she had snapped out of it for such a short time didn't make sense, but it had foolishly given me hope.

The idea of drinking my coffee or eating the toast I'd made no longer sounded appealing, so I left the food on the counter and grabbed my knife before heading to the door. Hopefully, Mom would eat the toast if I left it where it was.

I had to pause when I stepped into the hall because my legs were shaking so much. I leaned my head against the closed door and squeezed my eyes shut, letting out a deep breath. Mom's crazy rant rang in my ears, but I wasn't sure if it was in my head or if I could actually hear her through the door.

"Megan?" I opened my eyes to find Charlie staring at me. "Where the hell have you been? I haven't seen you since the other night at Dragon's. You're never home and..." She sank her teeth into her lower lip for a second before saying, "I was worried about you."

The night we'd gone to Dragon's with Jackson had only been a couple days ago, but at the moment it felt like years had passed. I couldn't believe how silly the fear I'd felt that night seemed now. In the face of everything else, that struggle in the bathroom felt like nothing.

I pushed myself off the door. "You don't need to worry about me. I'm fine."

"Okay..." Charlie lifted her eyebrows expectantly. "I'm going to need a little bit more than that. I mean, you've been MIA for days."

"I had to get another job." I waved for her to follow as I headed down the hall. Above us, the lights flickered, sending shadows across Charlie's face that made her already sharp features sharper. "I've been serving drinks at Dragon's, actually."

"What?" Her voice echoed through the hall and she looked around. "You can't be serious. That place was a dump." This time, her voice was lower.

"In case you haven't noticed, I'm running out of options."

I stopped in front of the elevator and pushed the button. The engine whined behind the door, the chains that pulled the elevator up rattling. One of these days, the thing was going to break for good.

"You're right. I'm sorry," she said, her voice low. "I've been a really shitty friend.

I glanced toward Charlie but didn't turn away from the elevator. "No, you haven't."

"Yes, I have."

The door opened and I stepped in. Charlie followed, and I turned to study her as the elevator made its way down. She looked pretty ashamed of herself, which was so not like her.

"What almost happened the other night had me really shaken, and it got even worse when I couldn't find you for days afterward. I started thinking about everything you've gone through, and how selfish I've been. Mom's been telling me for years that I'm spoiled and entitled, but I never listened. She was right. I mean, I have everything. Both my parents are alive and I have a nice place to live, plus extra credits whenever I need them. I've never lost anyone." Charlie looked down. "Can you forgive me?"

"Charlie—" She lifted her head and I gave her a smile. "—I was never mad at you."

"Thank God. I've been feeling like such a bitch. But I'm going to be better from here on out. I'm not going to be so spacey and selfish."

I laughed, and after the craziness of the morning, it was a nice feeling. "Okay."

The elevator finally reached the first floor and the door groaned when it opened. Charlie and I headed out together, walking side by side in silence until we'd made it out of the apartment building.

The morning sun was bright and already hot, making me dread work. There had to be a cooler settlement in this country—

and one that wasn't so close to the Regulator. Maybe Luke had the right idea and we should all get the hell out of here while we could.

Speaking of Luke...

I glanced at Charlie out of the corner of my eyes. "Have you seen your brother lately?"

She looked the other way and shrugged. "You know him. Never around."

I waited a couple beats, and wasn't at all surprised when Charlie's hazel eyes shot my way. Her cheeks were red and her lips pressed together, a telltale sign that she was lying.

"You know," I said accusingly.

"Know what?"

"About the apprenticeship."

Charlie turned to look at me, her eyes searching my face. "He told you?"

"He came into the bar the first night I was working and told me all about it. When did you find out?"

"Last night." Charlie sighed. "I was home when he stopped in to get some things. I've noticed that his stuff has slowly started to disappear, and I kind of assumed he'd met someone."

"That's what your mom thinks too."

"I know. I told Luke he needs to tell Mom and Dad, and he swears that he's going to eventually, but I have no idea when. He's planning on leaving really soon. As soon as he can register as a zombie slayer." Charlie shook her head like she thought her brother was insane.

Zombie slayers were the only people who could go in and out of settlements regularly and still benefit from the government. Otherwise, citizens stayed inside the safety of the walls—unless they were out on a run or doing something for the maintenance crew. Most people who lived outside the sanctioned settlements were unregistered, which meant they weren't entitled to help. Ever. No food, no medicine, and no vaccines. Nothing.

Zombie slayers got the best of both worlds, at least according to them. They could get help if they needed it, but they lived outside. They didn't have to answer to the government as much. It was an approved way to live because the government said we needed people who were willing to spend their days hunting down and killing the dead. Of course, the lifespan of a zombie slayer was usually short. They had to check in at their designated settlement at least once a month, and if they didn't they were presumed dead. When they checked in, they also had to report their kills for the month. It was how they earned credits. When they made a kill, they collected the ears of the dead as proof. It was chilling, but a harsh reminder of the reality we lived in.

I'd always thought it was a crazy way to live, but after everything that had happened over the last few days, I didn't think so. Not anymore.

"There's been a lot going on with me—" Charlie lifted her eyebrows but I waved her questions away before she could voice them. "I can't get into it right now, but I promise I'll tell you when things get better. Anyway, after all the shit I've learned over the last few days, I don't think Luke is crazy."

Charlie's eyes got huge. "What are you saying?"

"Nothing. I'm just saying that it will be okay. Luke will be back at least once a month. You'll see him." And maybe, if I could work things out, we could join him out there. Although, I didn't think Charlie was ready for that bomb just yet.

We lapsed into silence as we approached shantytown. The shacks were just coming alive, and the sounds of children crying and mother's urging them to get moving rang through the air, as well as the occasional cough and moan. Halfway through the town we passed the shrine where three people knelt, each one lost in their prayers. I watched them as we walked by, wondering what made them think this was the right god to pray to.

Almost as if she was reading my mind, Charlie nodded toward them. "It's strange, right? I mean, we never talk about it, but we all know it's nuts. *Angus*. Can you believe it?"

"They think he died saving the world." I shrugged even though I agreed with her. It was nuts.

"Do they believe he's going to come back one day and save them again?" Charlie pressed her lips together, her dark eyes on the people kneeling in front of the statue of my Uncle Angus. "They do realize it's impossible to come back from the dead, right?"

"Is it? There are zombies walking the earth right this second." I lifted an eyebrow at her and we both laughed nervously.

"Anyway, this wouldn't be the first religion that believed their deity lived as flesh and blood, died saving the human race, then came back."

"True..." Charlie shot the people praying to Angus one last look, then walked faster. "It's still weird."

She wasn't wrong.

We didn't talk again until we'd reached the edge of the shantytown, and when Charlie looked my way, I knew her mind was on something other than the Angus worshipers or her brother. She had an excited gleam in her eye.

"Is Donaghy still fighting at Dragon's?" she asked.

"Yup," I said, smacking my lips together at the end of the word and refusing to meet her gaze. My heart pounded faster just thinking about him, and I as afraid she would see it in my eyes.

Hopefully, she didn't notice the heat that had spread across my cheeks. Despite everything going wrong in my life, I was having a tough time forgetting the kiss Donaghy and I shared last night. It had been amazing. Thrilling. Like a very good dream. After what had happened with Colton, I never thought I'd find myself in this situation again. Even worse, I knew it was bound to lead to the same kind of heartache. Donaghy didn't belong here, and he'd be leaving soon.

"Maybe I should come see you. You working tonight?" Charlie paused before shaking her head. "No, not tonight. I'm finally starting my apprenticeship with Dad. It will have to be tomorrow."

"Apprenticeship?" Despite the unease in my stomach, I couldn't help giving Charlie a questioning look. I'd always thought she followed Al around just for show.

"Yeah, Dad has been on me to make a decision about my future. Then there are the lectures from Mom." She rolled her eyes like it was the most tedious thing she'd ever had to deal with, which was probably true, but there was a small smile on her lips that gave her away. "I finally gave in. I'm excited, I guess."

"That's good." It was nice that someone had some direction. Now, I wish I'd taken Joshua up on the offer of an apprenticeship two years ago. It would have given me access to the CDC if nothing else.

"Are you working tomorrow night?" Charlie asked hopefully.

"Yeah. Every night." Every day, every night. I never got a break. Just thinking about it weighed me down.

"If I came by, maybe you could introduce me to Donaghy."

My feet stopped moving. Seriously? She watched me out of the corner of her eye, trying to act subtle. She missed her target by a mile, though. It wasn't a surprise that Charlie would want to meet Donaghy, he was hot and any sane person could see it, but for some reason it took me by surprise.

"Meg?" She turned her whole face toward me and shot a questioning look my way. "What's wrong?"

"Nothing." I started walking again. "Yeah. I'll introduce you."

A pang squeezed my insides, but I ignored it. Donaghy had walked away from me because he was leaving soon, so it only made sense that he wouldn't let anything happen with Charlie. Still... I looked her up and down, and I couldn't help feeling a little inadequate. Charlie was exotically gorgeous.

"What's going on?" She narrowed her eyes on me. "Is something happening between you and Donaghy?"

"No," I said, a little too fast.

When her eyebrows shot up, I knew she wasn't buying it. "Holy shit! That's great." Charlie beamed at me. "Now I want to meet him even more."

"Nothing is happening." We reached the intersection where I needed to turn and stopped walking. "I'm serious."

"Okay." Charlie started was smiling from ear to ear as she walked backward, heading down the opposite street. "I totally believe you. I'm still coming, though."

I sighed. "Okay."

"See you tomorrow, then?" Charlie called as she spun on her heel and headed down the street.

"Yeah," I mumbled, shaking my head.

She waved once before trotting off, and I let out a sigh.

# CHAPTER NINETEEN

## Donaghy

**MY** night in Dragon's Lair was restless and not nearly as refreshing as sleeping at the Regulator's house had been.

My guards, who had barely been able to drag themselves into the bar after their night of partying, were still passed out when I woke. The snores the younger one let out were nasal and deep, and seemed to echo off the cement walls of the room. The sunlight that shone in through the one small window was low, telling me it wasn't nearly time for me to drag my ass out of bed, but no matter what I did, I couldn't block the snores out enough to get my body to relax.

"Asshole," I muttered as I rolled over and glared at the guard, whose mouth was wide open.

The door that led to the holding room was cracked, and between snores the sound of distant voices was just audible. They were deep, but not loud enough for me to make out their words. Not that I cared what they had to say. I just knew it meant Dragon was already up and I could get some breakfast. The prepackaged food he'd given me at every other meal tasted like shit, but at least it kept my stomach from growling the way it constantly had in DC.

I slid out of bed and headed across the room, not bothering to be quiet. Not only did I not give a shit if I woke up my guards, but I was pretty sure that a zombie horde couldn't have roused them at the moment.

The voices grew louder when I stepped into the other room, and even though I could only catch a word here and there, I knew with certainty that one of the men was Dragon. What I wasn't sure about was *who* he was talking to.

I moved through the dark holding room and past the empty cages. My footsteps were quiet, barely more than a slap against the stone floor. The closer I got, the louder the voices became, and for some reason that I couldn't quite put my finger on, I found myself straining to listen. They wouldn't be able to hear me coming, not with the noise they were making, and for some reason I wanted to take a moment and listen. Something about the few words I'd been able to catch had my interest piqued.

When I reached the door I stopped and held my breath, waiting to find out if I'd be able to hear anything through the thick wood.

"I want 'em out!" The voice of a man I didn't recognize boomed through the room.

"I know you're worried, but we can't rush this," Dragon said, his own tone much quieter. Calmer. Like he was trying to reassure the other man. "They're safe for now."

"They ain't safe. Nobody is safe here. Them assholes have got eyes everywhere."

"I don't know what you think is going to happen, but I'm watching them."

"An accident is gonna happen. A breach. A damn flu. Hell, you of all people know they don't give a shit. They can snatch somebody up like that—" The click of fingers being snapped cut through the words. "—and say whatever they want."

"I'm keeping an eye on them."

"It ain't 'nough. We gotta get out while we can."

"Are you willing to leave Axl behind?"

*Axl.* The name made my heart beat faster, and I pressed my ear against the door harder. That was Meg's dad, but how Dragon was involved and who he was talking to was a fucking mystery.

"No." Silence followed, but it was brief. "But I know he'd

want me to if it meant keepin' everybody else safe."

"Trust me." Dragon's voice was calmer than I'd ever heard it, and his tone reminded me of someone who was talking to a hysterical child. "Have I ever let you down? I've watched after Glitter, haven't I? Just like you asked."

There was a pause, and when the other man spoke again, something about his voice made me think he was smiling. "She's a good girl, ain't she?"

"She is. So is Meg. I promise that we will do everything in our power, but we need more time. My contact on the outside is getting the supplies together, but it's going to be a while before we have enough manpower and explosives. The CDC is a fortress."

*Explosives? The CDC?*

"What the hell?" I muttered just as the man in the other room said, "You got me out."

"It took us almost twenty years," Dragon said, his tone wracked with guilt.

"We don't got that long. Understand? What they're doin' now is bigger. Shit. You wouldn't believe the things I seen in there."

"I know."

Silence followed, and I held my breath again, waiting. But all I could hear was the sound of footsteps and a few muffled words here and there. After a second, I took a deep breath and eased the door open. Carefully. Slowly. When it was wide enough for me to get a good look out, I peered around the corner. Dragon and another man were behind the bar, still talking, but quieter now. The other guy was older. Lots of gray hair and a beard that matched, both of them wild.

Was this the man who had given Meg the note? It was possible, but how was Dragon mixed up in all this? And what did Glitter have to do with it?

Shit.

I stepped back before they spotted me and stood in the darkness of the room, trying to sort it all out. None of it made sense, and the more I learned about the situation, the more questions I seemed to have. I couldn't imagine how Meg felt.

I was still standing in the same place when the loud boom of someone knocking echoed through the bar. Dragon swore and I made my move. It seemed like a good opportunity to get another look at—and maybe talk to—the man with the gray hair.

I pushed the door open and stepped out just as the gray-haired man disappeared down the back hall. Dragon was heading for the front door, and when he spotted me, he waved me over. I would have rather followed the other man, but since I didn't have a good excuse, I headed after Dragon.

He ripped the door open and stepped back when the scent of death floated into the room. "What the hell?"

"A delivery for you. For the fight." A deep voice said. "In addition to the two you planned to throw in."

Dragon's body was blocking my view, but I didn't miss it when his dark eyes grew large. I took a step closer so I could get a good look, and when I did, I nearly shit my pants. Two men wearing enforcer's uniforms flanked a zombie so tall that they only came up to his shoulders. And these weren't short men. Six feet, probably. But the thing between them, which was desperately trying to break free of its chains, had to be seven or eight inches taller than that.

"You have to be kidding me," Dragon said, his eyes narrowing on the two men. "I like to keep things fair."

"This isn't a request."

Dragon stepped back as the guards pulled the zombie through the door. My feet felt like lead when I moved out of their way, and I couldn't take my eyes off the creature they were dragging past me. He was thin, but freakishly tall and new. In life I would have been able to take him without a problem, but depending on what strain of the virus he'd been infected with, he could be aggressive. Tough to beat even.

And there would be two others in there with me.

Dragon and I stayed next to the door while the guards pulled the dead man through the bar and into the other room.

"Looks like they finally decided to get rid of me," I mumbled, shaking my head.

Dragon's eyes moved from the door the zombie had just been pulled through so they could focus on me. "I think there's more to it than that." His gaze went past me, to the dark hallway his friend had just disappeared down. "I think this is a message."

"What kind of message?" The only message the government would want to send me was the one that said it was time for me to die. I refused to go easily, though.

Dragon shook his head instead of answering.

When he walked away, I didn't move. Despite what he'd said, I couldn't really see how this would affect anyone other than me. I was the asshole who was going to get his throat ripped out by the dead man's teeth.

# CHAPTER TWENTY

## Meg

**MY** crew had been MIA all day.
It was trash week, which meant a group of ten of us picking up stinking bags of garbage, most of which had been sitting in the sun for weeks by the time we got to them. More often than not, they'd also been ripped open by animals or people desperate for leftover scraps of food. Even with gloves on my hands, a mask to cover my nose and mouth, and an orange jumpsuit, the stink seemed to penetrate my skin.

By noon I was drenched in sweat and a hundred percent positive that I'd never feel cool—or clean—again. The worst part: this would be my assigned job for the week. That was how long it took to collect all the trash in the city.

I was beat by the time the shift was over. My arms and legs were shaking when I stripped my filthy clothes off and stepped under the hot stream of the decontamination shower. It would have been refreshing if the water was cool, but they claimed the chemicals they sprayed us down with needed hot water to work well. I was pretty sure they were just trying to torture us a little more.

I spotted my boss on the way out, my hair still dripping and stinking of chemicals, and my body so sore that all I wanted to do was go home and curl up in a ball. Still, I couldn't make myself leave without finding out what had happened to my crew.

"Hanson!"

The boss stopped and looked me up and down, frowning like he was upset to see me standing in front of him alive. "What do you want James?"

"My crew. The guys you sent me out with yesterday. Where are they?"

Hanson looked away. "Quit."

"Quit?" All three in one day? "Why?"

"Don't know, don't care. All it did was piss me off and put me behind." He headed off without saying anything else.

They quit...

I didn't believe it. Not only did it not make sense that all three of them would quit at the same time, but Matt had worked on the maintenance crew since he'd turned sixteen. Why, I didn't know, but I doubted he would just up and quit.

My stomach was uneasy the whole way home, and it got even worse when I found Mom once again passed out on the couch. This time, I left her where she was.

The feeling of dread stayed with me as I showered for the second time, trying to get the chemical smell out of my hair by using more shampoo than I should, and the worry hadn't eased by the time I left the apartment—once again wearing my black dress.

When I arrived at the bar, Donaghy was nowhere in sight, and a part of me was relieved. I was so preoccupied that I could barely focus on anything other than the thoughts in my head, and I had serious doubts I would be able to carry on a conversation right now, let alone try to unravel how I was feeling about him and the kiss we'd shared last night.

Like me, Helen was silent and tense. She didn't look my way when she slipped behind the bar, and even the drunks didn't get much of her attention tonight. Her blue eyes seemed to be continuously focused on the door across the room, and when she held her cigarette to her lips, there was a slight tremor in her hand.

I wondered if she and Dragon had a fight.

At first glance Glitter seemed to be her normal, chipper self.

She chatted with the patrons and shot Helen a few concerned looks that seemed to confirm my first impression about the older waitress having fought with her lover. After a while, though, as the night got busier, I caught Glitter looking my way a few times too. There was pity in her eyes, and concern. I couldn't figure out why she was looking at me, but the expression fed the heaviness in my stomach. It only got worse when Dragon entered the ring and the crowd moved away from the bar. I turned to face the older waitress, only to find her staring at me with the same expression in her eyes.

My heart beat faster. Something was going on, only I didn't know what.

I hadn't seen Donaghy yet. Had something happened to him?

No, Glitter and Helen would have told me. This couldn't be about the fighter. Dragon was in the ring now, getting ready to call him out, which meant that Donaghy was fine. Nothing had happened to him.

Then why was Helen looking at me like I was on the way to a funeral?

Dragon was still talking when the doors to the back room burst open. I turned toward the sound, hoping to get a glimpse of Donaghy so I could reassure myself that he was okay. The big men who doubled as bouncers pulled the cart forward, and the crowd parted for them. I couldn't see much from my place behind the bar, not through the crowds, but it had never really mattered to me before. There was never really much to see. Except today, that is. Today was different.

There were three zombies on the cart tonight, an extra treat for the spectators. The first two were small and nothing special as far as I could tell, although not much was visible other than the tops of their heads. The third zombie, however, was so tall that he dwarfed the other two.

"Do you see how big that one is?" I said, not even sure who I was talking to.

My eyes were on the dead as the men pulled the cart forward. Not only was Dragon upping the odds by adding a third zombie, but he was throwing in one that had to be taller than even Donaghy.

"Wasn't Dragon's choice." Helen's gravelly voice came from

my other side. When I glanced her way, the waitress's hand was shaking even harder than it had earlier as she took a drag off her cigarette. "Somebody brought that one in this morning. Told Dragon he had to add the thing to the fight today."

"Who?" I asked, turning to face the older woman completely.

She didn't meet my gaze as she sucked in another mouthful of chemicals. "Somebody high up. That's all I know." Smoke came out with the words, hitting me in the face, but I didn't care.

Why would someone *high up* have any say in the fight? Why would they care?

The dread that had been sitting in my stomach all day grew until I found myself wrapping my hands around my stomach. This had to be about Donaghy. Had they decided to finally finish him off? It would make sense, especially if they'd found a new fighter to showboat across what was left of the country.

By the time I turned back to face the ring, the zombies were chained up and ready for the fight. Donaghy made his way out of the back room and the crowd went nuts, screaming his name. Men and women slapped him on the back as he passed, but as usual, he kept his head down. The closer he got to the ring, the more my stomach ached.

I hadn't gotten a chance to say goodbye to him, and I suddenly found myself wishing that I'd paid more attention to the atmosphere when I'd come in tonight. I'd been too preoccupied with what was happening in my own life, and now I'd missed my opportunity.

When Donaghy stepped into the ring and took his place at Dragon's side, I saw that I'd been right. The third zombie was a good six inches taller than the fighter. Now that I was able to get a better look at the creature, though, I was relieved to see that the zombie was thin. Long and lanky. He might have towered over Donaghy, but he was all decaying arms and legs. Maybe there was still a chance.

"I've never even *met* anyone that tall," Glitter whispered.

"I have," I said, my eyes on the lanky zombie as he pulled against his chains, trying to get at the fighter. "My uncle was—" The words died on my lips when all the air whooshed from my lungs in one violent burst.

Joshua had been six feet seven inches tall, but thin. Gangly.

Just like the zombie in the ring was. He'd died shortly after Dad disappeared. Some kind of accident in the lab. He'd been exposed to the virus...

No.

I shook my head as I moved around the bar, my gaze on the tall zombie. The handlers pulled the levers, releasing the creatures from their chains, but the tall zombie's back was to me and I couldn't see his face. I needed to get a good look at him.

"Meg?" Glitter called after me. "Come back!"

I ignored her and pushed my way through the crowd, trying to get closer to the ring. All around me, men cheered, but I was too short to see what was going on. Suggestive comments were thrown my way, but they barely sank in as I shoved the stinking men and women aside with only one goal in mind. I had to know if it was him.

By the time I reached the edge of the ring, one of the two smaller zombies was already down, his head smashed into a putrid puddle of black blood and bone. Donaghy had the other one pinned to the ground, his foot pressed against the thing's back as he wrestled with the tall one. This one wasn't as decomposed as the other two were, meaning he'd been turned more recently. His blood was still thick and black, though. Thankfully. If it was brown, it would have meant that his heart could still be pumping, struggling, clinging to life even though he was already beyond saving.

Donaghy had the tall zombie by the neck as the thing snapped his teeth in the fighter's direction, but his back was still to me. His hair was shaggy and dark brown, with just a hint of gray at the temples. Just like Joshua's had been. Still, the color alone didn't prove anything. Lots of people had hair that color. It couldn't be my uncle. I was imagining things.

Still not satisfied, I pushed through the crowd, keeping close to the ring as I worked my way around to the other side. I turned the corner just as Donaghy twisted the creature around, and everything froze. The monster's face was decayed and his features distorted, his brown eyes milky and unseeing.

Still, something about his face *was* familiar.

No. It couldn't be. I was letting my imagination run wild. All the crazy things going on around me recently had me seeing things

199

that weren't real.

I gripped the side of the ring, my fingers aching from the pressure as I looked the zombie over, trying to find something that would dispute the evidence in front of me. His shirt was torn and stained, and there was nothing familiar about it. His pants, too, were simple and common.

Donaghy twisted the thing away, once again turning the creature's back to me. The struggle increased in intensity, and somehow the zombie managed to get his hand wrapped around the fighter's arm. His fingers dug in and I took a deep breath, praying he didn't break the skin. Donaghy twisted him again, and the lights from above flashed off the band on the zombie's ring finger, forcing all the air out of my lungs.

I knew that ring.

"No," I moaned just as Donaghy managed to get the zombie down.

People shot me looks of disgust, which only got more threatening a second later when the fighter slammed his boot into the zombie's head. A scream of agony ripped its way out of me, and my legs wobbled. If the crowd hadn't been pressed against me so tightly, I would have collapsed for sure.

Tears streamed down my face and my body shook, but somehow I managed to make my legs work. I pushed my way through the crowd, heading for the door to the cage as Donaghy moved to finish off the zombie that used to be my uncle. The heel of his boot slammed into Joshua's head and the splintering crack of bone echoed through the air. Somehow with the stomp of his boot, the fighter managed to crush my heart as well as the zombie's skull.

Donaghy turned to take care of the third and final zombie just as I reached the door. I grabbed for the clasp, my fingers shaking as they tried to get it undone. I was out of my mind. Clueless about what I planned to do. I just knew that my uncle was there. That he was dead.

Someone grabbed me from behind before I was able to get the door open, wrapping their arms around me. "Not so fast," a deep, male voice whispered in my ear, his tone firm but not threatening.

I was shaking and crying, but I didn't fight him when he pulled me away from the ring. I couldn't look away from the rotting corpse of Joshua, practically smeared across the floor of the ring. My legs wobbled, but the man at my back held me up.

"Easy now," the voice said in my ear. Soothing and calm. "I ain't gonna let you fall."

The third zombie went down and the crowd around me roared. The man holding me stepped back when Dragon pushed his way past us. Then the door was open, and even though I wanted to move, I couldn't.

"Gotta calm down. Don't let 'em know that you know."

I nodded as I swallowed down my anguish.

He was right. Whoever the man at my back was, he was right. I had to stay in control. I couldn't let anyone know that I recognized the zombie in the ring.

Running my arm across my face, I wiped away the tears. The man at my back loosened his grip, but didn't let go. Almost like he wanted to make sure I was able to hold myself up before he stepped away. My legs wobbled, but stayed firm when I put weight on them.

"I'm okay," I said, twisting to face the man.

Gray eyes almost hidden behind a mop of equally gray hair greeted me. The beard on his face was as thick and wild as the hair on his head was, masking his features. Still, something about him was familiar...

The note!

"You," I gasped just as the crowd pushed forward.

The man took a step back, leaving me alone as the crowd around us shifted and moved. I pushed against them, trying to stay next to the man who seemed to know everything going on in my life, but the current of bodies surrounding me was too strong. I blinked, and just like that the man was gone. Swallowed by a sea of people.

"Meg!" Donaghy was at my side a second later, concern written all over his face. "What the hell just happened? I saw you try to open the gate."

I swallowed and my gaze moved past him, to the ring where men were already cleaning up the mess that used to be my uncle. The crowd around us thinned, but there were still too many people who might hear what I had to say, and the gray man was right. I needed to be careful.

I leaned forward, pressing my lips against Donaghy's ear. "I can't tell you right now, but I need you to do something for me. Can you?" I pulled back long enough to meet his gaze, and he nodded. "Get the ring off the tall zombie's finger for me. Please."

Donaghy was frowning when I pulled away, but he only hesitated for a split second before heading back into the ring.

I watched as he said something to the men cleaning up the dead. One of them slapped the fighter on the back, and I recognized him from the day outside the walls. For the first time, found myself wondering what had happened to the other guy. The one who had been bitten. I hadn't seen him since then, and it looked like Dragon had already hired his replacement.

"Want a trophy, huh?" The man in the ring laughed and Donaghy gave him a rare smile. "Go on, then."

The fighter dug through the remains, his broad back and shoulders blocking my view. Less than ten seconds later, he was standing. When he climbed out of the ring, he grabbed my arm and wordlessly pulled me toward the back room.

Neither one of us said a word until we were inside the holding room and the door was shut behind us, and even then the only thing I could mutter was, "Did you get it?"

Donaghy nodded as he slipped the ring into my hand, his eyes holding mine and seeming to penetrate the darkness of the room.

I curled my fingers around the little band of gold, feeling like it weighed a hundred pounds. It was cool against my palm and moist with the black blood of the zombie Donaghy had ripped it from. Logically, I knew that creature wasn't my uncle. Not anymore. Of course, knowing that didn't ease the ache in my heart. It was like losing him all over again.

"You going to tell me what's going on?" Donaghy finally said.

I took a deep breath through my nose, then blew it out of my mouth, hoping to ease the pain in my chest. It didn't work. "That was my uncle."

Donaghy took a step back. "What?"

"There were all kinds of unanswered questions surrounding my Dad's disappearance. Questions I now know were justified. At the time, though, it was mainly my mom who was asking them. Add to that the many rumors we'd heard over the years about my uncle still being alive, and she seemed to come unraveled almost overnight.

"I don't know if Joshua believed the rumors or if he was just humoring Mom. He worked at the CDC—he was a doctor—and he started poking around. I wasn't even sure what he was doing, and I guess at this point none of us will ever know, but less than a week after Dad disappeared, there was an accident in one of the labs and Joshua was exposed to the newest strain of the virus."

"An accident?" Donaghy said, and I nodded. "And he died?"

"This new strain works faster than the others, and by the time Parvarti, my aunt, arrived to tell him goodbye, Joshua was past verbal communication. Since he was infected with the virus, they couldn't allow her to bury his body. They swore they would dispose of him humanely—"

My voice broke and I tightened my grip on the ring. I had no clue why Parv hadn't gotten it when she went to say goodbye, but I knew I had to give it to her now. And tell her—as well as everyone else in my family—what happened here tonight. I didn't know why the government delivered Joshua here, but it had to be a message. A very nasty one.

"Were you here when they brought him in?" I asked, tearing my gaze away from the floor so I could look at Donaghy once again. "Helen said someone brought him. Told Dragon he had to be added to the fight tonight."

"Yes." Donaghy let out a deep breath. "I thought they were trying to get rid of me. It was the only thing that made sense at the time."

"Maybe they were," I said, shrugging. "Two birds with one stone."

Donaghy was nodding when the door behind us was thrown open, and I spun around to find Dragon standing there.

His eyes were narrowed when he stepped inside, but when he saw us, confusion clouded his vision. "What the hell is going on in here? I expected to walk in and find you two going at it."

I slipped Joshua's ring onto my thumb even though it was covered in blood. "Nothing."

"Nothing?" Dragon stepped closer. "You're supposed to be working and you tell me nothing. You almost rip the door to the ring open during a fight, and all you have to say is *nothing*."

I slunk back, but Donaghy stepped in front of me before I could respond. "She was scared. Thought the zombie had gotten his teeth into me."

Dragon's eyes narrowed even more as they moved back and forth between the two of us. "Something going on here that I need to know about?"

"Just killing some time before I get shipped back to DC," Donaghy said, not looking at me. "Can't blame a guy for wanting to get laid by somebody who isn't covered in lice and losing most of their teeth. Right?"

I tried to curl into myself so I looked hurt by his words, and it was much easier than I expected it to be. My insides were raw and achy, only the pain had nothing to do with the implication that Donaghy was just using me for sex. It was because all I could think about was how I was going to tell my aunt what happened here tonight.

Dragon exhaled as he jerked his head toward the door. "Whatever you do, do it on your own time. Got it?"

"Yeah. Sorry." I slinked past Donaghy, not looking up to meet his or my angry boss's gaze.

Dragon didn't follow and neither did the fighter. The place was nearly empty, and the few patrons still at the bar were crowded around Glitter, hanging on her every word. The girl sure knew how to work the crowd. It got her tips, too.

She caught my gaze as I stepped behind the bar, and the look of pity in her gray eyes reminded me of the man who had stopped me from opening the cage. In the middle of everything, I'd totally forgotten about the sudden reappearance of the mysterious gray man. Where the hell had he come from and why? Was he watching over me like some fairy godmother of the apocalypse?

On the other side of the bar, Helen was watching me closely, almost like she wanted to make sure I wasn't going to fall apart. Her concern made sense now. Like Donaghy, she probably assumed they'd brought that zombie in to finish him off and she thought I'd take it hard. I would have too, although probably not as hard as this.

I looked away from the older woman and tried to focus on my job for a change. It would have been nice if it weren't such a mindless task. A distraction would have been welcome right about now.

# CHAPTER TWENTY-ONE

## Donaghy

I tried to head after Meg, but Dragon stepped between me and the door, blocking my way.

"You listen here," he said, speaking so low that I almost had to lean forward to hear him. "I'm the last person who would normally try to stop someone from getting his jollies, but the girls in my bar are off limits. Understand?"

"Off limits?" I repeated the words like I'd never heard them before.

Dragon nodded and I clenched my hands into fists, having to stop myself from punching him right in the damn face. I knew he was screwing Helen, so it only made sense that I'd have suspicions about his relationship with Glitter, but this was too far. Even if it meant a ticket back to DC, there was no way in hell I was going to let this asshole put his hands on Meg.

"Don't you fucking touch her," I growled, stepping closer.

Dragon's right eyebrow shot up, and his eyes narrowed to slits. "You telling me what to do in my own place?"

I clenched my jaw, holding back the angry words I wanted to hurl at him. If I got sent back to DC, I wouldn't be able to help Meg do anything. Not look for her Dad, and definitely not keep this asshole off her.

"No." The word shot itself from between my teeth with so much force that it felt like I'd spit in Dragon's face.

The bar owner grinned, showing off the gap in his mouth where his teeth used to be. "That's what I thought." He slapped me on the arm and I flinched when my fist almost shot out. "Besides, I have no intention of laying a finger on her."

I relaxed even though I wasn't sure if I believed him. "You don't?"

"No." Dragon rolled his shoulders back and the muscles popped. "I'm keeping an eye on her for someone. Making sure she's safe. Same as Glitter."

The conversation I heard this morning ran through my head. Maybe he was telling the truth. "Who?"

"Nobody." The other man waved his hand like he was trying to brush my question away. "Just an old friend."

Something wasn't sitting right with me, though, and it wasn't just the old friend or the fact that I suspected it was the same man who'd given that note to Meg. It had to do with what Dragon had said this morning, after the zombie got dropped off.

He turned to head back into the bar, but I stopped him in his tracks when I said, "You knew that zombie was Meg's uncle."

Dragon turned, slowly, his eyes once again narrowed.

I lifted my hands. "You're the one who said it was a message, then Meg told me it was her uncle and I connected the dots. It wasn't hard. What I want to know is: How did *you* know it was her uncle?"

Dragon's jaw ticked. "Helen works at the CDC."

That I hadn't known, but it still didn't explain much of anything. "So?"

"So I met the guy. Everybody knows the family, and everybody knows about the bullshit rumors going around. It made sense that they sent him here as some kind of message for the girl. What that message is, I don't know. Who knows what she's gotten herself mixed up in." Dragon took another step toward me. "What I do know is this: You better watch who you talk to about all this. You claim to like this girl, but you're not going to do anybody any favors by running your mouth. Least of all her."

Dragon's words were steady and his gaze even as he held mine, but I didn't buy it. He knew more than he was letting on, and it had something to do with the man he'd been talking to this morning.

At this point, though, I couldn't let him know that I was suspected anything.

"No worries." I matched his tone. "I'm just trying to look out for her too."

Dragon held my gaze for a few seconds longer before turning away. His jaw was clenched like he was holding in a barrage of curse words as he headed out into the bar.

I followed him, silently. Thinking it all through. I didn't know where this man fit into the puzzle that seemed to be Meg's life, but I was positive he did. According to everything I knew about her, the first time Meg had set foot in this place was the night she was attacked. I found it hard to believe she'd met Dragon anywhere else, and she'd never indicated that they knew each other outside this bar. But he had an *old friend* who wanted to make sure Meg was safe? Why? And who?

I needed to keep my ears open.

# CHAPTER TWENTY-TWO

## Meg

THE Atlanta evening was hot and muggy when I stopped in front of the gate. Overhead, the moon was tucked behind a blanket of clouds, barely allowing any rays through to illuminate the wall. I didn't need it. I'd climbed the ladder to the guard towers hundreds, if not thousands, of times over the years. Between Dad, Parvarti, and Al working the fence, there had been no shortage of people for me to visit, and I liked sitting up there. Watching the darkness of old Atlanta and imagining that life might one day be able to spread beyond these walls again. That there still existed the possibility that we could start over.

It seemed like a lost cause now.

The metal ladder groaned under me, its rusted rungs chafing my palms as I pulled myself up. The heaviness that had settled inside me this afternoon was not only still present, but worse than ever before. It grew with each rung I climbed, every inch bringing me closer and closer to my aunt.

I hadn't seen her all week. I knew she was avoiding going

home—avoiding all of us, probably—and I couldn't blame her. She was trying to move on and we were all reminders of what she'd lost.

The darkness didn't ease when I reached the top, so I paused to allow my eyes to adjust. Someone turned my way, cloaked in the shadows of the guard tower, and I blinked. Parv's small frame came into view after only a second, no more than a black outline against the dark sky.

"Megan?" Her voice was a total contrast of the person I'd known all these years. She was small and soft-spoken, but to me she had always seemed larger than life. Tough as nails and ready to take on anything. She'd had to be to rise to the rank of Judicial Officer of New Atlanta.

"It's me," I said, a sudden feeling of déjà vu coming over me. Hadn't I said those exact same words to Mom last night when I got home?

I pulled myself forward, keeping my body low so I didn't topple over the side and fall into the zombie world that existed beyond the wall. It was so dark that even though I was familiar with the area, I had to feel my way. Most people turned on a lantern up here. Maybe the darkness was comforting for Parv.

"What are you doing up here?" she asked as I settled in next to her.

She moved a few things around and a second later a match flared, the small spark turning into a tiny flame that lit the space just enough to allow me to make out my aunt's face. Shadows, long and black, played across her features, making her cheeks appear sunken and her eyes nothing more than dark pits. It sent a shiver down my spine that I couldn't shrug off until after the lantern had flared to life between us. Only then could I see my aunt clearly, and only then were her gentle brown eyes a comfort.

"I wanted to talk to you," I said, shifting so I had my legs pulled up against my chest. "You haven't been around much."

Parv exhaled as she nodded. "I know, I'm sorry. It's been hard pulling myself out of this. I've had to do it before, but this time…"

She swallowed and looked away, and I found myself wondering if she was talking about her family or someone else. I knew that everyone in her life had died from the initial outbreak, and that she never got to say goodbye to them, but something about the expression on her face told me that the loss she was referring to was something else altogether. Someone she had loved before Joshua, maybe?

"How's your mom?" Parv asked, her gaze focused on the dark city in front of us.

"She was better last night. A little more together. Even though she was out of it again this morning, I can't help hoping it's a good sign." Parv nodded in understanding. "She had this crazy dream that Angus came into her room. That he told her to get her shit together or something like that."

I chuckled, but it was cut short when Parv turned her whole body to face me.

"Angus came to her room?"

"In a dream," I said, wondering if I'd forgotten to mention that part.

"Right. Of course." Parv shook her head. "What did you want to talk to me about?"

"Um..."

For a second I couldn't think, too caught up in conspiracy theories that were as old as I was. Then the reason I was here came screaming back and I almost burst into tears. The last thing I wanted to do was kick someone when they were down, but that was exactly what I was about to do and I hated myself a little for it. Not that I had a choice.

"It's about Joshua," I finally said. "Something happened today."

Parv closed her eyes and nodded. "What is it? Just tell me."

I took a deep breath, and when I blew it out, the words came with it. Everything that had happened. Me getting a job, the note given to me by the stranger, the warnings I'd been given, how I was sent outside the fence, and finally seeing my uncle as a zombie this evening. The whole time I talked, Parv kept her eyes shut. They were clenched tight, but the emotions that played across her face were so raw and painful that I physically hurt for her.

When I was done, I slipped the ring off my thumb and held it out to her. The light from the lantern highlighted the design etched into the silver metal.

Parv opened her eyes, which were shimmering with tears, and took the ring from my hand, rubbing it between her fingers like just having it made her stronger.

"Thank you." She slipped it on her thumb, just like I had earlier, then took a deep breath. "I think I always suspected they hadn't taken care of him the way they said they would. Just like I always knew it was no accident. Maybe that's why it was so hard to deal with it." A tear slid down her cheek and she swiped it away almost violently. "You know, we resisted falling in love for a long time. We'd both been stung before and I guess we didn't think the pain was worth it. When we first got here, we were only living together out of convenience. We'd been together for months, on the road and in Colorado, but Joshua and I were both naturally quiet people, and we really hadn't taken the time to get to know each other.

"Time moved on and we became...comfortable. It was two years after we got to Atlanta before we admitted to one another how we felt. By then Luke and Charlie had already been born, and your mom was pregnant with Margot. I was in my mid-twenties and Joshua was pushing thirty, and we figured it would be a good time to start a family."

Parv stopped like the words were too hard to get out, and I held my breath. I'd never heard most of this stuff before. There wasn't a time that I could think back on and remember Parv and Joshua not being together, and I'd had no idea that they'd ever wanted children. They'd always been an odd couple. Joshua, taller than anyone I'd ever known and so pale that he looked like he spent his life in the lab, hidden away from the sun. Parv had barely come up to his chest, and next to him her dark skin had washed him out even more. But as far as I knew, they'd always been happy.

"You couldn't have kids?" I asked when she didn't say anything else.

Parv tore her gaze off the ring circling her thumb and focused on me. "It never happened for us."

There was so much space between those words that I couldn't help trying to search the gaps for some hidden meaning. I couldn't find one, of course. Maybe Parv had a baby when I was too young to remember and it had died. It happened so much in the early days that it seemed like a logical conclusion to jump to.

My aunt let out a deep breath, and when she inhaled she

looked like a stronger person. Like her old self. "Tell me more about this note and the man who gave it to you."

"Okay..." I hadn't come here to burden my aunt, but if she could figure some of this out, it might help all of us. "He was older. Sixty, maybe. Thin. Gray hair that was wild and a beard that was just as crazy. And he had these gray eyes that—" I broke off short of telling her that they had reminded me of Dad. I didn't want to sound like Mom. Crazy and out-of-touch with reality.

"That's it?" Parv asked. "Nothing else really stood out?"

"Other than the fact that he popped up again tonight in Dragon's? No."

"Did you tell anyone else about all this?"

"I talked to Al when I first got the note, but he freaked out. He tried to act like it was no big deal, but I could tell he was nervous."

"If you were in the apartment," Parv said. "It's understandable. We never know when they're listening."

*They*? Now who sounded like Mom?

"Who exactly are you talking about when you say *they*?"

"We aren't sure exactly. It could be just the government—Jackson's dad—or it could run deeper. The CDC. For all we know, it's all connected. We can't ignore the rumors that have surrounded Angus for years. That's why Joshua originally agreed to be Dr. Helton's apprentice. Before the virus hit, he'd worked as an ER doctor, and he was better suited for trauma than research. But they were low on doctors and needed help creating a vaccine, and we'd only been here for a few months when Dr. Helton approached him about it. The timing was good."

"Why?"

"There was this man named Jim who left Colorado with us." Parv paused and patted my leg. "He was a good friend of your biological father's, actually."

Jim? Hadn't that been the name of the zombie slayer Luke introduced me to? The one who'd said he knew my parents? No. It couldn't be. Could it? Everything else seemed to be connected these days, so I shouldn't be surprised, but how did Luke know him?

Parv sighed like the memories made it difficult for her to breathe. When she continued, her voice was quieter. "Anyway, we got separated from Jim on the way here, and when he finally arrived, he had a woman with him. Amira was deaf, but she could read lips, and while in quarantine a couple guards said some things in front of her about a *cabbage* and a *vegetable*. She'd gotten the impression that they were talking about a person. Since we'd already heard rumors that Angus was alive and being kept under lock and key, it seemed like a good idea to check it out. So, Joshua went to work with Dr. Helton at the CDC."

"He never found anything?"

"No," Parv said firmly. "But there were areas he was never allowed access to. Even after almost twenty years. Top secret sections that were off limits. Guarded."

What the hell was at the CDC that they didn't want people to see? Especially other doctors.

"Parv," I said, choosing my words carefully while inside me, something that felt an awful lot like hope tried to force itself to the surface. "Do you think my dad is still alive?"

My aunt held my gaze, her dark eyes boring into mine while my heart beat faster and faster with each passing second.

"I do." When she finally said it, the words were so soft that they almost got caught on the breeze. "After Jim got back and the rumors grew worse, Joshua tested Axl's blood. He was immune."

I squeezed my eyes shut when they filled with tears. All the horror of what Dad could be going through hit me with so much force that it felt like the wall under me had collapsed and I was being crushed under the rubble. If Parv was right, then Dad was being used as an experiment. Poked, prodded, possibly injected with things. He was probably in horrible pain.

"So the CDC knew Dad couldn't be infected?" I asked, my eyes still closed.

"They did."

"Why didn't they tell him?"

"Only they can answer that question for sure."

"Why now?" I whispered. "Why take him now? If he was immune, why didn't they take him back then?"

Parv's hand covered mine and I opened my eyes. "I think they didn't need him yet because they had Angus. Plus, the city was still new, so they were probably short on resources. I don't think Angus died the way the claimed, but instead they kept him as a prisoner for years. Used his blood to create new vaccines as the virus mutated. I think two prisoners would have been too hard for them to control, so they kept your father's immunity a secret instead. Either Angus has recently died for real—" Parv paused to take a deep breath. "—or the virus has finally mutated in a way that doesn't respond to Angus's blood. This is just a theory, but one Joshua and Al happened to agree with."

*Al.* So my uncle knew all this. No wonder he was terrified when I brought him that note.

"I can't believe this," I said, allowing the tears to stream down my cheeks. "Why did we stay if you guys thought this might happen?"

"Because we didn't know anything for sure, and even with the risk of something like this happening, this city was better than anything *out there.* You have no idea what we went through before we made it here, and we had to believe that we could have a real life inside the wall. Plus, by the time we formed these theories, Al and Lila already had two kids, and your parents had you and Margot to worry about. Leaving the city meant putting all your lives at risk. There were unsanctioned towns, but they got raided and overrun all the time. Plus, they didn't get help from the little bit of government that we did have. We briefly talked about going back to Colorado, but before we could figure out a way to make it happen, the town was breached. Everyone we knew there was killed." Parv squeezed my hand. "We did the best we could with the information we had."

"It's like putting a Band-Aid on an amputation," I muttered, repeating one of Al's favorite sayings.

Despite the sadness surrounding us, Parv let out a little laugh. "Al never has lost his sense of humor."

"I hope he never does," I said, wiping the tears from my face. "What about Mom? Did she know all this?"

"Yes and no." Parv sighed. "She would be furious if she knew your dad kept all this from her, but when we found out he was immune she was pregnant and he didn't want to scare her. Or dampen her good mood. Then she was happy for a long time, and after everything, I think he just didn't want that to change. Then Margot died…" I swallowed and Parv patted my hand again. "She heard the rumors about Angus and we all talked about it, but we kept the majority of what was going on a secret from her. It's how your dad wanted it."

"What now? What do we do about Dad? We can't just leave him in there, but how the hell are we going to get into the CDC?"

"I'm open for suggestions." Parv pulled her hand off mine and stared at the ring on her right thumb, putting it next to the matching one on her left ring finger. "We need someone on the inside. Problem is, there isn't anyone. Not anymore."

I started to nod, but stopped when I realized she was wrong. There was Jackson.

If anyone knew what was going on inside the CDC, it would be him. His father was in charge of the entire country, plus Jackson had been doing an apprenticeship at the CDC for years. Since he was fifteen. He had to know something, and if he didn't, he could get information easily enough.

Only I hadn't spoken to him in days and after what Ticker told me the other night, I wasn't planning to. Ever again if I could help it.

It couldn't be too late to smooth this whole thing out, though.

"I could talk to Jackson."

Parv put her hand on my leg again, only this time it was more forceful. As if she was trying to stop me from running off. "That's a big risk, Megan. I know you two have been close for a long time, but he's the Regulator's son and you know your dad never trusted him. We have no way of knowing how much Jackson knows or how deep into all this he really is. He could be innocent, or he could know every single dark secret his father has."

I thought about all the stuff Matt and Ticker told me, comparing it with the Jackson I always thought I knew. The one who'd been sweet and caring with me. The one who acted understanding. Matt had called him a sociopath. Could he be? If so, I would be taking a big risk.

But it could be my only chance...

"I'll be subtle," I said almost to myself, then turned to face my aunt. "I'll just feel him out."

"I don't think it's a good idea, Megan." Parv squeezed my knee before letting out a sigh. "But I have a feeling I won't be able to talk you out of this. You're too stubborn. Just like your mom. Both of them."

Her smile was small in the dim light of the lantern, and I

mimicked it.

"What next?" I asked after a few seconds of silence. "Are you going to talk to Al about all this?"

"I need to," she said, "but finding privacy is going to be tough. We need a place away from the prying eyes of the government, but with our jobs, that isn't going to be easy."

She had a point. Even up here we were taking a risk, and the apartment was totally out of the question. The streets would be too out in the open as well. Anyone could watch us or eavesdrop on our conversation. We needed a place that was either outside the reach of the government, or so insignificant that they would never even consider bugging it.

"What about Dragon's Lair?" I asked, an idea forming in my head. "There's no way anyone would care what goes on inside the bar."

Parv nodded slowly. "That could work, but I'd still need to get a message to Al. If we're on the right track, then there's no doubt in my mind that we're being watched, and you are for sure. We'd need it to be subtle. "

"Charlie can do it." It was the perfect solution. "She just started an apprenticeship with Al anyway, so no one would suspect that she's passing him a message. She already told me she's going to stop by the bar tomorrow for the fight. When she does, I'll give her a note to take to her dad."

"It could work," Parv said. "We'll shoot for eleven. Al will still be working, so no one will be suspicious if he heads to the entertainment district."

I got to my feet and stretched. Sharing my worries with my aunt had helped ease the heaviness in me some, and knowing that Parv, Al, and I were going to meet tomorrow gave me hope that we might be able to figure this whole thing out. But it was late and I had an early shift, followed by a few hours on my feet in Dragon's Lair. Plus, somewhere in the middle of all that, I needed to get in touch with Jackson and try to make up with him.

"I need to get some sleep," I said through a yawn.

My aunt stayed where she was as I made my way across the wall toward the ladder, keeping my body low so I didn't fall. My feet were still on the top rung when she called out to me.

I looked her way and she held the ring up. "Thanks for this. It

217

hurts, but I'm glad that I finally know what happened to him. It's nice to have some closure. I wasn't sure if I would ever get it."

"I know the feeling," I said, letting out a deep sigh.

"We'll find him," Parv said firmly. "I promise."

I nodded as I headed down the ladder, hoping that she was right, but unable to ignore the doubt inside me. All we had were theories right now, and no real plan to speak of. Hopefully, we could come up with something and fast.

# CHAPTER TWENTY-THREE

## Donaghy

THE sound of one of my guards trying to cough up a lung woke me at the ass crack of dawn. I threw my arm over my head, hoping to drown out the noise, and squeezed my eyes shut tighter, but it only made his coughs echo through my brain. The cement walls of the back room magnified the sound, and every time he hacked it vibrated through the air, bouncing off the stone until it slammed into me.

Now that Jackson had kicked me out of his house, waking up was more of a shock to my system than I would ever want to endure this early in the morning. The stink of death clung to everything in the bar, seeping from the holding room and making the stuffy atmosphere even more stifling. The sheets under me probably hadn't been that clean to begin with, but now they were soaked through with my sweat and sticking to my body like a bucket of glue had been poured over me. As much as I hated the prick, I found myself wishing Jackson and Meg hadn't gotten in a fight.

More coughs echoed through the air, this time coming from the opposite corner of the room. I pulled my arm away from my face as I twisted on the cot, the metal frame and springs groaning under me. The room was dark but not pitch black, and even with the shadows stretching across the small space, I could make out the other two beds. Both guards were curled up under blankets—just the sight of it made me sweat even more than I already was. The tremors moving through their bodies' rocked the wobbly beds so hard that they looked like they were on the verge of falling apart.

The guard let out another cough that rattled through his chest in terrifying sickly way. A second later, he groaned. I pushed myself up into a half-sitting position, trying to get a good look at the guy. His face was visible, but just barely, poking out of the blanket that was draped over him. He reminded me of an infant who'd been swaddled by his mother. His cheeks were flushed and his forehead was moist with sweat.

"You sick?" I asked despite my better judgment.

These assholes had gone out of their way to show how little they gave a shit about me, so I tried to tell myself I was just asking because I didn't want to get whatever this dude had. It wasn't true, though. Despite how hard I'd tried to own the I-didn't-give-a-damn-about-the-world attitude over the past year, it was all an act. My mom—God rest her soul—had raised me to care about people, and it was a habit I couldn't seem to shake. Even if the people around me didn't deserve it, I found myself unable to turn my back on them. Like when I'd stumbled upon Meg in the bathroom that night. Even if she hadn't looked helpless, I would have run to her aide. I would have killed the guy in exactly the same way even if I'd stepped into that room and found Meg ready to slit his throat herself, because that's what I'd been raised to do: look out for others.

On the other cot, the older guard pushed himself up, and his gaze moved across the room to the guard I was staring at. With the old guy up I was able to get a better look at him. He didn't seem any healthier than the first one did. The older man's skin was pale but his cheeks were pink. Sweat glistened on his face while tremors shook his body. He also had dark rings under his eyes that made it look like he'd dropped ten pounds over night.

"Shit. Everybody was—" He hacked for a few seconds before spitting a big wad of phlegm on the cement floor. "About every other person at that strip club was coughing like crazy last night.

Looks like we caught what they all had."

I found it impossible to respond when the conversation I'd heard in the Regulator's house came back to me. Was this the flu he and his nasal friend had been talking about? I knew I couldn't rule it out, even if I didn't totally understand the point of it all. After what had gone down the night before, I believed with everything in me that the people in charge would do *anything* to meet their goal. What the goal was, I still didn't know, but it was something big and something a hell of a lot different than finding a cure for this whole zombie crisis.

The guards continued to cough, but my brain was wide awake now and I knew I'd never be able to get it to turn off enough to go back to sleep. My nerves were shot and I needed to calm the hell down. It didn't matter how early it was, I wanted a drink.

I threw myself out of bed and headed for the other room, my bare feet slapping against the cement floor as I went. Despite the humidity clinging to the air, the stone was cold against my skin. So chilly, in fact, that I hadn't even made it out of the holding room when a shiver ran up my spine. It was like that old superstition about someone walking over your grave, and it wasn't very far-fetched either. There was a hell of a good chance that I wouldn't make it out of this settlement alive, and thinking that had me even more unsettled than anything else that had happened so far. Which was saying a lot.

The main room was dark except for a few lights that shone down on the rows of booze lined up behind the bar. The glass sparkled as I rounded the counter, heading straight for the bottles. One drink should do the trick.

My hand was trembling when I poured myself a glass of whiskey, so much so that liquid sloshed across the counter. I ignored the mess and threw the drink back, closing my eyes when it burned its way down my throat. I didn't move, waiting for the alcohol to work its magic. When it didn't work, I opened my eyes poured another glass, once again spilling it. I didn't clean it up before tossing the second drink back, closing my eyes in a futile attempt to block out reality.

"You better wipe that up or Dragon will piss himself." Helen's gravelly voice echoed through the room, and I swear I almost pissed *myself*.

"Shit."

I opened my eyes to find her headed my way, wearing scrubs and already smoking. Her blue eyes were only a shade lighter than the clothes, and her short hair was wet and slicked down against her scalp like she'd just gotten out of the shower. She sucked in a mouthful of chemicals, allowing them to set up home in her chest as she crossed the room.

When she stopped in front of me, she opened her mouth and let it all out in one puff of smoke. "Little early to be drinking."

A cough echoed through the bar from the other room and Helen's eyes darted toward it. The cigarette was halfway to her mouth when her lips turned down, her hand frozen inches from their target.

When she looked back at me, she didn't blink. "Sick?"

"Coughing like crazy." I put down the empty glass and tried to hide my shaking hand.

Helen's sharp gaze caught the movement and she frowned even more. "It's going around." Her eyes flitted back up to mine as she took another drag. She didn't blink until after she'd let the smoke back out. "We were busy as hell at the CDC yesterday. So much so that I was dragged to the ER to work instead of doing my usual job."

"I didn't even know you worked there until Dragon told me last night."

The older woman nodded once. "I'm a nurse. Twenty years ago when this shit started, I was working in the ER. Right here in Atlanta. I watched the beds fill up, watched people die slow, horrible deaths. Watched loved ones cry their eyes out before following the people they'd been mourning to the grave. The bodies piled up, in the halls first, then later in the rooms. Stacked one on top of the other as we ran out of places to put them. It got to the point where we couldn't even take patients back to the beds. We just saw them in the waiting room. Not that it mattered. By then, most of the staff was just as sick and we knew there was nothing we could do." She took another drag off her cigarette, her hand shaking slightly. When she spoke again, smoke came out with the words. "I kept on working until the very end, waiting for my turn."

"But it never came."

"Not yet, anyway." She swallowed before pointing back toward the room my guards were still coughing away in. "You be sure to steer clear of them. Understand? This thing is contagious, and once you get it, you can kiss your ass goodbye. There's no coming back from it."

My stomach dropped. "People are dying?"

"Not yet, but they will. This comes through every few years and it's always the same. I've been working at the CDC since day one, so I've watched it all happen." She paused to take another drag, but her eyes were still glued to mine. "I've seen it *all*."

The smoke that came out of her mouth was so thick that it blocked her lips from view, but the words were loud and clear. She knew something, just like Dragon did. I'd seen the way Helen looked at Meg when the girl wasn't paying attention, and it was obvious that the older woman knew something about Axl or the family. Maybe not where Meg's dad was exactly, but something for sure.

"You've worked at the CDC for twenty years?" I asked, holding her gaze. "You must be pretty high up, then."

Helen's lips twitched like she was holding in a smile. "Sure am."

"Seen a lot."

"Sure have."

I waited for her to say more, but she just watched me as she smoked. I knew she wasn't going to give me any real information, but maybe if I could get her to allude to something it would help give us an idea where to go next. If she worked there, she must have seen something.

"Dragon said you knew Meg's uncle." I held my breath and waited. It was a big leap, but it could pay off.

"Joshua was a good man." Helen barely blinked. "It's a shame what happened to him."

"That's all?"

"Didn't know him that well. He worked in the labs. See, I've been around since the beginning, and over time my duties have expanded to include some of the more restricted areas." She put the cigarette between her lips, not looking away. Her mouth closed around the cancer stick, puckering as she sucked the chemicals in. After a second, she opened her mouth and let the smoke out. It floated into the air, making her face fuzzy.

"Aren't you afraid of cancer?" I asked, nodding toward the cigarette.

The bootlegged cigarettes that had replaced the ones previously manufactured in factories, back before the days of zombies, didn't have filters. There were also no real regulations when it came to making them, meaning who knew what the hell went into them. It wasn't like the surgeon general was around anymore to stamp warnings on packages.

Helen shrugged as she took another drag. The cigarette had burned down to almost nothing now, and the thick smell of tobacco was pungent. "There are worse ways to die these days. Much, much worse ways." She stood up straight. "I have to be going. See you tonight for the fight."

Helen headed for the door, not looking back and still smoking.

She wasn't wrong, especially if she and Dragon were involved in what I was starting to think they were involved in. A plan to overthrow Star or something very similar.

# CHAPTER TWENTY-FOUR

## Meg

THE second day on trash duty was even worse than the first. Partly because it was hotter than it had been the day before, but mostly because we found ourselves in shantytown shoveling up piles of trash.

Here life was harder. The people who inhabited these sorry excuses for homes rarely had enough of anything. Food was often scarce and electricity nonexistent. They cleaned themselves no more than once a week, if at all, utilizing the city bathhouses. They didn't have enough credits to buy the necessities, let alone bags or cans to store their garbage in. Typically, the trash was tossed into the alleys that ran between the houses where it was left to bake in the sun, rotting slowly and filling the air with the stink of failure and wanting and disappointment.

I did my best to focus on the job at hand so I didn't have to think about *what* I was shoveling, but the smell made it almost impossible. By the time trash day rolled around, the stench of shantytown was so foul that it was probably only matched by the stink of the zombies.

"Water break!" my crew leader called out, his voice ringing

through the air and rising above the sound of shovels scraping against the ground.

I wiped the moisture from my forehead as I turned, using the sleeve of my jumpsuit even though I knew it was a bad idea. There was no way some of this filth hadn't gotten on my clothes, and odds were it was now smeared across my face.

Only two shacks over, the other people on trash detail were busy sucking down lukewarm water. My own mouth felt like sandpaper, but I'd only taken one step when someone popped out of the alley right in front of me. The shovel was still in my hand when I reared back, and my heart was beating like mad, but the beady eyes that greeted me made me freeze before I'd had a chance to bash the guy's face in.

"Ticker?" I said, reaching to pull my mask away from my mouth and nose, then thinking better of it. I looked around to make sure no one was watching, then grabbed his arm and pulled him behind a shack where we would be hidden from the rest of the workers. "What the hell are you doing here?"

Ticker's right shoulder jerked. "Hiding. Matt and Jimmy, they went missing. Gone. Just like Stevie. Ticker's not going to let them get him, though. Not again." His eyes darted back and forth, for once not stopping on my chest. Not that he would be able to see anything with the jumpsuit I was wearing, but the fact that he wasn't even trying said something about his state of mind.

He looked terrified, his eyes even beadier than usual as they bounced around, not focusing on anything for more than two seconds before moving on to look at something else. And the spasm in his shoulder was constant. Up, down. Twitch, twitch. He looked like he was on the verge of a dance or having some kind of fit. Like seizures that never went away but were only mildly annoying. Ticker had never owned his name as much as he did right now.

"Calm down, Ticker. Tell me what happened," I said, trying to get him to focus on my face. "Did it have something to do with what you guys told me at Dragon's?" If it did, it might not be a good idea to talk there after all. Maybe there was nowhere safe from the prying ears and eyes of this new government.

*Big Brother is watching…*

A shiver ran through me when I remembered the party slogan

from that old novel I'd read in school. One of the few books that had stuck with me even after all these years, and only partly because it had chilled me to the bone. It had *felt* familiar. The decrepit state of the world those characters had lived in, crumbling buildings and broken lives. The first time I'd read it, I'd felt like the author had looked into the future and seen how things would turn out. Walls that, although sturdy, appeared hastily thrown together, their parts growing more and more rusted with each passing season. The flickering of lights in the hall that led to my apartment and the elevator that groaned in protest when it worked at all. That book had felt like the most prophetic thing I'd ever come across, and I'd found myself thinking that if the people in this city were smart, they'd study and worship it rather than bothering to pray to a man that had been nothing more than a loud-mouth asshole who'd just happened to be immune to all this shit.

Ticker's shoulder jerked, but he didn't answer my question.

"Are Matt and Jimmy dead?" I asked as calmly as I could, even though under my dirt covered and sweat-soaked jumpsuit, a shiver had run up my spine.

The kid shook his head twice, then nodded. "Don't know. No. I don't think so. After we met up with you, we went to another bar. Saw some guys there. Some guys we knew from work. They asked about you. Asked what happened outside the walls. How you lived. It was real weird." Ticker bounced up and down on the balls of his feet. "Matt didn't like the questions. Then Jimmy, he isn't that bright, he told them that we'd just seen you. That we talked. The guys at the bar had a lot more questions after that, but we got out of there. Jimmy isn't that bright."

People were asking about me. I wasn't sure who'd sent them, but I knew they were checking up on me and it very well could have put my crew's lives in danger.

"I'm sorry, Ticker," I said reaching out to him before I remembered that my gloves were covered in garbage. I dropped my arm to my side, clenching my hand into a fist like I was ready to punch someone.

"Watch your back. You hear?" Ticker's shoulder jerked again, and this time, his whole head bobbed. "They'll kill us all if they think we know something."

"I will, Ticker. Thank you."

His head bobbed a few times as he backed away, his eyes darting around like crazy. Then, without saying another word or even looking back at me, he spun on his heel and took off, disappearing around a corner only a few houses away.

When he was gone, I let out a deep breath. This was getting out of hand. Ticker, Matt, and Jimmy hadn't really told me anything concrete. They'd only repeated rumors. They hadn't hurt anyone or told me anything that I couldn't have found out on my own. Sure it had added to my suspicions, but they'd had no way of knowing that was going to happen.

"James!" someone called, making me jump.

"Coming." I took a deep breath, barely noticing the stench that surrounded me, before heading back around the corner.

My crew leader greeted me with narrowed eyes as he held a cup of water out. "When we take a water break, you drink. If you don't, you'll die of heat exhaustion out here."

He shoved the cup in my hand, then yelled for everyone to get back to work. I didn't even taste the water when I downed it, and for the rest of the day, I was so preoccupied that I barely smelled the trash I was shoveling.

I DIDN'T HAVE A LOT OF TIME AFTER MY SHIFT, WHICH meant I found myself running through the streets toward my apartment. My clothes were stuck to my body and the stench of chemicals from the decontamination shower stung my nostrils, but I didn't slow. I needed to get showered and changed—and hopefully cool off in the process—and check on Mom. She'd been out cold last night when I got home from talking to Parvarti, and even though I wanted to know if she was as lucid as she'd been the night before, I couldn't help being relieved. I wanted her back, but right now I didn't know what to tell her about Dad or Parv, or the mysterious gray man who'd popped into my life twice now.

The apartment was so quiet when I stepped into the living room that at first, I was sure she wasn't going to be home. Before I'd even had a chance to shut the front door, hope had bubbled up inside me. Maybe she'd gone to work today. Maybe she was back to her normal self and we'd be able to catch up soon, and then I could quit this stinking job.

But when I pushed her bedroom door open, all that hope melted away. Mom was asleep, curled up in the center of the bed with her mouth hanging open. She looked more like someone who had passed out from exhaustion than someone who was taking an afternoon nap, but she hadn't done a single thing in weeks that would make her this tired. Something just wasn't right here. It couldn't be.

Only, I didn't have time to think it through. I needed to get moving if I wanted to see Jackson before heading to Dragon's Lair. We needed to mend our relationship if I was going to get any information out of him.

When I was showered and once again wearing the black dress — with the plaid shirt over it — I headed out. The long sleeve shirt was going to make me start sweating all over again, but I needed to wear it until I could spill the beans about my new job to Jackson.

His house was on the other side of the settlement, and just like I'd thought, I was sweating by the time I reached it. I stopped on the doorstep and looked up, marveling at the luxury in front of me.

Even though Jackson and I had been friends for years and I'd always trusted him, there was a part of me that had never felt comfortable inside the Regulator's mansion. It wasn't until I'd gotten older that I'd realized why, though. How they lived had always felt *wrong*. Most of the people in Atlanta lived in buildings that had been renovated after the walls went up, and their apartments were small and cheap, often not even painted. Most had community bathrooms, meaning people had to fight for showers. Only a small percentage of the population had a real apartment, but even the converted office buildings were better than the shacks a lot of people lived in. Those people had nothing.

Now, standing in front of the house of the person I'd always thought I knew so well, I realized that I should have taken more notice of stuff like this earlier. Jackson had always been so good at playing on my emotions that it was easy for me to brush things off on his father, but it shouldn't have been. In all the years that we'd known each other, Jackson had never once acknowledged the struggles other people in this city lived with on a daily basis. He'd never looked at the shantytown and compared it with his own

229

house, and he'd never acted the least bit guilty for taking so much and giving so little in return.

If I didn't need to get information out of Jackson, I'd be more than happy to have him out of my life completely.

But I did need him, so I took a deep breath and rang the doorbell, and less than a minute later, the door opened.

Jackson didn't smile when he saw me, and he didn't pull the door open wider or ask me to come in. His gaze was cold and guarded, and I was pretty sure that for the first time in our friendship, I was getting a glimpse of the real Jackson Star.

"Meg," he said flatly.

The sun's rays seemed to be intensified by the plaid shirt I was wearing, and his gaze wasn't helping. A bead of sweat ran down my back and I shifted from foot to foot, pushing the sleeves up in a futile attempt to cool off.

Jackson's gaze moved over my shirt and he pulled the door open a bit wider, but he didn't look concerned about my comfort. Just curious. "Why are you wearing that? It's ninety degrees."

"I'm an idiot." I let out a nervous laugh and unbuttoned the shirt.

My hands were shaking when I slid it off, and the expression that flashed in Jackson's eyes only made it worse. The look of indifference was gone, and it now seemed like he was trying to memorize how I looked.

"Why the hell are you wearing that?" he asked with a little more animation in his voice.

"I've been trying to figure out how to explain everything to you. Why I was upset the other night and why I pushed you away. Things have been so backward and upside down for me, and I've been feeling so alone for the last few weeks. I knew you would try to take the burden from me if I let you, and it just didn't seem fair. It still doesn't. We've been going around and around for years, and even though I always knew you wanted more out of our relationship, I also knew I couldn't give it to you. And I thought taking things from you when I wasn't ready to commit to more would be unfair, and I didn't want to hurt you, but I didn't have the energy to do more than just push you away." I took a deep breath, looking away from Jackson's intense gaze when heat spread across my cheeks. "I had to get a job in the entertainment district so Mom and I wouldn't lose our apartment. I've been waitressing at Dragon's Lair."

"What?" His voice was so sharp that I couldn't keep my gaze from meeting his. "Are you nuts, Meg? After you almost got attacked there?"

"See, I knew you'd argue and you wouldn't understand!" I said, closing the gap between us so I could grab his hand. It was a difficult thing to do knowing the damage these same hands had inflected on Stevie Jones, but I forced myself to commit. "But it's ended up being a good thing. It's made me realize how much I need you in my life."

The last sentence almost got stuck in my throat, but I tried to pretend the Jackson in front of me was the person I'd always thought he was. The one that I now knew had all been for show, but the one who'd made me care about him. The one I'd thought I loved like a brother.

Jackson's expression remained stony at first, but it only took a couple seconds for the coldness to melt away. He turned on the smile that I'd seen him flash other people so many times, and then pulled me into the house, holding my hand in his the whole time. The second I was engulfed in the artificially cool air, I exhaled. My skin was moist, and the whoosh from the vent above me was refreshing.

"So," I asked, looking up at him through lowered lashes, "do you forgive me?"

He let out a deep breath, acting like he was exasperated with me even though he was still smiling. I focused on his eyes, and the expression I saw there felt like an omen. Like the man in front of me knew he had a part to play, but deep inside he wanted nothing more than to gut me or maybe even commit other unspeakable acts. Like he'd done those things before and had not only enjoyed them, but had thrived on how they made him feel. Like they were what kept him alive.

"I wish you would have just told me all this," he finally said. "Even more than that, I wish you'd let me help. I could give you everything." He waved his free hand around the room, and I had to fight revulsion at what he was implying.

"I know," I said, looking down like I was ashamed or embarrassed instead of trying to hide the fear that was swirling around inside me. "I just need some time to think about it. Right now, all I know is that I've missed you so much." I fell against his chest, letting out a sigh that I hoped sounded like contentment.

"I missed you too."

He wrapped his arms around me, and his hands moved up and down my bare back. I had to force myself to stay still as the tips of his fingers traced my spine. His skin was warm against mine, and the movement was so slow that I couldn't help wondering if he was daydreaming about how he'd kill me. If he was fantasizing about severing that same spine he was tracing so he could render me helpless.

I squeezed my eyes shut when the urge to pray came over me. Who would I pray to if I did? Not Angus, I wasn't insane, but I couldn't think of anyone else to pray to either. Especially not when Jackson pulled me closer to him, his hand now reaching the back of my neck and his fingers curling around it like he might choke the life out of me. My heart, already beating wildly, leapt to my throat.

"I just want what's best for you," Jackson said against my head, his fingers gripping my neck tighter.

I swallowed, and suddenly his grip loosened. But at the same time, all the other muscles in his body grew tense. It was almost as if he was holding himself back, and I suddenly found myself terrified to be alone with him. The mansion was huge and no one knew I was here. He could take me somewhere and lock me away and no one would ever see me again. Parvarti would come looking for me, but she wouldn't find me and she'd most likely end up dead too.

But that thought was crazy. Wasn't it? Jackson may not be the person I thought he was, but he wasn't a murderer. He didn't have plans to end my life.

Suddenly, the fear I'd been feeling melted away and was replaced by regret and something else that I couldn't name at first. Loss? Yes, that was it. Tears filled my eyes when I realized I'd lost yet another person: my best friend. True, that person had never been real to begin with, but I hadn't known that. I'd always thought Jackson was someone I could count on, and now he was gone.

When I couldn't stand being in his arms any longer, I pulled back and wiped the tears from my cheeks. "I have to get moving,"

I said, unable to meet his gaze. "Work."

Jackson frowned and the darkness in his gaze was so unsettling that it sent a chill shooting through me. "I don't like the idea of you working in that hole."

"You're the one who took me to that hole to begin with," I said nudging him as I forced out a smile.

"Don't remind me." He shook his head. "Promise you'll think about what I said? I can give you everything, Meg. *Everything*."

For some reason, his words sounded more like a warning than a promise.

"I'll think about it," I lied as I backed toward the door.

Jackson walked me out, stopping on the doorstep. I gave him a wave as I headed down the street, but he didn't return it and he didn't move. He just stood in the open doorway, watching me with his arms crossed and his eyes narrowed like he was cooking up some nefarious plot. It gave me the creeps, so I walked faster, refusing to look back even though his gaze was so sharp it felt like needles poking into my back.

AFTER DONAGHY'S WIN AGAINST THREE ZOMBIES AT once, the bar was so busy that I forgot all about what Parvarti and I had planned until I caught sight of Charlie pushing her way through the crowd. Thank God I'd written the note before I left home today.

She bounced up to the bar, grinning from ear to ear and wearing a dress that put Glitter's to shame. Charlie's was also nothing more than strips, only it was white and the fabric was nearly transparent. The snowy material stood out among the filthy bodies packed into the room while contrasting beautifully with Charlie's olive skin. How the hell she had kept that dress clean on the walk over here was a mystery, but it was sure to be streaked with filth by the end of the night. Even the air was dirty in this place.

"I'm here!" she said when she stopped in front of me, her gaze darting around the room instead of focusing on me. "Where's Donaghy?"

"Getting ready for the fight." I reached over the bar and

grabbed her forearm, pulling her forward.

"What the hell?" she gasped as she tried to pull back.

"Stop," I hissed in her ear. I shoved the note into the palm of her hand. "Take this to your dad. *Now.* It's life or death."

Charlie's eyes were huge when she pulled back, and the nod she gave me was just subtle enough that I doubted anyone else had noticed it.

"I mean it," I said, loud enough for anyone nearby to hear me. "If you show your face in here again, I'll tell your parents."

Charlie's cheeks turned red, and even though she fixed an angry glare on me, the expression in her eyes said she knew what I was trying to do. "You've always been a buzz kill." She spun on her heel and shoved her way past men whose eyes were glued to her bronze skin. "Fuck you!"

*Nice touch, Charlie.* I almost rolled my eyes.

I turned to find Helen staring at me with her eyebrows raised.

"Tough love," I said with a shrug.

I went back to serving drinks, keeping one eye on the door. Around the room, coughs broke through the chatter and clinking of glasses, and more than once Helen and Dragon shared a concerned look.

The illness had spread quickly, just like it did every time this happened; only now all I could think about was the conversation Donaghy had overheard. Was it really possible that the CDC was behind this? It seemed even more far-fetched than the idea that they would take my father and hold him captive, but I couldn't deny the fact that we were very much in the dark when it came to what they were actually trying to achieve.

The minutes ticked by, and finally the fight got underway, allowing me room to breathe. I downed a shot while across the room Donaghy beat the shit out of two zombies. We hadn't had a chance to talk tonight, and despite my concern over everything that was going on, I found my gaze constantly moving toward him. The worry in my stomach that something might happen was impossible to ignore. He was undefeated, but that didn't mean things couldn't go terribly wrong in the blink of an eye.

The fight was still going on when I spotted my aunt. She pushed her way through the crowd like she was ten feet tall, ignoring the lewd comments that were thrown her way. Even though she was pushing fifty, her dark skin was smooth and her short hair was still as black as a raven's feathers.

She slid into the seat in front of me, subtly raising one eyebrow.

I nodded in response to the silent question. "Can I get you a drink?"

"Moonshine." Parv looked over her shoulder toward the ring, her brown eyes curious and sad at the same time. She must have been thinking about Joshua being there last night, and the memory squeezed my own heart painfully.

I poured her a glass that was more than three quarters of the way full and slid it over.

"Aren't you the Judicial Officer?" Helen asked from my side.

Parv and I both turned to face the other woman. Her eyes were focused on my aunt, and there was a softness in them that was usually reserved for Glitter and Dragon—or one of the many hopeless drunks who frequented the bar.

Parv nodded. "Checking out the fight. There have been some questions raised about whether or not it's humane."

"For the zombies or the fighters?" Helen asked.

Parv's eyes narrowed on the other woman's face. "Do I know you? I feel like we've met."

"I'm a nurse," Helen said, not looking away from Parv. "At the CDC. This is my night job."

Helen was a nurse? That was the first I'd heard of it.

"That's right," Parv whispered. "I remember now."

The two women stared at each other for a few seconds, each seemingly mesmerized by the other. My aunt looked away first, and the vulnerability in her eyes was only overshadowed by the questions swimming in them. Whatever thoughts were going through her head, though, she didn't voice them, and Helen didn't say anything else.

All around us the crowd roared, and a second later Dragon was announcing Donaghy's win, earning even more cheers from the crowd.

"Looks like you missed most of it," Helen said to Parv, nodding toward the ring before heading to the other end of the bar.

"How did you meet her?" I asked when the older waitress was

out of earshot.

"She was there the day I went in to see Joshua." Parv took a gulp of her moonshine, squeezing her eyes shut when the liquid burned its way down her throat.

Helen was at the CDC when Joshua turned? Did that mean she'd recognized him yesterday? Probably. Right? It was even possible that she had answers about what happened to him after Parv said goodbye. Where they'd taken him or how he'd ended up here. She could even know *how* he'd been infected...

Or where Dad was.

"Do you think she knows anything?" I asked, my eyes on Helen.

Dragon walked up to the older woman and the two talked, their heads close together like they didn't want anyone else to hear their conversation. A second later, my boss turned his gaze on my aunt.

"I don't know," Parv said. "I'm not sure I know anything anymore."

My attention was pulled from Dragon and Helen when Al walked through the front door. His gaze moved across the room, coming to stop on me before moving to Parv. His mouth was scrunched up in an expression that got lost somewhere between worry and confusion, and then he was heading our way. Helen and Dragon looked up when Al walked by them, and I would have had to be blind to not see the look they shot him, only I wasn't sure what it meant. I wasn't sure what any of this meant.

"What the hell is going on?" Al hissed when he stopped in front of us. His eyes turned to me, and the frown on his face was deeper than I'd ever seen it. Like a parent who was disappointed in their child. "And why the hell are you working here?"

"You know exactly why," I snapped, then lowered my voice so I didn't draw attention our way. "But that isn't why we're here. We're here because my Dad is missing, and we all know he's alive and that he's in the CDC."

The color drained from Al's face and he opened his mouth to say something, but no words came out. He looked around, scanning the bar. Thankfully, now that the fight was over the crowd had started to clear out, and the few drunks still sitting at the counter were more interested in their glasses. The handful of other patrons seemed to either be settling debts or discussing which strip club to go to.

"I told her everything," Parv said.

Al's mouth dropped open and he stared at my aunt like she'd gone insane, but I was starting to think that we'd all gone a little insane, or none of us at all. Either we were all out of our minds, or someone high up was very good at making people think they were out of their minds.

One way or another, I was going to find out.

"I know Dad is immune."

"Shit." My uncle looked around again, and he was still craning his neck when he said, "We need to talk about this, but not at the bar." He motioned toward the back of the room. "Table in the corner. Now."

Al pushed himself off the counter almost violently, heading off without looking back. Parv stood, letting out a sigh that sounded exhausted.

"I'll pour a few more drinks and head over," I said, and my aunt nodded in response.

My hands were shaking when I filled the glasses. Across the room, Parv and Al were already whispering, and I couldn't help wondering if there were details I still knew nothing about. Or maybe she was filling my uncle in on what had gone down here last night.

Liquid sloshed out as I crossed the room, the three glasses held between my trembling hands. I had to dodge tables and men who didn't seem to think getting out of my way was important. All around the bar, people coughed, causing a feeling of dread to move through me and settle in my stomach.

Dragon stood at Helen's side, his dark eyes moving between my aunt and uncle as he frowned. Then his gaze settled on me, and the heaviness in my stomach grew. Something in his gaze made my steps falter. He looked like he knew what we were doing here, like he'd expected it all along, and I couldn't help wondering if he and Helen were somehow involved in this.

Al looked up when I set the glass in front of him, his brown eyes swimming with pain and maybe even shimmering with tears. It was hard to tell in the dim light. "So it's true? Joshua was here?"

I slid into the empty chair and nodded somberly. "It's true."

237

"Shit." Al lowered his head, and this time I was sure there were tears in his eyes, and that he was trying to hide them from us.

My uncle put his good hand on his head, massaging his scalp. His other arm rested on the tabletop. He was technically on duty, so he was wearing the sword contraption on his stump. It had been a long time since I'd studied the thing—not since I was little and had been enthralled by the idea that my uncle might have been a pirate when he was younger. Seeing the blade now made that weight inside me grow. The metal was dull from age, and along the base where the blade met the cuff, a layer of rust had started to form. Al was a teenager when the virus started, goofy and young, he had bounced back after losing his family much better than a lot of people had. But he'd aged, just like the rest of us had, and along the way he'd probably started to think that he'd grown accustomed to the threat of death lurking around every corner. Only he hadn't, and the shock of loss was just as startling and painful now as it had been when the virus was first released on this world.

"I can't believe this is happening," Al said after nearly a minute of silence, his head was still down and his hand was still massaging his scalp. "After twenty years, I thought we were in the clear. I thought all our worries had been for nothing. Why are they doing this now?"

"I don't know," Parv responded. In the dim light of the bar, she suddenly looked ten years older than her actual age. The dark circles under her eyes that told me she'd been having a difficult time sleeping were more pronounced, and I noticed for the first time that she had creases at the corners of her eyes. "But we need to figure out how to get Axl out of the CDC."

"If he's there." Al, having pulled himself together, lifted his head and focused on my aunt. "All we have right now are theories."

"He's there," I said firmly. Theories or facts, I didn't doubt it anymore. The CDC had my Dad. "Between the stuff Donaghy overheard at Jackson's house and finding out that Dad is immune, I don't have a doubt."

Even though Al frowned, he nodded like he agreed with me. "It looks bad."

"What's bad is the fact that we have no real way of getting in."

Parv's gaze was suddenly focused on something behind me, and I twisted in my seat to find Helen and Dragon still standing in the same place. Still talking, their heads together like they were trying to block out the rest of the bar. "Maybe…"

"Can you trust her?" Al said.

"Trust who?" I turned back to face my aunt and uncle. "Are you talking about Helen?"

"Parv said she works at the CDC. Maybe she knows something."

"Maybe," I said. "But I don't know who to trust anymore. Plus, until tonight, I had no idea Helen was even a nurse. If she knew who I was, wouldn't she have said something?"

I thought back to all the conversations I'd had with Helen, and doubt clawed at my brain. There were times when she'd seemed to be trying to tell me something, but I hadn't paid a whole lot of attention to her. It had never occurred to me that the gnarled woman who served drinks in Dragon's Lair would have any real information to share.

"Can you trust her?" Al repeated.

"I don't know." I exhaled, my mind still flipping through every word and look Helen had thrown my way since I started here. Nothing felt off or suspicious. At least not until today. But I'd been understandably preoccupied. I could have missed something. "The best I can do at this point is feel her out."

"What about this gray man?" Parv asked. "What if he has some kind of access to the CDC?"

The gray man. He was an even bigger mystery than anything else that had happened, because I couldn't for the life of me figure out how he knew anything. He looked like someone who either lived in shantytown or slept in alleys, not a person who would know secrets. Who the hell was he?

"He obviously knows something, but I don't know what that is or how he got the information." I shook my head and the urge to massage my temples hit me hard. With all the new information swirling around in my head, I was starting to get a headache. "And it isn't like I know where to find him. He just pops up."

Al exhaled and sat back. He drummed his fingers against the table as he thought it all through, and I held my breath. Waiting. Praying that Al had an epiphany that would lead us to Dad.

"We're going to have to be smart about this. Take our time. Do some recon. And we absolutely cannot talk about this in the apartment building." He turned his brown eyes on me. "Don't tell your mom."

I hated the idea of keeping her in the dark. It wasn't fair, at least not to the person she was before Dad's disappearance. She'd always been strong and I knew that if they'd chosen to tell her the truth back when they'd found this all out, Mom could have handled it. Now, though, I had to agree with my uncle.

"You should have told her years ago," I said, even as I nodded in agreement.

"That's something you'll have to take up with your Dad," Al replied. "*When* we find him."

The pain in my head increased, then traveled through my body until it found a home in my stomach. Adding to the tension that had already coiled inside me.

*When we found Dad.*

I tried to hold onto that hope, but it was tough when we hadn't really accomplished anything with this conversation. In fact, I kind of felt like I had even more questions now than I'd had before I sat down with Al and Parvarti.

"So that's it?" I asked, looking back and forth between my aunt and uncle. "This is the best we have?"

"I'm open to suggestions," Parv said.

I didn't have any, and it made me feel more helpless than ever before.

Al got to his feet. "I'm sorry, kid, I wish I could do more."

"We all do." Parv stood too.

I got up without thinking about it, following their lead like I was a puppet and they were pulling the strings. Obviously, they considered this little meeting over, and I couldn't beg them to stay because I had nothing else to add. That didn't mean I was happy about it, though. In fact, I was so angry that I didn't trust myself to open my mouth without screaming.

Al and Parv traded a few comments about work and before heading out my uncle assured me that he'd poke around.

Parv started to follow him, but stopped at my side after only two steps. "I know it seems like we didn't get anywhere, but we did. If nothing else, you're not alone in this now."

"I know." She had a point, but I didn't feel much better about where I stood. "I just want to get Dad out of there before it's too late."

"We will." Parv gave my hand a squeeze before following my uncle.

I went back to the bar, ignoring Glitter, who was more chipper than I could stand right now, and doing my best to stay away from the customers even though I desperately needed the tips. I had too much going through my head to even think about being cordial.

Helen had disappeared sometime during my meeting with my aunt and uncle, and she stayed gone the rest of the night. If Dragon hadn't been missing too, I would have wondered where she was, but I had a suspicion they were going at it in his office. Again.

Oddly enough, Helen and Dragon weren't the only two people I didn't see after my aunt and uncle left. Donaghy, too, seemed to be nowhere in sight. Before the fight I was relieved that we hadn't had the opportunity to talk, but now I found myself constantly scanning the room in search of him. Maybe it was wrong to drag him deeper into all of this, but my aunt was wrong about one thing: I didn't feel lighter now that Al and Parv were in on this. It made me feel more helpless because they didn't have any more solutions than I did, and who the hell knew if or when we'd ever come up with something. Donaghy, with those icy blue eyes and the scar on his chin, as well as his quietly calm exterior, made me feel secure.

He came out of the back about a half hour before closing time. He was still shirtless, but his skin was moist, as if he'd just gotten out of the shower. Maybe he had. He didn't usually take a shower when the bar was still open, but I'd missed most of the fight and for all I knew he'd been covered in the black blood of his enemies.

He stopped in front of me, shaking his head as he slid onto a stool. "My guards are in bad shape."

I poured him a drink without being asked, and slid the glass across the counter. "They're sick?"

"Coughing like crazy. Feverish. They haven't left their cots all day, which tells me it's serious. Those two assholes love the entertainment district more than anything." He let out a deep breath. "This thing is going to get serious real fast."

He was right, but I didn't need to tell him that. Not with the man sitting at the end of the bar, coughing into his glass. Glitter served him whatever he wanted, but kept her distance. I'd even seen the girl use a rag to pick his empty glass up, and she'd spent more time scrubbing the dirty glasses today than any other night since I'd started working here. The water in the basin was hotter, and had more soap in it, too. It was like everyone working here had the same suspicions that Donaghy and I had about this flu.

"Did you know Helen works at the CDC?" I asked, tearing my gaze away from Glitter so I could look at the fighter again.

"Just found out." He shook his head. "She and Dragon..."

I perked up. Something about the expression in Donaghy's eyes told me he had the same suspicion I did. "What? Do you think they know something?"

"I think they are involved in a lot more than just serving booze and organizing fights. I'm just not sure what." Donaghy took a big gulp and I watched as his Adam's apple bobbed. When he'd set the glass down, he wiped his lips and said, "I'll keep my eyes open, but I have a strange feeling."

"Me too." I exhaled and leaned against the counter, suddenly feeling exhausted. "I'm starting to think that the best thing I can do is just get back on Jackson's good side. He'll be able to get me some information."

Donaghy sat up straighter. "After what those guys you work with told you? That would be dumb as shit, Meg. Don't risk it."

"I have to find my dad, and this could be the only way."

"Don't do it," Donaghy said again, he paused so he could study me for a second. "You don't still think Jackson's a good guy. Do you?"

"No..." My voice trailed off when I thought back to how Jackson had behaved this afternoon. He was the same, but different. I felt like I'd seen him without blinders on for the first time. "He had me fooled for so long. I can't believe I didn't see it before, but I think I know how he was able to hide it from me.

"How?"

"He saved me," I said, meeting the fighter's gaze.

"What?" Donaghy's eyes searched mine, swimming with concern and questions.

He wasn't the only one who had questions, though. I'd had a million going through my head for the past several weeks, but

242

most had been about my dad. So many that I hadn't really stopped to think about Jackson and how he had managed to fool me for all these years until now. I should have, though, especially after what I'd learned about Stevie Jones — AKA Ticker.

"The day my sister was killed, Jackson swooped in and saved me," I said, trying to do something I usually avoided: remember. "Mom was walking Margot and me home, and the streets were busy. Full of people who were doing the same thing: going home after a day of work or school. The horde came out of nowhere. One second the street was clear, and the next they were there. Dozens of them. They turned a corner and charged us. It happened so fast. The crowd went nuts, and Margot and I were ripped away from Mom. I held onto my little sister's hand as hard as I could while we ran. I tried to keep her close. She was crying, and all I wanted to do was to get her somewhere safe.

"When I lost her, it felt like someone with super-human strength ripped her hand out of mine. It was so violent and forceful that I almost felt like I'd been shoved away from her in the process. People surrounded me and I couldn't figure out where she'd gone. I screamed for her and searched the crowd, but it was as if she'd vanished.

"Then the crowd parted and the zombies were there. Snarling and growling. They'd already taken a few people out, and I can remember the smell of blood in the air. The dead were coming straight for me. Everyone around me was trying to look out for themselves and no one cared that I was alone. I tried to run, but there was nowhere to hide.

"That's when Jackson popped up out of nowhere. He grabbed my hand and pulled me through the crowd. A zombie was on top of us, but he took care of it and got me to safety. We hid in an alley, behind a dumpster, just the two of us. I could still hear the screaming from the street, and I was crying because I didn't know what had happened to Mom or Margot. Jackson held me and comforted me. He kept me safe.

"When it was over we went back out to the street. There were bodies everyone — both human and zombie — and the road was covered in blood. We found Margot's backpack lying in the middle of the street, covered in blood and ripped up. Jackson helped me look for my sister, and not too long after that Mom showed up. She had a big gash on her head, but she couldn't remember what had happened. She thought the crowd had trampled her. We searched all night for Margot, but never found her.

"After that, Jackson and I were inseparable. I knew people didn't like him, but he was always good to me. Sweet and caring. I thought I could see something in him that no one else could. I thought I knew him better."

I stopped talking and silence settled around us. Donaghy was frowning, thinking it all through, and I did too. Searching my memories of what had happened for facts I might have been ignoring for years.

It was odd, Jackson popping up like that when he didn't live in that part of the city, but it had always seemed almost divine to me before now. Like it was meant to be. Now, though, I had to wonder if it hadn't all been for show. Like he had planned the whole thing. No, not Jackson, but his father.

"We never found her," I said quietly. "Margot's body vanished. She was the only one from that day."

"You think they took her?" Donaghy asked, his voice barely more than a whisper.

*They.* It always came back to *they* lately. Only, I didn't know who *they* were and I didn't know who to trust or what to think.

"Maybe. Angus was immune, and I now know my father is too." Donaghy's eyebrows shot up and I shrugged. "My aunt and uncle filled me in on some details. Anyway, Margot could have been too."

Something like worry or fear or a feeling even more intense than that flashed in Donaghy's eyes. "If they took her, they could take you. You're part of that family too. What if you're immune?"

"I'm not." I almost laughed. "My last name is the only thing special about me. People get all bent out of shape when they hear that my last name is James, but the truth is, we aren't related by blood. My biological parents died on the way to Atlanta. Vivian and Axl James adopted me."

Understanding crossed Donaghy's face and he frowned. "That's it. That's why Jackson wants you."

"What?" I wasn't following his train of thought.

"Your name. *James.* You're the one who told me how power-hungry his dad is. Well, who has more power in this country than the Regulator?"

"Angus James," I whispered, shaking my head. "He's been dead for twenty years, and yet people still talk about him every day. They pray to him for God's sake."

"Having you at his son's side could ensure that the Stars would be able to stay in control. Hell, he might even be able to get The Church to back him if Jackson was married to you."

"Shit."

It had never occurred to me before now, but it should have. Jackson was usually careful not to bring my uncle up, or the crazy religion that for some reason thought Angus James was their savior, but Donaghy was right. If anyone in this settlement could sway people to side with the government, it would be someone with the last name James.

I MULLED OVER WHAT DONAGHY AND I TALKED ABOUT the whole walk home, so lost in contemplation that the coughs ringing through shantytown got little more than a fleeting thought from me. A thought that went in one ear when a hacking cough shook the metal walls of the shack I was walking by, passing through my head and flying out the other ear when the statue of my uncle came into view.

I slowed to almost a stop, my gaze on the carving and the gifts lined up around it. Credits were tucked under the base, the paper they were printed on flapping in the breeze like it was taunting the people around it.

To me it felt like that, anyway. The people living in this section of the city didn't have enough of anything to go around, and yet those credits would sit by this shrine until it rained hard enough for them to be washed away. No one dared touch them, no matter how lawless or needy they were. Even skeptics probably found themselves silently fearing that the spirit of Angus James would curse them to a death even more horrible than the one the virus had rained down on this country. They would instead starve, possibly right here in this very spot, kneeling in front of the statue and begging for help while the credits flapped in the breeze.

This religion was perhaps the most powerful thing in the

settlement, but it had never occurred to me until Donaghy brought it up. Mostly because it was something we didn't discuss in my family.

I couldn't remember a time when people hadn't prayed to the statue of Angus, but I had never realized that I was somehow a part of it—at least in the eyes of the fanatics—until I started school. Before that, I think my parents worked to shield me from The Church, because I never really made the connection with the statue and the uncle who had died saving humanity until I started school and it became impossible to avoid.

On that first day we took turns standing in front of the class, sharing with the other children our age our names and who we were. When my turn came, I'd been nervous enough, and it had only gotten worse when I'd said my name. While half the kids had maintained their sleepy boredom, the other half had perked up. It was like my name had some magical power I'd never been aware of until that moment.

"James?" one little girl, who I would later learn to avoid, had asked. "Like Angus James?"

"Yes." I'd nodded, unaware that this girl was the daughter of the high priestess of The Church. "Angus James was my uncle."

I'd raised my chin, proud that I shared the last name of the man who'd died saving us. That was a story I knew. One everyone knew. What I'd never been told by my parents, though, was that there were a lot of people who thought of Angus as some kind of god.

On that first day of school, I learned more than I did for the rest of my education. I learned all about The Church and their beliefs. How they thought Angus would come back and save them again one day, and I also learned that the religion was spreading faster than the virus had.

Back then, only a small portion of the population held those beliefs, but as the years passed and illnesses claimed even more lives, the religion spread. Now more than half of Atlanta bowed their heads when they sat down at the dinner table and said a prayer to Angus James.

I shivered and walked faster, leaving the shrine and the shantytown and the thoughts of religious zealots behind me. My building came into view, and the sight of Jackson leaning against the wall next to the door caused my footsteps to falter just a little.

The realization that he'd been using me all these years hurt, but it also scared me. Whether or not he knew what was going on in the CDC, he was part of this whole thing. His father had brought him in as an apprentice at a young age, and there was no way Jackson had been kept in the dark for all these years. Not completely, anyway. He had to know something about my father.

"Meg? Are you okay?" Jackson pushed himself off the wall when I was still ten feet away, and when he looked me up and down, the hair on my scalp prickled.

For years I'd interpreted looks like this as concern. As proof that he was better than his father. Now, though, I couldn't help wondering if it was something else. If Jackson was studying my moods and using the feelings I was so poor at hiding from him as a weapon against me.

"I'm fine," I lied. "Just tired and confused about life. Things have changed so much and I don't think I'm dealing with it all that well."

"I'm sorry. I know things have been hard for you." For once, the sympathetic look he gave me felt fake and rehearsed.

How had I allowed him to fool me for all these years? Other people could see through him. My parents had never been fans, and Donaghy saw it the second he laid eyes on Jackson. But I'd been blinded for years by the fact that he'd been there to save me when I needed him the most. Jackson had comforted me in the worst moments of my life, and I'd seen it as proof that deep down he was a good person. Had it all been an act just so he could use my name to gain more power?

I let out a deep breath, trying to act exhausted and confused, which wasn't a total lie. I was exhausted, and everything about Jackson seemed like a riddle to me now. But, I needed information out of him.

It was time for a different strategy.

I took a step closer and pressed myself up against him, laying my head on his chest. When I wrapped my arms around his waist, he returned the hug, but the familiarity of his embrace was gone. This man no longer felt like a friend. He felt like a stranger. Or worse, an enemy.

"You've always been so strong," I said. "Always been here for

247

me. Thank you."

I lifted my head, peering up at him through my eyelashes. Jackson was watching me, his face expressionless and his eyes so cold that it almost made me shiver. I forced out a smile as I lifted myself up on the tips of my toes, and when I pressed my lips against his, I had to squeeze my eyes shut and pretend he was someone else.

Jackson's hands were on my hips in a second, and then he was pulling me closer. His mouth moved over mine so quickly that it took my breath away. I tried to put everything I had into the kiss, but it was hard. All I could think about were the things Ticker said and the icy expression in Jackson's eyes when I'd gone to his house earlier today. I needed to do this, though. I needed him to trust me and let me into his life so I could look around. This was all about survival. About bending the situation to my will.

Jackson spun me around so my back was against the building, his hands snaking up my hips to my waist while his mouth devoured mine. He'd wanted this for so long and I knew it, and even though having his lips and hands on me made my skin crawl, I couldn't back down.

But the kiss was cut short only seconds after it started, and Jackson pulled away. Only he didn't step back, and his hands were now planted firmly against the wall on either side of me, caging me in. My lips were raw from his attack and he was out of breath, but the intensity that flashed in his eyes when he looked down at me had nothing to do with passion. He glared like he was trying to shoot fire from his eyes, looking more like his father than he ever had before. I tried to shrink away from his fury, but he had me trapped against the wall.

"Jackson?" I whispered, suddenly terrified of the person in front of me.

"I bet you think you're real smart," he said, the smile on his face not matching the fury in his eyes. "Well, fuck you." A laugh that was slightly maniacal popped out of his mouth and I cringed away from him. "That's what I should have done. I should have kept going. Seen how far you'd be willing to take this little charade. You would have screwed me if you thought it would get you what you wanted. Wouldn't you?" The last two words echoed through the streets, bouncing off the surrounding buildings.

"I don't know what you mean." I sounded smaller than a mouse, which was how I felt under his gaze. Tiny. Insignificant. Unable to fix even the smallest problem in my life.

Jackson let out a deep breath and stepped back. "It would have been a waste of time. If you think I'd ever consider betraying my father and what he's trying to accomplish here, you're even dumber than I thought. He's building something great, and I'm going to help him."

The truth of who this person was slammed into me. Matt had been right. Jackson was a sociopath. All these years I'd thought that deep down he was good. He wasn't, though. Never had been. He was exactly like his father. Manipulative and power hungry, and Jackson's friendship with me had always been about my last name and a desperate grab for even more power.

"*Anything* they do within the walls of the CDC is justified." Jackson's voice was low and menacing. Like a threat.

Tears filled my eyes when images of Dad flashed through my mind. Strapped down to a table, tubes and wires coming out of him.

"Is he there?" I whispered even though I knew Jackson would never tell me. There would be no reaching the man in front of me.

His hands dropped to his sides and he took a step back, giving me room to breathe. I did, sucking in a deep breath and holding it, waiting for him to answer. He didn't, though. He just ran his hands down his shirt, smoothing it out like it was a suit and he was getting ready to head into an important meeting.

He didn't meet my eyes again. Not even when he said, "It's late. I should get home." He took one step away before stopping, not even turning when he called over his shoulder, "When you see that fighter friend of yours tomorrow, be sure to tell him that I said good luck. From what I hear, the zombies they're tossing his way are bigger and newer."

He headed off, but I couldn't move. I wasn't sure if his last statement was intended as a warning or if it was his way of telling me that he knew Joshua had been thrown into the ring last night. Maybe it was both. After what I'd just witnessed, I didn't have a doubt in my mind that Jackson knew all the ins and outs of this settlement.

# CHAPTER TWENTY-FIVE

## Donaghy

**"WHAT** the hell are you doing?" Dragon growled. I rolled onto my side and peered at the other man through the cage surrounding the ring. The bar was still dark, so it must have been early, but I hadn't gotten much rest. The cot was a piece of shit, but it was a hell of a lot softer than the floor of the ring.

"Trying to get some sleep." I pushed myself up to sitting position, then rolled my neck, wincing at the cracking and popping noises that echoed through my head. "Those asshole guards of mine are hacking like crazy."

Dragon let out a deep breath. "Shit's going down."

"Happens every few years." I narrowed my eyes on the other man, trying to get a good look at him through the cage. Something in his voice said what I already knew: that this was more than just a bug sweeping across the settlement.

"Happens too often." He turned his back on me and headed toward the bar, nodding for me to follow. "Come get some breakfast."

I dragged myself out of the ring and headed after him,

wondering what he was thinking. I had my suspicions about the illness spreading through the settlement, but that was because of what I'd overheard at the Regulator's house. Dragon had other sources, though. Whether it was Helen or the gray man, I didn't know, but someone had let him in on the Regulator's dirty little secret: that they were using this flu to weed out the scum of the city.

I slid onto a stool just as Dragon pulled a couple prepackaged meals out from behind the bar. He tossed one my way, his brows pulled low and his face darker than usual. I didn't say anything before tearing into my meal. He clearly had stuff on his mind and so did I. Between Meg and what was going on with her family, and the fact that I couldn't stop thinking about her or how bad it hurt to know that I was leaving in a few days time, my head felt full.

We ate in silence, each of us lost in thoughts about the shit that was falling on this settlement and what it would mean for us. I knew what it would most likely mean for me: death by flu. That was a subject I hadn't broached with Meg. I'd been sleeping in the same room with my guards, and odds were good that I'd catch this thing.

Someone banged on the door, the sound echoing through the empty bar, and I swear I nearly shit my pants. It had startled me, coming out of nowhere when the silence was so thick and heavy it had felt untouchable, but there was another reason my heart started pounding like a stampede. No one came to a bar this early in the morning to deliver good news.

I stopped chewing and swallowed, wincing when the food nearly got stuck in my throat. My gaze was on the door as Dragon swore and headed around the counter.

I didn't move from my position on the stool. After the other morning, Dragon and I both knew exactly what was on the other side of that door, but what I didn't know was why. Was it another message for Meg, or a zombie for me?

Dragon pulled the door open and took a step back. The snarls that floated into the room weren't a surprise, but they still made my stomach threaten to eject the food I'd just eaten.

"You know the drill," a man said, but his voice was strained. "Move back. This one's determined to get a bite out of me."

Dragon took a couple steps back as the same two men from

the other morning dragged the zombie inside. The thing growled and struggled against his chains, fighting to get free as they pulled him forward. The zom's snarls were only interrupted by the constant cursing of the guards. If they were having a tough time controlling the bastard while he was chained, I was in for it.

I turned my back on them and returned to my meal, trying my best to ignore the swears and growls that vibrated through the room.

When Dragon stopped in front of me, I forced myself to look up, wanting to read his gaze. His eyes, dark and hard, gave nothing away, though.

"Is this another message?" I asked when he didn't say anything.

He shook his head, his gaze moving past me to the back of the room. "Not that I'm aware of."

"Great," I muttered, looking down at the pathetic meal in front of me. One of my last, most likely. "Maybe I would have been better off if I'd allowed myself to catch the flu."

"Don't kid yourself," Dragon said. "They'd still make you fight."

He was right about that.

I WAS DOING PUSHUPS WHEN MEG CAME STUMBLING into the bar. Her eyes were crazy and her normally neat hair was a wild mess. She looked like she'd been attacked or threatened, or she'd just heard the worst news of her life.

I was on my feet and out of the ring before she'd made it even halfway across the room, meeting her in the middle of the bar. Her little body slammed into mine so hard that some of the breath whooshed out of my lungs, but I pulled back and looked her over, trying to figure out if she was hurt.

"What's wrong?" I asked when I didn't see anything.

"Jackson." She swallowed and blinked like she was fighting back tears. "I talked to him last night."

"You did what?" This girl was either the bravest or dumbest person I'd ever met, I just wasn't sure which one. "I told you to stay away from him." My hands tightened on her shoulders when a million crazy thoughts flipped though my head. If he touched her, I wouldn't be able to stop myself. I'd kill him with my bare hands and die with a smile on my face when his puny father put a bullet through my brain.

"He threatened you," Meg blurted out, and all the thoughts in my head sizzled away. "At least I think he did. He said to tell you good luck."

From anyone else that would seem like a nice sentiment, but from this guy... Yeah, it was definitely a threat. I should have known he was behind the special delivery we had this morning.

"Shit," I muttered, but I couldn't help feeling relieved that Meg was okay. I was going to die, but it wasn't news to me. The second those guards knocked on the door this morning I knew my odds of seeing tomorrow were slim to none.

Across the room, someone coughed. Meg and I both turned, but I didn't know who it was. None of the men in the bar looked particularly healthy. Slouched, weak, shivering with fever. They were drunks who had dragged themselves here even though they'd felt like shit. Hell, they were probably used to feeling like shit and hadn't yet realized that this was different. This wasn't a hangover after two too many glasses of moonshine. This was death.

"Listen," I said, pulling Meg's attention my way. "Another zombie was brought in his morning and I have good feeling this one was intended for me."

Meg's green eyes grew even bigger, seeming to take up most of her face. "What?"

I wasn't sure if she didn't understand what I was telling her or if she just didn't want to accept it. Either way, I had a few things I wanted to say to her before I stepped into that ring tonight.

I pulled her to the side of the room and held her by the shoulders, looking her in the eye as I said, "This is probably the end for me."

Meg swallowed. Her lips parted but nothing came out, then she shook her head. This was exactly what I'd been trying to avoid: Meg once again feeling abandoned. Even though it wasn't my choice, I couldn't help feeling like an ass.

"We both knew it was coming," I said gently. "We knew they wouldn't let this go on forever."

"This is my fault," she whispered. "If you hadn't gotten involved with me, they probably wouldn't have worried about you. They'd let you go to Key West. They'd let you keep fighting."

"Maybe," I said, unable to lie, "but maybe not. We all knew this was temporary."

I let my hands fall from her shoulders as I looked around. The fight would be starting soon, but the crowd was thinner tonight than usual. Of the few people who had managed to drag themselves in, most didn't look so hot. It wasn't just the hacking that seemed to constantly echo through the air, either. I watched as across the room, a man in his fifties leaned against the wall, gasping for breath. He acted like he barely had the strength to stand.

"This flu is going to get worse before it gets better." I once again focused on Meg. "Remember what I heard at the Regulator's house?"

She nodded. "I know. Half my crew was out sick today."

"They did this."

"I know."

Meg let out a deep breath and looked across the room. "I'm sorry. I still feel like this is my fault."

"It's my fault. I'm the one who got sent to DC."

"You did it to save your sister," she let out a deep breath and turned back to face me. "I'm glad I met you."

"Me too."

I pulled her in for a hug even though I really wanted to kiss her. I would have done it too, if it hadn't been for the fact that I was sure it would make this goodbye that much harder on her. I wanted to be fair. Needed to be. It was the least I could do for her.

"How sweet," someone sneered from behind Meg.

I pulled back but kept my hand on her arm as together we turned to face Jackson. He was only a foot away from us, and behind him stood a group of people close to his age.

His brown eyes flashed as he looked back and forth between Meg and me. "I should have known you were screwing the convict."

I tried to push Meg behind me, but she stood her ground. "Donaghy is a friend."

The cocky prick only smiled. "We'll be in the VIP area."

He jerked his head toward the roped off section and headed that way. The group at his back followed, a few of them shooting us looks that ranged from hateful to curious. I didn't have to be told that they were all council brats; the air of importance that followed them said it all.

"You should get to work," I said as I watched the asshole step into the VIP section.

I hated the idea of her serving him, but she needed the money. There was no guarantee that she'd ever get her dad out of the CDC—assuming that's where he was—and she had a life to live. One that didn't involve me and the extra drama I'd brought to her life.

Meg turned back to face me, her green eyes pleading. "You can beat this. Whatever they throw your way, I know you can beat it."

After listening to the snarls and struggles of the zombie they'd brought in, I wasn't so sure, but I nodded anyway. "I'll do my best."

Meg took one step away before thinking better of it. This time when she turned back, she threw herself against me. I barely had time to think about it before she had her lips pressed against mine, but even when I was able to think it through, I couldn't stop her. All I could do was pull her closer to me. My arms engulfed her, pulling her against my chest as I moved my lips faster. She opened her mouth and I swept my tongue over hers, savoring the way she tasted and how strong her little body felt in my arms.

When I pulled back, we were both gasping.

"I had to do that one more time," she said, tears shimmering in her eyes before she turned away, pushing through the crowd. Leaving me standing by myself and hating what I was about to face.

I never thought the end would hurt this damn much.

My heartbeat hadn't slowed by the time Dragon came over to join me. After the other day, I expected some kind of lecture about how his girls were off limits, but he didn't say anything. I guess he figured that since I was about to die, kissing Meg didn't really matter all that much.

Dragon cracked his knuckles as he surveyed the room. I leaned against the wall and watched as Meg pushed her way through the crowd and headed toward the VIP section. Jackson and his friends filled the area that normally sat empty, and their catcalls were loud enough that I could hear them from all the way across the room.

"You ready for this fight?" Dragon asked, looking my way out of the corner of his eye.

"Do I have a choice?"

I glanced through the open doorway at my back, taking in the zombies that were loaded onto the cart. They were struggling to get free, their chains clinking against each other. The one they'd brought in this morning was much more aggressive than the others. He snarled. He pulled at the lock like he still had enough mental function to get it open. He looked at me, his eyes barely milky enough to cover the blue of his irises.

"No choice," Dragon said. "We play by the rules the best we can or we all die." He turned to face me, his upper lip curling enough to show the gap where his teeth used to be. "Our day will come though."

Our day will come?

I narrowed my eyes on him, studying his face for any hint of what he was trying to say. He was definitely trying to tell me something, but what that was I didn't have a damn clue. One thing I did know: *my* day wasn't going to come. Not unless getting shipped back to DC or being ripped apart by a zom could be considered *my day*. My future was shitty enough before I got here, but now that I was mixed up in this business with Meg and her family, I'd pretty much signed my own death warrant. All I could hope for now was a quick and relatively painless end.

"Take this," Dragon said after a second of silence.

I looked down to find him holding a switchblade, and I almost stepped back. If he got caught arming me, they probably wouldn't even bother sending him to DC.

"What the hell are you doing?" I asked, shaking my head as I looked around. No one was paying any attention to us, thankfully.

Dragon pressed the knife into my palm, looking around like I just had to make sure no one was watching, and I was forced to take the damn thing. If I made a scene, people would notice and he'd be dead. Me too, probably.

"Don't use it unless you absolutely have to." His eyes were

still searching the room and my gaze was trained on his mouth. The black hole that had once been teeth was hypnotizing when he talked. "If anyone sees it, you didn't get it from me."

Dragon was helping me? It didn't make any damn sense. Not that anything really had since setting foot in this ass-backwards settlement.

I slipped the knife into my pocket, but I couldn't stop myself from asking, "Why?"

"Because the people pulling the strings think they are in charge, but it won't always be that way. *We* will rise up."

Dragon headed toward the ring, the crowd parting for him like he was a modern day prophet. The words he'd just uttered rang in my ears, seeming to echo that sentiment.

I didn't move. The man was nuts. That was the only explanation, but right now I was thankful that he was just a little bit out of his mind. Crazy or not, he might have just saved my ass. I could take old zombies. I could probably even take one new zombie as long as I had a way to defend myself. But in a ring with no weapons and a freshly turned zombie, especially if it was a newer strain of the virus, I was fucked.

The wheels of the cart creaked behind me, and I stepped aside so Dragon's cronies could pull the zoms out of the holding room. The newer one was still tugging on his chains, but he was on his feet the second he saw the people. He lunged, his chains pulling tight and stopping him from going anywhere, but not stopping him from gnashing his teeth.

His fight continued the whole time the men worked to get him chained up inside the ring, and more than once one of them came close to getting a chunk bitten out of them. I'd never seen a zombie so aggressive or determined. They were all blood thirsty, but this one didn't get distracted by the noise surrounding him the way they usually did.

When Dragon called my name, I headed out. Every inch of my skin was covered in a layer of sweat and my stomach hadn't been this uneasy since my first few fights. I looked toward the bar, but Meg wasn't there, and when I turned back, I saw why. She was serving drinks to the VIPs. Jackson and his group of council brats. The asshole had his arm around the shoulder of some blonde girl while one of his friends talked to Meg. I was too far away to be able to hear what the little prick was saying to her, but with the way her hands were clenched into fists, I had a feeling it was a good thing I was out of hearing range. If I could have heard it, I probably would have broken the asshole's nose.

In the ring the lights were so bright that they momentarily drowned out the faces of the crowd. My eyes would adjust before too long, but right now, I wished they wouldn't. Having Jackson and his asshole friends here was a distraction I didn't need.

Dragon asked the crowd if they were ready and cheers echoed through the air, making every muscle in my body tense in anticipation. He backed out while I turned my focus to the zoms. All three of them pulled at their chains, trying to break free, but the one in the middle fought twice as hard.

The door clanged shut, and in the blink of an eye the dead were charging me. It only took a split second for me to realize they hadn't released the newest one. Even though I tried to see it as an advantage—if I could get at least one of the others down before they let him out, I might be okay—I knew they were just biding their time. Waiting for me to be distracted so they could let the other one loose.

The first one to reach me was so rotten that the skin had started to peel off his face. He chomped and reached for me, but thankfully, he only had three fingers on his right hand. I grabbed him around the wrist and jerked my hand to the left, and the cracking of bone echoed in my ears. He snarled and tried to get me with his other hand, but I repeated the process. The second zom was almost on top of me when I threw the first at him, and they both went down. They writhed on the floor, trying to get up, but I didn't give them a chance. When I slammed the heel of my boot into the first one's skull, I was rewarded with a crunch and the thing stopped moving, his motionless body sprawled out across the other one, pinning the bastard to the ground.

Chains clanged to my right and I spun around to face the sound. The newer zombie was free, but he didn't charge. He just stood there, watching me like he was biding his time, his milky eyes narrowed but his dilated pupils focused and alert. The bright lights reflected off his smooth head as he tilted it to the side, his gaze moving to the zombies at my feet, then back to my face. When he opened his mouth, spittle flew out with his roar.

"Shit." I took a step back.

The virus must not have turned him completely yet or he wouldn't be able reason like this. The dark veins in his arms told me he was beyond saving, but I was willing to bet that if I cut him, his blood wouldn't be black yet. It was the most dangerous stage of this new strain. Whoever had brought this zombie in knew exactly what they were doing.

Lucky for me, being locked in a cage with the asshole meant it wasn't exactly possible for him to take me by surprise. Which meant that when the thing finally did charge me, I was ready for him.

I held my ground until the last possible second, then darted out of the monster's way. He flew past me, slamming into the fence at my back. When I spun around, the grinning face of Jackson momentarily distracted me, but a snarl brought me back. This time when the zombie headed my way, I lifted my leg and slammed my boot square into the center of his chest.

He let out a howl when he once again went crashing into the cage, but I wasn't sure if it was from anger or pain. He tried to jump at me again, but I slammed my shoulder into his chest and held him back. His face was inches from my ear when he snapped his teeth, so close that spit sprayed across my cheek. I jerked my head away while keeping my shoulder pressed against him, and in a moment of horror, I realized that deep in his chest, his heart was still pounding away. The rhythm was odd, slower than normal, the beats somehow longer and more spaced out, but not struggling. Even as the zombie jerked back and forth, trying to break free, I knew that he shouldn't be able to move this quickly with his heart beating at such a slow pace.

What the hell had this virus created?

I pulled him off the fence and threw him to the ground, then stood over him, my feet on his arms so he was pinned to the floor. With him restrained, I was able to take a moment and really look him over. A line of crimson liquid dripped from the cut on the side of his face, bright enough to almost make me step back. That was wrong. His blood shouldn't have been red like this. It was supposed to be dark brown, well on its way to turning black.

This was unlike any zombie I had ever seen.

I gave him a closer look, my own heart pounding so hard it

echoed in my ears. On first glance I'd thought he was bald, but now that I was able to get a better look at him, I realized that wasn't right. There was *no* hair on his body at all. None on his head or chest, and he had no eyebrows or eyelashes either. On top of that, his skin was so thin it almost looked transparent, reminding me of the eighty-year-old man who had lived next door to my family when I was young. Only, the creature's skin didn't rip easily the way an old person's did, and the texture was different. Not soft and thin, but leathery. Like the sun had hardened it.

In one violent twist that caught me totally by surprise, the zombie threw me back. He was on his feet so fast that it almost looked like he had superpowers, and all I could think as he charged at me was that he was planning to rip me apart with his bare hands.

This time when he reached me, I didn't mess around. I slammed my fist into his face just like I would if he were a living person who was trying to attack me. He stumbled back but didn't fall; only it didn't matter because I ran at him, keeping my body low. My shoulder slammed into his stomach and he doubled over. I wrapped my arms around his torso and lifted. His feet left the ground, flailing under him, and his hands clawed at my back for a second before I threw him across the ring. He slammed into the cage and the chain link rattled all around us. The creature landed on his stomach and scrambled to get up, but I was on him before he could. I sank one knee into his spine to hold him down, then grabbed his head between my hands. One violent twist was all it took to end it. A crack echoed through the air when his neck snapped and his body went limp. I got to my feet, panting as I stepped back. Staring down at his now lifeless eyes.

The room was silent except for the sound of the other zombie, still at my back and still trapped under his fallen comrade. I was gasping for breath when I turned to take care of him. Two stomps to the skull and he was gone too, but still no one made a sound. The stunned silence that had fallen over the room made perfect sense considering what just happened.

I had just killed a zombie without destroying his brain.

Was he even a zombie?

The gate clinked when Dragon opened it, but I didn't look his

261

way. Instead, I lifted my head, focusing on Jackson. Around him, his friends looked just as stunned as the rest of the room did, but the little prick was smiling. A sick, evil grin that made his eyes flash like hellfire was burning in them. The disappointment that swam in his gaze was a total contradiction to that smile, and it caused a shudder to move up my spine.

THE WATER I SPLASHED AGAINST MY FACE WASN'T COOL, but it was refreshing. I squeezed my eyes shut and splashed more, running my damp hands in circles across my face, hoping to wash away all of the blood spatter. When I opened my eyes, the water in the sink was gray.

I stepped back and took a deep breath before looking at my reflection. My face was pretty clean, but there was still a sprinkling on my arms and chest. Only they weren't all black. A burst of red painted my right bicep, so bright it stood out even among the lines of black on my skin.

"What the hell was that thing?" I asked my reflection.

Like me, he didn't have any answers.

"Donaghy?" Meg's voice echoed through the room and I turned to find her standing behind me. "You did it."

"I did."

I held her gaze, not sure what to say now that I'd made it through the fight. We'd kissed. It wasn't the first time, but there was something significant about it. Something that didn't just tell me how she felt about me, but made me accept the truth of how I felt about her. I wanted this girl. Despite the crazy and danger surrounding her life, and how it would most likely leave us both with a lot of heartache, I wanted Meg.

She stepped closer, her fingers brushing the red on my bicep. "What was that?"

"I don't know." I shook my head. "It was fast and powerful, and it's heart was still beating. It was like some kind of crazy hybrid zombie."

"Is this what they're doing in the CDC?" Meg's green eyes searched mine.

The thought hadn't occurred to me, but mainly because I

hadn't had time in the middle of the ring to really process it all. But it made sense. I never believed Jackson's father wanted to stop the zombies. With the threat out there, people were forced to stay behind the wall and do as they were told, which gave the Regulator all the power. But if he didn't want to create a vaccine, why he would kidnap people who were immune was an utter mystery. Until now. That thing, whatever it had been, wasn't natural.

"I don't think there's any other explanation for it." I let out a deep breath and ran my still damp hand over my head. My hair was starting to grow back after being shaved in DC, but it was still soft against my palm. "I've been out there for weeks. On the road, traveling from settlement to settlement. I've never seen anything like that."

"We have to stop them."

"We will." I pulled her close and she rested her head on my chest.

The back room at Dragon's was dark and reeked of death, and my guards were still coughing their heads off, but right now, I wouldn't want to be anywhere else.

# CHAPTER TWENTY-SIX

## Meg

**THE** city seemed darker than usual, which made no sense considering the full moon was shining its soft rays on the street in front of me. Then again, maybe it had to do with the long shadows that seemed to stretch toward me from every nook and cranny I passed, reaching out like they were trying to pull me into their black depths.

I walked faster, the sound of my heels clicking against the street not doing anything to calm my pounding heart. I was still shaken from the evening. First, knowing that they'd sent a zombie in hopes of finishing off Donaghy, then seeing Jackson and realizing he'd had a hand in it. The creature in the ring had been the final straw. It moved faster than any zombie we'd ever seen, regardless of the strain, and it had purpose. Like he'd been told his only reason for existing was to rip Donaghy's throat out. He wasn't human, but he wasn't one of the dead either.

Arms wrapped around me from behind, catching me totally off guard and ripping me right out of my heels. My scream echoed through the still night and I kicked my leg back, but before my foot could make contact, my attacker threw me to the ground. My body slammed into the concrete. The force of the impact vibrated through my bones and knocked the wind out of me. The throb that moved through me was immobilizing, and the scream I tried to let out was nothing more than a strangled gasp.

I tried to move. Tried to drag myself away from the footsteps that came up behind me. I managed to make it halfway to my hands and knees, pulling myself forward as pebbles dug into my palms and legs. I only gained inches, though, and then the man was on me again. He grabbed me by the arms and flipped me over so violently that the back of my skull banged against the ground, causing a bright, white light to flash across my vision. Blackness followed, closing in on me from all sides. I struggled against it, trying to fight back, but found myself being pulled into an abyss so dark and deep that I wasn't sure I'd ever be able to escape.

*No!*

I blinked and forced myself to stay conscious. I could feel it as my brain clawed itself from the abyss, and when my eyes finally focused, I found my attacker leaning over me. He was nothing but bright eyes and lips in a sea of black, and I was so disoriented that it took longer than it should for me to realize why. He was wearing a mask.

"Don't move," he said, his mouth seeming to float above his body.

"Stop." My voice trembled so much that I wasn't even sure the word I tried to mutter was actually a word.

I batted at him, but the man above me only laughed as his hands ran up my thighs. The knife strapped to my leg was pulled off and tossed aside. When it clanked against the pavement, getting lost in the darkness, I wanted to scream.

I did scream when the man pushed my skirt up around my waist, but it did nothing to help my situation. He pushed my dress higher and I howled and kicked and batted at him, my arms and legs flailing uselessly as I tried to fight him off. I didn't make any progress. His weight was heavy on my stomach when he leaned forward, his knees digging into my arms and making it impossible for me to get any movement at all. Warm air brushed my chest when my dress went even higher.

"Just hold still and it will all be over faster," he said, his bright eyes and mouth hovering over me.

Every move he made seemed to be in slow motion, and the thoughts in my head weren't much faster or clearer, but one thing did stick out: *This man doesn't stink.*

I forced my eyes to stay open even though they wanted to close. The man moved back, and I focused on his hands. His palms were flat against my stomach, and as starkly white as my own skin was. Clean. No dirt caked under his nails.

*Why is he so clean?*

He sat back, the weight of his body pressing against my knees as he worked to undo his pants. "You brought this on yourself."

The epiphany that slammed into me with those words was so sharp it felt like a knife cutting into my brain.

Someone sent him here to punish me. Maybe even kill me...

Someone from the government.

*Jackson.*

That thought had just crashed into me when another face came into view, hovering over my attacker's shoulder. This one wasn't as clean, but it was familiar. Gray eyes flashed like violent storm clouds just before my attacker was ripped off me.

I inhaled, filling my lungs until they felt like they would burst as I pulled my dress down. To my right, the scuffle was loud and violent, knocking over trashcans that rattled against the sidewalk and spilled their foul-smelling contents all over the ground. I rolled to my side, my head still pounding and the world around me spinning faster than the two men wrestling each other on the ground. Flashes of black and gray swirled together, highlighted by the moon, and I squeezed my eyes shut when a wave of nausea rolled through me.

When I opened my eyes again, the gray man was standing. His shoulders heaved as he stared down at the other man, now nothing more than a tangle of black on the pavement.

I pushed myself up, barely clinging to consciousness but knowing that I needed to talk to this man before he once again disappeared. "You saved me."

The gray man turned away from the body in front of him and knelt at my side. His eyes, now calm and full of concern, moved over me before he nodded once. "You alright?"

"I—I think so." I touched the back of my head, which

throbbed, and felt a bump. No blood, though. That was good. "Who are you?"

"Just an old friend," he said, once again looking me over. "You sure you ain't hurt?"

A painful twinge squeezed my insides. Dad used to say *ain't*. God, if only I could stop seeing him in everything that happened. Donaghy's scar and the way Glitter puckered her lips, not to mention this man's eyes. Now he was starting to sound like Dad, too. Maybe I was losing my mind.

"I'll be okay," I said, getting to my feet and pulling my skirt down the rest of the way. My hands trembled when I grabbed my shoes and put them on, but I refused to think about what had almost happened or the fact that Jackson was responsible for this. I was okay.

The gray man stood too, and a second later he let out a low chuckle. "You're just like your mamma. She was tough as nails, too."

"You knew my mom?" I wasn't sure if he was referring to Hadley Lucas or Vivian James, though.

"Long time ago."

The gray man glanced over his shoulder, then grabbed my elbow. He started walking, leading me forward. I didn't ask where he was taking me. Probably because I knew. Home. He wasn't going to hurt me. The opposite, really. He wanted me to be safe.

We reached shantytown, our footsteps joining the moans, coughs, and snores of the people who lived here. Neither one of us spoke, but I looked his way every few seconds, trying to memorize his face and store it away for later. Trying to figure out how this man fit into my life.

The only discernable change in his mood was when we came to the shrine of Angus. Two people, coughing so much they were barely able to stay upright, were kneeling in front of the little statue. Their lips moved in silent prayer, their hands folded in front of them as they asked for salvation or forgiveness or something else, only they knew for sure.

The gray man slowed for a split second, his eyes on them. Then he shook his head and kept walking.

When we finally reached my building, he stopped and looked up. "Can't go in."

He let go of my arm and took a step back, and I found my legs steadier than I'd thought they would be. My head was pounding, though, and I had a suspicion it would be a couple days before the ache went away.

"Can you tell me who you are?" I asked, when it hit me that he was about to walk away and I had no idea when I would see him again.

He turned his gaze on me, and the eyes that stared back were sharp and familiar, but my fuzzy brain refused to allow me to make the connection. It was there. The answer was so close that I could almost reach out and grab it, but no matter how hard I tried to bring it into focus, I couldn't seem to catch it.

"Watch out for yourself," he said instead of answering my question. "Tell the others to watch their backs, too. They got it out for the whole lot of you. Pretty soon, they're gonna get tired of tryin' to make it look like an accident and just get rid of you."

"Who?"

He took a step back. "The CDC."

The CDC?

*Dad.*

"Is my dad there?" I asked, stumbling after the gray man as he turned and headed down the street. "I just want to know if he's alive!"

My voice echoed down the dark street, but the gray man kept walking, not even looking back at me. I stood in the middle of the road on wobbly legs, watching as he disappeared into the darkness. Totally unable to run after him with my head pounding the way it was.

When he was gone, I dragged myself inside, but it took a few minutes for my head to clear enough to hit the button for the elevator. The thing groaned and I held my breath, waiting to see if it was going to work. After what seemed like forever, the lobby went silent and the door slid open. One of these days, this thing was going to break for good. I was just glad it wasn't today. I wasn't sure I'd be able to drag myself up the stairs with the way my head was throbbing.

Mom was up and sitting on the couch when I got in, and she jumped to her feet the second she saw me. "Meg? What happened?"

269

"It's no big deal," I said as I headed past her into the kitchen.

My head wouldn't stop pounding and my bottom lip wasn't much better. It was going to be fat tomorrow for sure. Under the kitchen lights, I was able to see all the cuts and scratches on my arms and legs from my struggle. I got lucky once again.

Mom stopped at my side when I turned on the faucet. I needed a shower, but it was late and I was exhausted, so the water from the sink and a washcloth would have to do.

"What happened?" Mom asked, her voice calmer this time.

When I turned, she took the wet cloth out of my hand and pressed it to my throbbing lip. I winced, but she didn't blink. That's when it hit me: She was back. The mom I'd grown up with. Her brown eyes were bright and alert, assessing my injuries with the same cool exterior she'd always shown when I was a kid.

"I was jumped." I kept my eyes away from hers so she wouldn't know that the man had wanted more than just credits from me.

"Did he get what he wanted?" The way she winced told me that she could see right through me.

"No." I exhaled. "Someone saved me."

"You got lucky." The breath she let out was full of relief, and I stole a glance at her face. She was still looking me over like she was making sure I was in one piece.

"I'll be fine," I said, trying to reassure her.

Mom nodded and allowed me to take the cloth from her hand. I used it to clean the dirt off my arms and legs while she leaned against the counter with her arms crossed. In this light, I was once again struck by how much weight she'd lost. She was bony now, her breasts almost looking clownish on her thin frame. I'd always known they were fake, but I hadn't thought about why she had them done until now. She used to be a stripper before. That must have been why.

"Tell me something I don't know," I said when I turned to rinse the washcloth. "Something about you before the virus hit. Or maybe something about you and Dad that I've never heard before. Something happy."

Mom's gaze moved toward the floor and she grinned for a second before saying, "Your uncle was a bully when I first met him. He didn't like me, and he didn't want your dad and me to be together, but it happened anyway." When I turned to face her, the cool cloth still pressed against my throbbing skull, Mom's smile was wider. "There were times when I thought Angus hated me. He loved to get under my skin, and I know he had moments when he resented me for taking Axl's attention. But the day he was bitten — the day we found out he was immune — he sacrificed himself to save me."

Her smile grew bigger and I joined in. I'd thought she was going to tell me something about Dad, but it had turned out to be about Angus instead. It was strange, and I wasn't sure what to make of it, but it was nice too.

"I stopped drinking the water in the bedroom," Mom said, pulling me from my thoughts.

"Why's that?" I was only partially paying attention, still lost in my own musings about the past and how much things had changed in recent weeks.

"I had another dream about Angus, and he told me to start boiling the water. He said the filters weren't safe. I've felt better since then. More with it."

I stood up straighter. Could it have been that simple? There had been times, especially over the last week, when it had seemed like Mom's paranoia was about more than just losing Dad. There were even moments when I'd wondered if someone was drugging her. She'd been so out of it. What if someone *had* slipped her drugs?

*Pretty soon they're gonna get tired of tryin' to make it look like an accident and just get rid of you.* The gray man's warning rang in my ears.

What if *they* were trying to get rid of Mom slowly? Make her look nuts so that when she disappeared, people would just assume that she'd finally lost it. At this point, I wasn't willing to discard any theory.

"I'm glad," I said, trying to keep a straight face. Either way, the good news was that she seemed even more with it today than she had the other night. "I missed you."

Mom smiled and opened her arms, and I found myself falling against her. She wrapped me in a bony hug that was comforting despite the slight unfamiliarity of it.

"I'm going to change out all the filters on the sinks tomorrow,"

Mom said against my head. "But just in case, we should boil the water."

"I think that's a good idea." I buried my face against her chest as tears came to my eyes. There was a part of me that wanted to tell her everything. To let it all spill out so she could help shoulder the burden, and so she'd know that she wasn't alone in all this.

I didn't, though. Not yet. First I needed to talk to Parv and Al, and tell everyone to be careful. Then I'd find out what they thought about bringing Mom into the loop.

IT WAS ANOTHER DAY TOO SCORCHING TO BE PICKING up trash, and my aching body wasn't making it any better. The scrapes and cuts covering my legs from last night's attack weren't bad, but the back of my head was still tender and my lip was throbbing and swollen. The eyes of every person I passed swam with questions, but they didn't ask. They probably just assumed that I'd mouthed off to a boyfriend or something like that.

Luckily, we weren't shoveling up trash today. We'd reached a nicer part of the city where people had kindly taken the time to bag their garbage, and unlike the shantytown from the past couple days, the buildings in this section were tall, former offices and apartments that had long ago been renovated to fit the needs of New Atlanta. They cast shadows across the road, helping shade us from the sun while we worked. Another blessing. There were no good days on garbage detail, but some were worse than others. Shantytown was as bad as it got.

The good news: Mom left the apartment at the same time that I did this morning. If she could get her old position back, it might be possible for me to quit this stinking job.

"Holy shit!" someone to my right called out.

I dropped the fifty-pound bag of trash I'd been dragging toward the truck and looked up to find a little guy who couldn't be older than sixteen staring into an alley only ten feet away from me. My sweaty hair got plastered across my eyes, and I batted it away as best as I could, trying not to get garbage all over my face. Again. The guy's expression was a little green.

"What's wrong?" the crew leader called, his voice slightly

muffled from his mask.

"Body." The kid turned away, and the little bit of his face that was visible was scrunched up in disgust. "Looks pretty fresh."

"Shit." The crew leader dropped his bag of trash as he turned on his heel, heading over to where the boy stood. He peered down the alley, annoyance flashing in his eyes as he shook his head. "I'll have to call it in. Everybody keep working! No reason to gawk at the poor bastard."

He took off for the truck, which was parked a block down, ripping his gloves off in the process and swearing up a storm as he went. I took a few deep breaths before lifting the bag I had just dropped. The muscles in my arms throbbed.

All around me, people did exactly what the crew leader had said *not* to do: hurried over to get a glimpse of the body. I ignored them and headed for the truck, sweating like crazy and praying Mom could get her job back so I didn't have to do this again tomorrow.

"We have a body out here," the crew leader was saying into the radio as I approached the truck. "South Peachtree Street."

Static broke through just as I tossed my bag in the back, but I didn't wait for the response before heading back to get more.

"Did you see that guy?" a girl about ten years older than me asked as she passed me. The load slung over her shoulder was so small a toddler could have carried it. "Gross."

"No," I gasped.

A crowd was still gathered around the alley, and since I honestly wasn't interested in seeing a dead person—Didn't I see them every night at Dragon's?—I tried to move past. But just as I was stepping around the people crowded near the body, a girl squealed and jumped back.

"Don't poke it!"

I spun toward the group, all ready to tell them to have a little respect, but the words died on my lips when I caught a glimpse of pale, blond hair.

"No."

I was moving before I could think better of it, pushing people out of my way so I could get a better look. Knowing before I even saw his face that it was Jimmy and he was here not only because of me, but as a warning *to* me.

273

Someone swore when I shoved them aside, but I didn't care. My eyes were glued to the blond head just barely sticking out from the pile of black bags. When I stepped closer, shockingly blue eyes stared up at me from a baby face and my stomach convulsed.

"No," I said again, this time backing away.

"You okay?"

"Did you know him?"

"Who is it?"

Questions were thrown at me, but I didn't stay long enough to answer. I turned and ran, ripping my mask off and tossing it aside, then my gloves. My jumpsuit was unzipped before I'd made it to the end of the street. The crew leader called after me, but I didn't stop or look back or even think about pausing. I ran, shoving the jumpsuit down as I went, almost tripping over the fabric when it bunched around my ankles. Somehow, I managed to kick it free without falling on my face. I didn't care that I was only in a pair of skimpy shorts and tank top after that, because all I could think about was finding Ticker.

I was gasping for breath by the time I made it to shantytown, and I could barely focus enough to remember where I'd seen him. I passed shack after shack, squeezing between metal and wood siding as I called his name, barely able to breathe let alone think. My leg caught on something, but I barely felt the sharp prick of the cut when it sliced across my skin.

"Ticker!" I stopped and called his name as loud as I could, spinning in a circle.

Until now, I hadn't realized how many shacks had sprung up. Blocks and blocks of them were lined up in front of me, shoved so close together that there was barely any room between them. It was unreal.

The hacking sound of illness was rampant. Echoing off the walls of the buildings. Even worse was the smell. We'd picked up the garbage in this area already, so I knew for sure the faint stench of decay had nothing to do with trash. Death had fallen across the city.

"The flu," I said, almost to myself because I had a feeling there weren't many people around to hear it. Right now they were either at work or too sick to understand me, or they'd already passed over to the other side.

Based on the way they were living, maybe it was better. Maybe we all would have been better off if the virus that had swept the country twenty years ago had destroyed the human population. We sure hadn't done a better job the second time around.

"Meg?"

I turned at the sound of Ticker's voice and found him standing two streets over, just visible through a break in the houses. His beady eyes were bright and alert as they scanned the area, and the second he was sure I'd seen him, he ducked down so he was out of sight. I squeezed between two houses, then down another alley, and finally Ticker was in front of me. Kneeling in the dirt.

"What are you doing?" he whispered, his gaze moved across my face, over the cuts and bruises.

"I was attacked last night," I said as I crouched down in front of him, panting. "And Jimmy... They found his body today. I was picking up garbage and he was there. They put him there so I'd see. So I'd know he was dead!"

Ticker's shoulder jerked. "He's dead."

"He's dead."

"Can't find Matt. He's still missing. Ticker's not going to bite it, though. Ticker's getting out."

"Getting out? How?" Anyone who left the city had to go through the main gate, and I could pretty much guarantee that they had someone keeping an eye out for Ticker. Probably for me, too.

"Zombie slayer. Ticker has credits saved. You want out of the city, all you need are credits."

"When are you going?" I asked as his eyes flew back and forth like crazy, bouncing past me and down the street like he was sure he would get jumped at any moment.

"Tomorrow. Ticker's had enough of this city. Ticker's done."

I didn't blame him. If my Dad weren't trapped in the CDC, I'd be out of here too.

I grabbed his hand and gave it a squeeze. "Be careful. Okay, Ticker?"

"You be careful." He raised himself up just enough so he could get a good look around. "Watch your back. Ticker thinks you should get a gun. If you can find one."

"Thanks. That's a good idea."

He nodded once, his beady eyes barely stopping on me before he took off. Seconds later, he darted down an alley and disappeared from sight.

I stayed where I was, kneeling in the middle of shantytown with the sun beating down on me. Flies buzzed overhead, occasionally landing on me, but mostly just trying to get into the surrounding houses. Every time a breeze swept down the street, it brought the stink of death with it, and it was foreboding enough to send a shiver shooting through me.

Ticker was right. I needed a gun.

# CHAPTER TWENTY-SEVEN

## Donaghy

THE lifeless eyes of the younger guard stared up at me. It was different than looking at a zombie, though. The walking dead had a strange spark in their milky eyes that made them seem alive, even if their heart was no longer beating. The guard's, however, were blank. Empty. Like whoever used to be in there had been drained out.

On the other side of the room, the older guard wheezed. Every breath out of his mouth seemed to take more effort than the last, and with each inhale his chest rattled even more. He was losing his fight with this flu and we all knew it. Even worse, at this point, I was pretty sure he was praying for the end.

"I'll wait until he's gone to have the other body removed," Dragon said, nodding to the older guard who was barely hanging on. "No reason to have the undertakers here more than they need to be."

Even though the idea of leaving the dead guy here made me cringe, I had to agree with Dragon. This flu had swept through the city, and I was sure the people in charge of removing bodies were having trouble keeping up.

"Any signs of it slowing?" I asked as I followed Dragon into the other room.

He shook his head as he ducked behind the bar. "Not that I can see, but if this one follows the same pattern as the last few, we should be nearing the end."

"There's a pattern?" I asked, sliding onto a stool while the other man filled shot glasses.

We'd fallen into what could almost be called a friendship over the last couple days. Dragon had proven himself to be reliable, even if I still suspected that he was slightly unhinged, and I had proven that I could keep my mouth shut when he helped me. With my guards dying, I didn't know when I'd be leaving, and despite all the close calls since I'd been here, it was the best place I could imagine getting stuck.

"There's a pattern to everything if you look for it." Dragon's brown eyes held mine as he slid a glass across the counter. "But this especially."

He didn't look away until he'd thrown the shot back, and then it was only so he could refill his glass. "They aren't timed any certain way, which is why a lot of people probably don't notice the pattern. The last flu was five years ago, and the one before that seven. The first one was only three years after the walls were built. But see, the number of years isn't what we should be looking at, it's the population."

I watched Dragon closely for any sign that he was testing me, but there wasn't any. He believed every word, and so did I. His theory pretty much confirmed what I'd heard at the Regulator's house.

"You think the government released this flu so they could downsize the population?"

"A lower population is easier to control. People who are grieving over lost loved ones even more so." He leaned forward, his gaze holding mine. "I know you've seen it too."

"Yeah." I threw the shot back and took a deep breath. "Yesterday you said our time was coming. What did you mean?"

After the conversation I'd overheard the other morning, I knew Dragon was involved in something, but how deep he was in was the question I hadn't dared ask.

Dragon's sharp gaze sliced through me. "Those in charge aren't looking out for us. The opposite, really. They use the people they need, then toss them aside like they're nothing. They leave widows and orphans to live in filth, not caring that they can make the world better. And they can. We can't let it go on."

I shook my head, not sure what to say or what to ask. "What about Meg? Does this have something to do with her or her family?"

Dragon leaned back, not taking his eyes off me for even a second. "What do you think?"

"I think that almost everything I've seen or heard since getting here has something to do with her family, and it's damn suspicious. Too suspicious to ignore." I threw my shot back, letting it hit my stomach and ease the tension there before saying, "And I think you know more than you're letting on."

Dragon opened his mouth and I braced myself for the truth, but before he could say anything, the front door was thrown open. We both turned at the sound, my body already tense and my brain ready to get yet another surprise from the government. The guards standing there weren't a shock, but the person with them was. No zombies this time. Just Jackson Star.

"Sorry to interrupt. But we just got some unfortunate news from Dayton." The prick gave me a condescendingly sympathetic smile as he crossed the room toward me. "I thought it should come straight from me."

Dread squeezed my insides and I braced myself for what I knew was coming. The look on Jackson's face said it all, and after my win last night there was no doubt in my mind that this asshole wanted to destroy me. Slowly if possible, but above all else, he wanted to inflict pain on me.

"Say it," I growled.

"Your sister was killed sometime last night. Someone broke into her apartment, and she had no one to protect her." Jackson shook his head as his mouth morphed into a parody of a frown. "A tragedy. She was so young. Had so much ahead of her. The Judicial Officer in Dayton called me personally to let me know. If only you had been there to save her the way you saved Meg. Not that you can save Meg from *everything*."

The flash of triumph in his eyes made me jump to my feet. My shoulders were heaving, and I was ready to explode. Red covered my vision, and I knew that at any second I was going to charge this asshole. Beat him to death and then die happy.

Dragon grabbed my arm. "Thank you for letting us know."

I clenched my hands into fists, ready to punch him too. *Us?* How the hell was he involved in any of this? He didn't know Patty. He hadn't been the one to hold her when Mom died or to feed her when Kurt checked out. Dragon hadn't seen the bruises on her face and arms and legs after that asshole had his way with her. No, that had been me. I was the one who should have been there to take care of her. To keep her safe. But I failed. Not only did I get my ass sent to DC, but I got mixed up in something that found her all the way back home in Dayton.

Jackson didn't move for what felt like hours. Dragon's grip on my arm tightened, and behind the Regulator's son, the enforcers who had come with him shifted awkwardly. The asshole actually grinned when I didn't move, and I knew he was daring me. Daring me to screw up again so those pricks behind him could shoot me in the head. They'd be justified and everyone in this room knew it.

I let out a deep breath, working to blow all the pain out of my body, and then sank back onto the stool. Dragon let me go and a second later, footsteps shuffled out the door. My head was down, so I didn't see the expression on Jackson's face when he left, but I could picture the one from last night perfectly. He had a backup plan and I knew it. He'd be disappointed, but that evil smile of his would be there to light up his face and tell me that he had more than one trick up his sleeve.

"I'm sorry," Dragon said when we were alone.

"I should have been there for her."

"There isn't much in this life that we have control over. Not anymore."

"I had control over this."

"No. You didn't." I looked up to find Dragon shaking his head. "I read your file and I know what you were in for. That's the only reason I agreed to this exchange program." He flashed a toothless grin my way. "Well, that and the credits I knew it would bring in. But that's not the point."

"What's the point?" The ache that had started in my gut had now moved to my chest, and I was pretty sure I was on the verge of a heart attack. All I could picture was Patty the way she'd looked after the first time she was attacked. Split lip and bruised body. Crying. That was probably how she'd looked when she'd died too.

"The point is, we need people like you if we want to start over for real."

"We can't start over for real." I shook my head. "Star's in control."

"We can. Just not here."

I narrowed my eyes on Dragon. "You suggesting we leave? Start an unsanctioned town?"

"No. I'm suggesting we join one. One that's already established and growing stronger. One that wants to work toward a better future and maybe, one day, defeat Star."

It seemed ironic coming from the guy who was running this dive, but there was a lot about Dragon I didn't understand. The first time I'd set foot in his basement I knew that.

"Who are you?"

Dragon grinned. "I'm the black dragon, and I'm about to rain fire down on all of Atlanta."

"You're nuts." I got to my feet and headed to the back so I could grieve by myself. One of my guards was dead and the other was on the verge, but I'd rather cry in front of them than in front of Dragon.

He didn't try to stop me. Not that he could have.

# CHAPTER TWENTY-EIGHT

## Meg

**MIKE** lived one floor below me, but I'd only been to his place a few times. With Dad. I'd always known my father was involved in the black market of New Atlanta, but I'd never really asked questions. With stuff like that it was better to live in ignorance. That is, until you were in the position I now found myself in. Thankfully, I'd paid enough attention back then to know where I needed to go now.

Standing outside the closed door, I shifted from foot to foot and glanced up and down the hall, almost as if I expected to see someone standing in the shadows. No one was around though, and even if someone did happen to see me here, there was no real reason for suspicion. It wasn't illegal to visit someone in the middle of the day, and as far as any strangers passing by knew, that's all I was doing. Still, my heart was beating twice as hard as it usually did, and my palms were moist with sweat.

What I was about to do wasn't necessarily what was making me nervous, though. The thing that was making it all so much more nerve wracking was the utter silence that had fallen over this building. It felt empty. Deserted. Like a graveyard. It seemed that the flu hadn't just wreaked havoc on the shantytown, which just went to show that no one was really safe these days.

When I finally got up the nerve to knock, the sound of my knuckles hitting the wood echoed through the hall. I jumped even though I knew I was the one who'd made the noise. My heart beat faster, the sound of it echoing in my ears. I took a step back and looked up, toward the peephole. If someone did happen to be home in the middle of the day, they were going to look through that little hole before they opened the door.

"Please, please, please," I whispered, crossing my fingers.

It seemed to take forever, although it was probably less than a minute, but finally the sound of the deadbolt clicking cut through the silence that surrounded me. The lock followed a second later, but when the door was finally pulled open, the safety chain was still on.

A pair of blue eyes peered at me through the gap, moving over me slowly. "What do you want?" the woman asked.

"Hi." I took a step closer as I shot another quick look up and down the hall. "I'm looking for Mike."

The woman didn't blink, but she also didn't respond.

Did I have the wrong apartment? I was certain this was the right place, but maybe Mike didn't live here anymore. Maybe he'd died or been shipped off to DC for selling weapons. Anything was possible, and it had been a few years since I'd come here with Dad.

"I need something," I said, then held my breath.

I couldn't just come right out and ask for a gun, especially not if this woman had nothing to do with the black market, but I wasn't ready to give up yet. After seeing Jimmy's body in that alley, I was afraid to walk away empty-handed. Twice in the last week, my knife had proven insignificant.

When the woman in front of me still didn't respond, I tried one last tactic. "My dad was Axl James. I need help."

The woman blinked again, but this time it looked more like she was startled than she was studying me. A second later the door slammed in my face. My shoulders slumped and I let out a deep breath. Maybe I didn't have the right place, or maybe this woman didn't want to get mixed up in whatever had happened to Dad. At this point, I almost couldn't blame her.

I turned to leave, but a click from the other side of the door made me freeze. I spun back around, and a second later the door was pulled open.

"Come in," the woman hissed, her blue eyes darting around as I rushed through the door.

She shut it before I'd even had a chance to register where I was, and it wasn't until it slammed behind me that I started to worry. With all the shit going on around me, how did I know I could trust this woman or Mike? Dad had worked with them, but everything had been fine for the past twenty years, and then the world around me seemed to explode. For all I knew, these people were just as bad as Jackson and his father.

The lock clicked and I spun around, coming face to face with the woman who had answered the door. She was in her forties, fit despite the saggy skin on her neck and the dark circles under her eyes. Her hair had once been blonde, but now it was a dull color that was somewhere between gold and gray, and her eyes, although bright, looked sunken.

She coughed once, turning her head away. "What do you want?"

I swallowed. "A gun."

"And Axl was your dad?" The woman didn't even blink when she looked me over.

"Yes."

"Megan, right?"

I nodded.

She moved past me, further into the apartment. "I only have one."

"Where's Mike?" I asked as I watched her cross the room.

Her entire body jerked, but her steps didn't falter. "Dead. Last night." She coughed again. "I'm not too far behind him."

"I'm sorry."

Something in my voice must have reached her, because she paused long enough to look back over her shoulder. The sadness in her eyes reminded me of Mom and how she looked every time someone talked about Dad. Like a piece of her had been ripped away.

"Me too," the woman whispered.

She disappeared down the hall, leaving me alone, and I shuffled from foot to foot while I waited for her to return. Random items lined the walls in the living and dining room. Bottles of booze from the old world, bootlegged cigarettes by the carton, moonshine, batteries, and prepackaged meals. The illegal stuff was probably hidden, but it looked like everything in this apartment was worth something to the right person.

Footsteps headed my way, and a few seconds later the woman was back, a pistol in her hand. "This should be easy for you to use, but there are only five rounds." She held it out to me.

"I've shot one before," I said as I shoved my hand in my pocket and pulled out all the credits I had in the world. How I'd pay for rent I didn't know, but I did know I needed the protection this gun would provide. "This is all I have." My hands were trembling. Hopefully, it would be enough.

She shook her head as she shoved the gun in my hand. "I'm dead. Even if this flu doesn't kill me, I'm finished." The resignation in her voice was painful. "Take anything else you might need."

She jerked her head toward the stuff stacked along the wall, and even though I felt slightly guilty about taking advantage of her, I turned toward it. "Thanks."

She nodded, watching me as I shoved the gun into a box of prepackaged meals. My scalp prickled under her scrutiny, but I was too desperate to be humble right now. I needed this stuff.

When I turned back to face the woman, she nodded. "I hope everything turns out okay for you."

It sounded more like: *you're screwed.*

"Thanks," I mumbled again as I hurried to the door.

I couldn't wait to get out of the apartment, but once I was in the hall I was only able to breathe a little bit easier. The box in my hands weighed me down, but not because of the food packed inside it. Because the gun resting on top of those meals was enough to get my ass shipped off to DC, only I had serious doubts that Jackson would let me leave this city. I had to get it home and hidden as soon as possible.

AFTER STASHING THE GUN IN THE BACK OF MY CLOSET, I was too wound up to hang out at the apartment by myself, so I headed to Dragon's. My shift wasn't supposed to start for hours, but I didn't want to be alone right now. Not after getting attacked last night and not after finding Jimmy's body. Not only did I want to be around people I trusted not to hurt me, but I wanted to tell Donaghy what had happened. He knew all my secrets and I felt like we'd reached a point where we were closer than friends—even if I wasn't exactly sure how to categorize our relationship.

The atmosphere in the bar was darker than usual, but I wasn't sure why. Glitter was behind the counter, serving drinks in her skimpy little dress, but she was missing the usual bounce in her step. Dragon was nowhere to be seen and neither was Helen, although I could only assume she was still working her day job at the CDC. After what had happened today, I needed to make it a point to get to know the older waitress better. To find out if I could trust her, and what she might know—if anything—about my dad.

Donaghy was nowhere in sight, so I headed into the back room. The growl of the zombies made me freeze, but once my eyes adjusted I saw that there were only the normal two. No more bald creatures of the CDC's making, and no little surprises for me. Thank God. Maybe Jackson had decided to admit defeat.

The room with the cots was quiet, and two of the beds empty. Donaghy's guards had barely been clinging to life the day before, so I could only assume that they'd died sometime in the night or early this morning. Thankfully, their bodies were gone.

The fighter occupied the third cot. He sat on the edge of the bed, his elbows on his knees as he held his head in the palms of his hands. He didn't move or look my way when I crossed the room to him, and every inch of him was tense. Something about his body language made my heart beat faster. Had he caught the flu? He looked okay. He wasn't coughing and his skin was still bright with life. His face even looked pinker than usual.

"Donaghy?" I whispered as I moved across the room. "Are you okay?"

His gaze stayed glued to the floor. "Wonderful. My whole fucking life has fallen apart, but as long as you find your family it will all be worth it."

The bitterness in his voice took me by surprise, and I found my legs unable to move closer to him. Not since I'd opened up to him about my family had he spoken to me with so much distance. His tone was cold. Detached. He sounded like the fighter I had first met, the one who kept everyone at arm's length so he didn't have to feel anything.

No. That wasn't right. There *was* feeling in his voice, only it was hatred and pain. The warmth I'd felt in his arms just yesterday had vanished completely, leaving the room — and the fighter — feeling cold.

Something had happened.

"What's wrong?" I asked as I closed the distance between us, going against my better judgment.

His body was rigid before I started walking, but the closer I got, the more he tensed until he looked like he'd been carved out of stone. I knelt at his side, hesitantly touching his arm. His muscles flexed under my fingertips, making the tattoos that swirled around his biceps jump. His skin was warm, but not hot. He wasn't sick, but something had happened.

"What is it?" I whispered. "What happened?"

"You." The word was harsh and sharp, like a knife cutting into me. It sliced down my middle and penetrated my chest, slashing my already raw heart in half.

"Donaghy, I—"

He twisted to face me so fast that it knocked me on my ass, and the expression on his face made it impossible for me to regain my composure. I sat on the hard, dirty floor as he got to his feet, pushing past me. Pacing. His hands were on his head, massaging his skull like he wanted to crush it so he could forget. The pain was written across every inch of him.

"You did this. Spoiled. Selfish. It doesn't matter if you destroy everyone around you as long as you find the people who matter to you. Who gives a fuck about the rest of the world when Megan James needs help?" He shook his head, his hands still on his skull when he closed his eyes and let out a deep breath. "And I fell for it. I let you bat your eyes and shake your ass in my direction and snare me in your trap. Like an idiot!"

"Donaghy, I don't know—" My sobs made it impossible to talk, but I needed to. I needed to find out what had happened and why he was hurting, and tell him I was sorry and that I hadn't meant to bring him down with me. "Please."

It was the only word I could get out, and it was so distorted that I didn't think he'd understand it, and when he reared toward

288

me, his eyes blazing with anger and pain, I wasn't sure if he had.

"Is that all you can say? Is that all you can do? Ask for help like a child? Why couldn't you have taken care of yourself? Why couldn't I have let you?"

His eyes landed on my face and he blinked. We stared at each other in total silence. The room around us got hotter by the second while the sobs that were threatening to break their way out tried to suffocate me.

Then, like magic, the anger melted away and the Donaghy I knew was back. His gaze moved over me, from my face to my scratched up arms and legs, and then he was in front of me. On his knees, his hands gentle as they moved up my arms.

"What happened? Oh my God, what happened?"

The tears I'd been trying to hold back broke through the dam and slid down my cheeks. "I was attacked. Last night. On the way home. I think Jackson sent the man. He said I brought it on myself. He had me down. My dress—" Donaghy pulled me against him, swearing under his breath. "The gray man saved me. Nothing happened. Nothing happened."

"Nothing happened?" he said against my head. "Look at you. You're covered in cuts."

"But I'm okay." I wiggled out of his arms even though it felt good to be comforted. Something much bigger had happened to him, and I needed to know what and why and how I could help him get through it. "What happened to you?"

Concern for me warred against the pain in his eyes. "Patty."

His sister. Dear God. Was it possible that Jackson's influence could reach all the way to Dayton? Could Jackson seeing Donaghy and me together have caused *this*?

"Is she…?"

Donaghy nodded, and a second later his face crumpled. His eyes filled with tears and he fell into my arms. The sobs that came out of him were so violent they nearly shook the whole room. It was like watching a building collapse, having this big man sobbing into my shoulder.

All I could do was hug him. Wrap my arms around him and hold his body against mine as he shook with grief and pain and disappointment. He cursed Jackson and the zombies, his stepfather and even himself. He screamed for justice. Swore that he'd avenge his sister. He sobbed like a child who had lost the only thing he'd ever loved.

By the time he was finished crying, my back was stiff from sitting on the floor and my legs had lost all feeling. Donaghy, the biggest and strongest person I'd ever known, pulled back and wiped his face with the back of his hand. I expected him to look ashamed, maybe not even be able to meet my gaze, but he looked me straight in the eye.

"I'm sorry for what I said. None of this is your fault, and I don't blame you. I just needed someone to be mad at."

"I know." I took his face between my hands while shifting just a little, hoping to get the blood flowing in my legs. "It's okay."

He shook his head but didn't speak, and neither did I. Words felt insignificant in the current situation. Like putting a Band-Aid on an amputation...

"Jackson did this," Donaghy finally said. He ran his hand up my arm to my cheek, his thumb moving over the small cut on my lip. It throbbed, but not enough for me to pull away. "He did this to both of us. He was here. He came to tell me that my sister was dead, and he said something about you. I didn't get it at the time, but now I know."

"He isn't going to stop until we're dead, is he?"

Donaghy shook his head. "I don't know."

"At least you're leaving soon. Maybe then you'll be safe." Even thinking the words felt like I was betraying myself, because I didn't want Donaghy to go. Saying them out loud, though, felt like they would crush me.

His eyes went to the empty cots on the other side of the room, and he shook his head. "I don't know what they'll do with me now. My guards are dead, so there's no one to take me to Key West. I think I'm stuck here for the time being."

A shiver went down my spine. I thought about Mike, the black market runner who was dead, and the silence that had surrounded me in the shantytown. And Jimmy.

"I found Jimmy's body today," I said, turning my gaze back to Donaghy. "While I was working on maintenance duty."

"Jimmy?" He shook his head, but the movement was slow and the confusion in his eyes probably had more to do with the fact that his thoughts were still on his sister.

"The blond guy from my crew."

"The big dumb one." Donaghy's head bobbed. "That's right. So he's dead?"

"And Matt is missing. Ticker was hiding in shantytown, but I found him today and told him about Jimmy. He's getting out. Paying a zombie slayer to smuggle him out of the city."

Donaghy let out a deep breath, then got to his feet, pulling me with him as he settled onto the cot. Even though it wasn't very soft, it was a relief to not be on the hard, stone floor anymore. One side of my ass had gone numb, so I shifted my position in hopes of getting the blood flowing. Pins and needles moved down my thigh to my leg as the circulation returned.

"Hopefully, it works or Ticker will soon be joining his friends," Donaghy said. "Along with a lot of other people. The city is infected. People are dying left and right. Helen said the CDC has been so busy that it's hard to keep up."

"That's another thing. How well have you gotten to know Helen since you've been here? I need someone on the inside. Someone who works at the CDC. But I'm not sure who to trust and I don't know Helen all that well."

"I think—" He glanced toward the door like he wanted to make sure no one was listening in on us, but we were alone. "I think you can trust Helen and Dragon with anything you might need. They know something about all this, Meg. What, I'm not sure. But they are involved somehow."

He paused, my hand held in his as he thought something through. Something about the expression on his face made my hand tighten around his.

"There was a man here," Donaghy finally said, lowering his voice even though no one was around to hear his words, "yesterday morning before they brought that zombie in. He had wild gray hair and a beard. He and Dragon were talking about stuff I didn't totally understand, but your dad's name came up."

My heart jumped. Could it have been the gray man? Did he really know where to find my dad? "What did they say about him?"

"The man with the gray hair said he wanted some people out—out where or who those people are, I don't know—but Dragon asked him if he'd be willing to leave Axl behind." My

291

hand tightened around Donaghy's even more, but he didn't flinch. "The gray man said he knew Axl would want to be left behind if it meant keeping everyone else safe."

"They're talking about the CDC." I lowered my voice and moved closer to Donaghy, taking a quick look around to make sure we were still alone. "He's there. I know he is."

"I think you may be right."

The only question now was: What were we supposed to do about it?

Silence fell over us as we mulled over the events of the day. He was stuck here, at least for the time being, which should buy us some time. If we could get Dad out, then we might not have to say goodbye.

"We could leave," I said, turning to face Donaghy. "If we can get my Dad out, we can leave just like Ticker. Find a zombie slayer and pay him to smuggle us out."

I thought about Luke and the man who had been with him on my first day working in the bar—Jim. Maybe he'd be willing to help.

"I'm a convict," Donaghy said.

"I don't care, and if we can get far enough away from the city, they won't be able to find us. We can start over. People do it. Live in unsanctioned areas."

"Dragon said something about an unsanctioned town this morning, right before Jackson came and told me about Patty." Donaghy's Adam's apple bobbed. "I think he has a place in mind."

"And you say we can trust him?"

"I think so."

"Then we need to make this happen. We need to talk to him about it, and we need to figure out how to get Dad out of the CDC."

"Tonight," Donaghy agreed. "We'll talk to Dragon and Helen tonight after the fight."

"Okay."

I gave his hand another squeeze as hope swirled through me. Suddenly, it felt like the pieces of the puzzle I'd been working on were finally making sense. The picture wasn't whole yet, but I was getting there. Making progress. We were on the right track.

"You sure you're okay?" Donaghy asked, reaching out to

touch my face.

I tried not to wince when his fingers brushed the small cut on my cheek, but the gesture caught me by surprise and I jerked away before I could stop myself.

"Shit, I'm sorry," he said, just as I replied, "I'm fine."

"You're not fine." Donaghy shook his head. "If the gray man hadn't shown up, you would have been in real trouble. I feel like I should have been there."

"How?" I asked, shaking my head even though his words caused a warm glow to move through me. "You have no control over Jackson, and it's not like you're free to roam the settlement. This was beyond your control." I took a deep breath when the truth of what I was about to say hit me hard. "Plus, you might not always be here to save me."

Donaghy's mouth turned down and sadness filled his blue eyes. He touched my face again, his thumb running down my cheek in a gesture that was so gentle it didn't even sting. "I want to be."

"I know." We'd never been this forthcoming with one another before, and it was scary, but I wanted to be honest. "I want you to be here too, I just don't know what's going to happen."

My gaze moved over him, past his cool blue eyes and down his chiseled features to the little scar on his chin. A memory clawed its way to the surface of my brain, slow and fuzzy, coming into focus a little at a time. I had a dream last night. About that scar. Or, more accurately, about a man who had a scar in the same place. There were moments in the dream when the person was Dad, and other times when it was Donaghy. The two seemed to have been interchangeable in my brain, making it hard to know who was who. But I did know this: we'd been running from something, and in my dream I knew that all I needed to do was stay close to the man with the scar. That he would keep me safe.

When I ran my fingertip down the scar, Donaghy's stubble was rough against my skin. "How did you get this?"

"When I was little, before this whole mess even started. I fell off a playground and cut my chin. My mom had to rush me to the emergency room." The corner of his mouth pulled up. "I had to get ten stitches."

"So long ago," I whispered, tracing my way back up.

I didn't stop when I reached the top of the scar, though, but instead traced Donaghy's bottom lip. His eyes searched mine, the wanting in them speaking volumes.

I hiked up my skirt and scooted over, climbing on his lap so I was straddling him. His eyes stayed locked on mine as he moved hands up my legs to my thighs, then to my back. I leaned forward and he met me halfway, his mouth covering mine as he pulled me against him until my chest was flush with his, our hearts beating together as we kissed.

I ran my hands down Donaghy's arms, then back up, feeling the hard bulge of his muscles as he caressed my back. He was wearing a shirt, which was a rare thing for him, and I wanted it gone. I dragged my fingernails down his chest, and he broke away when I grabbed the hem of his shirt and pulled it over his head. His lips were back on mine before I'd even had a chance to toss the shirt aside.

His lips moved faster over mine, and it only took seconds for him to shift flip me over so I was on my back, lying on the cot. Then Donaghy was above me, his body pressed against mine in a perfectly pleasurable way as we kissed. Fingers traced their way up my leg to my thigh and moved under my skirt. I shifted, trying to give him access to my body, but he didn't take it any further. All he did was kiss me. Slow, sweet caresses that were broken every so often by fiery desperation when his tongue swept over mine. All the while his hand moved up my thigh, then back down, and his body rocked against mine as the fire inside me grew until I felt like I was going to burst into flames.

"Donaghy," I gasped when his mouth left mine for the first time. My battered lips were sore from last night's attack, coupled with the passionate assault Donaghy was in the process of giving them.

He trailed kisses down my neck to my chest, following the deep V of my neckline. His hands had migrated up to my ribcage, his fingertips brushing the underside of my breasts. There they stayed, splayed out teasingly. So close, but not moving up any further as he ran his tongue over my exposed skin, never once taking the opportunity to move the fabric of my dress aside so he could have more of me.

"Donaghy," I gasped again when he didn't answer. "You're

driving me crazy."

"I know," was his only response as his lips moved back up my body. Kissing every inch of my bare skin, his teeth nipping at my collarbone and his tongue tracing my lips before his mouth once again attacked mine.

We stayed that way for a long time, Donaghy teasing me. Driving me mad. I tried to move his hands, always so close to the bull's-eye but never quite reaching it, but he refused to be deterred. I even tried other ways to shift gears. Running my hand down his chest to his stomach, dipping my fingers past the waistband of his pants.

He groaned, but pulled my hand away. "No."

"Why?" I asked against his lips.

"Not here. Not in a hellhole like this. You deserve better."

His lips covered mine once again, making it impossible to respond. Not that there was much to say to that. I wasn't sure if there was anywhere better than where we were, not anymore.

# CHAPTER TWENTY-NINE

## Donaghy

**AFTER** the day's events, the make out session hadn't just useful for letting out some of this pent up sexual frustration; it had been therapeutic.

I had wanted so badly to take Meg's clothes off. Even now, after the heat had died down and we were no longer kissing, I couldn't stop thinking about it. Her head was resting on my chest and she was running her fingers up and down my stomach, but the only thing my brain could focus on was what it would feel like to flip her onto her back and strip her down so I could plunge into her. I knew it would feel good, but I also knew it wouldn't feel right.

I had to be better than that.

"Is Donaghy your first name?" she asked out of nowhere.

I cleared my throat and shook my head, partly to answer her, but also to try and get my brain to think about something other than screwing the girl at my side.

"No." My voice came out strained, so I cleared my throat again.

Meg pushed herself up so she was looking me in the eye. "What is it?"

"Michael Donaghy Fallon," I said. "Donaghy was my mom's maiden name. She'd always planned on using it as a middle name, but she hadn't intended to call me that. Only, I was premature. When I was born, I weighed less than two pounds." Meg's eyebrows shot up and I nodded. "Donaghy means fighter. She said from the moment I was born, that's what I was. A fighter. So, that's who I became."

Meg smiled. "I love it."

"Seems ironic now, doesn't?" I shook my head. "My name meaning fighter, and here I am. Doing this."

"I think it's your destiny. Without you, I probably would have been killed in that bathroom. I think you were sent here to save me."

When I wrapped my arms around her, Meg put her head down on my chest and hugged me back. I was glad, because I couldn't stand the thought of her seeing the tears in my eyes. Not because I was ashamed, but because I wasn't sure where they'd come from. Was it the thought that Meg might have died without me, or the realization that Patty had? Both, maybe. Whether or not it was destiny, I didn't know, but I knew that I was here now and I had to do everything I could to embrace it.

"Patty was the most forgiving person I've ever known," I said, the tears in my voice making the words shake. "Thinking that I let her down would most likely kill me if I didn't remember that. I know, more than I know anything else in this life, that she would want me to move forward and be happy."

"Of course she would." Meg's arms tightened around my chest.

"What about you?" I asked, hoping to move on to a happier subject. "You said Vivian and Axl James aren't your biological parents. What happened to your mom and dad?"

Meg's shoulders moved when she shrugged. "The apocalypse, I guess. My entire family was in Colorado when they found out Angus was immune, and they knew they had to bring him to the CDC if humanity was going to have a chance at surviving. My mom was pregnant with me at the time. Dad died along the way and Mom right after I was born. Complications. Joshua—" She paused to suck in a deep breath. "—couldn't save her. Before she died, she asked Vivian and Axl to raise me. That's about it, really.

Except that I'm named after Dad's sister. I don't know the whole store, apparently it's a sad one, but Megan is how my parents met."

"I'm sorry." I should have known there were no really happy stories anymore.

"It's fine," Meg said. She pushed herself up so she could look me in the eye again. "If they had survived, I would have loved them and had a great life, but I've had a pretty great life with my adopted parents too. Despite everything, I mean. I've been loved and protected, and that's about the most you can hope for these days."

"That's the truth," I said.

Meg smiled before leaning forward to kiss me again. I'd just managed to banish the thoughts of her naked body, and all it took was her lips pressed against mine for them to come screaming back. My hands went to her back without thinking, then down and over the curve of her ass. When I reached bare skin, I swear to God she spread her legs for me.

"I want you," she said against my lips.

Her own hand had migrated down my chest to my stomach, working its way south. Every ounce of blood in my body had switched directions, flooding to my crotch and taking my brain cells with it. I slid my hand up the inside of her thigh. She pushed her fingers past the waistband of my pants. My fingertips had just brushed warmth when the door flew open behind us.

"Son of a bitch," Dragon growled as he charged across the room. "What the fuck did I tell you?"

Meg rolled off me just as Dragon reached the cot. He grabbed my arm and yanked me to my feet so fast that Meg toppled to the floor and I almost tripped over my own two feet and fell on my face.

"I told you the girls in my bar are off limits." The words hissed their way through the hole where his teeth used to be.

"Dragon," Meg said, hauling herself off the floor. "What the hell? I'm a big girl, and you have no right to tell me who I can and can't sleep with."

The man whirled around to face her, letting me go. "What did you say to me?"

Meg blinked at the fury in his voice. "I said, I'm a big girl."

"You're my responsibility, and the last thing I need is for you to get knocked up by some asshole convict who's on his way out. Do you have any idea what Jackson would do if he found out about this?"

"Jackson?" Meg shook her head. "Wait, what? What do you know?"

Dragon's face went a whole shade lighter and he took a step back. I'd never seen the man look like he wanted to unsay or undo something before, but he did now. He'd let something slip, but I wasn't sure what and I could tell by looking at her that neither was Meg.

Dragon licked his lips and looked between Meg and me. "Nothing. I just know that after last night, the Regulator's son has it in for both of you. I'm just looking out for you."

"Bullshit," I said before Meg could respond. "You know more. I know you do because I heard you the other morning, talking to that man about Axl. You know where Meg's dad is, don't you?"

She looked like she was holding her breath. When Dragon didn't respond, she let all the air out of her lungs and stepped forward.

"Tell me what's going on," she said through clenched teeth.

"I can't." Dragon's voice was low, but he looked more sure of himself than he had a second ago. "Not yet. I swear to you that when the time comes, I will tell you everything. But there are things happening that will put you in danger, and I swore I'd look out for you."

"Who?" Meg asked. "Who told you to look out for me?"

"A friend."

"The gray man," I said.

Dragon's eyes clouded over but he didn't respond before he turned his back on us and headed for the door. "Get to work or you're fired. *Now.*"

Meg didn't follow him, and once we were alone she turned to face me. "What now?"

"Helen," I said. "Talk to Helen tonight. Every chance you can get."

"She's going to be on Dragon's side."

"I know, but I think she'll be more sympathetic to your

situation. At the very least, she may give you an idea of what's happening."

JUST LIKE THE ROMP IN THE BACK ROOM WITH MEG, THE fight tonight felt so therapeutic that I might as well have been stretched out on a leather couch and spilling my guts to some disinterested man with a notepad. Every time I slammed my fist into the zombie in front of me, I pretended it was Jackson or that asshole JO's son from Dayton. Picturing Patty, her innocent face cut and bruised, or looking at the other side of the room to see Meg's swollen lip kept the adrenaline moving through my veins. The throbbing in my knuckles felt like aloe on a burn, and the spray of black blood across the ring was more exhilarating than it had ever been before.

The pricks of this world thought they had us where they wanted us. They thought they could prey on the weak and take whoever and whatever they wanted. But they were wrong and I wanted to prove it to them.

By the time I had smashed in the skull of the last zombie, I was having a hard time catching my breath. My body was on fire. I'd never felt anger like this before. It threatened to burn me alive from the inside out and made it difficult for me to see straight. Even when Dragon came into the ring and announced my win, I couldn't get my vision to focus. The world around me was red. Painted with the blood I wanted to spill. Jackson's and that asshole who had killed Patty.

# CHAPTER THIRTY

## Meg

**I'D** planned on spending the fight chatting with Helen and attempting to wrangle some information out of her, but instead my eyes were glued to the ring the entire time. Donaghy was more amped up than usual. His punches seemed to come harder, his eyes not really focusing on the creatures in front of him, but instead looking through them. It was like his brain was somewhere else. His fists hitting someone else.

It didn't take a genius to figure out who or where.

The fight was over in record time, but the cheers were minimal when Dragon announced the winner. Mostly because the crowd was thinner than it had ever been before. The coughing had disappeared, but so had a lot of the population. It was like they had all vanished in the blink of an eye. Here one day, gone the next, never to be thought of again and definitely not to be missed.

"They're bulldozing it," Helen said from behind me, her scratchy voice cutting through my thoughts.

I turned away from the ring as Donaghy headed back to get cleaned up. He was even more covered in blood than usual, so he'd most likely take a shower. The idea of joining him popped into my head, but it floated away the second I set eyes on the older waitress. The *National Newspaper* was in her hands, and her blue eyes were focused on it as a cigarette dangled from her barely closed lips. They moved slowly as she scanned the article in front of her, the cigarette bobbing up and down with the silent words, ashes barely missing the newspaper before dropping to the floor.

"What?" Glitter asked before I could. Her pink hair was slicked back and brighter today, the dark blonde roots no longer visible.

"Shantytown." Helen shook her head and closed her lips long enough to suck in a mouthful of poison. She blew smoke out of the side of her mouth before reading the story. "'The population has been reduced enough to get rid of the shacks and move the remaining citizens into apartments. The removal of bodies will start next week, along with a census to find out how many people were taken by the most recent flu epidemic. Once apartments have been freed up, the relocation process will begin. The government expects it to take only a few days, and as soon as shantytown is no longer inhabited, a bulldozer will be brought in to remove the shacks. The CDC blames the unsanitary living conditions for the spread of the illness, and the bulk of the deaths, and the Regulator has declared that measures must be taken to prevent another outbreak of this or any other flu. He has pledged to keep on top of the housing situation from now on, and is in the process of writing up a bill that will ban the building of any unregulated homes within the city.'" Helen's mouth scrunched up and she snorted. "Assholes. Like they don't know how many people died."

"Was it worse than the last one?" I asked.

The older woman shrugged and tossed the paper on the counter before plucking the cigarette out of her mouth. "I'm willing to bet the number of deaths will be about the same, although who knows what the *National Newspaper* will report about it. I'll get the real figures at work, though."

Most of the patrons had left the bar, leaving only a handful staring into their glasses at the end of the counter. Tips were going to be shitty tonight, not that it mattered. I was more interested in clues about what was going on than credits at the moment.

"You're that high up?" I asked. "At the CDC, I mean."

Helen was in the middle of inhaling more smoke into her lungs—I swear they had to be black as night. She pulled the cigarette out of her mouth and held her most recent breath in as she stared at me, almost like she was trying to give the chemicals a chance to poison her lungs.

She let the smoke out in one breath. "I am."

I swallowed, my heart beating erratically in my chest. The expression in her eyes said she was dying to say more, but she didn't. She just pressed her lips together and stared at me, one arm crossed over her chest and the elbow of the other arm tucked into her side while between her fingers the cigarette burned.

"Do you have access to all the top secret areas?"

Helen nodded once.

Behind her, Glitter shuffled her feet. "Helen, I—"

The older woman waved her off. "It's okay, honey. Let her ask her questions. I don't have to answer them if I don't want to."

"Why wouldn't you want to answer me if you have the answers I'm looking for?" I was well aware that the question came out sounding like a riddle, but I had a feeling Helen knew what I was getting at.

"Sometimes, the truth hurts. And I'm not talking about hurting emotionally." She put the cigarette between her lips and took another drag. "I wouldn't want to tell you anything that would get you hurt, if you know what I mean."

Heat moved up my neck to my face as anger swirled through me. She knew something, just like Dragon did, but neither one of them was going to tell me. My father's life was in danger, but they weren't going to help me even though they could.

"So you and Dragon are never going to tell me what's going on?" I snapped. "I'm just going to have to figure it out on my own, is that it?"

Helen shook her head. "No. In fact, trying to figure it out on your own is the last thing you should do."

"What exactly is the first thing I should do? Since you're so quick with the advice."

"Wait. You won't be in the dark forever, but if we move too fast on this, something bad could happen."

"Something bad could happen if we move too slow, too," I snapped, waving my hand at my face, which was bruised and cut up.

Not one of my coworkers had asked me how I'd gotten hurt, but since Donaghy had seen the gray man in here the other day, I had a good feeling they all knew where my injuries had come from. Because whoever the gray man was, he was hiding here and he was plotting something with Dragon and Helen. Maybe even Glitter.

"You're okay, right?" Glitter asked as her big, gray eyes swept over my face.

"Wonderful." I let out a deep breath. "Just wonderful."

No matter what Helen said, I wasn't going to just sit back and do nothing. Not anymore. Tonight I would talk to Mom about everything that was going on, and she and I would decide what our next move would be together. I was tired of waiting on other people. Screw Helen and Dragon, and screw the gray man. He may have saved me a couple times, but he wasn't looking out for my best interest or he would have told me what was going on in the CDC by now.

I turned away from the other waitresses and scanned the room. Dragon was talking to the big men who doubled as bouncers, but Donaghy was nowhere in sight. He must still be in the shower.

When I headed across the room, Glitter called after me, but I heard Helen tell her to let me be. Good. I was done talking. It was time for action.

The holding room was quiet now that Donaghy had taken the zombies out, and when I shoved the door to the back room open, the small space was filled with steam. The pitter-patter of water as it hit the shower floor echoed off the walls, loud in the tiny room.

When I stepped into the bathroom, I stopped dead in my tracks. There was no shower curtain on the stall, giving me a perfect view of Donaghy. He stood under the trickling stream of water with his back to me, stripped down to nothing. His head was bowed and the water ran down his back, magnifying the lines of his tattoo. Every inch of him was muscular and firm. Like he'd been carved out of the strongest marble.

My breath caught in my throat and I couldn't make myself leave. The anger I'd been feeling was still there, but it now felt muted by the desire swimming through me. Donaghy wanted to wait for a reason I couldn't comprehend, but I had no desire to wait. I hadn't wanted to wait earlier, and certainly didn't want to now. After losing Colton, I never thought I'd want another man, but I did, and he was here and I knew firsthand that time was an abstract thing. This moment could be our last. Every moment could be our last.

I slipped my shoes off and shimmied out of my underwear, dropping them to the floor next to my heels. When I pulled my dress over my head, I tossed it aside just before stepping into the shower.

The water was lukewarm, but refreshing in the muggy atmosphere of the bar. Donaghy didn't move, unaware that I was even here, but the second my hands touched his back he stiffened. He lifted his head slowly, turning it so he could look over his shoulder at me. He didn't twist to face me, but his eyes held mine as I ran my hands down his back, not stopping until they were on his ass, my fingers curling around his hips. The urge to move them around to the front made my legs tremble.

"Meg."

He didn't say anything else, but his shoulders rose when he took a deep breath, and he squeezed his eyes shut like he was trying to decide what to do. Like if he didn't look at me, he'd be able to resist.

Not if I had anything to say about it.

The shower was small, but there was enough room for me to squeeze around him so we were facing each other. I moved my hand too, dragging it along his hip to the front where I curled my fingers around him. He let out a deep breath at the intimate touch, groaning. Keeping his eyes shut tight as I slid my hand up and down. I watched his face the whole time; saw the conflicting desires in his expression. Saw the need. I moved my hand faster.

"God."

It was the only word he muttered before he lost the war raging inside him and his mouth covered mine. My back slammed into the wall from the force of his kiss, the cold tile contrasting with the heat his hands brought to my body as they moved up my stomach to cup my breasts. His movements were frenzied, desperate and passionate and needy. His hands were everywhere, exploring every inch of my body that he'd managed to resist earlier. His lips following their lead. The power of his actions forcing gasps from me, and moans. My legs were weak and trembling, barely keeping me up, and I had to hold on to him to stop myself from collapsing on the floor at his feet.

Then he was lifting me, one arm around my back while the other held me up. I wrapped my legs around his waist as he pushed inside me. The water fell on us in fat drops and my back hit the wall from the force of his thrusts. My lips were sore, but I couldn't stop kissing him. His grunts mixed with my moans, the two sounds echoing through the room like a symphony of ecstasy as our bodies moved together.

It was quick, but satisfying, coming to an end when we both cried out together. Donaghy's arm tightened around my waist as my nails dug into his back. I was afraid I'd drawn blood, but I couldn't form words to ask him if he was okay, and when I opened my eyes, I couldn't look away either. Donaghy's gaze held mine prisoner. He didn't put me down. Didn't speak. Didn't move from under the stream even though the water had cooled even more. We stared at each other, both of us breathing heavily.

A door slammed, but it was muted—probably in the holding room—and Donaghy finally set me on my feet. "Dragon's going to fire you."

Neither one of us made a move to leave the shower.

"I don't care," I said. "I can't keep waiting. I'm telling my mom everything tonight. I have to get my dad out. Now."

Fear flashed in Donaghy's eyes, the emotion so strong it felt like it would knock me on my ass. He grabbed my arms and shook his head. "No. Meg, you can't do something like that. Give Dragon time. I know he'll come through. He's planning something. I know it."

"What if my dad dies before whatever he's planning comes together?" I shivered, but it was only partly from the water that had now turned icy. Thinking about my dad dying while I did nothing made me sick. Sick and cold.

"He won't die." Dragon's voice boomed through the room, and we both turned toward the sound. The man stood there, his bulky form taking up most of the doorway. "Get out and put some clothes on. Then we'll talk."

He was gone before we could reply.

Donaghy flipped the water off and we took turns using the small towel that hung on the wall. It didn't get me totally dry, but it was better than nothing.

I was pulling my dress over my head when Donaghy said, "I'm sorry."

"Why are you sorry?" I turned toward him, adjusting my dress so nothing important was exposed.

"I didn't want this for you." He waved to the filthy room at my back. "I told you. You deserve better than getting screwed by a convict in the back room of a shithole like this."

"What about you?" I snapped. "You don't? Why do you assume that I deserve better, but you deserve nothing?"

"That's not it. It's just—"

"No, that is it. We *both* deserve better. We *all* do. Everyone in this whole settlement. Everyone in this whole, shitty world. We all deserve better than this."

"Shit," a voice said behind me. "You sound just like your mama. Guess the apple don't fall far from the tree."

The gray man. I spun around, knowing who it was before I'd even laid eyes on him, and there he stood yet again. Grinning at me as he shook his head. At his side stood Dragon, not smiling, and the gray man mimicked the frown when he turned his eyes on Donaghy.

"You again." I threw my hands in the air in frustration. "Who the hell are you?"

"In time," the gray man said. "Right now, I need you to go home."

"No. I'm not going home until you tell me what's going on, and who you are, and most importantly, where my dad is."

"No," the gray man said, taking a step forward. It wasn't menacing or I would have shrunk away from him. Everything about his attitude was protective. Just like it always had been with me. "You're gonna go home and get your mama. You get Al and that rich girl he married too, and their daughter. And Ram— Parvarti. Don't talk in the apartment. They'll hear you and know what we're up to. Write a note or take 'em downstairs. Whatever makes 'em understand. Got it?"

He'd been ready to call Parv something else, but I didn't know what. Ram? Like a sheep? Maybe it was an old nickname. I'd never heard it, but apparently there was a lot from the past that I had never been told. Either way, I'd have to worry about silly names later, but right now the urgency in his voice had my attention.

"Okay." I nodded, and then shook my head. There were so many question swirling through my brain right now that it was hard to think straight. "Then what? What do I tell them all?"

"Tell 'em to come here. Not tonight, that'll be too suspicious. In the mornin'. Act like things are normal. Split up, don't come together."

It was happening. Finally, after days and days of confusion and questions, it was going to happen.

"Are we going to get my dad?" I asked as my heart beat faster. The gray man nodded once. "Fuck yeah we are."

I wanted to jump up and down, I wanted to curl up into a ball and cry, I wanted to punch the gray man for not answering my questions, and I wanted to drag Donaghy back into the shower and screw him again.

With all the options in front of me seeming insane, I chose to take a deep breath and nod. "Okay."

I turned to face Donaghy, who pulled me in for a hug before I could utter a word. "You okay?"

"I'm okay," I said against his chest. His lips touched my head and behind me, the gray man grunted. I ignored him and looked up into the fighter's blue eyes. "I have to go."

"I know."

The kiss he gave me was so deep that I could feel it in my toes. It went straight through me like a bolt of lightning, leaving shivers behind.

"Shit," the gray man muttered. I pulled away from the kiss at the sound of footsteps and found the gray man crossing the room to us.

"Hands off, asshole," he growled, his eyes on Donaghy.

"It's okay," Dragon said. "I told you. We can trust him."

The gray man's mouth puckered up, making me think of Dad. His eyes were still on Donaghy when he said, "You gonna help us, lover boy?"

"I'll do whatever I have to if it helps Meg."

The gray man's lip curled into a sneer, but he nodded. "I'll let Axl deal with you." His expression softened when he turned his eyes on me. "You gotta go now."

I nodded as I pulled away from Donaghy. My gaze moved across the three men standing in front of me and to the door, and for the first time, I noticed Helen and Glitter standing there. Did they know too? Who the gray man was and where Dad was being held, what they were doing with him? How and why and who these people were was a mystery, but one that would be solved in the morning. I just had to get through a few more hours, and then I'd have answers and I'd know the plan. The plan to rescue my Dad.

Then maybe we could leave this city. All of us.

THE CLOSER I GOT TO THE APARTMENT, THE MORE MY legs shook. On the walk home I decided that a note would be the best of course of action. I considered getting everyone to go down into the basement with me, but since I didn't know how they were monitoring us or who was listening, or how often, I was afraid that if I pulled everyone out to talk it would clue them into what we're doing. Whoever *they* were.

It was late, meaning the apartment building was quiet, but not late enough that everyone should have been in bed. Dragon had sent me home early, and it wasn't quite eleven thirty yet.

I stopped outside Al and Lila's door, trying to decide if I should talk to them first. Mom would take longer—and a lot more writing—but Al and Lila already knew a lot of what was going on. Plus, Al might not even be home and I doubted Parv was. This would give Charlie time to go out and get them.

I knocked, jumping when the sound echoed down the hall, and only seconds later footsteps headed my way on the other side of the door.

The lock clicked, and Lila pulled the door open. She blinked in surprise when she saw me. "Megan? It's late. Is everything okay?"

"Yeah." I let out a nervous laugh and pushed past her, pantomiming writing so she'd know I needed paper and a pencil.

Even though I knew I wouldn't be able to figure out how they were keeping tabs on us, I found myself looking around. Everything look normal, though.

My aunt's eyes flashed with worry, but she didn't hesitate. "Looking for Charlie?" she asked as she pulled a piece of paper and a pen out of a drawer.

"Yeah. We had a fight the other night at the bar and I wanted to apologize." I started writing, but since I was talking too, the words were slow to come out. "I feel bad."

"She's in her room." Lila sucked her bottom lip into her mouth. "You want me to get her?"

"Okay." I wrote faster. "Thanks."

My aunt glanced at the note as she walked by and the color drained from her face. She moved faster, and I was still writing like crazy when her knock rang through the apartment.

"Charlie, Megan is here to talk to you." Lila's voice trembled.

We needed to keep it together. Just until morning.

I was just writing the last sentence when footsteps came up behind me. Charlie and Lila stopped at my side and I added a period, then slid the paper across the counter.

"What's going on Meg?" Charlie asked as she started scanning the words.

At her side, my aunt did the same. After only a couple seconds, she grabbed Charlie's hand and held it in hers.

"I wanted to say I'm sorry about the other night. You know how shitty things have been for me, and I was being a bitch."

The words tumbled out so fast I didn't even know what I was saying, but I knew I was repeating myself. Giving them time to read the note, then time to respond. Charlie threw a few comments in as my aunt started writing, making it sound like she was still pissed, even tired of my temper tantrums—her words. Good. I needed her to storm out. To go find Al and Parv, and get them back here or at the very least make sure they met us at the bar in the morning.

Lila slid the paper over to me with shaky hands just as she said, "Charlie, you aren't being fair to Megan. She's been through a lot, and a little forgiveness goes a long way."

Charlie took a step toward the door as I read the note. *We'll be there.*

"You're always on Meg's side," Charlie said, her eyes darting around like she was trying to figure out who was listening. Like me, she seemed clueless.

The expression on her face reminded me of Mom. I needed to apologize, to let her know how sorry I was for thinking she was crazy.

"It's the right thing to do." Lila's eyes were big and wide and focused on her daughter as Charlie stopped in front of the door, her hand resting on the knob. Lila looked like she was afraid she'd never see her again.

"I'm out of here," Charlie yelled, her voice bouncing off the walls. She shot her mom one terrified look, then pulled the door open and hurried out, slamming it behind her.

I let out a deep breath. "I'm sorry, Lila."

Her hand clutched mine and I had to look away from the tears in her eyes. That was when it hit me how dangerous this situation had gotten. If Jackson or his father found out we were on to them, and plotting something to boot, we'd all disappear.

"It will be okay," Lila said, barely speaking above a whisper. "Go check on your mom."

My steps were heavy when I left the apartment and crossed the hall. I had the note in my hand to save me some writing. Hopefully, Mom's plan to boil the water had worked and she was coherent.

"Mom," I called when I slipped inside.

I shut the door behind me and locked it. No one responded, which made my heart beat wildly.

I walked deeper into the apartment, calling out a second time and holding my breath while I waited. Footsteps padded down the hall and I let out a deep breath when Mom walked into the living room. She was clean and put together, her face pink and bright with life, and her brown eyes alert. So alert that she noticed the fear on my face the second she saw me.

"Megan? What's wrong?"

"I got in a fight with Charlie."

I put my finger to my lips and motioned for her to come over. Then I started writing. I'd already decided I wouldn't tell her everything yet. Not all the stuff Al and Parv and Dad had been hiding especially. Let them explain why they'd all decided to lie to her. No, right now I was just going to fill her in on the fact that we were pretty sure Dad was alive and in the CDC, that she'd been right when she'd thought someone was listening in on her, and that we had to go in the morning.

Mom stood quietly at my side while I wrote. I said a few words here and there, just in case someone was listening, trying to

313

sound angry and hurt. I called Charlie a bitch and acted like I was mad at Mom for leaving me alone all this time. I could tell that one hurt her, but I was too busy writing and talking to feel bad about it.

When I was done, Mom took the paper and scanned it, her eyes getting bigger the more she read. When she reached the end of the note, she lowered it and took my hand, giving it a squeeze.

We just stood there like that, staring at each other with our hearts pounding and words feeling totally insignificant. There was only one thing that mattered to me, and I was sure Mom had the same thought floating through her head. It was the last thing I'd written on the note. The one I'd underlined and the one that made my eyes tear up.

*We're going to save Dad. Then we're getting out of the city. Together.*

# CHAPTER THIRTY-ONE

## Donaghy

**AFTER** Meg left, I tried to get some information out of Dragon and the gray man, but they weren't talking. Especially the man with the stormy eyes. Every time he looked my way he acted like he was trying to hold himself back from punching me in the face. Even though I was younger and stronger, I found myself shrinking away from him. He had a glare like a bulldog.

Eventually, the gray man disappeared—although to where, I didn't know—and I was able to relax. Glitter and Helen were cleaning up, and Dragon was counting the credits he'd made from the evening's fight. It didn't seem like much, but that wasn't a big surprise. The bar had been pretty empty.

"Shitty night," Dragon muttered as he shoved the credits into a lock box.

"You're worried about credits with everything else going on?" I shook my head.

"The credits," he said as he turned on me, "will help us reach our goals. We need supplies, and supplies aren't free."

I arched my eyebrows at him. "So that's why you do this?"

"That's why I have you here." Dragon pointed his glass at me. "I was happy with the way things were. We had plenty of credits, but the place was never too crowded. We could do what we wanted pretty much. Except buy all the supplies we needed at once. I was okay taking my time, because we had plenty of it, then Axl disappeared and things got pushed up. Can't wait forever."

"So you know where he is and you're going to help Meg get him back?"

Dragon grinned over the rim of his glass, revealing the hole where his teeth used to be. "Yes."

The word pushed its way through the gap, making him sound like a snake. Only, he was a snake that was on our side, and I had a feeling his venom was reserved for the CDC.

Helen leaned over the bar and patted my arm. "Don't worry, honey. It's all going to be okay. We know what we're doing."

"I'm not the one you need to reassure."

The door banged open behind me, and I spun around as a group of guards rushed in. At my back, Glitter yelped and Dragon swore. Helen told the younger girl to get behind her.

"What the hell is this?" Dragon asked, his voice booming through the room.

My heart pounded in my ears, and it only got louder when the guards headed my way. They grabbed me and dragged me off the chair, shoving me to the ground. My face was pressed against the cold, stone floor as they pulled my arms behind my back. A knee dug into my spine and I swore.

"Get off!" I growled and struggled against them, flailing around on the floor like a fish out of water, but making no progress.

My curses rang through the air as they jerked me to my feet, my hands now bound behind my back and a man on each side of me. More guards stood just inside the door holding guns, and behind the bar Dragon stood frowning. At his side, Glitter and Helen were holding onto each other. The younger girl was crying, but Helen looked like she was ready to strangle someone.

"Perfect." The slimy way the word rang through the air left little doubt who had said it, and when the guards spun me around, I wasn't the least surprised to find Jackson walking toward me. "It's come to my attention that you're supposed to be on your way to Key West, but your guards have met an untimely end." The corner of his mouth twitched like he found the idea of my guards dying funny. "We wanted to make sure you had a proper send off."

Jackson gave the room a quick once over, then spun on his heal and headed for the door, barking for his men to follow him.

The guards dragged me forward, their fingers digging into my arms. My feet were bare, and they slapped against the cement floor as I moved. I fought, but no matter what I couldn't get away. Not that it mattered. What would I do if I did manage to get free? Get shot. That's what.

That would kill Meg.

Meg! "Shit." I fought against them harder even though I knew it was stupid and pointless. "Tell Meg I'm sorry!" I called over my shoulder. "Tell her—"

My words were cut off when the guards jerked me forward, pulling on my arms harder. Not that mattered. I wasn't sure what else to tell her. Not be upset? That would be a pointless gesture. Not to look for me? That might clue Jackson in on what was going on. I had nothing to say beyond what I'd already yelled.

Pebbles and trash dug into the bottoms of my feet when the guards dragged me outside. A truck sat waiting, the engine already running and the back so full of armed men that it made my head spin. Was all this for me?

I was shoved into the back where I fell to my knees at the guards' feet. When I looked up I was met with angry glares, and alarm shot through me only a second before one of the men kicked me in the gut. I grunted and hunched over, my stomach throbbing from the impact. A second kick got me in the side. With my arms tied behind my back, it was impossible for me to protect myself from their blows, and I turned my face only to have knuckles slam into my eye.

"Enough." Jackson barked. "We need him in one piece."

I stayed curled in a ball and seconds later the truck lurched forward. We barreled down the road, bumping over the potholes and debris, but I didn't move. Every inch of me hurt, and I wasn't dumb enough to think that I was headed to Key West or any other settlement. If anything, I'd guess that I had about ten minutes left to live.

Patty was dead, so I shouldn't care that my own life was finally at an end. If it hadn't been for Meg, I probably wouldn't, either. But thinking about leaving her after everything she'd been through hurt worse than the kick to the gut had.

The truck stopped and I was jerked to my feet. I expected to see the outside world looming in front of me, or possibly a horde of the undead waiting to rip me apart. It would have made sense if these assholes had thrown me to the dead so they could watch them tear me to pieces. But to my utter shock—and then complete terror—I found the CDC looming in front of me.

"You know what to do with him," Jackson said when he stepped out of the cab, not even bother to look my way.

Just like before, I was dragged forward. Out of the truck and through a side entrance to the building. We ended up in a hall that was long and sterile. The lights from above reflected off the white walls and floors, nearly blinding me. We passed what seemed like an endless number of dark windows and brightly lit labs where men and women were hard at work even though it was well after midnight. All of them were hunched over microscopes or computers and wore white coats.

When we finally stopped, it was in front of a closed door. The words posted above it screamed at me: *Authorized personnel only. Top Secret Clearance Required for Entry.*

The man in front of me typed a few numbers into the keypad, and the small, red light turned green. Then the door popped open and I was dragged inside.

The windows we passed this time revealed rooms of horror. Some held zombies that were so decayed they looked like skeletons with strips of rotten flesh clinging to their bones, while others held newer victims who could almost pass for human. They all snarled and chomped their teeth as we went by, banging against the windows as they tried to get at us.

About halfway down the hall, a zombie smashed into the glass on my right, and I cringed away when recognition slammed into me. It was the man who used to work for Dragon. The one who was bitten that day Meg and I were outside the wall together.

The next few rooms held creatures similar to the one I'd fought in the ring. Hairless, their nearly transparent skin shining under the lights and making the dark veins in their arms and legs stand out. They didn't try to get at us the way the others had, but instead watched as we passed, their eyes intelligent and calculating despite the disease flowing through their veins.

The last of these creatures that we passed was slightly different, but it was still obvious that he'd been infected by the same strain of the virus. His head was smooth just like the others, but there was still a sprinkling of dark hair on his chest and legs. His eyebrows hadn't fallen out either, and the five o'clock shadow on his face contrasted with his smooth head. My eyes met his as I was dragged by, and for the second time a jolt of recognition shot through me. Even worse, I saw the same thing in his eyes. Matt. The missing man from Meg's crew.

The teenage girl in the room at the end of the hall was even worse than all the zombies combined. She was secured to the table by straps that barely cover her nakedness, and the inside of her arms were covered in scars that reminded me of Glitter. The girl was hooked up to machines, countless tubes running from her arms. When her eyes met mine they were alert, and the sadness in them was so thick that I actually found myself hurting for her. Whoever she was, her existence looked horrific and torturous.

The window just past the girl revealed an empty room, and that's where the men dragged me. Just like the door that had led into this hall, there was a keypad on the wall. The guard holding me tightened his grip, while another one punched in a few numbers, and the door popped open with a hiss that reminded me of Dragon's basement.

Alarm shot through me when the guard tried to drag me forward. I jerked back, my side throbbing from my earlier beating. My wrists were still tied, too, but somehow I managed to get one arm free. I shoved the guard away, then kicked the second one in the stomach. The man went down and I stumbled across the hall, away from the open door and the room that most definitely held a lifetime of torture for me. I'd only made it one step before someone tackled me from behind, and I slammed face-first against the glass window in front of me.

Voices screamed in my ears, calling me scum and throwing threats at me while my face was pressed harder against the glass. On the other side of the window, a man with gray eyes watched it all unfold. Unlike the girl, he wasn't restrained, but he obviously wasn't here of his own free will, either. He was wearing a hospital gown and his feet were bare. Like me, this man was a prisoner.

The guards pulled me back, dragging me across the hall

toward my own cell, but I couldn't tear my gaze away from the face in front of me. The scar on his chin stood out, screaming at me from the other side of the glass. It was in almost the exact same place as mine, and seeing it nearly knocked the wind out of me.

"Axl!" I yelled, pulling against the men holding me. "Axl James!"

The man got to his feet just as I was shoved into my own room. I stumbled forward, falling to my knees, but before I could stand the guards were on me. They pushed me against the ground, holding me down as they unbound my hands. I had to grit my teeth to keep from screaming. When my hands were finally free, the men hurried out.

Behind me, the door slammed shut, but I was on my feet seconds later and running to the window. Across from me stood the man with the scar. When our eyes met, he nodded, and I swear to God I wanted to cry.

I'd found Meg's dad, only there was nothing I could do about it.

# CHAPTER THIRTY-TWO

## Meg

**AFTER** lying in the darkness for what felt like days, totally unable to shut my brain off, I crawled out of bed. There was no point trying to sleep. I threw some clothes on and grabbed the small bagged I'd packed before stumbling out into the living room. In it, buried under some extra clothes in the hope of hiding it from prying eyes, I'd stashed the gun.

Mom was up, sitting on the couch and so wide-eyed that it looked like she hadn't gotten a wink of sleep. She smiled when she saw me. It was a sad smile that didn't reach her eyes, but was enough to warm me all the way through. She patted the cushion at her side and I went over to join her, putting my bag at her feet before settling in. She slipped her arm around my shoulders and I rested my head against her chest. I tried to will myself to relax, hoping to catch a little bit of rest. I doubted it would work, but at least I didn't feel alone. That in itself was a relief.

We couldn't talk. Not with the threat that someone might be listening in on us hanging over our heads. Not that it mattered. Until we had more information, I wasn't even sure what questions to ask anymore. There were too many now, the weight of them making me feel like I had an anchor around my shoulders.

Time stretched on, it's passing marked only by the ticking of the clock in the kitchen. It was the only sound in the room other than our breathing, and even though it was quiet, I was afraid it would drive me mad if we didn't get out of here soon.

Only it wasn't even two o'clock yet. We had at least until seven before we could safely leave the apartment and not raise the alarm. Any earlier than that would seem off.

Somehow, against all odds, I eventually found my body relaxing and my eyelids growing heavy with the need to sleep. I exhaled and willed my body to drift off, embracing the floating feeling that comes just before exhaustion takes over.

That's where I was when the knock rang through the apartment. It jerked me back to reality and I bolted upright while Mom jumped to her feet, and in an instant my exhaustion was gone. Our eyes met, but neither one of us said a word at first.

Finally, Mom whispered, "Who in the world could that be?"

I glanced toward the clock, my heart going crazy. It was four in the morning, which meant that whoever was on the other side of that door couldn't be bringing good news. Maybe it was Al or Parv, but I doubted it. Charlie had definitely told them what was going on by now, and they'd never risk showing up here in the middle of the night.

The second knock was so loud it felt like it was echoing through the room. Mom jumped and my heart mimicked her. I slid my hand into my bag and wrapped my fingers around the gun. It felt heavy in my hands. Hot even.

"We need to get it," she said, shooting me a worried look as she headed to the door. "It's going to be okay."

The expression in her eyes told me that she was as unsure about that as I was.

"I'm ready." I tightened my grip on the gun, but left it in my bag. She didn't know I had it, and I didn't want her to.

Mom paused at the door, giving me one last look before easing it open. The safety chain pulled taut, stopping the door from opening more than a couple inches. Mom reared back when a face appeared in the gap.

I had the gun halfway out of my bag when a strangled laugh

broke out of her. "Al! You scared the shit out of me."

"Open the door." My uncle's eyes were big and round when they moved between Mom and me. "We have to go. *Now*."

Al pulled back so Mom could shut the door. Her hands shook when she undid the safety chain, and only a second later the door was shoved open and Al charged inside.

"Get your stuff." His voice was low, but urgent, and he couldn't stop looking around. It was the same expression he'd had on his face when I'd shown him the note.

I was halfway to the door before I realized my uncle wasn't alone. Charlie and Lila were in the hall, and behind them, Parvarti had her gun drawn. The sight of her standing in my hallway, armed and ready, wasn't what had my heart beating faster, though. It was the sight of my boss standing behind her.

"Dragon?" I'd only taken one more step forward when Mom grabbed my arm and pulled me out the door.

We moved down the hall as a group, my feet stumbling over one another as we moved. Dragon was in the lead while Parv took up the rear. Her gun was still drawn, but I kept mine safely tucked in my bag. She was the JO, which meant she had a weapon permit. If I got caught with a gun Jackson would be able to do whatever he wanted with me.

Just thinking about it sent a shiver down my spine.

Mom stayed close to my side, and none of us spoke as we moved. Our footsteps echoed through the stairwell on the way down, matching the pounding of my heart, and my anxiety only grew when we stepped outside. The city was pitch black, and the now mostly abandoned shantytown deathly silent as we made our way past it. The normal sounds of people scraping by had been replaced by stillness, and the scent of garbage and urine could no longer overcome the smell of death that permeated the walls of the shacks.

The walk to the entertainment district seemed to take no time at all, but I didn't even realize we'd made it there until the red door that led into Dragon's Lair was looming in front of me.

My boss didn't say a word when he shoved the door open, and even once we were all safely inside, I couldn't calm down. Something happened. Something big, or he wouldn't have come to the apartment in the middle of the night like this.

"What is it?" Mom was the first to speak, her voice echoing through the empty bar.

Dragon locked the door, then turned to face us. "Not here."

He nodded toward the back as he hurried by, and we once again lapsed into silence as we followed. I knew where he was going, but everyone else was probably as confused as hell when he led us down the stinking hall and past the bathroom.

We stopped outside the basement door, my heart never slowing as Dragon typed in the code. A few seconds later, the door opened with a hiss and he headed down.

"Whoever's at the back, be sure to shut the door behind you," my boss called over his shoulder.

Unlike last time, the basement light was already on, but we didn't stop in the pristine room either. Dragon kept moving, passing the tubs and barrels and shelves of booze, not stopping until he reached the door I'd noticed last time we were down here. Once again, he punched a code in and the door popped open. My boss walked on without looking back, his only statement a reminder that we should be sure to shut the door once we were all safely inside.

I followed, staying close to Mom and keeping my hand on the gun. Unlike the basement, the hall we walked through wasn't pristine. Cobwebs and dirt clogged the corners, but the corridor was so dark that I couldn't get a good sense of where we were headed. It seemed to go on forever, and when it finally stopped it was so abrupt that I almost slammed into Dragon's back. He opened yet another door, this one not locked, and climbed a rickety set of stairs that creaked under our feet with each step. The air in here was stale and dusty, tickling my nostrils when I inhaled.

When we finally emerged at the top of steps, we were in a dark and filthy room. The windows had been boarded up, allowing only slivers of moonlight in through the cracks, and along one wall sat a cot similar to the ones in the back room of the bar. There was also a table and two chairs, a few candles that were scattered around cast a soft glow across the dark room. In the center of the table sat a pile of prepackaged meals.

Someone was living here.

"Where are we?" I asked, finally breaking the silence that had settled over us.

"On the other side of the wall." Dragon turned to face us, his eyes moving over my family slowly before stopping on me. "They took Donaghy."

I blinked, then shook my head, unable to believe his words. "What? No."

"Who's Donaghy?" Mom asked.

"The fighter?" Al looked at me. "What does he have to do with this?"

"Who took him?" Parv asked calmly.

"We—" I swallowed, having a hard time talking through the lump in my throat. It was a ball of tears, and they were trying to choke me, but I had to keep it together. No matter how much it hurt, and it did hurt. So much more than it should have considering we'd just met. "He and I have gotten close. He was helping me."

"Shit," Al muttered. He shook his head, but his face was distorted thanks to the tears in my eyes.

"Who took him?" Parv asked for the second time, her gaze on my boss.

Mom slipped her hand into mine and I tried to absorb some of her strength so I didn't fall apart. She was the strongest person I knew, despite the horror we'd been through since Dad's disappearance. I had to be strong like her. Had to focus and not lose control.

"Jackson," I said, answering for Dragon.

My boss nodded. "That's right."

"Took him to the CDC probably." Helen's gravelly voice echoed from behind us.

I spun around to find her standing in the shadows on the other side of the room. Glitter was at her side, wearing more clothes than I'd ever seen her in, and next to her stood the gray man. His hair had been tamed since the last time we talked, and his beard was gone, but it was him for sure. Even in the darkness of the room, his smoky gray eyes stood out.

Mom's hand slipped from mine and went to her mouth. Her eyes were huge. Terrified or shocked, I wasn't sure. She took a step forward, her legs slightly shaky as her head moved from side to side. She wobbled and I reached for her, afraid she might faint. The recognition on her face matched the expression in the gray man's eyes, and I looked and forth between the two, waiting for someone to finally tell me who he was. It was obvious Mom knew him.

"Angus?" she finally said, the name a scratch whisper. "Is that you?"

The gray man smiled, but it was sad and made his eyes look even stormier than they had before. "Hi there, Blondie."

"Oh my God," Lila whispered.

Angus? The gray man was my uncle? I couldn't believe it, but it had to be true, because Mom was crying and she was running toward him. She threw herself against him and the gray man—Angus—wrapped her in a hug. Her body shook with silent tears, and above her head my uncle's eyes shimmered as well.

Lila, Al, and Parvarti were right behind Mom, each of them as shocked as she was at the sudden reappearance of my uncle. They all hugged, their arms around each other and their bodies shaking with pain that was two decades old. Angus kept one arm around Mom while he hugged Lila, then patted Uncle Al on the shoulder. When he got to Parv, he called her Rambo and engulfed her in a one-arm hug that swallowed her small frame.

It all made sense, now. Why this man saved me, and why he reminded me of Dad. He was my uncle, and even though they looked different, there were so many similarities between him and his brother. His eyes, the way he puckered his lips as he looked everyone over. Even the way he spoke to me. I couldn't believe I hadn't noticed it before, but I should have. It should have been so obvious.

Charlie slipped her hand into mine and shook her head. "I can't believe this. Twenty years. He's been alive all this time?"

"In the CDC," Dragon said, crossing his arms. "We got him out a few months ago. It took years of planning and recon, but thanks to Helen, we figured out who we could trust and how to make it work. That's why they took your dad." He turned his gaze on me. "They needed his blood once Angus was gone. If we'd known he was immune, we could have foreseen it. But we had no idea."

"He's alive then?" I asked, suddenly unable to hold in the tears. Charlie gave my hand a little squeeze. "He's alive?"

"He is, and we have a plan, but getting Axl out is going to mean the end of our time in New Atlanta. We won't be able to stick around the way we did with Angus."

"I don't care. We have to do it," I said. "We have to save him."

"It ain't gonna be easy to get him." My uncle's voice boomed through the room. His arm was still around Mom, who was still crying and shaking her head. "You done it twice already, and they've changed things up since then, made it tougher. But we can get him out. We gotta."

"Twice?" Lila wiped tears from her cheeks and Uncle Al gave her a squeeze.

"Who else did you sneak out?" Parv asked.

Angus's gaze moved to Glitter, who was hugging herself and staring at the floor. Helen slipped her arm around the girl's shoulders.

"My daughter," Angus said.

The girl ventured a look at my uncle, her expression was shy, but affectionate, and Angus beamed at her.

"Daughter?" Mom shook her head as she wiped the tears from her cheeks. "How do you have a daughter? And Axl is immune? None of this makes sense!"

"It's a long story." Helen exhaled as she leg Glitter across the room. Both waitresses sank into chairs, and the older one nodded to the empty ones. "You should all sit. There's a lot to tell you, and a lot to think about. It's going to be a long night."

We obeyed, silently taking seats around the table. As a whole, we were in shock. Angus was alive. All the rumors had been true and somehow, against all logic, my uncle had come back from the dead like that crazy prophecy of The Church's had been true all along.

Was he here to save us? I didn't know, but I knew that Helen was right; we had a long night ahead of us. Two decades had passed since my family arrived in New Atlanta, and all that time Angus had been alive. Held prisoner and used like his life meant nothing. Jackson's father was behind it, I had no doubt, just like I had no doubt that the same thing was happening to my Dad at this very moment. How Dragon and Helen had gotten involved was another mystery, but right now I was willing to sit silently and listen to whatever they had to say. They'd both promised that when the time was right, all my questions would be answered, and the time had finally come. The time to save Dad, and now Donaghy too.

## To be continued...

# TWISTED MEMORIES

### *Twisted* Book Two

# ACKNOWLEDGEMENTS

When I finished writing *Silent World*, I already knew I was going to continue the story. Part of it was the constant hounding from readers, you know who you are, but another part was that I felt like it *needed* to keep going. I knew that the idea to skip ahead twenty years was risky, but I felt very strongly that this was where the story *had* to pick up. That, of course, meant packing a lot into the plot, and will mean packing a lot of backstory into the plot of the next book, and I'm very excited with how it turned out!

But I couldn't have done it alone. Thank you Erin Rose, my bestie and first reader who read, loved, and gushed about *Twisted World*. Also, Jen Naumann, who was nice enough to let me bounce the plot idea off her before I even started writing the book, and then both read and loved it when it was finally done. Thank you Jan Strohecker for offering to beta read and asking all the right questions, they really helped me fill in a few plot gaps, and Laura Johnsen and Mary Jones for searching for typos for me.

A very special thanks goes to my son, Carter, who told me—more than a year ago—that I should call one of my books *Twisted World*. I thought it was a good title, but needed the right plot for it. This one is perfect. Also, my other three children and my husband, who are proud of everything I've done and who are tireless in their efforts to promote me to friends, teachers, coworkers, students, and parents of friends. I love you all!

I hope that everyone enjoys this book, and I promise to get the next one done as soon as possible, but please be patient with me. I have a big move coming up and will do my best to work writing into my schedule, but I can't make any promises about when I'll get the next book out.

# ABOUT THE AUTHOR

Kate L. Mary is an award-winning author of New Adult and Young Adult fiction, ranging from Post-apocalyptic tales of the undead, to Speculative Fiction and Contemporary Romance. Her Young Adult book, *When We Were Human*, was a 2015 Children's Moonbeam Book Awards Silver Medal winner for Young Adult Fantasy/Sci-Fi Fiction, and a 2016 Readers' Favorite Gold Medal winner for Young Adult Science Fiction. Don't miss out on the *Broken World* series, an Amazon bestseller and fan favorite.

For more information about Kate, check out her website: www.KateLMary.com